D0804968

LOIS RICHER

A Baby by Easter

&

A Family for Summer

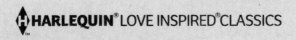
HARLEQUIN® LOVE INSPIRED®CLASSICS

Recycling programs
for this product may
not exist in your area.

First published as A Baby by Easter by Harlequin Books in 2011 and A Family for Summer by Harlequin Books in 2011.

ISBN-13: 978-0-373-20854-8

A Baby by Easter & A Family for Summer

Copyright © 2017 by Harlequin Books S.A.

The publisher acknowledges the copyright holder of the individual works as follows:

A Baby by Easter
Copyright © 2011 by Lois M. Richer

A Family for Summer
Copyright © 2011 by Lois M. Richer

Printed in U.S.A.

www.Harlequin.com

CONTENTS

Lois Richer loves traveling, swimming and quilting, but mostly she loves writing stories that show God's boundless love for His precious children. As she says, "His love never changes or gives up. It's always waiting for me. My stories feature imperfect characters learning that love doesn't mean attaining perfection. Love is about keeping on keeping on." You can contact Lois via email, loisricher@gmail.com, or on Facebook (loisricherauthor).

A BABY BY EASTER

It's in Christ that we find out who we are and what we are living for. Long before we first heard of Christ and got our hopes up, He had His eye on us for glorious living, part of the overall purpose He is working out in everything and everyone.
—*Ephesians* 1:11–12

This story is for those generous souls
who open homes and hearts to kids of all ages
who crave love and affection. Your dedication
will be revealed in tomorrow's generation.

Chapter One

Evenings in Tucson were a lot cooler than the Los Angeles' dusk Susannah Wells was used to.

Remember, Suze, we foster kids never know about tomorrow. Save whatever you can so you'll be prepared.

Susannah squeezed her hand in her pocket, fingering the last bits of change leftover from her meager savings. Connie's advice about money had been right on, like so much other guidance she'd given in those long-ago days when they'd shared a room in their North Dakota foster home.

What advice would Connie have for her this time—or would she even want to be bothered with her former foster sister?

Susannah hugged her thinly clad arms around her waist and breathed in the heady scent of hot pink oleanders. Deliberately she forced one foot in front of the other. Moving quickly wasn't an option when the world occasionally tilted too far to the right. Beads of moisture on her forehead chilled her hot skin, making her shiver.

The bus driver had said two blocks—surely she'd come at least that far?

Suddenly off balance, Susannah stopped to steady herself. She focused her blurry eyes on the paper in her hand, peering to confirm that the numbers on the page were the same as those on the house. Her sluggish brain responded as if obscured by fog. She squinted for a second look.

This was it.

Susannah's heart sank a little lower. Such a grand home. How could she possibly walk into that perfectly manicured courtyard, knock on that elegant glass and wrought-iron door and ask Connie for help?

You're not worth helping, but you don't have a choice.

Nothing harder to stomach than the truth. Susannah knew that too well. She gritted her teeth, pushed open the gate and moved forward. Droplets of perspiration ran into her eyes, blurring her vision. She swiped them away with a quick brush of her hand, afraid to release the branches of the hedge for more than a second, lest she flop to the ground. She was cold, and yet she was so hot.

What was wrong with her?

Finally she stood at the entrance. Music floated out from the brightly lit house. Or maybe the melody was just stuck in her head.

Susannah lifted a hand and tapped gingerly, inhaling as the world spun faster.

The door opened, light and laughter flooding out.

"Yes?" A man's voice, rich and smooth, like butterscotch candy, flowed over her. It was hard to see his face, but light brown eyes gleamed through the dusk. "Can I help you?"

"Connie," Susannah whispered.

Then everything went black.

* * *

David Foster stared at the unconscious woman lying on his best friend Wade's doorstep. Wade's wife, Connie, always had someone stopping by, friends from the foster home where she'd once lived, acquaintances she'd met and offered to help, even total strangers who'd heard about her charities. This frail woman must fit into one of those categories.

But Connie and Wade were celebrating their return from Brazil with a houseful of guests. He didn't want to disturb them. As Wade's lawyer, David was accustomed to handling things for his friend. He decided he'd handle this guest, for now.

He bent and scooped the young woman into his arms.

"Who's that?" Darla asked. His little sister had a habit of soundlessly appearing at his elbow.

"I don't know," he murmured, leading the way to the study. "One of Connie's friends, I guess. She fainted. I think she's sick."

"Oh." Darla watched as he laid the young woman on the sofa. "Can I help, Davy?"

David smiled, brushed his hand over her shiny brown hair in a fond caress. Darla loved to help. Though nineteen, a skiing accident had left Darla with a brain injury that cut her mental age in half. David's goal in life was to make his sister's life as rich and happy as possible. It was becoming a challenge.

"Sure you can help, sweetie. Why don't you go in the bathroom over there and get a wet cloth?" he suggested. "You can wipe her forehead. She seems to have a fever."

"Okay."

Darla hurried to do as asked, her mood bright because of Connie's party. "Like this?" she asked him, dabbing the cloth on the woman's face.

"Very gently. That's good." He watched for a few moments. "She had a bag," he mused. "It must have dropped. Can you take care of her while I go look for it?"

"Yes." Darla hummed quietly as she gently removed the traces of dust and grime from the visitor's pale skin. Not that it mattered—their guest was gorgeous.

"I'll be right back." David hurried toward the front door, his mind filled with questions.

She was tiny, light as a feather. Her delicate features made him think of fashion magazine covers—thin, high cheekbones, full lips and wide-set eyes. She'd pulled her golden blond hair back and plaited it so it fell down her back, but little wisps had worked free to frame her face in delicate curls. He caught himself speculating what the color of her eyes would turn out to be when those incredible lashes lifted.

She's obviously needy, and your docket is full.

Boy, did he know that.

A denim backpack lay outside on the step. David bent to pick it up. Well used, even ragged. Like her clothes.

He carried the bag inside, quickening his step. Darla couldn't be left alone for long. He stepped into the room.

"You're Sleeping Beauty, aren't you?" his sister whispered as she slid her cloth over the girl's thin, ringless fingers. "You need Prince Charming to wake you up."

David knew what was coming. He tried to stall by taking the woman's pulse.

"She'll wake up in a few minutes, sis."

"No," Darla said, eyes darkening as her temper

flared. "She needs you to kiss her, Davy. That's how Sleeping Beauty wakes up."

David sighed. Apparently he'd read her that particular fairy tale one too many times.

"It would be wrong of me to kiss her, Darla," he said firmly, ignoring the allure of full pink lips. "I don't know her. She wouldn't want a strange man to kiss her. Women don't like that."

"It's the only way to get her to wake up." Darla was growing agitated.

David closed the study door and prayed their visitor would soon rouse. He didn't want a scene at his friends' party. And Darla would make one. She'd grown used to getting her own way, and when she didn't, she tantrumed. That was the main reason she'd gone through so many caregivers in the past six months. None of the helpers he'd hired had been strong enough to stand up to Darla's iron will.

Like he was?

"Kiss her." Darla scowled at him, her mouth tight.

"No." David kept his voice firm. "It's no good getting angry, Darla. I'm not going to kiss her. This isn't a fairy tale, and she's not Sleeping Beauty. She's real and she might be quite ill. Look how she's shivering." He lifted a coverlet from the sofa and laid it over the small form.

"You have to kiss her." Darla stamped her foot. "I want you to." She swung out her hand. It connected with a lamp, which shattered against a table.

"Darla! Now you've broken Connie's lamp. Stop this immediately." David reached for her arm to keep her from wrecking anything else, but Darla was quick. She sidestepped him.

"Kiss her," she ordered, her face stormy as any thundercloud.

"Nobody's going to kiss me," a soft voice murmured. "And I wish you'd stop yelling. You sound like a spoiled brat."

Darla glowered at their visitor. Then she grinned. "Sometimes I am," she admitted shamelessly.

"Why? It's not very nice to live with people who are spoiled." The woman shifted the cover over her shoulders then swung her feet to the floor as she sat up. Her face paled a little and her fingers tightened on a sofa cushion.

"Easy," David murmured. "Not too fast. You fainted. Remember?"

"Unfortunately I do remember. What an entrance." She tilted her head back to rest it as she studied him.

Her eyes were a deep, vivid green. Their shadowed intensity reminded David of the Amazon forest—he'd once taken a trip there with Wade and their friend Jared. Before his world had become consumed by responsibility.

"My name is David Foster," he said. "This is my sister, Darla."

"I'm Susannah Wells. So this isn't Connie Ladden's home?" She looked defeated.

"Oh, yes. Connie and Wade *Abbot* live here," he assured her.

"They're having a party," Darla butted in. She frowned. "Did you come for the party? You don't have a party dress on. You're not supposed to come to a party if you don't dress nice," she chided.

"Darla." David frowned at her.

"She's only saying the truth. You're not supposed to

show up at a party dressed as I am." Susannah smiled at him tentatively then turned to Darla. "But I didn't know it was a party, you see. Anyway, I don't have party dresses."

"Not even one?" Clearly this mystified Darla. "I have lots."

"Lucky you." Susannah frowned. "Maybe I should leave and come back tomorrow."

"You can't." Darla flopped down beside her.

Susannah blinked. "Why can't I?"

"'Cause you don't have any place to go. Do you?" Darla asked.

David tried to intervene but Susannah merely waved her hand at him to wait.

"How do you know that, Darla?" she asked, brows lowering.

"I'm a detective today."

"Oh." The visitor glanced at him, her confusion evident.

David shrugged but didn't speak.

"I'm Detective Darla Foster. You don't have any suitcases. All you have is a backpack." Darla trailed one finger over the frayed embroidery work on the bag. "If you had a hotel, you would go there and wash first. But you came here dirty. I washed your face." She lifted the wet washcloth off the floor and held it out to show the grime. "See?"

A ruby flush moved from the V of Susannah's neck up to her chin and over her thin cheeks.

"There was a wind," she muttered, avoiding David's gaze. "It was so dusty."

"It's none of our business," he assured her hastily,

giving Darla a warning look. "Except that I don't think you're well. Should I call a doctor?"

"You actually know doctors who make house calls?" Her big eyes expressed incredulity.

"Dr. Boo came to my house. She asks too many questions." Darla's bottom lip jutted out. "Detectives don't like Dr. Boo."

"Dr. Boone," David clarified, interpreting Susannah's stare as a query. "Actually she's here. Shall I call her?"

"No." The word came out fast. Susannah donned a quick smile to cover. "I'm not very good with doctors. I'll be fine. I think I caught a little cold, that's all. But they never hang around for long."

"You're shivering." David didn't miss the way she hugged the coverlet around her shoulders as if craving warmth, or the way her stomach issued a noisy rumble. "And hungry, by the sounds of it. Shall I go get Connie?"

"Oh, please, I don't want to disturb her party." Susannah shook her head. "Can't I just stay here quietly until everyone's gone?"

"You don't want to go to the party?" Darla frowned, then grinned. "Me, neither," she declared. She patted Susannah's arm. "Let's have our own party. Davy, you get Silver," she ordered.

"Silver?" Susannah looked horrified. "I don't want money!"

"Silver is Wade's daughter." Darla giggled. "She's nice."

"I think Connie took Silver up to bed a while ago." David held his breath, wondering if that would engender another explosion.

And that was exactly his problem. He worried too much about Darla's temper and not enough about insisting she modify her behavior. But it was so hard to be firm with her. She was his baby sister. She'd lost so much since the accident. All he wanted was to make her world easier, to see her happy.

Still, it was his job to take care of her, no matter what. Which meant that tomorrow David would start scouting the agencies—again—to find someone to be with his sister when he couldn't be.

Lowered voices drew him back to the present. Two heads, one dark, one blond, bent together as his sister laid out her plans for their impromptu party.

"Darla?" David waited until she lifted her head and smiled her dazzling smile at him. "I'm going to find something for Susannah to eat. Will you stay *here*?" He emphasized the word so she'd understand she wasn't to leave the study.

"Okay." Darla tore a piece of paper off the pad by the telephone and began scribbling. "Here's our order, Davy. Crackers and cheese and soup. Chicken soup. Eighty-six percent of doctors say chicken soup is an effective aid in treating cold and flu."

Darla had a knack for reciting television commercials verbatim.

"Cold and flu—is that what I have?" Susannah asked, tongue in cheek. "How do you know?"

"I'm a nurse. We just know." Darla pulled the cover tighter around her patient's shoulders.

David hid his smile at Susannah's surprise.

"I thought you were a detective," he said.

"Not anymore." Darla glared at him. "Food, Davy.

This child is starving," she said in her bossy grand-
mother voice.

"Yes, ma'am." He choked back his laughter. Darla
had always been able to make him laugh. He headed
for the door. "I'll be right back." He thought he heard a
giggle from the blond woman before he closed the door,
but it was quickly smothered.

David went searching for Connie and caught her between guests.

"There's a woman in the study, a Susannah Wells,"
he began, but got no further.

"Really? Suze? How wonderful." Connie beamed
with happiness. It faded a little as she glanced around
the room. "We're about to eat dinner. I can't leave right
now." She thought a moment. "Bring her to the table,
will you, David? I'll get another place set."

Before Connie could continue, David stopped her.

"I don't think that's a good idea," he said softly. "I
don't think she's well. She fainted when I opened the
door and she's been shivering ever since."

"Oh, dear." Connie looked distracted. "Cora just
gave me the nod. I need to get everyone seated."

"Then go ahead. Darla and I will keep Ms. Susannah entertained until you're free." David smiled at her.
"Don't worry. Darla has everything under control. She's
a nurse."

"Ah." Connie grinned in understanding and stood
on her tiptoes to kiss his cheek. "What would we do
without Darla, David?"

"I don't know," he answered her, perfectly serious.
"Go enjoy dinner and don't worry about your friend.
I'll look after her."

"You always look after everyone." Connie touched

his cheek. "Thank you for all you do for us. You're a dear."

David watched her hurry away. He couldn't help but envy Connie. She and Wade shared the kind of home he'd always wanted—one filled with love and joy, hope and the laughter of friends and family. But he shook himself out of it. Having a family was a dream he'd given up.

For Darla.

He escaped to the kitchen. A whisper of concern that Darla might cause problems lingered at the back of his mind as he hurriedly filled a tray and carried it to the study. He hadn't gotten what she'd asked for, but she would have to manage. He pushed open the study door—and froze.

"You could marry Davy. He would look after you. He looks after me." Darla's bright voice dropped. "He had a girlfriend. They were going to get married, but she didn't want me. She wanted Davy to send me away."

David almost groaned. How had she found out? He'd been so careful—

"I'm sure your brother is very nice, Darla. And I'm glad he's taking care of you. But I don't want to marry him. I don't want to marry anyone," Susannah said. "I only came to Connie's to see if I could stay here for a while."

"But Davy needs someone to love him. Somebody else but me." Darla's face crumpled, the way it always did before she lost her temper. David was about to step forward when Susannah reached out and hugged his sister.

"Thank you for offering, Darla. You're very generous. I think your brother is lucky to have you love him."

Susannah brushed the bangs from Darla's sad face. "If I end up staying with Connie, I promise I'll see you lots. We could go to that playground you talked about—" Susannah suddenly lurched up from the sofa and stumbled toward the bathroom. The door slammed closed.

"What's wrong?" Darla jumped to her feet. She saw him and rushed over. "What's wrong with her, Davy? Did I do something?"

"No, sweetie. You didn't do anything." He set the tray on a nearby table, then hugged Darla close. "I told you. She's sick."

"But I don't want Susannah to be sick. I want us to be friends and do things together." Tears welled in Darla's brown eyes. "Susannah doesn't think I'm dumb. She talks to me like you do, Davy."

David could hardly stand the plaintive tone in his sister's voice. But he dared not promise Darla anything. Not until he'd learned a lot more about Susannah Wells.

As he hugged Darla, the sounds of retching penetrated the silence. Susannah sounded really ill. Maybe he should have ignored her wishes and called the doctor in anyway.

"Davy?" Darla peered up at him, her eyes glossy from tears. "Do you think she's going to die like Mama and Papa?"

"No, honey. Susannah's just sick. But she'll get better." He squeezed her shoulders, wishing he could make everything right with Darla's world.

A moment later the bathroom door opened and Susannah emerged, paler than before, if that was even possible. She sat on the sofa gingerly, as if afraid she'd jar something loose.

"I'm sorry," she whispered. "I shouldn't have come."

"Of course you should have come." Connie breezed into the room and wrapped Susannah in her arms. "I'm so glad to see you, Suze. But you're ill." She leaned back to study the circles of red now dotting Susannah's cheeks. "I'll call the doctor."

"No."

David noted Susannah's quick intake of breath, the way she vehemently shook her head as her fingers clenched the sofa cushion. He wondered again why she was so nervous.

"But honey, you're obviously unwell. Maybe you have a virus."

Susannah began to laugh, but tears soon fell and the laughter turned to sobs. "I don't have a virus, Connie." She risked a quick look at David.

He understood immediately. He grasped Darla's hand.

"We'll leave you two alone."

"No!" Darla jerked away from him and sat down beside Susannah. "I want to help my friend. Can I help you?" she asked quietly, sliding her fingers into Susannah's.

David had never seen his sister bond with anyone like this. He prayed Susannah wouldn't reject her offer of friendship.

"You already have helped me, Darla." Susannah smiled. "You looked after me and helped me the way a very good friend would, even though I hardly know you."

"I know you," Darla insisted. "You're Sleeping Beauty."

"I'm not really." Susannah caressed Darla's cheek. She glanced at him, then Connie. "I'm just an idiot who's made another huge mistake."

"Davy says everybody makes mistakes. He said that's how we learn." Darla faced Connie. "I made a mistake and broke your lamp. I'm sorry."

"That's okay, honey. You and I will go shopping for a new one." Connie smiled her forgiveness, then turned back to Susannah. "Can you tell me what's wrong, Suze? Because you're very pale and I still think you need to see a doctor."

"I've already seen one." The blond head dipped. "I know what's wrong with me."

"Tell me and we'll do whatever it takes to get you well," Connie promised.

"If only it were that easy," Susannah whispered.

"There's me and Davy and Connie and Wade and Silver. That's lots of people to help." Darla twisted, trying to peer into Susannah's face. "We can all help you. That's what friends do."

David had to smile at the certainty in his sister's voice. But his smile quickly died.

"I'm pregnant." The words burst out of Susannah in a rush. Then she lifted her head and looked him straight in the eye, as if awaiting his condemnation.

But it wasn't condemnation David felt. It was hurt. He'd prayed so long, so hard, for a family, a wife, a child. And he'd lost all chance of that—not once, but twice.

How could God deny him the longing of his heart, yet give this homeless, ill woman a child she was in no way prepared to care for?

"Come on, Darla," he said. "We're going home now. Connie and Susannah need to talk. Alone."

Darla must have heard intransigence in his voice because she didn't argue. She leaned over and kissed both women on the cheek, whispered something to Susannah, then placidly followed him from the room. She walked home beside him in silence, peeking at him from time to time. It was only when they'd stepped through the front door that Darla finally spoke.

"I know what it means, Davy. Susannah's going to have a baby."

"Yes." He felt horrible about his attitude, but he just didn't want to get involved with Connie's friend. He had enough responsibility with Darla. He couldn't—wouldn't—take on any more.

"Is it hard to have a baby?" she asked.

"Yes. I guess so."

"Then we have to help Susannah, don't we? That's what the Bible says." Darla took his hand and held it between hers. "She's my friend, and I want to help her."

"I don't think there's much that we can do, sis." Brain injury or not, Darla had always tried to fix the world. David loved that. Loved her. "It's not our problem."

"Yes, it is our problem. We have to show love." Darla let go of his hand and stepped back. Her face was set in stern lines, her dark eyes glowing with the unyielding resolve he'd run into before. "I'm going to help Susannah. I'm going to ask God to show me how."

Then she turned and walked to her room, determination in every step.

David went into his study but he didn't turn on the lights. Instead he stood in the dark, thinking. Finally he could contain his hurt no longer.

"I don't want to take on anyone else's problems, God," he whispered. "I was Silver's guardian for four years while Wade worked in South America. When Dad died, I took over his law firm, and then managed Mom's care until she passed away. Then Darla had her accident and it was up to me again. I can't take on any more."

"I'll be good, Davy," Darla whispered.

He whirled around, saw her standing in the doorway with tears coursing down her cheeks and cursed his stupidity.

"Oh, Darla, honey, I didn't mean—"

"I promise I won't be bad anymore. I won't yell or break things or be nasty, if we could have Susannah look after me. Please?" She stood in her white cotton nightgown, a penitent child where a woman should have been. She'd lost so much.

His heart ached to make her world better. But not this way.

"Sweetie, I don't think Susannah is going to be able to work. I think she'll have to rest and get well."

"For a little while, till she's not sick. But then Susannah will want to work. She told me she came to see if Connie could help her get a job." Darla dragged on his arm. "Ms. Evans said she isn't ever coming back here to stay with me again, so we have a job, Davy. Please, could we get Susannah?"

David had never been able to deny his sister her heart's desire. Not since the day she'd been born. Certainly not since her accident. But David couldn't promise this. Darla took every spare moment he had and then some. He had to be her buffer, protect her and make sure her world was safe and secure. He couldn't take on the responsibility for a pregnant woman, too. He just couldn't take on another obligation for anything or anyone else.

Can't or won't? his conscience probed.

"Please, Davy?"

"I'm not saying yes," he warned. "I'm saying I'll think about it. But don't get your hopes up, Darla, because I don't believe Susannah will want to do it."

And I don't want her here. I don't want to be responsible if she works too hard or you cause her problems and that child is jeopardized. I don't want more responsibility.

"Thank you, Davy." Darla flung her arms around him and hugged him as hard as she could.

"I haven't said Susannah can come, remember."

"I know." She tipped her head back and grinned like the old Darla would have. "But I'm going to pray God will change your mind." She kissed him, then raced toward the kitchen. "I didn't have dinner. I'm hungry."

Darla's faith.

David wished his own was as strong.

Chapter Two

"So you thought you were married to this man?" Connie said.

"Nick. Yes." Susannah nodded.

"But—"

"I know it sounds stupid and gullible," Susannah muttered and hung her head. "He said he didn't want a fuss, that he wanted our wedding to be just us, private and intimate."

"But to lie about marriage—I am so sorry." Connie touched her hand in wordless sympathy.

"So am I—sorry that I was so dumb. Nick arranged everything that I asked for—the minister, the church, everything. But it wasn't real. None of it was." Susannah pushed away the rest of the soup David had brought. She shook her head. "I thought Nick loved me. I guess I should have known better."

"Why? When you're in love, you do trust the one you love." Connie's fingers smoothed hers. "That's natural, exactly how God meant love to be."

"Only God didn't mean love for me." Guilt settled

on Susannah for ruining her friend's party. "Shouldn't you go back to your guests?"

"I told them an emergency had arisen."

"I'm an emergency? Yuk." Susannah made a face.

"Just like the old days, huh?" Connie teased. She shook her head. "Don't worry. They're friends and well used to my 'emergencies.' Wade will take care of them."

"Is he nice?" Susannah asked softly, studying her friend's glowing face with a twinge of envy.

"Wade is—wonderful." Connie's face radiated happiness.

"How did you meet?"

"Silver is Wade's daughter. Wade had to leave her here while he worked in South America. David was her guardian. He hired me to be Silver's nanny."

"How romantic. Like Cinderella." Susannah thought Darla would have loved that.

"Not at first. When Wade came home he was nothing like I expected. But God knew what he was doing when he put us together. We were married a year ago." Connie held out her hand. "My engagement ring was Wade's mother's."

"It's beautiful." Susannah thought of the cheap gold circlet she'd tucked into her bag. Nick had promised he'd get something nicer later on. Another lie. "Nick died and I didn't have anywhere else to go."

"Oh, Suze, I'm so glad you came here. You were only seventeen when you ran away from our foster home. What have you been doing?" Connie asked, her voice grave. "I called home several times, but Mom said she didn't know where you'd gone."

"I got in with the wrong group and went to Los Angeles. It took me a while to get my head on straight, but eventually I got a job in a nursing home. That's where I met Nick." She inhaled to ease the constriction in her throat. No more tears.

Connie squeezed her fingers. "How did you find me?"

"I finally phoned Mom day before yesterday."

"She misses you." Connie's eyes blazed with sympathy.

"I miss her, too." Susannah sniffed. "I was stupid to run away. So stupid."

"Everybody makes mistakes."

"Even you?" Susannah asked, glancing around.

"Especially me." Connie laughed. "I'll tell you later about my mistakes." Her voice grew serious. "But what about the baby, Suze? When are you due?"

"April. Around Easter."

"An Easter baby."

Susannah gulped. "I'm on my own and I have about two nickels to rub together. I guess, first of all, I need to find a job. Do you know of any?"

"First of all you need to get better," Connie said in her familiar "mother" tone. "Do you want to keep your baby?"

"I don't think any child would want a mother like me." She deliberately didn't look at Connie.

"But you'd make a wonderful mother!" her friend protested.

"Hardly," Susannah scoffed. "Look how I messed up my own family. I'm so not the poster woman for motherhood."

"You were nine the day they brought you to our foster home. I told you then and I'll tell you again, *you* did not break up your family, Suze. Nothing you did caused your father to leave you, or your mother to start drinking. And you did not start that fire." Connie tucked a finger under her chin and forced her to look up.

Susannah couldn't stop the tears. "Why did God let this happen to me, Connie?"

"Oh, sweetheart." Connie wrapped comforting arms around her shoulders and hugged her close, rocking back and forth as she had when Susannah was younger.

"I feel like He hates me," Susannah sobbed.

"God? No way." Connie let go and leaned back. "Listen to me, kiddo, and hear me well. God does not hate you. He loves you more than you could ever imagine."

"But I've messed up—"

"There are no 'buts' where God is concerned. He loves you. Period." Connie pressed the tendrils away from Susannah's face, then cupped her cheeks and peered straight into her eyes. "God has a plan. He's going to work all of this out for your benefit."

"You sound so sure."

"I am sure. Positive." Connie smiled. "But until He shows us the next step, I have the perfect guest room upstairs. You'll stay as long as you need to. Now finish that soup and try to swallow a few of the crackers," she insisted. "You're thinner now than you were when you first came to North Dakota, and you were a stick then. Eat."

"Still as bossy," Susannah teased, her heart swelling at the relief of being able to count on a friend.

"Still needing bossing," Connie shot back, laughing. "You need taking care of, and I'm just the person to do it." She watched while Susannah ate. "What was Darla saying about Sleeping Beauty?"

Susannah shrugged but couldn't stop her blush. "I

passed out on the doorstep. Her brother carried me in here. When I came to, she was demanding he kiss me, like Sleeping Beauty." Susannah crunched another cracker, enjoying the feeling of having enough to satisfy her hunger. It had been ages since she'd been able to eat her fill.

"She loves that story." Connie smiled fondly.

"Darla is a bit old for fairy tales," Susannah mused. "Something's wrong with her, right?"

"She had a skiing accident." Connie's voice filled with sadness. "It happened a few months after her mother died. Their father was already gone so David had to handle everything. He's been looking after her the best he can, but it's been a challenge for him."

"What do you mean?" Susannah struggled to decipher the cautious tone in Connie's voice.

"Well, David was engaged. Twice."

"Oh." Not much wonder, Susannah thought. He was very good-looking.

"Each time his fiancées backed out because of Darla."

"They wanted him to dump her into some home?" Indignation filled Susannah. "Typical."

"Why do you say that, Suze?"

"It was like that where I worked," Susannah fumed. "So often the seniors were seen as burdens because they took a little extra time and attention, or couldn't remember as well."

"Well, in Darla's case, David's fiancées might have had a point," Connie said, her voice quiet.

"Oh?" Susannah frowned. "Why?"

"Darla has had—" Connie paused "—difficulty adjusting to her world since the accident."

"But surely she goes to a program of some sort?" Susannah asked.

"She does. The problem is Darla. She has trouble working with anyone. Her temper gets very bad. I'm sure that's what happened with my lamp." Connie inclined her head toward the shattered glass.

"When I came to, she was yelling." Susannah frowned. "But she didn't act up when I was speaking with her. She was sweet and quite charming."

"That's the way she is, until someone doesn't do as she wants. Then she balks and makes a scene. It's part of her brain injury. She's had a number of workers try to teach her stronger self-control." Connie made a face. "With little success, so far. They keep quitting."

"Well, maybe David hasn't found the right people to work with her," Susannah said. "He seemed kind of frustrated by her."

"Maybe he is," Connie agreed, "but he devotes himself to his sister."

"To the exclusion of everything else?" Was that why he looked so tired?

"Yes, sometimes. David is convinced it's his duty to his parents to ensure Darla's happiness, even if he has to sacrifice his own." Connie pulled a vacuum hose from a cupboard and cleaned up the shards of glass before tucking the lampshade into a closet.

"Aren't you mad about the lamp?" Susannah asked curiously.

"It was just a thing." Connie loaded the used dishes onto the tray. "People are more important than things. Come."

Connie opened a door that led to a staircase. Susannah followed her, curious to see the rest of this lovely house.

"We'll sneak up to your room this way." Connie shot her a conspiratorial grin.

Their footsteps were muffled by thickly carpeted stairs. Connie grasped her hand and led her to a beautiful room tucked under the eaves.

"This used to be my room," she said. Her face reflected a flurry of emotions as she sank onto the window seat. "I spent a lot of time right here, praying."

"Are you happy, Connie?" Susannah asked, sitting beside her. "Truly?"

"Happier than I ever imagined I'd be." Connie hugged her. "You will be, too, Suze. But you have to give God time to work things out for you. You have to have faith that He has great things in store for your future."

"That's hard, given my past," Susannah muttered.

"That's when it's most important to read your Bible and pray," Connie murmured. "You have a lot of decisions to make. But you don't have to rush. You can stay right here, get well and figure things out in your own time."

"Is it hard—being a mother?" The question slipped out in spite of her determination not to ask.

But the prospect of motherhood scared her silly.

"You're worried about the baby, aren't you, Suze. Why?" Connie moved to sit on the bed, patting the space beside her. When Susannah sat down, she hugged her close. "What's really bothering you?"

"My role model for motherhood wasn't exactly nurturing. Nothing mattered to my mother more than her next drink." She heard the resentment in her own voice but couldn't control it. "Nothing."

"Suze, honey, you can't hold on to the bitterness."

"Can't I?" Susannah opened her bag and pulled out her wallet. She flipped it to two pictures nestled inside. "They're dead, Connie. Because of me."

"No."

"Yes." Susannah nodded. "I should have been there."

"Then you would have died, too." Connie gripped her hand.

"But if only I hadn't chosen—"

"The fire wasn't your fault, Susannah." Connie's soft voice hardened. "No matter what your mother said when you were a kid."

Susannah had gone round and round this argument in her head for years. But nothing erased the little voice of blame in the back of her brain. Her hand rested for an instant on her stomach.

"A new life," Connie murmured. "Hard to wrap your mind around it?"

"Very," Susannah agreed with a grimace. "Even harder to imagine coping."

"You'll do fine," Connie assured her.

"It's easy for you to say that. You spent all those years in our foster home caring for everybody else. I don't know anything about caring for a baby, except that you need to feed it and change it." Just saying that made Susannah feel helpless. "What if it gets sick?"

"Then you'll get help." Connie patted her shoulder. "One thing I've learned with Silver is that there are no easy answers, no recipe you can follow. You do your best, pray really hard and have faith that God will answer. And He does. David told me that when he first hired me."

"Really?" So David Foster was a man of faith, too.

"David is one of the good guys. My husband is another. So is their friend Jared." Connie smiled with pride. "They're the kind of men who do the right thing, no matter what. Integrity. They have it in spades."

Susannah couldn't dislodge the image of the tall dark-haired man with the slow spreading grin that started with a slight lift at the corners of his mouth, followed by a gradual widening until it reached his toffee eyes. David Foster had the kind of smile that took forever to get where it was going, but once it got there, it took your breath.

"A lawyer with integrity," she mused. "How novel."

Connie drew back the quilt and patted a pillow. "Come on, into bed. Your eyelids are drooping. Rest. We'll talk again whenever you're ready."

"Did I say thank you?" Tears swelled Susannah's throat.

"What are sisters for?" Connie hugged her. "Don't worry about anything, Suze. You're here now. Relax. In due time you can start planning for the future. Just remember—you're not alone."

A moment later she was gone, the door whispering closed behind her. Susannah stood up, tiredness washing over her. Then she spied the bathroom door.

Five minutes later she was up to her neck in bubbles in a huge tub, enjoying the relaxing lavender fragrance as jets pulsed water over her weary flesh.

Are You really watching out for me, God?

She thought over the past months and the tumble from joy to despair that she'd experienced. Unbidden, thoughts of David's troubles rose. How difficult to lose both your parents, and then the sister you'd known and loved. They had that in common—loss.

Susannah hadn't said anything to Darla or Connie, but when David had carried her into the house, she had come to, for a second. And in that moment, she *had* felt like Sleeping Beauty. Awakening to a whole new perspective on life.

Which was really stupid. She didn't want anything to do with love. Certainly not the romantic fairy-tale kind—that only led to disappointment and pain.

Susannah Wells had never had a fairy-tale life and she doubted it was about to start now, just because a nice man and his sister had cared for her. She didn't deserve a picture-perfect life.

And you won't have one. You're pregnant, Susannah. David Foster won't give you a second look.

Not that she wanted him to. Depend on yourself. She'd learned that lesson very well a long time ago.

Wearied by all the questions that had no answers, Susannah rose, drained the tub and prepared for bed. But when she finally climbed in between the sheets, she felt wide awake. She pulled open the drawer of the nightstand to search for something to read. A Bible lay there.

She picked it up with no idea of where to start reading. She let it fall open on the bed. Isaiah 43.

I, I am the One who forgives all your sins, for My sake, I will not remember your sins.

God forgave her? That's what Connie had said. But maybe it was only an accident that she was reading these words. Susannah closed the Bible, let it fall open again.

2 Corinthians.

God is the Father who is full of mercy and all comfort. He comforts us every time we have trouble, so when others have trouble, we can comfort them with the same comfort God gives us.

So many times she'd asked herself, where is God? According to this, He was right here, comforting her with Connie's house. He was the father who didn't walk out when life got rough.

A flicker of hope burst into flame inside Susannah's heart.

Maybe God could forgive the stupid choices she'd made. Maybe...but she doubted it. She wasn't like Connie—good and smart and worth saving.

God had let her get duped by Nick. Why?

Because she wasn't worth loving. Her whole life was proof of that.

Susannah let her tears flow far into the night.

Chapter Three

David screeched to a halt in front of his home and jumped out of the car.

"I'm sorry, Mr. Foster. I only went to get Darla a drink because she said she was thirsty. When I came back, she was gone." The caregiver wrung her hands. "I've looked everywhere. She's not in the house or the yard."

"Okay. Okay." He forced his brain to focus. "Show me what she was doing."

"Here."

He studied the reams of pictures Darla had drawn. Nothing made sense to him.

"What were you talking about?" he asked.

"Actually I was reading."

"Reading what?" Suspicions rose.

"*Sleeping Beauty*. From that big book she likes so much." The woman pointed. "I tried to read something else, but she wouldn't listen.

Two weeks of Darla nagging him to visit Connie's. Suddenly it all made sense to David.

"Wait here a moment, would you please?" He picked

up the phone and dialed, chagrined when Susannah
Wells answered. "This is David Foster. By chance, did
Darla walk over there?"

"Connie is just now calling your office," Susannah
explained. "We were having lunch by the pool when
Darla showed up. She was quite upset. Connie didn't
want to make it worse so she included her in our lunch.
Not that you need to worry," she added.

"Why's that?"

"Darla calmed down immediately once we got her
busy. Connie has tons of puzzles. Darla seems fasci-
nated by them, too."

Puzzles? Since when?

"I'll be over in a few minutes to pick her up," he said.
"I'm sorry she bothered you."

"Darla's no bother at all," Susannah said. She paused,
then spoke slowly, thoughtfully. "It would be nice if
she could stay for a while, though, if that won't upset
your plans."

Ha! David's plans had gone on hold the moment he'd
received the call.

"I'm afraid I've been at loose ends, taking up too
much of Connie's time," Susannah explained. "Having
Darla here would free Connie to attend to her own issues. She wouldn't have to keep babysitting me."

"You're feeling better?" Not that he wanted to know.
He'd spent hours shoving the memory of Susannah's
face out of his brain.

"Oh, yes. Much recovered." She chuckled. "Especially with Darla here. She's got a wicked sense of
humor."

"Mmm." What was he supposed to say to that?
"Well, I'll come and get her out of your hair."

"Really, it's not— Oh, here's Connie."

"David?" Connie sounded breathless.

"Sorry for the invasion," he apologized.

"Invasion? Darla's like a refreshing breeze off the mountains. Which, given today's heat, I could use. This is not autumn in Tucson as I've known it." She chuckled.

"Hang around, you'll get used to it." He swallowed. "Connie—"

She cut him off.

"David, I was thinking—" He could almost hear the wheels grinding in Connie's head. "Couldn't Darla stay? Susannah and I are enjoying the visit as much as she. In fact, I've just had the most wonderful idea."

"Oh?" He glanced at his watch, not really listening to Connie's plan. Ten minutes before his next client arrived in his office. Could he get back in ten minutes?

"…Susannah would be great at it. They really connect."

"I'm sorry, Connie," he interrupted. "What did you say?"

"I said, why don't you ask Susannah about caring for Darla after school? She has her certification as a special care aide. And she's very level-headed. They get along so well. I'm sure Darla would love it."

"I don't think a pregnant woman—"

"Don't be silly. This is October and Susannah's not due until Easter. I think it would be perfect," Connie enthused. She lowered her voice. "Susannah really needs a job, David. Working with Darla is taxing but it would only be for a few hours a day and it would keep her mind occupied. The hours Darla spends at her school would also give Susannah some time on her own."

David hated the whole idea. He didn't want a pregnant woman in his employ, someone else to be responsible for. Especially someone he was faintly attracted to.

Faintly?

David shut off the mocking laughter in his head and refocused. His sister had to have someone, and clearly the woman the agency had sent over wasn't going to work out. Again.

"Will you consider it?" Connie asked. "Please?"

"I can't decide this right now. I left the office in a rush and I've got an urgent appointment in a few minutes." David thought for a moment. "Could Darla stay there for the afternoon, just till I get home? Then I'm going to have to talk to her. This can't happen again."

"I'll make sure she stays. You go do your work. We'll be fine," Connie insisted. "But promise me you'll think about my suggestion. It would be so perfect."

"Connie, Darla is bigger than Susannah. And stronger, judging by what I saw. She could hurt your friend. Not intentionally, but she does lash out."

"But that's the funny thing. She hasn't with Susannah. Maybe because of the baby, I don't know." Connie sighed. "I know how you like to dot all the *i*'s, David. Go back to your office. Think on it. We'll be here."

"Thanks. You're a good friend, Connie." David hung up and wasted a few minutes musing on the idea.

"Am I fired?"

He blinked and saw the helper he'd hired staring at him.

"Because if I'm not, I quit. I can't do this. She's—violent."

"She just gets a little frustrated. I'm sorry if Darla scared you. Here." He handed her a wad of money. "That should cover your expenses. Thanks a lot."

By the time David returned to his office, his father's former client was antsy and David had his work cut out assuring the high-profile man that his case wouldn't suffer just because his father wasn't handling it. David worked steadily until he suddenly noticed the office was quiet and the clock said ten to six.

He was so far behind he could have used another three hours to catch up. But no way was he going to add to Connie's responsibilities by shirking his. Traffic was backed up and by the time he arrived on their street the sun had long since dipped below the craggy red Rincon Mountain tips.

"I'm so sorry," he began as the door opened. He stopped. Susannah. "Hello." She looked infinitely better than she had last time. In fact, she glowed.

"Hello, yourself." She didn't smile. "We're about to sit down to dinner."

"Then I won't bother you." He could feel the ice in her voice. "If you'll call Darla?"

"No, I won't." She stepped forward and pulled the door closed behind her, forcing him to take a step back. "You can't make her leave now."

"Why not?" The peremptory tone of her voice confused him.

"Darla's spent a huge amount of time helping prepare this meal," Susannah informed him. "It's only fair she should get to enjoy it."

"I'm not sure this is about fairness. But—"

She cut him off.

"Look, I get that you don't like me, that you think I'm some kind of a tramp. It was evident in the way you looked at me when I told Connie I was pregnant."

Her face flushed red but she didn't stop glaring at him.
"Fine. No problem. But this isn't about me."

If that's what she thought, her perceptions were way
off. David had lost valuable billing time in the past
two weeks thinking about Susannah Wells, and not one
thought had been negative.

"Did you hear me?" she asked, frowning.

"This isn't about you," he repeated, noting the way
the porch light reflected the emerald sparks in her eyes.
The deep hollows under her cheeks had filled out a little
and that pallid, sickly look was completely gone. Her
blond hair shone like a swath of hammered gold as it
tumbled down her back.

"It isn't about you, either. It's about Darla. She's tried
very hard to make up for worrying you by leaving your
house without telling anyone. Helping with dinner is her
way of making up." Susannah lowered her voice as the
door creaked open. "Can't you let her have that much?"

She made it sound like he was some kind of an ogre.
David fumed. But he kept his lips buttoned because
Darla's dark head appeared in the doorway.

"Can we stay for dinner, Davy? Connie invited,
I didn't ask." His sister stood in front of him, hands
clasped at her waist as she waited. She looked different
and it took David a minute to figure out why. Her hair. It
had been styled in a way that showed off her pretty eyes.

"Do you deserve to stay?" he asked, waiting for her
to blow up.

But Darla simply shook her head.

"No, I don't," she murmured. "I promised not to
leave the house without asking, and I broke my promise. I'm sorry, Davy."

"Are you really?" he asked, suspicious of the meek

tone in her voice. He glanced at Susannah but she was watching Darla, her face an expressionless mask.

"I really am." Darla peeked at Susannah who gave a slight nod. "I got mad because Ms. Matchett said my fairy-tale book was silly. We argued, and she said I was a dummy." Her bottom lip trembled, but after a moment she collected herself. "I didn't like her calling me that so I left. But I shouldn't have. I'm sorry, Davy."

His hands tightened into balls of anger. Dummy. The one put-down Darla hated most of all. No wonder she'd run.

"I was really scared, Darla," he said quietly. "I didn't know if you'd been hurt or got lost or what had happened. I was ready to call the police."

"The police?" Her eyes grew huge, then flared. "But I didn't do anything wrong!" She stamped her foot.

Susannah cleared her throat. Darla's entire demeanor altered.

"I'm sorry, Davy," she said. "I did do something wrong. I know it. And I won't do that ever again. I promise. Okay?"

Those big brown eyes—they always got to him. Peering up at him so adoringly from the first day he'd seen her in her bassinet. The innocence was still there.

"Okay. I forgive you."

She threw her arms around him in an exuberant hug and nearly squeezed the breath out of him. Behind her, Susannah hid her grin behind her hand.

"Thank you, Davy." Darla was all smiles now. "So can we stay for dinner? I helped," she said proudly.

"If Connie says it's okay," he muttered, knowing he'd been bested.

"She will."

He watched his sister and Susannah share a grin before Darla hurried into the house.

"She was very hurt by that Matchett person's comment," Susannah murmured.

He nodded.

"She hates to be called dumb." He studied her. "What did you say to her?"

"What makes you think I said anything?" She preceded him into the house.

"Connie seems to think the two of you have developed some kind of rapport." He couldn't help but notice the way Susannah's face tightened.

"You don't like that, do you?" she challenged. "You don't think someone like me should be anywhere around Darla."

"I don't think that at all," he argued.

"Darla is a lot smarter than you give her credit for, Mr. Foster."

"My name is David."

Susannah paused in the foyer, her face serious. "Your sister is very smart, David. She craves your attention. She feels alone and she desperately wants to please you." She tilted her head to one side, watching him. "I'm no psychiatrist, but I think Darla wants to prove to you that she's good at something. Hence the reciting of commercials and such."

"That's—interesting," he said.

"She could do so many things." Susannah's voice grew intense. "But she says you won't let her try. You're afraid she'll hurt herself. That's hard on her."

"Uh—"

"You don't think I know what I'm talking about. I get that. I guess I wouldn't listen to me, either. I don't have any credentials and I'm not exactly a walking advertisement for responsibility. But please, don't write off Darla's ideas too quickly. That's worse to her than being called dumb."

She'd put her hand on his arm as she spoke, imploring him to listen. David glanced at it. Susannah only then seemed aware of what she'd done and hurriedly jerked her hand away.

"Never mind," she whispered and hurried toward the others.

All through dinner David kept watch over his sister and the woman she seemed to adore. Darla told Susannah all about the pottery she'd made in her therapy classes, but it was the first time David had heard that she missed working with clay.

Or that she didn't like the outfit she wore. His choice. Susannah Wells had been busy.

"Aren't they great together?" Connie sat by him in the family room, watching Susannah and Darla with Silver outside in the courtyard. "Darla has a way with flowers, David. She repotted several cacti with Hornby this afternoon and you know he never lets anyone help him do that."

Just yesterday David had refused to let Darla weed the flower garden, afraid she'd hurt herself on the prickly thorns of the cholla.

Was Susannah right? Was he holding her back?

No. Susannah was full of advice, but she wasn't the one who had to rescue Darla when something bad happened, or calm her when life didn't go her way.

"She's been asking Susannah questions about the baby all day." Connie chuckled. "She's very excited."

"Connie." David frowned as he struggled to find the right words. "I'm sure Susannah is a nice person. And I'm guessing something bad landed her here, but—"

"Something bad? You could say that," Connie said, her voice harsh. "She married a guy she thought loved her. When he found out she was pregnant, he told her they weren't actually married at all and he kicked her out." She smiled grimly. "Susannah has a long history of those she trusts letting her down, so much so that she doesn't believe she's worthy of love."

"I'm sorry." He didn't know what else to say.

"Give her a chance, David," Connie pleaded. "Susannah's smart, she's funny, but most of all, she is good for Darla. Isn't that the kind of caregiver you want?"

What he wanted was a stranger, someone with no ties to him, who would come in, do her job and leave without affecting him. Susannah was beautiful, he'd already noticed that. And she was pregnant.

There would be complications if he hired her. Lots of them.

I don't have to get personally involved, other than making sure she's medically fit for work and that she can handle Darla. There's no need for me to treat Susannah Wells as anything more than an employee.

Somewhere in the recesses of his brain David heard mocking laughter.

Like he hadn't already noticed her intense eyes, fine-limbed figure or model-perfect face.

"David?" Connie's voice prodded him back to reality.

Laughter, sweet and carefree, floated into the family room from the courtyard. Susannah. She stood in a patch of light, gilded by the silvery beams, her delicate features faintly pink from the exertion of tossing a ball. She looked the same age as Darla.

"How old is she?" he asked.

"Twenty-two. Just." Connie frowned. "Does her age matter?"

Three years older than Darla. And about to be a mother.

"Come on, Darla," Susannah cheered. "You can throw it all the way from there. I know you can."

And Darla did.

"I'll give her a trial period of two weeks," David told Connie. "If she finds the work too hard or Darla too difficult, she can back out. I just hope Darla doesn't change her mind and blow up."

"I don't think that's going to happen, David." Connie laughed. "Just look at the two of them."

Susannah and Darla stood together, arms around each other's waists as they watched Silver dive into the pool. Susannah said something to Darla, who was now clad in a swimsuit. When had that happened?

David jumped to his feet. Darla was scared of water. She panicked when it closed over her head and after being rescued, always took hours of calming. And then came the nightmares.

"No!" he yelled.

But he was too late. Darla jumped into the pool. The water closed over her body. David rushed outside, furious that he hadn't been paying enough attention. He saw her black swimsuit sink to the bottom and yanked off his shirt.

"Wait." Susannah pulled on his arm. "Give her a chance."

"She hates it," he hissed. "She freezes underwater."

But after what seemed an eternity, Darla resurfaced and began to move, pushing herself across the pool until she reached the other side. She grabbed the side, gasping for air but grinning.

"I did it." She pumped her fist in the air. "Did you see, Susannah? I did it."

"I knew you would." Susannah smiled at her, watching as Darla darted through the shallow water to chase Silver. "You have to believe in her, David," she murmured. "Otherwise, how will she believe in herself?"

Then Susannah turned away, found a lounger and sank into it, her attention wholly focused on the pair in the pool.

She was right.

That was the thing that shocked David the most. This girl, seven years his junior with no training, not only saw Darla's potential but helped his sister find it.

He walked toward her.

"I'd like to offer you a job," he said. "But only if you are checked out by a doctor and he okays you to work with Darla. It would be only a few hours a day with perhaps some time on Saturdays." He told her how much he was willing to pay.

"There's a catch, isn't there?" Susannah said after a long silence, during which she studied him with those intense green eyes. "What is it?"

David didn't hesitate.

"Every activity you plan has to be approved by me," he told her.

"Every one?" She smiled. "Wow, you are a control freak, aren't you?"

"I insist on keeping my sister safe," he said firmly. "That's my condition."

"I see." Susannah's scrutiny didn't diminish. After a long silence she frowned. "Did you ever consider that you might be keeping her too safe?"

"No." He wasn't going to start out with her questioning his rules. "I'd like to start with a trial period of two weeks. Do you want the job or not?"

She kept him waiting, a blond beauty whose pink cheeks had been freshly kissed by the sun. Finally she nodded once. "Yes."

"Good. As soon as you get the doctor's approval, you can start." He turned to leave.

"I have a condition of my own."

He wheeled around, frustrated by the way she challenged him. "Which is?"

"When you disagree with my suggestions, and you will disagree," Susannah said, her smile kicking up the corners of her pretty lips, "will you at least try to understand that I'm making them for Darla's benefit?"

What did she think—that he was some bitter, angry, power monger who had to lord it over everyone to feel complete?

"I'll listen," David agreed, staring at her midriff. "As long as you promise you won't take any undue chances."

"With the baby?" Her face tightened. "No," she said firmly. "I want my baby to be healthy. I won't risk anything for that. That's one thing I don't intend to mess up."

"Then we have a deal."

David turned and walked away.

That's one thing I don't intend to mess up.

For the rest of the day, David couldn't stop speculating on Susannah's comment. What—or who—had let Susannah down, making her believe she had to earn love?

He found no satisfactory answers to stop his thoughts about Darla's newest caregiver—at least, that's how he *should* be thinking of the beautiful Susannah Wells.

Chapter Four

Two weeks later Susannah stirred under the November sun, stretched and blinked. The scene in front of her brought her wide awake.

"Do you like it?" Darla preened, scissors dangling from one finger.

"Um, it's different." Susannah slid her legs to one side and slowly rose. Thankfully her recent light-headedness seemed to have abated. She lifted the scissors from Darla's hands and put them on the patio table. "Let's put these away."

She'd slept a full eight hours last night. It wasn't as if she was tired. And yet, one minute of sun and she went out like a light. Sleeping on the job. David would be furious.

"Why did you cut off the bottom of your dress, sweetie?" Susannah asked.

"I don't like this dress," Darla grumbled. She flopped down into a chair. "Davy says it's nice but I think it's ugly."

"Because it's black?" Susannah asked. "But you look good in black. You have the right coloring."

Darla didn't look at her. Instead she drew her knees to her chin and peered into space.

"Why so serious?" Susannah laid a hand on the shiny dark head. "What are you thinking about, honey?"

"When my mom died, it was like today," Darla whispered. "There were leaves falling off the trees."

And you wore a black dress.

"Black isn't only for funerals, you know, Darla," she soothed. "Evening wear is often black because it looks so dressy. And a lot of women wear black to look slimmer."

"Am I fat?" Darla asked, eyes widening.

"No! Of course you're not. I didn't mean that." Susannah couldn't tell what was going on in the girl's mind, so she waited.

"Black clothes don't show marks when you spill stuff," the whisper came a minute later.

"Oh?" Something told Susannah to proceed very carefully.

"Davy and me went out for pizza last night. It was good, but I spilled."

"I'm sure the pizza people didn't care. Restaurants are used to spills," Susannah encouraged. "Besides, everyone gets messy eating pizza."

"Davy didn't. He had on a white shirt." Darla wouldn't look at her. "I wore my soccer shirt. It got stains. I looked like a baby."

Darla was worried about her appearance?

"Davy was embarr—" She frowned, unable to find the word.

"Embarrassed? I don't think David gets embarrassed." Susannah wasn't sure she completely understood what was behind these comments. But it was time to find out why her clothes bothered Darla. She held out a hand. "Come on."

"Where are we going?" Darla asked, taking Susannah's hand to help her rise.

"To look at your closet."

"Okay." Darla picked up the scissors.

"Without those," she added hastily.

"Oh." Darla put them back, then led the way to her room.

As they poked through the contents of the closet for the rest of the afternoon, Susannah watched Darla's reaction to each item. Mostly negative. Susannah had no idea how much time had passed when a sardonic voice in the doorway asked, "Did you lose something?"

"Oh. Hi." Darla had a point, Susannah decided. David looked as neat and pristine as he'd probably looked when he left the house this morning. She felt rumpled and dingy even being in the same room. "We're taking inventory."

"Ah." He blinked. "I'm going to change. You won't— er, leave the room like that, will you?"

"I think so." Susannah winked at Darla. "Has a certain carefree look, don't you think?"

But Darla didn't laugh. Instead she rose and began scooping up handfuls of hangers and placing them on the rod in her closet.

"I'll make it good, Davy," she said as she scurried back and forth.

"What happened to your dress?" he asked, staring at the ragged, sawed-off hem.

"Oh, that," Susannah said, noting Darla's flush of embarrassment. "I'm afraid that's a fashion plan gone wrong."

"You did it deliberately?" Pure shock robbed all expression from his face.

"It was unplanned," she hedged. "But the dress didn't work in its original state anyway."

"It worked for—never mind." His mouth drooped before he quickly closed it. He turned to leave, then stopped and turned back, dark eyes suspicious. "Did anything else happen today?"

"We did a little work in the back flower bed. Darla's really good at planting and we both like mums, so we planted a few pots."

"Then I owe you some money." He nodded. "If you'll meet me downstairs in a few minutes, I'll pay you."

"Good idea. I want to talk to you anyway." Susannah frowned. Was that fear flickering through his tawny eyes? Of her? "Five minutes?"

He nodded and left.

"Davy paid for my clothes. He likes them. So do I," Darla insisted loudly. She hurried to get the clothes hung, and in her haste the hangers dangled helter-skelter.

"Hey, slow down," Susannah chuckled. "I helped create this mess. I'm going to help you clean it up." By showing Darla how to group clothes, they reorganized the closet and rearranged the drawers. She paused when she pulled out an old pair of almost-white jeans tucked at the back of the closet. "How come you never wear these, Darla?"

"Davy doesn't like them. And I'm too big." Darla took them from her and relegated them to their hiding place. She took off the dress she'd cut and drew on another exactly the same except it was navy instead of black.

Clearly Darla didn't want to irritate the brother who had done so much for her. A lump of pity swelled in Susannah's throat. Darla was willing to be unhappy rather than tell her brother she hated her clothes.

They walked downstairs together. Mrs. Peters, David's housekeeper, asked Darla to set the table just as he came loping down the stairs.

"Now how much do I owe you for the flowers?"

Susannah glanced down the hall, grabbed his elbow and drew him into his study. She closed the door.

"We have to make this quick before she finishes the table."

"Make what quick?" he asked, one eyebrow elegantly arched.

"Listen, I want to take Darla shopping," she explained.

"Shopping?" He nodded. "More flowers?"

"New clothes." She held up a hand. "You're going to say her clothes are almost new. I'm sure someone at the goodwill center will appreciate that."

"You cut her dress because you don't like her clothes," he guessed, a frown line marring the smooth perfection of his forehead. "Um——"

"Darla cut it. Because she hates it. And the rest of her clothes." Susannah flopped onto a couch and crossed her feet under her. "I can't say I blame her."

His chest puffed out. His face got that indignant look and his caramel eyes turned brittle. Susannah gulped. Okay, that could have been worded differently.

"What I mean is——"

"You mean her clothes aren't trendy. No holes in her jeans, no skintight shirts," he snapped. "Ms. Wells, my sister's clothes are from an expensive store. They are the best——"

"—money can buy," she finished. "I'm sure they are." She sat back and waited for him to cool down.

David continued to glare at her. Eventually he sat down and sighed. "Explain, please."

"Did you choose Darla's clothes? No, let me guess. You told a sales associate what you wanted and she picked them out." Susannah chuckled at the evidence radiating across his face. "I thought so. Probably a commissioned sales woman."

"What difference would that make?" he demanded. "I got the best for my sister. Darla doesn't need to alter her own clothes."

"She might be happier if she could tear them all apart," she mused.

"What? Where is this going?" He looked defensive and frustrated. That was not her goal. Susannah straightened, leaned forward.

"After she cut her dress, Darla told me she wore black the day of her mother's funeral. Then she talked a lot about spilling and messes." She inhaled a deep breath for courage. "Did you notice when you were in her room how many of her clothes are black, brown or gray?"

"Good serviceable colors," David said.

"For men's suits!" Susannah blew the straggling wisps of hair off her forehead and tried again. "Your sister is, what, three years younger than me? Can you imagine me in any of her clothes?"

"No."

Susannah surveyed her jeans. "I don't have good clothes, David. I bought most of mine at a thrift store. But you're right," she said flatly, "I wouldn't wear Darla's clothes if you gave them to me."

David glared at her. "Why don't you just come right out and say what you mean?"

"Did Darla choose any of those clothes?"

"I don't recall." He frowned, his gaze on some past memory. "Her arm was still bothering her and she had some bandages yet to be removed when we shopped. We went for snaps and zips she could manage." Then he refocused. "Does it matter?"

"Yes!"

"Because?" He waited, shuffling one foot in front of the other.

"Because she should be young and carefree. Instead she wears the clothes of a forty-year-old," Susannah snapped, unable to hold in her irritation. "Because she needs to dress in something that lets her personality shine through. Because Darla is smothering under this blanket you keep putting over her."

"Well. Don't hold back." David stiffened, his face frozen.

"I wouldn't even if I could," she assured him. "I'm here to help Darla. That's what I'm trying to do."

"I'm not sure you fully understand Darla's situation," David said crisply. "Until about eight months ago, she could barely walk. She'd been wearing jogging suits while she did rehab. By the time she finished that, she'd outgrown everything she owned."

He'd done his best. That was the thing that kept Susannah from screaming at him to lighten up. No matter what, David Foster had done the very best he could for his sister. Because he loved her. Connie was right. He did have integrity. How could you fault that?

But Darla was her concern, not sparing David's feelings. Susannah leaned forward, intent on making him understand what she'd only begun to decipher.

"Darla is smart and funny. She's got a sweet heart and she loves people. But she doesn't have any confidence in herself." Susannah touched his arm. "She gets frustrated because she wants so badly to be what you want, and yet somehow, she just can't get there."

"I don't want her to be anything," he protested.

"You want her to be neat and tidy." Susannah pressed on, determined to make him see what she saw.

"That's wrong?" David asked.

"How many teens do you know who fit that designation? By nature teens are exploring, innovating, trying to figure out their world. Darla is no different." Susannah said. "Except that she thinks you're embarrassed when she spills something."

"I'm not embarrassed about anything to do with my sister." She saw the truth in his frank stare. "I thought…"

The complete uncertainty washing over his face gripped a soft spot in her heart.

"David, listen to me and, just for a moment, pretend that I know what I'm talking about." She drew in a breath of courage. "Most teen girls love fashion, they love color. They experiment with style, trying to achieve the looks they see in magazines. It's part of figuring out who they are. I'll bet Darla used to do that, didn't she?"

"She always liked red," he said slowly.

"I didn't see anything red in her closet."

"No." His solemn voice said he'd absorbed what she'd hinted at. "Go on."

"With her current wardrobe, Darla couldn't experiment if she wanted to," Susannah told him. "Her clothes are like a mute button on a TV. They squash everything unique and wonderful about her."

"But—" David stopped, closed his mouth and stared at her.

His silence encouraged Susannah to continue, though she softened her tone.

"I think her accident left her trying to figure out how she fits into her new world. She's struggling to make what she is inside match with those boring clothes."

"So how should she dress?" he asked, his eyes on her worn jeans.

"I want her to express herself. If she's in a happy mood, I want her to be able to pull on something bright and cheerful. If she's feeling down, I want her to express that, instead of becoming so frustrated she blows out of control and tantrums."

A timid knock interrupted.

"Are you mad at me for cutting my dress, Davy?" Darla peeked around the door, her big brown eyes soulful as a puppy's. "I'm sorry."

"It's okay, Dar. It was just a dress." David patted the seat beside him. "Come here for a minute, will you?"

Susannah wanted to cry as the tall, beautiful girl shuffled across the room, shoulders down, misery written all over her demeanor when she flopped down beside her brother.

"Ms. Wells has been telling me she thinks you need some new clothes."

"Really?" Darla jerked upright, her face brightening.

"Would you like to go shopping?" he asked.

For a moment hope glittered in Darla's dark eyes but it fizzled out when she shook her head.

"No. I have lots of clothes. I hung them all up, Davy."

"I know you did, honey. That's great." He smoothed her hair back. "You know, Dar, when we got those clothes you were still getting better from your accident and you had trouble with zippers and buttons." He laid an arm around her shoulders and hugged her. "But you're much better now. I think we should get you some new things, especially with Thanksgiving and Christmas coming. What do you think?"

"Connie's going to have a party. I could get a new dress for that." Darla's face cleared and she grinned. "Okay, Davy."

Susannah wanted to cheer. He'd phrased it just right. Everyone got new clothes for the holidays. It was a natural decision, revealing no reflection on the ugly things now in Darla's wardrobe. Little by little they could be shifted out.

"Can Susannah get a party dress, too?"

Susannah blinked, then shook her head. "Oh, no, I don't—"

"Why not?" David smiled at Darla.

"I don't want a new dress," Susannah protested. "With the baby, that is—" She blushed and avoided his stare. "I won't fit in anything for very long and—"

"There are such things as maternity dresses," he said mildly. "Besides, you'll need something for Connie's Christmas party. It's quite a fancy affair. Tomorrow's Saturday. That's a good day for shopping. I'll pay you overtime."

"No, you won't." Distressed by the way this had turned on her, Susannah rose. "I'm sure the two of you will manage very well tomorrow."

"Oh, no. You're not sticking me with a shopping trip

on my own. We'll pick you up at ten. Right, Darla?" He grinned at his sister, who grinned right back.

"Right. I'm going to tell Mrs. Peters." She rushed away, all arms and legs and excitement, exactly as a teenage girl would.

Susannah stared after her, amazed by the change. When she felt David watching her, she looked away from the intensity of his gaze and walked toward the front door.

"We could start at Bayley's Store for Women," he said, following her.

Her hand on the doorknob, Susannah froze. She turned and looked at him.

"For more of the same?" she asked.

"Point made." He sighed. "Okay, you can pick the stores. But nothing too..."

Susannah couldn't help but roll her eyes. "David, could you just lighten up? Try to remember what it was like when you were her age. It wasn't that long ago," she teased gently.

She thought she saw humor in those toffee-toned eyes, but before she could be sure, David blinked.

"Ten o'clock, remember. How much did you spend on the flowers?" He pulled out his wallet and handed her some money. "Will this cover it?"

"It's too much." Susannah held out her hand, offering it back. But David shook his head.

"No, it isn't. I'm pretty sure you stopped somewhere along the way for a drink, didn't you? And something to eat?"

"How do you know that?" she asked. He grinned, his smile dazzling her. She was momentarily stunned by how great he looked when he smiled.

"Because I'm getting to know you." He reached out and touched the corner of her mouth. "And because you have a little smear of chocolate right here."

"Oh." Her stomach shivered and it had nothing to do with the baby or morning sickness. "Right. Well, I guess I'll see you tomorrow," she said. "Bye."

Susannah turned and literally fled from the man whose touch had just sent warmth flooding through her. Her skin burned where he'd brushed his fingers.

She'd thought David stern and taciturn, but he'd surprised her. Maybe under all that lawyerly reserve and rule making, David Foster wasn't quite the ogre she'd thought.

David shifted uncomfortably on the dinky little chair someone had thought to provide for men stuck waiting while women tried on clothes. He'd like to leave, but he wanted to vet every outfit his sister tried on. So far, his decisions had not been popular with Susannah, who, by the way, seemed perfectly at home on her little perch.

"Uh, I don't think so," he said, when Darla emerged in a swirling lime-green tank top and matching pants.

"Oh, why not?" Susannah asked. "Too much color?"

"No. The pants don't fit her properly. They're too short." He didn't understand the droll look Darla and Susannah exchanged.

"It's a capri pant," Susannah explained. "They're supposed to be that length. It's the fashion."

"Oh." Fashion. He felt like he was drowning.

"So?" Susannah nudged him with her elbow.

"Do you like it?" he asked his sister, studying her face.

"Yes." At least she was definite. "Emmaline wears clothes like this at my school. She's pretty."

"You look pretty, too," he told her. And she did.

Contrary to David's expectations, Susannah's choices for his sister were not outlandish or edgy. Nor were they as expensive as the clothes he'd chosen. He was amazed at Susannah's patience as she taught Darla to choose the things that brought out her natural beauty. With each outfit, as Darla caught a glimpse of herself in the mirror, she grew more graceful. More and more she was becoming the sister he remembered, leaving behind the mulish child he'd battled with for the last eight months.

It wouldn't last, of course. Darla had a long way to go. But she was learning, and Susannah had lasted much longer than any of Darla's other caregivers.

"You should be proud. She's a very beautiful woman," Susannah murmured.

Woman? His sister?

David did a double take at the girl in the red dress now preening in the mirror. But Susannah was right. Darla looked more like a young woman than a girl. She was growing up and he'd have to face all that implied.

"I want Susannah to try on this dress." Darla held out a garment of swirling patterns in deep, rich green. "It has room for the baby," she said.

"It's very beautiful, Darla, and I appreciate you thinking of me," Susannah said quietly. "But I can't try it on. It's too expensive."

"I want you to. It's a present." Darla the woman disappeared, and the petulant girl returned, face turning red when Susannah continued to shake her head. "Davy, buy it," she insisted, thrusting the hanger at her brother.

"Darla, I can't accept it." Susannah was firm but insistent. "Please put it back on the rack."

"No. It's your dress." Darla was working herself up into a snit.

David rose, preparing to leave.

"Sit down please, David. We're not finished yet." Susannah never even looked at him, but her firm tone and calm manner left him in no doubt as to who was in charge.

David sat.

"Put the dress back, please, Darla. Then we need to look at shoes." Susannah blandly continued to survey the list in her hand.

Darla was still angry but now she looked confused.

"I want you to have a new dress, too," she said, her voice quieter as she stood in front of Susannah.

"I know you do, sweetie. And it's very kind of you, but this shopping day is for you. When I decide to get a new dress, I promise you and I will go shopping for it. But not today." She paused, studied the girl. "Okay?"

Darla's internal battle was written all over her face. But Susannah's calm tone and manner won. Darla returned the dress to the rack, changed back into her own clothes and calmly waited while the sales clerk totaled her purchases.

David handed over his credit card in total bemusement. How did Susannah do it?

"Can we have lunch before we start shoe shopping?" he asked as they stored the many packages in his vehicle. "I'm starving."

"That's because you didn't eat a good breakfast. Breakfast is the most important meal of the day. More than half of North Americans skip breakfast." Darla told him, stuffing her last package into the trunk.

"Half?" Susannah sputtered.

David looked at her. She was trying to hide her laughter.

"Yes, half," Darla insisted.

"Then I guess I'm one of those statistics," Susannah told her. "I'm starving, too. And your stomach is growling." She giggled out loud and soon Darla was giggling with her.

Shaking his head, David led them to a restaurant and left Susannah to deal with Darla's insistence on chocolate cake while he scoured the menu for himself. He'd forgotten how nice it was to relax over a meal.

Susannah didn't insist Darla choose anything, he discovered. She commented on the results of certain choices, and then left the decision totally up to Darla, who glanced at him for approval.

"You decide," David said quietly.

And she did, visibly gaining confidence as she discarded the chocolate cake in favor of another choice.

"I don't like soup," she told the server. "It's messy. Can I have something else?"

They settled on a salad to go with her cheeseburger and fries. Usually David ordered something she could munch on right away, but Darla seemed perfectly content to talk as they waited for their food. After a moment she excused herself and went to wash her hands.

"How do you do it?" David asked Susannah the moment his sister was out of hearing range. "She hasn't tantrumed with you once, though I thought we'd have one in the store."

"I did, too," Susannah confessed with a grin. "And if she had, I would have sat there and waited it out."

"Really?" He couldn't imagine sitting through one of Darla's tantrums.

"It's a behavior she's learned, David. She needs time to unlearn it." She shrugged. "If we make her responsible for her actions, she'll soon realize that the results she gets are determined by her. I want her to learn independence."

"We had a big argument about her bedtime last night," he admitted. "She thinks she should stay up longer. Maybe she should," he admitted. "I guess I still think of her as a little kid."

"She is in some ways." Susannah sipped her lemonade. "Why don't you let her choose a time on the condition that she has to get up in the morning when her alarm clock rings without your help? Make her responsible."

"Good idea." He sipped his coffee. "I can't believe you learned all this caring for the elderly."

"Some of it," she admitted. "But most of what I know about behavior, I learned in our foster home. And I took some university classes for a semester. They helped. I'm going to take some more. I want to get a degree in psychology."

He was intrigued by her. More than a boss should be.

"The bathroom is really pretty," Darla told them as she slipped back into her seat. "Lots of red."

Their food arrived and conversation became sporadic. David dug into his steak, then paused to notice that Susannah picked certain items off her plate and set them aside but eagerly bit into a sour pickle.

"So it's true what they say about pregnancies and pickles," he teased.

She flushed a rich ruby flood of color that tinted her skin from the V neckline of her sweater to the roots of her hair. Finally she nodded.

"It's true. For me anyway."

"I don't like pickles," Darla said. "You can have mine, Susannah."

"Thank you." Susannah laid the pickles on one slice of toast, then spread peanut butter on the other. She put them together, cut the whole thing in half and then took a bite.

"That's lunch?"

She blushed again when she caught him staring at her. "It's very good. You should try it."

"I'll take your word for it." Then it dawned on him. "Some foods bother you."

"Mostly the smell of some foods," she murmured, eyeing his steak with her nose turned up. She returned to munching contentedly on her sandwich.

"Connie said you'd seen the doctor I researched. She says everything is okay." It sounded like he was prying, he realized—which he was.

"I'm fine," she said. She set down her sandwich and stared at him. "The baby is fine. I'm very healthy. There's nothing to worry about."

"There's always something to worry about," he muttered, pushing away his plate.

"Why?" Susannah dabbed absently at a dribble of pickle juice and waited for an answer. "I thought Connie told me you believe in God."

"I do."

"People who believe in God usually talk about the faith they have in Him to lead them," she mused, perking up when a dessert cart arrived at the table next to theirs. "What are you worried about?"

"A new study says ninety percent of the things people worry about will never happen," Darla chimed in.

Susannah tucked her chin against her neck but not fast enough to hide her grin. David was beginning to wish he'd never said a word about worry, so he grabbed at their server's suggestions for dessert and bought everyone a huge piece of key lime pie. With the meal finished, he begged off shoe shopping and agreed to meet the two women in a little courtyard area outside. Better to trust Susannah than sit through another round of fashion do's and don'ts.

He was enjoying a well-creamed cup of coffee and working out a schedule of Darla's activities on his smartphone when Susannah arrived lugging several bags, visibly weary. He took them from her and insisted she sit down.

"Where's Darla?" he asked, searching the area behind her.

"She's coming. She met a friend and they're buying an ice cream cone. Her friend's mother will meet us here shortly." Susannah chose a seat in a shady spot where she could study the dangling seed pods of a desert willow. "You were working," she said. "Don't let me bother you."

"No bother." He stuffed the device in his pocket. "I just got an email about Darla's after-school soccer group. I guess I forgot to reregister her."

"Does she have to go?" Susannah asked.

"She loves soccer." He frowned. "Doesn't she?"

"Yes." Susannah didn't meet his stare. "But there are so many more things she wants to try."

"Such as?" He could feel the tension crawling across his shoulders. What was wrong with the status quo? Why did she have to change everything?

"Did you know she wants to do pottery again?"

"I know she liked it before. But it's not very active and Darla needs to keep her muscles toned. Soccer is good for that," he explained.

"Swimming is better."

David tensed. Why was she always so eager to push him?

"I'm not comfortable with her swimming. At least not without me present," he said, waving when Darla emerged from the store. "For now I think we'll stick to the activities she knows."

"The ones you've decided are safe for her, right?" Susannah smiled at Darla but her tone was troubled. "I hope you don't regret it," she said quietly.

David was going to ask what she meant but Darla snagged his attention, showing him the massive cone she was trying to eat before it melted. She giggled and laughed, teased Susannah about the pickle juice that had spattered her shirt and insisted David taste her triple-fudge-and-marshmallow ice cream.

David discarded Susannah's comment. Darla was happy, like a big kid enjoying the pleasures of life. That was exactly what he wanted for her.

Wasn't it?

Unbidden, the image of Darla twirling in front of the store's floor-length mirror in her red dress fluttered through his mind. Not a kid, a woman. He felt the intensity of a stare and caught Susannah looking at him.

She was good for his sister. He didn't deny that. But there were things in Darla's life that *were* working, things that didn't need changing. One of those was soccer.

He urged them back to the car and drove Susannah

to Connie's, anxious to escape her probing questions and retreat to the normalcy of his home.

But that night, when the house had quieted and there was no one to disturb his thoughts, David couldn't dislodge Susannah's warning from his brain.

I hope you don't regret it.

"Maybe I'm not supposed to worry about things, Lord," he whispered as he sat in the dark, watching stars diamond-stud the black velvet of the night sky. "But I am worried. She's changing everything. What if Susannah's wrong about Darla?"

But what if she was right?

Chapter Five

This is wrong.

It wasn't the first time Susannah had thought those words as she stood in the church basement and watched Darla try to interact with the young girls in the club.

It wasn't that they were mean or did anything to Darla. In fact, they were most impressed with Darla's new outfit and offered many compliments.

The problem was Darla didn't fit here and she knew it. The other girls were younger, faster and more nimble with their handicrafts. Darla tried, but only halfheartedly, and when her kite didn't work out, she crushed it and threw it into the trash in a fit of anger.

Susannah saw the glint in her eye and the set of her jaw and knew the girl was not happy. The ride home was tense. On an impulse she pulled into a park.

"Let's go for a walk," she said.

After they'd gone a short way, Darla stopped.

"I hate girls' club. I can't do it." She stamped her foot, caught Susannah's eye and sighed. "I'm sorry," she said, flopping onto the grass.

"Actually, I think you did very well at girls' club,

but maybe you've been there long enough," Susannah mused, sitting beside her. Maybe here Darla would open up and speak of things she did want to do.

"Davy likes girls' club. He says it's safe."

"I suppose it is safe," Susannah said, striving to sound noncommittal.

"It's for little kids. I'm not little." After a few minutes Darla began talking about the bed of flowers nearby. She described each one.

"You know a lot about flowers." Susannah's mind had begun to whirl with ideas but she gave nothing away. She'd have to talk to David first, get his permission. And that would probably not be easy.

"I like them. Flowers don't make me feel stupid," Darla muttered. Then her face brightened. "There's the ice cream man. I love ice cream. Maybe they have pistachio. Can I get one, Susannah?" Darla begged.

"I don't know if I have enough cash. Maybe you should find out how much a cone costs first?" Susannah stayed where she was, swamped by a rush of tiredness as Darla raced across the grass.

In a few minutes Darla came rushing back. Susannah held out her wallet and Darla counted out what she needed. It seemed a lot to Susannah. She'd been trying to save every cent she could for the baby but these little side trips were digging into that meager account.

Still, it was worth it to see Darla's proud face as she returned with two fudge bars.

"One for you and one for me."

"Thank you." Susannah took the bar, impressed again by Darla's kind heart. "That's very kind of you to share. Didn't they have pistachio?"

"I'd rather have a fudge one with you," Darla said.

She'd given up her first choice to share. Susannah felt proud as any new mom.

While they ate their cones, Darla talked about her brother.

"Davy's an awfully good brother," she said, her eyes soft with love. "He was on a vacation when my dad died. Davy had to come home and take over his work. When my mom got sick, Davy looked after her, too." Her smile dimmed. "And he always looks after me."

"He loves you a lot."

"I love him, too," Darla said. "I wish he would have gotten married. But Erin didn't want me around." Darla peeked sideways at Susannah, her guilt obvious.

"What happened?" She kept her voice even.

"I wasn't nice. I spilled ketchup on her shirt. Her favorite shirt." A glower replaced Darla's sunny smile. "She told Davy I was a baby, too young to make pots."

"Pots? Oh, you mean pottery?" She shrugged. "Maybe you were too young, honey. I'm afraid I don't know anything about it."

"I do. A man came to my school and showed us how to make pots. He said mine was the best," she said proudly. "Davy put it in the garden."

"You mean the blue one?" Susannah asked, surprised by the information.

"Uh-huh. It was going to be a fountain but it dried too hard and I couldn't put a hole in it." She sighed. "The teacher told me I should try again."

"Maybe you should."

"You mean it, Susannah? You'll let me do pottery?" Darla leaned over and hugged her tightly. "Oh, thank you."

Susannah ignored the blob of chocolate on her shirt-front and hugged back. "It isn't up to me, so don't get in a rush. I have to ask your brother. He's the boss and if he says no—"

She left it hanging. Finished with the ice cream, they rinsed off under a tap and then drove home. Darla immediately stormed David with a demand to make pottery.

As Susannah watched them, she grew very conscious of the way he surveyed her, his gaze resting on the twin ice cream stains the two of them wore. Well, so what? They'd had fun.

His mouth pursed in that thin line that meant he was going to deny Darla's request out of hand. Susannah had to do something.

"Darla, would you show me the pot you made? I'd really like to see it again." She followed the young woman to the back garden to admire the shiny blue pot that held a barrel cactus. "It would have made a lovely fountain," she agreed.

After much discussion about pottery, Mrs. Peters came to ask Darla's help. Darla left, and David turned to her. Susannah stiffened, knowing what was coming.

"Why this sudden need for pottery?" David asked. He pointed to a chair. "Please sit down. You look worn out."

Just what every woman wanted to hear.

"It's not *my* need, it's Darla's," she said, folding into the comfortable garden chair with relief. "She didn't have the best time at the girls' club—again."

"What happened," he demanded. "What did she do?"

"Darla didn't *do* anything," Susannah told him. "But she's too big for that club and she knows it. It doesn't interest her." She straightened and told him in a rush, "I don't think she should go anymore."

"What?" He glared at her. "Why not?"

"David, Darla can do so much more than play with little girls. She's lost some faculties, but she still has lots of skills and interests. Plants, for instance," she said, cutting off the question she knew was coming.

"I suppose I could clear out some of the things my mother planted," he said, studying the lovely garden.

"You could, but she needs more than that." Susannah struggled to explain what she'd begun to understand about Darla. "What would you do if you didn't have your work, David?" she asked.

"Me?" He shrugged. "I always wanted to fly. I have my private license. Why?"

"You have options. Darla is trying to figure out what hers are," Susannah told him. "She wants to do something that makes her feel good about herself, something that shows for her efforts and maybe something that helps others. She needs to feel confident about herself first, though."

"I don't think pottery is an option right now," he mused. "I don't think there are any classes going that she could attend. What else do you have in mind to help her learn this confidence?"

"Swimming." She shook her head at him. "I know *you're* afraid for her, but I think she's ready to challenge herself. She's ashamed that she can't go with her class when they go for swimming lessons. She knows she's missing out, David. Think how much self-esteem she'd have if she went with the class and had no problem in the water."

She knew he understood. He was clever and thoughtful and he wanted Darla to be happy. But something was holding him back.

"What if she panics?" he demanded in a tense voice.

"What if she does? They have trained staff who deal with that all the time. Darla isn't the first one to be afraid of water." Susannah touched his hand. "I know you want to keep her safe. And she will be. But she needs personal and physical challenges to grow and develop."

"But swimming?" He drew back from her touch, his face shadowed by the awning above.

A thought crossed Susannah's mind. "Do you swim, David?"

"Why do you ask?" He looked at her then, straight and head on.

"I ask because it seems like you're projecting your fears onto Darla. And I know that isn't what you want to do." She waited a few moments, watching the truth fill his face. "What happened?" she murmured.

"Are you psychoanalyzing me, Ms. Wells?"

"Do you have something to hide, Mr. Foster?"

It took several moments before he let out a deep breath.

"I was twenty-five. Old enough I suppose, but I never expected—" He shook his head. "My mother was a swimmer. We used to have a pool back here. She loved that pool, did laps every day. I came home one afternoon and found her floating on the water. She'd had a stroke."

"I'm so sorry." He was in his own world now, tied up in a knot of guilt. Susannah tried to nudge him out. "Did she recover?"

"Not really. She was paralyzed till she died. She never swam again."

"But that wasn't your fault." Something in his face didn't compute. "David?"

"I was so scared," he blurted. "I did all the wrong things. It took forever to get her out of the water because I was afraid of hurting her. I should have done more resuscitation but when she didn't come to, I panicked." He stared at her. "If it hadn't been for my friend Jared showing up, she would have died."

"So you had the pool filled in and you've been blaming yourself and trying desperately to stop anything like that from happening to Darla." Susannah smiled sadly. "But you're drowning her with your rules and regulations, David."

He held her gaze, not looking away even when Darla returned.

"It's late. I'd better go." Susannah rose slowly, forcing herself not to give away the fact that the yard was spinning.

"Can Susannah stay for dinner, Davy?" Darla asked.

"Not tonight, thanks," Susannah said before he could refuse. "I think I'm going to go home and lie down."

"Shall I drive you?" David's face was drawn and serious.

"Don't be silly. It's just a couple of blocks." She headed for the front door.

"All the same, you look pale. I think you should ride." He told Darla to stay with Mrs. Peters, then took Susannah's elbow and escorted her to his car.

"This is silly. I'm fine," she protested, but he ignored her.

"You're overdoing it. That was not my intent when you took this job. Maybe you should cut back. I can find someone else to work with Darla." He backed out of his driveway and pulled onto the street.

"Look, the doctor assures me that part of pregnancy is the occasional tiredness. I'm really fine." She saw him glance at her stomach and pulled down her shirt defensively. "I'm not some delicate flower. I'm tough, resilient." She breathed a mocking laugh. "I survived Nick. I can handle having a baby."

"Nick's the guy who left you?" he asked as he pulled up in front of Connie's house.

"He was the man I thought I married." Shame washed over her. "I stupidly thought he loved me."

"Why stupidly?" David turned in his seat to face her. "Why wouldn't he love you?"

"Because I'm a total failure," she told him, trying to suppress the tears. "People like me aren't the type who get happily ever after. I'm not like Connie. She took her life and made something of it. I messed up."

Susannah was too ashamed to sit there and let him see her give way to tears so she hastily exited the car.

"Thanks for the ride. Good night."

She hurried away, listening for the sound of the car leaving. But in her room, when she glanced out of the window, she saw him still sitting there, a puzzled look on his face.

A long time passed before he finally left.

"And now it's finally clear to him what a twit I am." Susannah sighed and started a bath. Some days were better forgotten. This was definitely one of them.

She caught a glimpse of herself in the mirror just before she stepped into the tub.

"Your mother is an idiot," she whispered, allowing the tears to fall unheeded. "Not the kind of mommy you deserve at all."

* * *

"Darla, did Susannah seem okay today?" David pretended nonchalance as he waited for his sister's response later that evening.

"I dunno." Darla looked up. "She gets tired sometimes. I pretend I am, too, so she can rest."

"That's nice of you. What did you do today?" He listened as Darla recited their activities. "That doesn't seem too bad."

"No. But I don't think Susannah has much money. When we were in the park, I wanted an ice cream cone, but when she opened her wallet, I saw that she only had enough money for me to have a cone. So I got two little bars instead. One for each of us."

"I'm proud of you for thinking of that." David's chest swelled.

"Yeah." She grinned at him.

"Maybe she doesn't carry much money with her," he mused.

"She always puts some of her money in a little can at Connie's. It's her baby can. She's saving." Darla grabbed the remote. "Can I watch my TV program now?"

"Sure."

Susannah didn't have much money. Well, of course she didn't. He'd forgotten to give her money for gas. Darla's old hot rod would bankrupt Midas.

Come to think of it, Susannah wouldn't have an easy time with those bucket seats a few months down the road, either. Maybe it was time to trade it in. The car had been secondhand when he'd got it for Darla, just before her skiing accident. It still ran, but he didn't like the idea of Susannah possibly getting stopped somewhere.

You're worried about her safety now? The chiding voice in the back of his head mocked.

David returned to the television room, oblivious to Darla's program. He wanted to shut that voice down, but the memory of Susannah's face when he'd driven her home, the pain in her voice as she'd spoken about the louse who dumped her, the thought of her innocent child caught in the midst of it all—well, David couldn't get rid of those thoughts.

"Davy?" Darla shut off the television. "Can I talk to you?"

"Of course. You can always talk to me." He patted the sofa and waited for her to curl up beside him. "What's up?"

"I was wondering who will be the daddy for Susannah's baby."

"Umm, what makes you ask, honey?" he side-stepped.

"Well, today I saw her watching a little boy when we were in the park. What if her baby is a boy? Boys need daddies to play with them and teach them stuff that mommies can't." Darla's nose scrunched up as she mulled over the problem.

"Well, maybe the father will come when the baby's born."

But Darla shook her head.

"Nope. His name was Nick and he died. I heard Aunt Connie telling Uncle Wade. He was a scoun—" She squeezed her eyes closed, trying to recall the word, but finally gave up. "I can't remember," she finally admitted.

The baby's father was dead—meaning there was no chance for Susannah to get support from him, financially or otherwise. And he *was* a scoundrel, David thought as his back teeth clenched.

You're not getting involved. You don't need any more responsibilities.

"*Scoundrel.* I think he was a bad man," Darla continued. "Don't you?"

"I don't know." He shouldn't even be listening to this, but David was curious. More curious than he should have been.

"I don't think a nice man would tell Susannah to get out. That's mean." Darla snuggled up to him. "She let me touch her tummy where the baby is growing."

"Oh." David smoothed her hair. Was it wrong to talk about this? He found himself eager to hear every detail about the beautiful blonde and her child. Maybe because he felt he'd never have his own child.

"Susannah said she doesn't know anything about how to be a mommy," Darla said. "But I think she'll be a good mother. She's really nice to me, even when I'm not nice."

"I think Susannah's nice, too, Dar." Wasn't that an understatement.

He kissed the top of her head, surprised when she jumped up. "Hey, where are you going?"

"To make some popcorn. I'm hungry." She scurried away in her jeans and bright red shirt, her bare feet slapping against the hardwood.

David could count on one hand the evenings they'd shared like this before Susannah. Evenings were usually a battle zone, but since Connie's friend had shown up Darla was more like her old self. Susannah was doing amazing work.

His mind suddenly replayed what Darla had told him.

So this Nick had told Susannah to get out? Knowing she was pregnant?

No wonder she sometimes seemed like a glass ornament, brittle and ready to shatter. Her tough veneer was just a facade, perhaps to shield herself from being hurt again. Connie had hinted at something in her past. Something ugly.

But David wasn't going to get involved.

Keep telling yourself that.

He had to. Though David felt a rush of relief that no bitter, angry boyfriend or husband was likely to come after Susannah, though he was glad that she and Darla would be safe from that, and though he was also grateful for the progress she was making with his sister—well, the rest of it was her life.

And none of his business.

"What are you thinking about, Davy?" Darla flopped at his feet, her cheeks bulging with popcorn.

He snatched one of the fluffy white bits and popped it into his mouth.

"I'm thinking about buying a different car for you and Susannah to use."

"Good. Susannah will be glad, too," Darla told him. "She says the seat hurts her back. And she has to sit on a cushion to see."

The things you could learn if you only paid attention.

"Davy?"

"Yeah?"

"Could you think about something else now?" Darla said, her brown eyes on him, sizing him up.

"What's that?" He was half-afraid to ask.

"I don't want to go to girls' club anymore. I'm too

big." She thrust her feet in front of her and stared at her poppy-red toenails.

"Okay. I'll tell them you won't be coming." He waited, knowing Darla was forming another thought.

"Do you think I'm too dumb to swim, Davy?"

He might have known.

"What do you think?"

"I don't know. At first I was scared to try, but Susannah says new things often scare us but that doesn't mean we shouldn't try them." Darla stared at him quizzically. "Do you think I can learn to not be afraid in the water, Davy?" The yearning in her voice was his undoing.

"I think you're very smart. I think that if you try hard, listen to the teacher and don't get frustrated, you can do a whole lot of things you never thought you could do," he said with certainty.

"I think maybe I can, too," she whispered. And then she grinned at him and held up her hand for a high five.

"I'll check on lessons tomorrow," he promised.

"Good. Because I don't like watching when my class goes swimming." Suddenly her eyes danced with excitement. "I'm going to surprise them when I swim right to the other end of the big pool!"

David could hardly believe the transformation in his sister.

What a difference Susannah Wells had made in their lives.

David wasn't going to get involved in her life, but that didn't have to stop him from praying that God would help her.

Her and her baby.

The beginning of a family.

He shut down that thought. A family was the one

thing he couldn't have. He knew that wasn't God's plan for his life and had accepted it.

No point in dwelling on the impossible.

Chapter Six

"There are tons of flowers," Darla burbled, her voice rising. "And you know what else they had at the botanical garden?"

"No. What?"

On Friday afternoon Susannah drove the almost-new station wagon away from the school with a light heart. It was so much easier to handle than David's other car. She had no idea what had prompted him to change vehicles, but she was glad of it.

"There's a butterfly room. It's a special glass room with plants and fish and stuff, and butterflies live there. They came and sat on me!" Darla rushed on, enthusiastic about her latest school trip.

Susannah let her talk as they drove home, knowing that she needed to spill all the things that were tumbling around in her head. They were still bubbling over when David arrived.

"Can we go back tomorrow, Davy? I want to show you the butterflies."

"I'm sorry, Dar, I can't. Tomorrow's my day for my boys." He turned to Susannah. "Actually I was going to ask you if you could come tomorrow. I'm big brother to three boys and we do something special once a month. Tomorrow it's a hockey game in Phoenix. I just got the tickets."

Big brother? David? Surprise kept her silent.

"Darla doesn't like hockey so she doesn't want to come. Do you have other plans, Susannah?" he asked.

He was always so polite, yet somehow distant. As if he didn't want to get too involved in her world. Not that Susannah blamed him. Her world was messed up.

"Susannah?" Darla poked her in the arm. "Are you sick?"

"No." She smiled to ease Darla's worried expression. "I was just thinking that I'd like to see your botanical gardens tomorrow. I should see some of the sights while I'm here."

"Are you thinking of leaving Tucson?" David suddenly seemed to stumble over his words. "Not that you owe me any answers. But I would like a bit of notice to find someone else to stay with Darla."

"I don't want you to go away, Susannah." Darla's face darkened. Her hands fisted at her sides and her body stiffened. "You can't go."

"I never said I was going anywhere right now," Susannah reminded quietly. "But if I had to leave, I hope you would wish me the best."

Darla thought about it for several moments. Finally the anger drained away and her sunny smile flashed again.

"I would," she agreed, winding her arm around Susannah's waist. She leaned her head on her shoulder. "You're my best friend, and I like doing things with you. Please stay." She glanced over one shoulder at David before she leaned near to whisper, "I want to see your baby when it's born."

Susannah flushed. David would not want to hear that. He might be glad she was here to watch Darla, but Susannah didn't need him to say out loud how much he disapproved of her. It was evident in the distant way he acted.

"The baby won't be here for a long time," Susannah murmured, with a quick peek at his face. It was hard to read anything in those inscrutable eyes. "So how about I go with you tomorrow and see those butterflies? They sound fun."

"They are." Darla once more launched into a description that lasted until Mrs. Peters came to say good-night and reminded them of the potluck supper at church.

"I forgot all about that supper. Go change, Dar." David waited until she ran up the stairs, then beckoned to Susannah to follow him to the kitchen. "I've wanted to hear tonight's speaker for a long time. He worked on a mission in the Amazon."

"You know the Amazon?"

"I took a trip there with Wade and Jared just after we all finished college." He smiled. A certain wistfulness tinged his voice. "It was amazing. Unfortunately we had to leave early."

Was that when his father had died? She hated to ask and bring up painful memories.

"You never went back?" she asked.

"Haven't had time so far." He pulled an envelope out of a drawer and handed it to her. "This is yours."

"What's this?" she asked, confused when she saw the money tucked inside. "You already paid me for the last two weeks."

"Wages, yes. That's for incidentals. Like gas for the car, the botanical garden tomorrow and the numerous ice creams and other treats my sister seems to inhale. I never expected you to pay for them, Susannah. I just didn't think about it until Darla reminded me." He glanced once at her midsection. "I'm sure you're trying to save—for the baby, I mean."

"I am, but it doesn't seem right to take this." Susannah set the envelope on the table. "You already pay me very well for doing almost nothing."

"Nothing?" He said with incredulity. "It's a lot more than nothing to me. It's been ages since I've been so caught up at work."

"Oh, good." She blushed under his praise.

"It means a great deal to me to know Darla's safe and happy under your care, Susannah. And she's learning, too. Take it. Please." He handed her the envelope again. "You'll get the same every week. And if you need more for some activity, please tell me."

"Well—thank you." She tucked it into her bag while mentally calculating how much more she'd need to save before she could get the sonogram the doctor had recommended.

An awkward silence yawned.

"Are you feeling all right? She's not too much for you?" David asked in a careful voice.

"I'm fine. Darla's wonderful. She goes out of her way to watch out for me," Susannah told him. "She's always bringing me a cushion or a glass of water. She fusses too much. She shouldn't waste her attention on me."

He'd been packing items into a cooler, but he stopped and turned to study her, his brow furrowed.

"Waste?" He shook his head. "Darla loves you."

"She shouldn't."

"Why?" His eyes were wide with surprise.

"You wouldn't understand," she murmured, trying to think up some way to get out of this conversation.

"Because you think I've had the perfect life?" His dark eyes flashed with intensity. "I'm a spoiled rich kid because I never went through foster care like you and Connie?"

"No." She did meet his stare. "I don't believe anyone has a perfect life. No one I know anyway."

"Then?" He stood where he was, waiting, palms up, for some answer.

"Look, you had your life mapped out in front of you and you followed that map." It frustrated her to have to put into words what hurt so deeply. "You weren't like me. You didn't mess up over and over. Your choices were smart. Mine weren't."

"But you were a kid and that was ages ago," he said. "You've changed."

"Have I? I hope so. But the results of my stupid decisions live on," she said, laying a hand over her stomach as if she could protect her baby. "They're certainly not the decisions a mother wants to tell her child."

"Susannah, that's ridiculous. Everyone makes mistakes—"

"You didn't," she said, daring him to contradict.

"I'm ready." Darla stood in the doorway, her smile fading. "Are you arguing?" she asked, her voice worried.

"No. Just discussing." David touched her nose. "You look very pretty," he complimented.

"It's the same color as Susannah's shirt," she said proudly. "We both like pink."

Susannah's heart lifted, as it always did in the presence of this lovely girl. "Connie made this shirt. She's decided she is going to sew me a whole new wardrobe and she won't take no for an answer."

"Connie's like Davy." Darla peeked through her lashes at her big brother. "He doesn't take no, either."

"Hey! No dissing me." He smiled at Susannah. "You look very nice."

"Thank you." She fought to keep from blushing again, but that didn't stop her heart from bouncing with pleasure at the compliment. How stupid was that—to be glad a man who looked down on you thought you looked nice? Pregnancy was fooling with her brain.

"Darla, why don't you go put on your coat?" David said. When she'd left, he turned to Susannah. "Would you like to come to the potluck with us?" he asked as he closed the lid on the cooler. "I'm sure the presentation will be worth seeing."

"Go with you?" Susannah didn't understand for a moment. "Oh, you mean to watch her? Sure, I—"

"No, that's okay—Darla will be fine. I meant would you like to come to the potluck supper and presentation with Darla and me." He leaned back against the granite counter and waited, lips tilted up in a quirky smile.

Susannah debated. It might be okay for tonight, but later, when the baby was showing more, everyone would wonder. Maybe the speculation would ruin his business and then she'd be responsible...but she was tired of hiding out at Connie's or the mall.

"I didn't realize it was such a major decision," he chuckled.

"I would like to go," she said so fast her tongue couldn't rescind it. "Thank you very much."

"You're welcome." Just for a second, he gazed at her in a way that made her face feel warm. Then his attention moved to his sister as she came back into the room. "Ready?" he asked.

"Yes. I put the soda in the trunk," Darla told him. She giggled as she told Susannah, "Davy bought root beer for his boys to have when they visit, but they don't like it. Neither do I," she said, her nose wrinkling. "We're taking it to the potluck."

"And if they don't like it, they can pass it on," David said, urging them toward the car. "I'm sick of looking at those cases taking up room in the garage." He stowed the cooler, then held the car doors while Darla and Susannah climbed inside. Once seated, he grinned at her. "Just one of the bad choices *I've* made," he said as they pulled out of the driveway and headed toward the church.

"What about that man you hired to put the carpet in your office?" Darla asked.

David winced. "Okay, two bad choices," he admitted. "He was the worst carpet layer I've ever seen. Can we let it go?"

But Darla was beginning to enjoy herself and Susannah was, too.

"Mrs. Peter's Christmas sweater?" Darla giggled.

"I didn't know she was allergic to cashmere!" he protested.

"Asking Mr. Hornby to fix the mess you made in the garden?" Darla laughed out loud at the chagrin on his face.

"He wasn't supposed to do it all at once." David's pained look spoke volumes. "I wasn't trying to kill him." Darla laughed until they pulled into the church parking lot.

"What about the cat?" she asked, ignoring his groan.

When David refused to answer, Susannah asked Darla, "What about a cat?"

"He got me a gift. A sweet cat, all white. I called her Snow White 'cause she loved to sleep." Darla's face softened, her dark eyes began to glow. "Davy *said* she was a special cat, that she'd be my best friend. That was when I was really sick. I had to stay home and I hurt a lot. Holding Snow White made me feel better."

They'd arrived at the church. David climbed out of the car, but after one look at Darla's face, he shook his head and left them to carry the cooler into the church. Susannah nudged the girl's arm.

"What happened?" This she had to hear.

"Well, Snow White ran away a whole bunch of times. If Mrs. Peter's opened the door, that cat would race outside and she didn't come back." Darla frowned. "I didn't hurt her or anything."

"I know you wouldn't do that," Susannah assured her.

"No, I wouldn't," Darla huffed. "Well, every time Snow White would run away, Davy would go and look for her. Sometimes it took a long time and I could hear him calling and calling. But he always brought her home. Except one night."

Surely the poor thing hadn't been hurt? Susannah bit her lip. She had a special affection for cats, honed by years of sitting in the barn on her foster family's farm, crying over her mother's refusal to answer her letters.

"It's okay, Susannah, you don't have to be sad." Darla

bent her head trying to see into Susannah's eyes. "It's not bad," she rushed to reassure.

"You'd better explain, Dar. I can see she already thinks the worst." David leaned against the car while Darla explained.

"Well, Snow White had babies. She didn't want to stay with me. She just wanted to come to my house and eat so she could feed her babies," Darla explained. "Mrs. Murphy was away and the boy she hired didn't take care of Snow White very well so Snow White had to take care of her family herself."

"By mooching off of us," David grumbled.

"When Mrs. Murphy came home and saw Davy picking up Snow White and carrying her away, she got really mad at him. It was her cat, you see. She called the police and she followed him home. She was yelling and her face was all red."

"How was I supposed to know it was her cat? I didn't even know the woman, let alone that she had a cat." Obviously disgruntled, David picked a fuzz ball off his sweater. "It was wandering around, yowling all the time. I thought we could give it a home. I paid over a hundred dollars for shots for that animal."

"That's okay, Davy. Snow White was grateful." Darla patted his arm.

"Well, Mrs. Murphy wasn't." His averted his face. "Calling the police on me was a bit extreme."

"Yes, that must have been—er—challenging." Susannah struggled to suppress her mirth.

"Snow White scratched Davy and tore his pants. Then Mrs. Murphy hit him with a broom." Darla reached out and touched him. "I'm sorry, Davy."

"So am I," David said in an aggrieved tone. "I fed

that great hulking thing fresh fish for two weeks and neither that cat nor her mistress said thank you even once."

"Snow White still comes over for a visit sometimes," Darla interjected. "But not if Davy's home."

"And don't think I'm unhappy about that." He gave a snort of derision.

Susannah couldn't help it, she burst out laughing. The thought of this big, accomplished, well-respected man avoiding a little white cat made her giggle. She could not imagine him prowling the streets, calling the cat and enduring all manner of indignities from Mrs. Murphy.

"Now that you know my mistakes, let's go inside. I'd like to eat some of that food before it's gone," David said with a hint of a grin in his eyes.

He walked around the car to open Susannah's door and help her out. She was very conscious of David's helping hand under her elbow.

She walked up the sidewalk with David and Darla, mentally steeling herself for what was to come. This was one reason why she'd refused to go to church with Connie; she feared people would start asking questions that she didn't want to answer.

But no one asked her a thing. David introduced her by name as their friend, and that seemed to be enough for people. Everyone she spoke to welcomed her and invited her to enjoy herself. And she did.

It was only later, when Susannah was seated in a pew beside David that she began to feel self-conscious as the speaker, Rick Green, talked about God's love.

"It was my privilege to teach these people that nothing they've done could erase the love of God," he said confidently. "Nothing."

He spoke at length about conditions along the river and the many trials he endured in his work. His pictures were a graphic testimony to his endurance. But Susannah kept hearing her mother's voice screaming condemnation.

It's your fault. It's your fault.

As always, a punch of pain accompanied the words and she squeezed her eyes closed to brace against it.

The social worker had insisted the deaths of her sisters, Cara and Misty, weren't her fault. But even after all these years, in the recesses of her heart, Susannah couldn't rid herself of the guilt that dogged her.

It *was* her fault. She *should* have been there.

She was a failure.

A hand pressed against hers, warm, comforting.

She opened her eyes and found David staring at her, concern in his gaze.

"Are you all right?" he whispered.

She dredged up a smile and nodded as she eased her fingers from his, forcing herself to pretend a calm she didn't feel. Why did his touch affect her so deeply?

After several moments of scrutiny he finally returned his attention to the speaker, but he kept giving her little sideways looks, as if he thought she might faint or do something equally inappropriate.

"Hear me tonight," Rick Green said softly. "There is nothing God wouldn't do for you. In fact, He's already done it by sending His son to die for you. All you have to do is accept His love."

By the time the meeting broke up, Susannah had regained her equilibrium. She was able to tease Darla and smile at David who still looked concerned. Connie and Wade joined them.

"You must have loved your trip down to the Amazon, judging by those amazing pictures," Susannah said to Wade.

"We did," Wade agreed. "Especially the piranhas." He held up a threatening hand and began tickling the back of Darla's neck. In a fit of giggles, she wiggled away.

"You know, we never did get to finish that trip because of Dad's heart attack," David mused. "We should go back sometime."

"I second that." A tall, lean man with sandy blond hair exchanged a complicated handshake with the other two men, hugged Connie and Darla and then held out a hand to Susannah. "I'm Jared Hornby," he said.

"Oh. I've heard a lot about you." Susannah shook his hand. She could see the easy camaraderie between the three men. "Darla shared some information, too," she added.

"Aw, kiddo! Can't you ever keep a secret," Jared asked Darla and grinned when she said, "No."

"I'm not putting money in that basket. I just don't agree with raising money to feed kids who live in this country." A shrill voice broke through their conversation, carrying from the foyer into the sanctuary. "Did you see the pictures of those children in the Amazon, how poor they are? It seems criminal to me that in this country of plenty, we give our hard-earned money to people who have social assistance and all kinds of government handouts. If they won't look after their own children, then the government can take over. Not a dime should go to that Mary's Kids Foundation."

"Uh-oh," Connie murmured. Mary's Kids was one of the charities she'd recently set up with a friend to help kids on the streets of Tucson. "I'll go—"

"I'm afraid I have to disagree with you there, Mrs. Beesom." David's voice carried clearly, his tone calm. "Needy kids are needy wherever they are, whether in Tucson or the Amazon. We should be ashamed that we've let American children get to the point where they are so desperate to eat that they have to rob and steal. It's disgraceful that in America a child isn't cared for by the whole community."

Susannah moved with the rest toward the foyer. She couldn't help admiring David's casual stance. There was no hint of anger in his voice or manner, though she saw a flicker of golden fire in the depths of his eyes.

"Disgraceful? Well, that's just silly. They have mothers and fathers," Mrs. Beesom blustered.

"That isn't the point," he said quietly. "The point is that there are children hurting around the world. It's our God-given responsibility to do whatever we can to alleviate the hurt of children whenever we can, no matter where they live."

"But—"

David wasn't finished.

"Thank God Connie Abbot has taken it upon herself to show God's love to the children of Tucson, just as this gentleman has been showing love to those he meets in the Amazon. We should all be doing more to support both of them."

After a couple of coughs and a few murmured amens, the foyer quickly cleared, but not before people dropped donations into both baskets.

Susannah followed Connie and Wade outside. The group paused in the parking lot.

"Look guys, I'm so sorry," Connie murmured, her embarrassment obvious. "I had no idea that would happen. I should have removed everything about Mary's Kids from the bulletin board."

"Don't be silly, Connie," David said. "She should have thought first."

"I'm sure David saw it as an opportunity to try and educate narrow-minded people rather than let their bigotry go unchallenged, didn't you, old man?" Jared slapped him on the back. "You always were a defender of the weak."

"I'm not a saint." David brushed away the praise. "What say we go out for coffee? I'm buying."

"But I don't drink coffee, Davy," Darla complained.

Everyone burst out laughing. David assured his sister they'd find her something to drink. As they drove to the coffee house, Susannah couldn't help but replay the scene in her mind.

She'd always seen David as cool and distant. But his defense of Connie's charity tonight showed her a new side. She assumed he thought her stupid, beneath him. But the truth was, he had never verbally condemned or judged her. Maybe she was misreading him, and shutting him out without giving him a chance to show who he really was.

David was great with Darla—understanding and gentle. He went out of his way to empathize with his sister's issues. He was exactly the kind of man who could listen and then help you figure out the next step. Connie was a great friend, but Susannah was sure that if she told her the plans she had to adopt her baby, Connie would try to change her mind. Susannah needed another confidant, someone who could advise her about adoption. Someone who wouldn't try to sway her, who would listen and even help

Tonight, David had shown he could empathize.

Tomorrow, Susannah would find out if he would help her.

Chapter Seven

"Surprise!"

On Saturday evening, David stared at the array of food on his kitchen counter and was dumbfounded.

He'd never expected this when he'd called to ask Susannah if she and Darla wanted to join him and the boys for dinner.

"I thought a barbecue might be more fun for your little brothers than being stuck in a stuffy restaurant." Susannah's cheeks burned a hot pink. But whether from effort or something else, he couldn't tell.

"We made a dinner," Darla told him, beaming with pride.

"You certainly did." He glanced at his three little brothers who were eyeing the fixings for a wonderful grilled meal with huge eyes. "But I'm sure they'd rather go out, wouldn't you, guys?" he teased.

"No way." Their team had won the hockey game and they were high on excitement. "Can we have both a burger and a hot dog?" the eldest asked in awe. "And some of the other stuff?"

"If you can find room after all that junk food you ate." He told them to wash up, then went out to the patio.

David couldn't remember the last time he'd worked so hard over a grill—nor the last time he'd heard so much laughter in his backyard.

Nor had he ever seen Susannah so happy. She insisted on dashing around, making sure everyone had enough to eat until David finally ordered her to sit down and enjoy her own meal.

She had a way with the boys. She didn't duck their questions about her baby, or try to change the subject. She answered honestly and they seemed to appreciate that. In fact, David was gratified to see them ask her to remain at the table while they cleared the dishes. He stacked the dishwasher himself, so he could listen in on their conversation.

"Boy, David, Susannah's sure pretty. What happened to her husband?" Caden, the eldest, asked.

"He died, I think." David wasn't sure he wanted to reveal more about Susannah without her permission. "Thanks for pitching in, guys."

"It was nothing." Charles, the youngest, peered out the window where Darla and Susannah sat together on the deck swing. "Does she live here?"

"No. She comes over to watch Darla when I can't be here," he explained.

"Darla's different than the last time we saw her," Cory said. "She doesn't look so sad. And she didn't yell even once."

"Yeah. She's fun," Caden agreed. "And she's pretty now."

Like she wasn't before? David choked back his brotherly ire and picked up the platter of cookies Susannah had left on the top of the fridge.

"We've barely got enough time to eat these before I have to get you home," he said as he shepherded them outside. "Your mom said no later than eight, remember?"

They grumbled but devoured the cookies as they asked Darla about the butterfly exhibit. To David's surprise, his sister knew a lot about it and was able to clearly explain what she and Susannah had seen.

"I won't be more than half an hour," he told Susannah before leaving. "The boys' place isn't too far away."

"We'll be here," Susannah promised. She hugged each of the boys, then handed Caden a bag. "Extra cookies in case you want a snack tomorrow. And there might be some fudge brownies in there, too," she added with a wink.

"Really?" Caden's eyes widened. "Thanks a lot."

David shooed them out to the car, but stopped when Susannah's hand pressed his arm.

"They're not allergic or anything, are they?" she asked.

"To chocolate?" He grinned. "More like addicted. Thanks for doing that. It was very thoughtful. They don't get treats like that very often."

"It was mostly Darla," she said. "I just helped."

He thought about that as he took the boys home. It seemed Susannah "just helped" everyone. He knew from Wade that Susannah took over meals when their housekeeper had the day off. Which was a good thing because Connie, for all her achievements, was no cook.

Susannah "just helped" Darla take swimming lessons, with the result that Darla had zipped through the first four levels and was almost done with the fifth. She'd "just helped" his little brothers enjoy a wonderful barbecue in a homey atmosphere, gently urging them out of their shells, until all three boys had lost their shyness.

Susannah Wells was quite a woman.

David pulled into the garage and waited for the door to close.

He liked her. He really liked her. Susannah didn't pretend to be someone else. She didn't seem to bear a grudge, though she had plenty of reason to. She was honest with Darla, yet wonderfully calm and soothing.

Like a sister.

Only David didn't think of Susannah as a sister.

Careful.

He found her inside, staring into space.

"Oh, you're back," she said, startled, as if she'd been deep in thought. "Darla's upstairs having a bath."

"Good. She was pretty sticky from all the cookies." Something was going on. He could see it in her eyes. "Do you—"

"Could I talk to you?" she blurted. "Confidentially, as a lawyer?"

"Okay," he said cautiously.

"I'll pay you and everything," she promised, "but I don't want what I say to leave this room." A desperate look washed over her delicate features, as if she'd been brooding over something and finally felt driven to bring it to light.

"As your lawyer, I'm forbidden to release anything you tell me to anyone else," he assured her. "Would you like some tea while we talk?" He had to do something to try to ease her discomfort. The uncertainty in her voice touched him. He wanted to help her, to ease the strain in her lovely eyes. He wanted to give her some of the joy she so freely encouraged in others.

"Yes. Please." Susannah waited until he'd made the tea and set everything on the table in front of them.

"Talk to me, Susannah. Please? I promise I'll try to help," he said when silence continued to reign.

"I need to know how to give up my baby for adoption."

The question hit him squarely in the gut.

Give away her child?

David forced his face to remain neutral, but inside his brain churned with questions.

"I can't keep it, that's for sure." She twisted her fingers together, staring at them as if she hoped to find answers there.

"Do you have someone in mind? Connie and Wade?" he guessed.

"No!" Susannah stared at him. "You can't tell them about this. Not a word."

"I'm not going to say anything to anyone, Susannah. I promise. Relax." He laid his hands over hers to help her calm down. "It's just—this is a bit of a surprise. I don't understand. Maybe you could explain some more?"

"No." She yanked her hands away and jumped to her feet. "I shouldn't have bothered you. I'll figure things out. But please, don't tell Connie."

"Susannah." David saw a myriad of conflicting emotions on her face. He could tell she was really struggling with her decision, with her feelings. "As your lawyer, I *can't* talk to Connie or anyone else. That's the law." He rose, touched her shoulder. "I really want to help you.

But in order to give you the best advice I can, I need to know more about what's driving your decision."

She frowned, her uncertainty obvious. His heart gave a lurch as he watched her struggle to find some trust.

"Let's just talk. No decisions, no judging—just talking," he coaxed quietly. "You don't have to decide anything right now. But I'd like to know what you're thinking and feeling. This is a big decision."

He found himself holding his breath. Would she trust him?

"I know exactly how big it is," she said. Finally she sat down. "I've been fighting it for a while. But I think the best thing for my baby would be for me to find a good family to raise it."

So now he was going to arrange an adoption?

So much for not getting involved, buddy.

With grim determination, David shut down the voice in his head. The truth was he was already involved in Susannah's life way more than he'd ever imagined he'd be. Over the past few weeks he'd caught himself watching to be sure she drank the freshly squeezed juice with which he'd insisted Mrs. Peters stock the fridge, and that she'd sampled the variety of organic fruit he kept buying at the health food store. He'd even checked the house for repairs that needed doing so she wouldn't trip on something, or hurt herself.

If he had to, David could recite every detail Darla had ever mentioned about Susannah's baby. Yeah, he wasn't getting involved.

"I would prefer if the adopters didn't know about my mistakes." The words emerged in a quiet, painful whisper.

"Okay." He nodded. "Now tell me why."

"Why?" She gave a half laugh, chewed on her bottom lip then looked directly at him. "Because my past is not the kind of fairy-tale reading a child needs."

"I meant why do you want to have someone adopt your baby?" he clarified.

"Isn't it obvious?" She frowned at him. "I can't be the kind of mother this baby needs."

"Why not?" he asked, pouring tea for both of them.

"I shouldn't even be a mother," she whispered.

"And yet you will be."

"I know." She nodded soberly. "But I can't provide the best environment for a child." Her eyes brimmed with shame.

"You're not a criminal. You haven't hurt anyone. You like kids and you're good with people." He shook his head. "I don't understand what possibly disqualifies you as a mother."

"Look around, David," she said, a tinge of bitterness edging her voice. "Look at what your parents provided for you and Darla. I'll bet your mother stayed home to care for you, didn't she?"

"Actually she was a partner in my father's firm." David smiled at the cascade of memories. "Best litigator I've ever known. But she would not do wills or family law. Absolutely refused."

"Oh." Susannah swallowed. "Well, anyway, I meant your parents provided a home and income for their children. They had a reputation that covered you."

"You have a bad reputation?" he asked, half in jest.

Susannah's eyes, dark and swirling with secrets, met his. After a moment she nodded. "Did Connie ever tell you about our foster home?" She glanced away, focusing on something outside the window.

"A little. How much she was loved, cared for. How much she appreciated what they did for her. That kind of thing. Why?" He didn't understand where this was going.

"I was sent to that foster home after a house fire—which was my fault." Susannah straightened. Her shoulders went back. Her jaw tightened. "Do you know where I was when the fire started?"

David gave a grim shake of his head.

"I snuck into a theater," she said, her voice brimming with unshed tears. "I ran away. My—mother was at home. She got badly burned in that fire, because of me."

Years of past misery now darkened her gorgeous eyes to green-black shadows. Pain oozed from her. David wanted to help but he didn't know the words to dissolve this kind of agony. It had festered too long.

"Susannah—"

"There's another reason I can't keep my baby." Susannah dragged her hand away from his and tucked it under her.

"What is that?" David asked, longing to hold her, to ease her obvious distress.

"My mother was not a good mother. I might be like her."

David wanted to laugh at the utter ridiculousness of it. But Susannah's face made it clear how serious she was.

"You are not like her, Susannah," he said, certain of that truth.

"I don't drink, but maybe—"

He shook his head and continued shaking it as she listed other faults she thought she might have inherited.

"No way."

"How can you say that?" A hint of defiance colored her voice. "You barely know me."

"I actually know you quite well, Susannah Wells." He smiled at her blink of surprise. "You are sweet and gentle with Darla when she's acting her worst. You go out of your way to make three boys you don't even know the most fantastic barbecue. You listen when I whine and complain and you never stop looking for opportunities to help anyone who needs a hand." He touched her cheek. "You'll make a wonderful mother."

She was silent a long time, head bent as she thought about it. But when she lifted her golden head and looked at him, David knew she hadn't heard him, not in her heart where the insecurities had taken root.

"You don't know what kind of mother I'll be, and neither do I. And I'm not going to risk the life of my baby. My track record isn't good. I'm not worthy of motherhood and I won't risk my baby." She gathered her jacket. "So are you going to help me figure out how to do an adoption, or should I find someone else?"

David rose, determined to make her see herself the way others saw her.

"In the past you made some bad choices, Susannah," he said seriously. "Maybe partly because of what you were told and partly because you were afraid to expect better of yourself."

"So?" Her long hair twisted up on the top of her head lent her a quiet dignity, its sheen a golden crown under the kitchen lights.

"I wish you could believe that your past doesn't determine your future. I wish you could let go of all those feelings of unworthiness," he told her, letting his soul speak. "You have so much inside you to give. You just need to trust God to help you and give yourself another chance."

"God isn't going to be bothered with me."

"God is bothered with everyone," he assured her quietly.

"And what if I blow that chance? I've done it a hundred times before. What happens to my baby then?" she challenged him. Then she cleared her voice. "Are you going to help me with this adoption or not?"

"Of course I'll help you. After all you've done for us, I would feel ashamed not to. You're the best thing I could ever have wished for Darla." He bent and brushed his lips against her silky cheek, surprised by the rush of longing he felt to make her world better. "Thank you."

She lifted a hand and touched her cheek where he'd kissed her.

"You're welcome," she whispered.

Then she was gone.

David stood in the kitchen and let his spirit talk to God because he couldn't find the words to convey all that was in his heart.

Sometime later he became aware he was not alone.

"Davy?"

"Yes, sweetie?"

Darla stood behind him, her face very sad.

"What's wrong?"

"Why does Susannah want to give away her baby, Davy?"

"That's a secret, sis. You can't ever talk about it. Not to anyone."

"Okay. But I love Susannah's baby."

"I know." He gathered her in his arms and let her cry on his shoulder, his sweet baby sister who was alive and getting better every day thanks to a small woman who oozed love.

Oh, Susannah, his heart wept.

"I'll only talk about it to God," Darla promised, sniffing. "He'll help. Let's ask Him."

So right then and there they prayed for Susannah and the child she was afraid to love.

But even that didn't ease David's concern over the heart-wrenching choices Susannah was determined to make.

"There's got to be something I can do," he prayed after Darla had gone to bed. "Show me some way to help her avoid making this tragic mistake."

Being Susannah's friend/lawyer hardly seemed enough.

Chapter Eight

"I can't believe you actually brought my sister to this place."

All signs of last week's gentle, understanding man whom Susannah had trusted with her deepest secrets was gone. She'd felt so close to him, even more so after that kiss. Her brain said it was all part of his thank-you, but her heart had sensed the tenderness in him, felt the gentleness of his eyes when his lips touched her. What a difference a week made.

Susannah tried to explain.

"They have a wonderful program with pottery here. Darla can finally dig her fingers into the clay and create as she wants to. She's ecstatic."

"Do you see who these people are? Drunks. Addicts. Criminals. Pottery is fine, but here?" He cast a disparaging glance at the disheveled young man working beside Darla's table. "He looks like he's been living on the street."

"He has. Burt's had some bad luck." Susannah hated the way David looked at the man—because Burt could have been her not so long ago.

"I'm sure he has." David took her arm and steered her to a corner. "This could be dangerous, Susannah. I don't like Darla in a place like this. You know she's had a couple of tantrums this past week."

"She's not going to be perfect all the time," she replied. "No one is."

"I didn't say *perfect*." He tightened his lips as a woman walked past, talking to herself in a high, screechy voice. "What if Darla gets upset and acts up? One of them could take exception and attack her. There is mental illness here."

"You're being ridiculous," she snapped, irritated by his attitude. "Connie's come here to New Horizons many times. No one's ever bothered her."

"Connie isn't a nineteen-year-old girl who—"

"Hi, Davy." Darla wound her arm through his, her face beaming with happiness. "This is my friend, Oliver. He likes to make pottery, too, but Oliver is way better at it than I am."

"Hey." Oliver gave David the once-over, then shook his head. "He's mad," he said to Darla. "I told you he was."

"Davy?" Darla shifted so she could stare into his eyes. "Are you mad?"

"He is," Oliver asserted. "His face is tight and his eyes are all crinkled and mad-looking. I'm leaving." He trotted to the far side of the room where he sat down in a chair and watched them.

"Why are you mad, Davy? Oliver is my friend. I thought you'd be nice to him." Storm clouds rolled across Darla's face.

"We *were* nice, Darla," Susannah intervened before David could give voice to his thoughts about this place.

"I'm sure Oliver is fine. Can we show David what you made this afternoon? I think it's going to be beautiful."

After a sidelong look at her friend, Darla proudly led the way to the massive vase she'd begun creating from coils of clay.

"Oliver showed me how to put them together. Oliver knows a lot about clay." Darla glanced around the room, but Oliver had disappeared.

"He was a sculptor," Susannah murmured for David's ears only. "His fiancée died in a car crash. He's had a hard time since then."

"It's very nice, Dar." David walked around the piece. "How big is it going to be?"

"Big. That's why Oliver has to help," Darla said, her forehead pleated in a frown.

"Why? You're the one creating it." David didn't have to say he disapproved of Oliver. It was there in his tone.

And Darla picked up on it.

"You don't know about Oliver, Davy. You think 'cause he's different than other people that he isn't smart. But he's really smart about pottery." Darla pointed. "That's his work."

Susannah felt a ping of satisfaction at the surprise filling David's eyes as he studied the massive sculpture.

"Very nice."

"I told you, Oliver is good." Darla touched her work with pride. "I'm going to be good, too."

"You already are," Susannah said.

"You have to put pots in the kiln. But this pot will be too high," Darla explained. "Oliver is going to show me how to make it so I can fire it and put it together after. No one will even know it was two pieces."

"I see. Well, I guess you would have to know kilns

to know how to do that," he admitted. "Are you finished for today?"

"Not quite," Susannah intervened. "We need to pay the course fee today. This week was just a trial period. That's why I asked you to meet us here. I thought you'd like to see what Darla would be doing."

"Fine," he said in an inflexible voice. "But I don't think we'll pay the fee today. We should talk about it first."

"But, Davy, I can't come and work here if we don't pay." Darla's voice rose with each word.

Susannah knew David expected her to do something to help Darla regain control, but the truth was, she was angry, too. She'd spent weeks searching for some way Susannah could make pottery with the guidance of someone who knew about clay and could help her realize her dreams.

Now that they'd found it, David objected because it wasn't up to his social standards?

"Come on," he said, reaching for her arm. "Let's go home and discuss it."

"No." Darla glared at him and yanked her arm away. "I want you to give the money for classes so I can come back here." Her voice had risen but she was not yet in the full throes of a tantrum.

"Excuse me?"

They turned as one to stare at the small, wizened gentleman who stood behind David.

"Are you having a problem here, Susannah?" He grinned at her, his almost toothless smile lighting up his wrinkled and worn face. "Can't have that baby of yours upset, now can we?"

"I think we're okay, Robert." She smiled, loving the way he'd rushed to her defense. Nobody but Connie had done that before.

"Well, you tell me if there's a problem, because we don't want arguing and fighting here." He waved a hand encompassing the room. "People come here to feel safe. If this man is bothering you—"

"This is Darla's brother, David Foster. David, this is Robert. He's a friend of mine."

"Robert. What line of work are you in?" David's tone offended Susannah, but she kept silent.

"Oh, I retired years ago. I just come here for a cup of coffee and a chat. Susannah will tell you I like to chat. And do woodworking." He winked at Susannah. "One of these days I'm going to get this little mama working on the lathe."

"It's nice of you to offer, Robert," Susannah said, patting his hand. "But I think I should learn something about pottery first. Darla's so good at it."

"Excuse us. We have to go." David waited until the old man wished them a good day, then turned to Darla. "You can make a scene if you want to, but I am leaving. This is not a place where you should be. I want you to go home. Now." He glared at Susannah, then turned and walked out of the room.

"Davy!" Darla wailed.

"We'll talk to him at home," Susannah whispered to Darla, concerned by the girl's white face. "You can tell him all about the center and explain it."

"Davy doesn't want me to explain," Darla said, tears edging her voice. She walked out of the room biting her lip to keep control. "Davy's already decided that I can't come here. He's embarrassed of me."

It was pointless to argue with her—especially since Susannah wasn't sure she was wrong. So she said nothing. She drove the girl home and helped her carry in her clay tools before hugging her goodbye.

"I have to go now, but it will be all right, Darla," she whispered, hoping she was right.

"I'm going to pray and ask God to help," Darla said before she fled upstairs.

Susannah bit her lip and turned to leave.

"Don't leave yet. I want to talk to you." David motioned to his study.

"Fine." Susannah followed him, tired and wishing she could crawl into a hot bath instead.

She smoothed a hand over her hair as she sank into the nearest chair. She noticed the clay stuck to her shoe, the streak of brown on her sleeve.

David sat down behind his desk, elegant, completely unmussed. That irritated her even more.

"Well? What do you need to say?" She crossed her feet. "It's been a long day. I'm tired. I'd like to go home."

"I want to know what on earth possessed you to take my sister to that place," he demanded, his voice icy.

"Pottery. Pottery possessed me," she shot back. "That and your sister's love of it. Which is something you seem to have difficulty grasping. If you'd only seen her face while she was working," she mourned.

"She can do pottery somewhere else." There was no give in his tone.

"That's the thing, David." Susannah was tired of his attitude. "She can't. Other programs have already begun. They won't allow her to join late."

"So she waits."

"And does what? Goes to more girls' clubs where she is miserable?" Susannah rose. "I suggest you think long and hard about denying her this opportunity."

"Did you even look at Oliver? Didn't you recognize him?" David's scathing tone left her in no doubt that he had recognized the sculptor.

"I told you he was well-known for his work with clay." Susannah fiddled with the strap on her purse, wishing she'd hadn't already eaten the apple she'd put in her bag earlier.

"Oh, Oliver is famous for more than pottery." A smug look washed over David's face. "He has some actions pending for damaging a building downtown. That's what I mean about being unsuitable."

"You don't even know the circumstances and yet you've already passed sentence on him." Susannah shook her head. "I wonder how judgmental you'd be if it was Darla who'd damaged something and was being charged. I wonder if you wouldn't make sure she got all the chances you could give her or if you'd just toss her away the way you seem to be willing to cross Oliver off your 'worthwhile human being' list." Another thought intruded, making her even angrier. "Or is it me you're really afraid of, of my being among like kind like that? Maybe I'll revert to my old habits."

"In my opinion," he said, his voice harsh and unyielding, "it is a bad decision on your part to make friends there and associate with those kinds of people."

"Those kind of people." She smiled. "I *am* those kind of people, David. Worthless, useless—society's write-offs."

"I didn't mean—"

"Yes, you did, David." Susannah had to get out of there before she said something horrible, something that she couldn't retract. Most of all, she had to forget the man who had so tenderly kissed her cheek.

She held his gaze for a moment more, then left, closing the door silently behind her. She walked home slowly, allowing the tears to fall without even trying to stop them.

So now she knew what he really thought. She'd suspected it all along—so why did it hurt so much that this man she admired more than any she'd ever known could write her off as worthless so easily?

David couldn't sleep.

Over and over he kept hearing her.

I am that kind of people. Worthless. Useless. Society's write-offs.

He'd argued when Susannah claimed herself unworthy to be a mother—but he'd just confirmed her judgment.

Irritated with himself and the persistent squawk of his brain telling him not to get involved, David went downstairs, brewed some tea and carried it to the family room. To his surprise, Darla was there.

"What are you doing up?" he asked.

She didn't answer. Her deep brown eyes studied him for a long time, long enough to make him shift uncomfortable.

"I don't like you today," she said finally. "You were mean to Susannah. She tried really hard to help me, and you were rude."

"I wasn't trying to be rude," he began, but Darla wouldn't let him get away with that.

"Yes, you were. You wanted to make yourself better than all the other people at the center. That was rude."

When had his sister acquired such understanding?

"I was afraid for you," he admitted simply.

"Don't you know Susannah? Don't you know she would never let anything happen to me? Even if it was going to, which it wasn't. The center is a good place."

Her voice touched a chord deep inside David and reverberated through his mind. For the first time since the accident, Darla was confronting him with her anger instead of throwing a tantrum.

"Susannah is the best friend I ever had and you're going to make her go away."

"I hope not." That was the last thing he wanted.

"You made her feel like I feel when people call me a dummy," Darla said bluntly.

"I never said—"

"And you made our friends at the center feel like that, too. They're not dummies, Davy," she said, her face earnest. "And it doesn't matter if you say it or not. When you talk the way you did, they know what you mean."

How could he argue with that? He'd been a jerk.

"Susannah knows that. She talks to Oliver and Burt and the others like she talks to me, like she talks to you." Darla bowed her head. "When she talks to us, she makes us feel strong. She makes us feel like we can do things. Lots of things."

Meaning he didn't do that for her?

"You're my brother and I love you lots, but sometimes you say things that hurt people," Darla said, her voice grave. "Today you made Susannah feel bad and I don't like that. You should apologize."

"But—"

"My Sunday school teacher said God wants people to help one another."

"Darla, it's not that simple."

"Everybody at the center likes Susannah because

she knows that sometimes you just need help." She narrowed her gaze. "I don't think they like you, Davy."

"Sweetie," he said, "it's not that I didn't like them."

"Then why do you think they'll do bad things? When I make mistakes, do you think I'll do bad things?"

"No, but—"

"Susannah says everybody makes mistakes." *Even you,* Darla's eyes seemed to say. "But people can change. That's what Susannah says."

Susannah. She had pitted his own sister against him now.

Susannah didn't do that. I did.

"The Bible says you're supposed to love everybody, no matter what. Doesn't it, Davy?" she challenged.

"Yes, but—"

"Then you should have love in your heart for Oliver and Burt and Susannah and everyone. You should expect them to do good things, not bad things." She crossed her arms over her chest, her face set.

Darla had just summed up the Christian life in action.

Shamed by his words and his attitude, and the fact that God had used his little sister to show him his own arrogance, David rose and moved to sit beside Darla.

"You know what?" he said as he took her hand.

"What?" she demanded.

"I think you're the smartest woman I know."

"Really?" A beatific smile lit up her face.

He kissed her cheek and hugged her as he praised God for Darla. "I'll apologize to Susannah tomorrow."

"Good. And Davy?" She pulled back, her face worried.

"Yes, sweetie?" He tucked a strand of her glossy hair behind one ear. "What is it?"

"It's her birthday tomorrow. Connie told me she's having a surprise party for Susannah tomorrow night and we're invited." Darla beamed with the excitement of keeping a secret. "I wasn't going to tell you if you were mean, but if you apologize, that's okay. Can we get Susannah a gift?"

"We'll go in the morning," he promised. "Now, let's get some sleep."

"I already know what I want to give Susannah," Darla said. "A dress for Thanksgiving. That green one we saw."

"That will be nice."

"Uh-huh." She flung her arms around him and hugged him so tightly David almost lost his balance. "Good night, Davy," she called.

He spent a long time thinking about the nurturer that was Susannah Wells, and about how he'd treated her. And about that kiss he had planted on her cheek…

She was amazing. Nothing seemed to faze the woman. She thrived on helping anyone who needed her.

How could such a nurturing woman ever give up her child?

She couldn't. It would haunt her for the rest of her life.

David knew then that he couldn't help her find adoptive parents for her baby. He wanted Susannah to keep the child, to make a new life for both of them, a life of second chances.

He'd talk to her about that tomorrow. Right after he apologized.

Chapter Nine

"Connie, you shouldn't have done this!" Susannah said, looking at the gifts piled in the living room. The dining table was set with fancy dishes.

"It's your birthday and we're having a party. Get over it." Connie grinned.

"But you're having your Thanksgiving party tomorrow night." Susannah wished she hadn't spent the afternoon sleeping—perhaps she could have put a stop to all this fuss. "This is a lot of extra work."

"It's not work. It's fun." Connie grabbed Susannah's hands and whirled her around. She stopped abruptly. "Oops, sorry. I keep forgetting this little one makes you dizzy." Tenderly she set her hand over Susannah's ever-increasing baby bump. "What a miracle."

Her baby was a miracle? But weren't miracles for those God thought special? Susannah found herself blown away by the thought that God had singled her out, specially gifted her with this child.

Could God have trusted *her* with such a gift?

An instant later the wonder dissolved as reality hit. This baby might be a gift, but it was a gift she couldn't keep.

Guilt assailed Susannah.

"Suze? You feeling okay?"

"Yes, thanks."

"Sure?" Connie's fingertips brushed her forehead before smoothing back her hair. "You don't feel warm."

"I'm absolutely fine." She pulled back. "Don't fuss."

"I have to take care of my best friend, don't I?"

The doorbell rang and a moment later Darla's excited voice, followed by David's lower rumble echoed through the house. Her stomach clenched just as the baby kicked her in the ribs.

"Surprise!" Obviously delighted with her secret, Connie beamed. "I take it Darla didn't squeal on me when she called this morning?"

"Not a word." Susannah hadn't told Connie about her argument with David because she didn't want her friend fighting her battles. She schooled her expression into a placid mask and followed Connie from the room to welcome her guests.

David's gaze caught hers. He smiled at her, eyes melting to butterscotch. There was nothing in his manner to suggest the least problem between them. In fact, he looked happy to see her. Susannah's heart jumped when he continued to stare at her. She swallowed hard and felt a little sick. Not a pregnancy sickness—more a kind of this-can't-be-happening, heart-dropping sickness.

How could he look at her like that, as if he thought she was something special, when she knew he thought she was nothing, nobody? And why did one man get the full package—height, good looks—along with a strong sense of who he was, a sense that would never make him feel unworthy of anything?

"Happy birthday," he said in that low growl she'd become accustomed to. He handed her a small silver box. An envelope was attached. "For you."

His fingers brushed hers. Susannah pulled away, burning at the contact. "Thank you," she whispered.

"I hope you have a great year."

What did that mean? Was that sweet grin a prelude to firing her?

"This is from me." Darla edged in front of him and held out a beautifully wrapped flat box. "Can we open the gifts now?" she asked Connie, impatience showing in her dancing feet.

"Yeah, can we?" Silver echoed, just as excited.

"Why not?" Connie led the way to the family room.

"Open Davy's first," Darla directed.

Embarrassed at being on display, Susannah lifted the lid of the box and found a lovely glass bottle of expensive perfume tucked inside, the kind she sometimes dabbed on at the cosmetics counter but could never afford to buy.

"Thank you," she said, avoiding his gaze.

"You're welcome," David said.

Susannah found nothing in those calm, smooth tones to give away his thoughts. Didn't he feel anything after their argument?

"Now open mine." Darla thrust the box into her hands and flopped down beside her. "I picked it out myself. And I paid for it."

"You shouldn't have spent your money on—oh, my." Susannah lifted out the dress she'd refused to try on in the store the day they'd chosen Darla's new clothes. The green-into-turquoise swirls were just as gorgeous as they had been that day, the fabric just as luxurious. "It's beautiful, Darla. Thank you."

Never had she been more conscious of the shabbiness of her clothes. Connie had tried to help out, but she hadn't had time to sew more than a pair of pants and two simple cotton shirts.

"Put it on," Darla ordered. She pushed the box off Susannah's lap and grabbed her hand. "I want you to put it on."

"But Connie has dinner—" Susannah looked at her friend.

"We can wait," Connie assured her. "It's lovely. Go try it on."

"C'mon, Silver," Darla said, grabbing Connie's stepdaughter's hand.

So up the stairs the three of them went. Susannah was glad to escape. She could feel David's stare boring into her back.

"I might not fit it, Darla," she warned as she peeled off her clothes. "With the baby, I'm—"

"It will fit," Darla assured her. "You'll see."

And in fact, Susannah thought it fit very well, skimming over her body in a swish of fabric. She twirled back and forth in front of the mirror, unable to believe her reflection.

"Put your hair up," Darla ordered.

She clipped her mass of curls to the top of her head with a huge bronze barrette. Then she slipped her feet into a pair of low sandals. They were old, but they suited the dress.

"You look so pretty, Susannah. Let's go show the others," Darla implored. She and Silver raced back downstairs.

Susannah followed more slowly, oddly proud. She knew that for the first time in a very long time, she looked good.

"You're lovely, Susannah." David's low, intimate voice brought a flush to her cheeks.

"It's the dress." Susannah couldn't look at him.

"No." Darla shook her head. "My mom used to say you had to be beautiful inside to be truly beautiful outside." With a quick press, she hugged her then drew away.

Connie coaxed Susannah to sit down and open the rest of her gifts. There was a lovely bracelet from Silver, matching earrings from Connie and Wade, and two new maternity pantsuits, which Connie had sewn.

"It's so much. Thank you, everyone. I think this is the best birthday I've ever had," she said, looking at David as she spritzed a little of the perfume on her wrists.

David's dark-honey gaze locked with hers. Susannah gulped, but she couldn't look away. She felt as if he could see right to the pain she'd tucked deep inside her soul, pain that still stung because her mother couldn't forgive enough to send her only living daughter a birthday greeting. Susannah had tried so hard to gain her forgiveness, to be a good daughter. But it always went back to the fire. Her fault.

And just like that, the guilt returned, clawing its way up her spine and around her throat, like ivy on steroids, choking the breath out of her.

You don't deserve a birthday party. Or anything else.

"Okay, now it's time for dinner." Connie swatted at Wade's shoulder. "Don't you make that face at me. I didn't cook it."

"Well, now I know what to give thanks for tomorrow." He smirked and ushered them into the dining room.

The meal was a delight. Connie wouldn't allow Susannah to move. Wade and Silver helped her carry in the many dishes of Chinese food and insisted everyone sample some of each.

"How did you know I was craving chicken balls?" Susannah asked, savoring the tangy sweet-and-sour sauce. "You'll have to roll me out of here."

"Not just yet." Connie beckoned to Darla and Silver who scurried into the kitchen with Wade behind.

"I wonder if I could talk to you later, Susannah," David murmured.

He was going to fire her. She knew it. He was so disgusted with her choice of the center for Darla, he was probably going to find someone else to do her job. Fierce, deep pain ripped through her.

Fool, he's not your friend. He's just a man who tolerated you because Darla liked you. You should have expected this. It's what you deserve.

"Fine. Later," she answered. There was no time to say anything else because an enormous cake appeared in the doorway, candles glowing merrily. Four voices broke out in song. "Thank you," she said when they were finished. "Thank you very much." And she meant it.

"Cut it, Susannah. I want to taste it." Darla wiggled on her chair. "I love cake!"

"Me, too," she said.

Who threw Darla's birthday party? David? The errant thought made Susannah pause before she slid the knife into the cake as she tried to picture what kind of party he would give her, what sort of cake they'd get her...

And then she remembered it was none of her business anymore.

David sat in the corner, sipped his coffee and paid little attention to the game he was supposed to be playing. All he could think about was how beautiful Susannah was, how she glowed in the soft lamplight of the family room.

She kept twiddling with her hair, trying to decide her next move. As a result, more and more tendrils had tumbled free and now curled around her long, slim neck. Her skin gleamed with the same porcelain translucence as the old master's paintings he'd seen in museums. Every so often she laid a delicate palm over her stomach and a funny, tender smile caressed her lips.

Once she'd caught him staring and turned an intense peach shade, the color of an Easter sunrise. David quickly looked away, pretending to concentrate on the task at hand.

Pointless. The mental image would not leave him.

"You won, Susannah!"

"I did?" She stared at Connie as if she couldn't imagine winning anything.

And once more David was reminded of her words, of her inability to grasp her own worth.

"Let's play charades now," Darla crowed.

David rose and left her to explain her favorite game. He wandered out to the back patio, studied the gleam of the water in the moon's bright light and tried to think about something other than Susannah Wells.

"You wanted to talk to me?" She stood behind him, her small body tense, her face a mask of no emotion.

"Will you sit down?"

"I'd rather walk a bit, if you don't mind?" She tried to smile and failed.

"Sure." David waited while she lifted the latch on the back gate. He held it open for her, breathing in her scent as she walked past.

"I eat so much and I don't get enough exercise. I'm going to have to go on a serious diet after the ba—" She cut herself off and said no more.

"I think you look beautiful."

"You do?" She'd been walking fast, trying to put some distance between them. But suddenly she stopped, turned and stared at him. "Me?"

"Pregnancy only enhances your beauty." He was surprised by how much he wanted her to believe him.

"Oh. Well, thank you." She stood there, a tiny furrow marring the perfection of her forehead. Then she shivered.

He slid off his jacket and laid it over her shoulders, watching her snuggle into the warmth as they walked down the street. "We won't stay out long. I'll just say my piece and go."

Susannah didn't say anything. But her wide green eyes darkened to the murky tones of the deep forest at dusk.

"I would like to apologize, Susannah."

"What?" She stared at him, shock swelling her pupils.

"I should never have said what I did at the center. I was way out of line." Shame filled David all over again. "Here I am, telling some woman in church to have a little Christian charity for Connie's work and I don't walk my talk. I've been worse than anyone for judging people and I'm sorry you had to hear that." He handed her an envelope. "This contains Darla's fee, and yours, for the pottery class."

"But—" Susannah's fine golden eyebrows rose. "I don't know how to do pottery."

He shrugged. "Use the money for whatever you feel is right. But please accept my apology for what I said."

"It doesn't matter." She turned and began walking toward Connie's home.

"Yes, Susannah, it does. It matters a lot that I hurt you." He caught her arm and coaxed her to stop so he could look into her eyes. "I know you're doing your best for Darla, and I appreciate it. There is no one else I'd feel as comfortable having with her as you, and I will never, ever question your judgment again. I promise."

She stared at him for a long time. Finally a tiny grin appeared.

"Ever? We'll see," she teased. Then her green eyes tipped down to his hand. Somehow he'd slid it down her arm until his fingers meshed with hers.

As if they were…good friends.

"They're not bad, you know." She whispered her plea for him to understand. "People won't give them a chance because they made some mistakes, but they're trying. Oliver hasn't had an easy life, but he's working it through."

"I know." He nodded. "And you're helping. I admire that."

"You do?" Susannah looked dumbfounded at first. Then she looked embarrassed. "I don't do anything."

"Give yourself some credit, will you?" he said. "Because of you, their paths, like Darla's, are a little easier. You take the time to find out what's bothering them, and then you put it right. That matters."

She didn't argue. She simply stood in place and studied him as if he were some foreign substance newly arrived on planet earth.

"I envy you, Susannah. Do you know that?" It cost a lot to admit it, but then David owed her a lot. He took her chin and tilted her face up so he could look into those amazing eyes. "You seem to intrinsically know what to do to soothe people. That's a gift from God, a serious gift. There aren't a lot of people who leave you feeling better about yourself than when they arrived. But you do."

She lowered her eyelids, hiding her expression. But her smooth cheeks turned a pearly pink in the shadows of a streetlight and she drew her hand away from his.

"I think you would make an awesome mother to your baby. I don't think there would be a child on earth that could have a woman more determined to give her baby all the love it needs to make it through this world." He took both her forearms then and tugged so she would look at him. "Won't you reconsider this adoption thing, Susannah? Please?"

He held his breath, hoping. Praying.

"I can't." She drew away. "And I don't want to talk about this anymore. Connie might overhear." She frowned at him. "You promised."

"I won't break my word." He waited while she lifted the hook on the gate, and then followed her through. "But I wish you'd reconsider."

Susannah closed the gate. She slid his jacket off her

shoulders and handed it to him. Her small pointed chin lifted in determination.

"It would never work." Her face closed up tight, the radiance that had lit her from the inside dimmed, quashed by some fear he couldn't see.

"Susannah—"

She shook her head.

"I'm not who you think I am, David."

"I don't think you are who you think you are, either," he replied. "Nor do I think you have any idea of what you could become."

She gazed at him for a moment longer, then walked into the house.

His heart pinched at the sadness of it. Susannah wouldn't let herself consider keeping her child. Wouldn't believe in herself that much. And he wasn't exactly sure why, except that the problem was rooted in her past—rooted firmly.

But what could he do?

Instead of returning inside he sat down beside the pool to think. As usual, images of Susannah filled his mind. He saw again that tender, bemused smile flickering over her face, the bewildered yet amazed way she touched her midsection.

A baby, a tiny, innocent child. A son. Or a daughter to whom she would give life and upon whom she could pour out the love she gave so freely to others.

Darla had told him Susannah had begun to talk about her child, and had mentioned how Susannah often offered to hold other women's children at the center.

To give up her child would leave a scar. One that would wound far deeper than the pain sweet Susannah now carried from her past.

And that was something David could not even con-
template, let alone allow. To see this beautiful woman
retreat back to the scared, sad person who'd arrived here
only a few months ago tore at his heart.

Don't get involved, his head reminded.

Only David knew it wasn't a matter of involvement
now. Susannah had breached his defenses, pushed her
way past all his intentions to remain aloof, and availed
herself into his world through Darla. Susannah had become part of his days, sneaked into his dreams and
made his heart wish for things he couldn't have.

It was silly, impossible to think of a future with her.
His brain had long since accepted that God's choice for
his life's path didn't lie that way. He had responsibilities. Love wasn't for him. Hadn't he learned that lesson twice? If only that lesson would sink into the secret
parts of him that longed to experience being a husband
and a father.

But that silly longing for something he couldn't have
didn't mean he should give up trying to persuade Susannah that adoption was not the way to go.

All David had to figure out was how to do that.

He'd start with money. A little nest egg for her baby.
Maybe if she felt she had something to fall back on, that
she wasn't teetering on the brink—maybe then Susannah wouldn't feel so compelled to give up her child for
adoption.

Maybe.

Chapter Ten

Susannah felt only relief when Thanksgiving and Christmas slid past in a rush that left her little time to think.

Pregnancy was a confusing business and no one was more confused than she. Especially with the increased fluttering her baby now made.

Her baby.

She had to stop thinking of it that way. It could never be hers.

On New Year's, Susannah decided to make plans for her future and wrote lists of actions she needed to take. But in the days following, she rewrote them over and over, depending on where her moods took her.

Those moods took her a lot of places. Into the pool late at night when she couldn't sleep. To the ice cream shop to taste weird flavors. To a crochet class at the center where she struggled to make a baby blanket the instructor insisted was "simple."

When no answer from her mother arrived to respond to the plea for forgiveness she'd sent earlier, Susannah found herself weepy and tearful, unable to accept Connie's assurance that God loved her. How could God love someone who'd made the mistakes she had? Her mother sure didn't love her. Susannah couldn't even love herself.

But she loved her baby. She loved that life inside her with every ounce of passion in her body. She would do anything, anything to protect it, including finding new parents for her baby—if only she could.

But that wasn't her only problem. Susannah was growing fearful of her burgeoning feelings for David Foster. Especially since he'd become so thoughtful, so—nice. But though she enjoyed being around him, enjoyed the way he made her feel part of his and Darla's world—Susannah would not let those feelings grow. She couldn't. She couldn't afford a repeat mistake—not with this baby's future at stake.

So Susannah was confused, wary and seven months pregnant when she arrived at David's office late one January morning. Thus far they'd always talked when he came home at the end of the day. But today he'd asked her to come to his office.

As she entered the exquisitely appointed building, she was enthralled by a granite wall down which water trickled. In contrast to the Tucson desert, lush plants thrived all around it with light from the massive windows. The office felt grand—and she felt totally out of place.

"Hello, Susannah. Welcome." David escorted her to his office, his hand firm but gentle against her back.

"It's beautiful in here," she whispered.

"Thank you." He seated her in a cranberry velvet chair that folded around her weary body, and then asked his secretary to bring them tea.

The girl flirted with David, batting her long lashes, making sure to bend over in front of him when she set down the tea and sumptuous-looking lemon and poppy

seed muffins. Susannah disliked the secretary immediately and she refused both tea and muffins, though
her stomach grumbled a complaint.

"I'd rather have coffee," she said when David held out
a steaming white china cup that probably cost the earth.

"You're supposed to cut down on coffee, aren't you?"
He set the cup in front of her, undaunted by her glower.

"Who told you that?" she demanded, then sighed.
"Darla."

"She loves to talk about you and your baby. And I
like to hear," he added.

"You do?" That shocked her. "Why?"

"Who doesn't like to hear about a new life preparing to join our world?" One brown eyebrow lifted. "It's
generous of you to share the details of your pregnancy
with her." He leaned back in his chair as he sipped his
tea. "I imagine it's quite amazing to have a life growing inside you."

"It is," she admitted. Susannah tilted her head down
to hide her smile of pure delight. It was astonishing, in
fact. But she felt embarrassed to tell him that. Especially here, where she was so out of place.

She hoped the coffee table hid her feet as she slipped
off her shoes. Even they didn't seem to fit anymore.

"You're probably wondering why I asked you here."
His voice changed from gentle concern to businesslike.

"Yes." In fact, curiosity was eating her up.

"I've done quite a bit of research into adoptions." He
caught her surprise. "I had to," he explained. "It's not
exactly my field."

"Oh." So she'd put him to a lot of trouble. How much
would all that cost? He kept telling her not to worry
about the cost, but she did worry.

"The thing is, Susannah, I need some direction. There are so many kinds of adoptions. I'm not sure which you prefer." He handed her a file filled with papers. "These describe open and closed adoptions and what choices, responsibilities and rights the mother had in specific cases."

"Okay." She set the sheaf down on the glass table. She'd think about it later. She picked up her teacup. Suddenly she was very thirsty.

"There are many variations," he continued. "For instance, do you want contact with your baby after you give it away?"

He made her baby sound like a used toy she was getting rid of.

"I don't know," Susannah murmured.

"Do you want to be involved in raising your child or are you intending to hand over all rights to the child's future and give the adoptive parents total freedom?" David leaned back in his chair and studied her.

"I don't—"

"Will you want the adoptive parents to tell the child about you or do you prefer your baby never know its real mother?"

"Uh—" Susannah frowned.

Never know anything about her? Never know that she loved her child desperately, that she yearned to keep it for her very own, to shower on it all the love she kept hidden inside? An arrow of pain pierced her heart. She laid a protective hand on her stomach.

"I—I'm not sure about that yet," she whispered.

"Will you release medical records?" he asked.

"I don't know." So many questions. She was growing more confused.

"Grandparents?"

"No!" At least she knew the answer to that question. Her hand squeezed tight against her purse where the condemning letter lay. "Never."

"You don't want the child to be able to trace his family roots someday?" David asked, his face puzzled.

"My father left when I was four. I doubt even I could trace his whereabouts," she told him, her body clenching with tension.

"What about your mother? Wouldn't she—"

"She's in prison." She watched his eyes, steeling herself to see disgust. But David never flinched.

"Do you ever see her?" he asked.

"She doesn't want to see me." Susannah's cheeks burned. She picked up her cup again and sipped just to have something to do with her hands. "She hates me."

"I see." Those dark eyes pinned her down, as if she was a witness on the stand. "So no family history. That's what you want for your child?"

Susannah almost gagged.

"It will be better that way," she blurted. "It's what I have to do."

"Actually you don't. That's what I'm trying to clarify," he said, leaning forward so his elbows were on his knees. "You have choices, Susannah. Lots of them. Your child is yours. You make the decisions. I'll do whatever you want."

"Okay." She nodded.

"But I have to be certain you understand what you're doing," he said, his voice solemn. "I would be failing you as your lawyer if later you regretted your decision."

"Let's not go over that again," she said, rising. She stepped away from the coffee table, searching with her feet for her shoes. But as she tried to slip her foot into one, she lost her balance and reached out to grab something to steady herself.

That something was him.

"Easy." His arm slid around her waist. "Sit down and I'll put them on for you."

"I can manage." She drew back and wished she hadn't. Her head whirled. Being this near to him made her want all kinds of things—like someone to care about her, someone to love her.

Stupid. David Foster wasn't interested in her. He was just being nice.

"Do you ever let someone help you without an argument?" His mouth tipped in a crooked grin. With gentleness and great care, he helped her sit. Then he knelt down in front of her to slide on her sandals. "You should put your feet up," he murmured, brushing his fingers against her calf. "Your ankles are swollen."

"All of me is swollen. I look like a truck."

David chuckled. Susannah burst into tears.

"Stop laughing at me!"

"I'm not laughing at you." Somehow he was there beside her, holding her close, allowing her to weep all over his expensive suit jacket. "I'm laughing at the way you mistake things. You are beautiful, Susannah, one of the most beautiful women I've ever known. Motherhood has only made you more beautiful."

"I can never be a mother." Grief swamped her.

"Talk to me, Susannah." David cupped her face in his hand. "Tell me what this is really about," he said in a soft, tender voice. "Tell me the whole story."

The burden was so heavy. And Susannah was so tired.

The words emerged of their own volition. She stared into his concerned face and let it pour out of her.

"I was the oldest. I promised my sisters I'd always be there for them. They were only four and seven. Little girls who needed someone to watch out for them. But I didn't do that. I ran away." Loathing scathed her voice. "They died because of me."

"No." He seemed dazed, incredulous.

She smiled bitterly. "Believe it. They're dead."

"You said there was a fire," he said. "How could that be your fault?"

"Easy." She pulled out of his hold and gathered her courage. When he knew, he would send her away. Might as well just get it over with. "I wanted to get away from the chaos. I was so tired of having to figure out what was for dinner, what we were supposed to wear to school, how we were going to pay the electric bill. Scared of being scared all the time."

She'd never told anyone that, not even Connie.

"Those are things your mother should have handled."

"She couldn't, so I did." Tears glossed her eyes, but she refused to shed them. She forced herself to continue. "My sisters died because of me, David. It was my fault. I killed them."

Give me words, Lord, because I don't have any, David prayed silently. His heart ached to ease the inner torment her eyes revealed.

"Susannah—"

"Now do you understand why I cannot—I will not—raise this child?"

David studied the weeping woman in front of him. He doubted Susannah even realized that she was cradling her baby as she spoke. He couldn't begin to imagine how one small woman could bear so much pain.

"Why don't you say anything? Are you disgusted? Revolted?" she asked, anger sparking her eyes. "Well, so am I. And I will never let a child of mine feel that way."

Help her!

"Susannah, how old were you when they died?"

"Nine. I was their big sister. S'ana they used to call me when they hugged me at night." A flicker of a smile appeared and vanished. "I tried so hard to keep them safe."

"Of course you did," he whispered, smoothing damp curls from her brow. "You protected them and loved them as much or more than your mom did, didn't you? You would have done anything for them."

She stared at him, nodding in a dazed manner as if she'd never thought of it in those terms.

"You were a great big sister, Susannah. But doesn't it seem to you, now that you're older and can look back, that nine was far too young to be responsible for two other children?" David held his breath as she frowned, tilted her head to one side.

"I was responsible," she repeated, confusion evident.

"You weren't, sweetheart. You were not their mother."

She simply looked at him.

"Your mother was there, right?" He waited for her nod. "She was in the house when you left?"

"Yes."

"Doing what?" He had to get to the bottom of it, had to make her see.

Susannah was quiet for a long time. Finally she lifted her eyes and looked at him. "She was drunk. She was often drunk."

He touched her cheek. "But that didn't make it your job to do any of those things you said, Susannah. It was only your job to love your sisters, and it sounds to me like you did. Very much. Enough to take care of them the very best you could. All by yourself."

"You make me sound like some kind of hero," she protested. "I wasn't. I left them. I ran away."

"What nine-year-old doesn't run away from home at least once? I did." He took her hand in his, marveling at the coldness of it. Such a small, frail hand, a frail body to house such a big heart. "Maybe you shouldn't have sneaked out, but that does not make you responsible for their deaths."

"Legally, you mean." Was that hope dawning?

"I mean you were not responsible in any way, shape or form. Not legally and not morally," David insisted. "You were a child, as your sisters were. The guilty person was your mother, Susannah."

"No." She shook her head with determination. "She couldn't help it. When my dad walked out she was so hurt. She was always crying."

"So she got drunk to dull the pain?"

"I guess so." Susannah blinked away the tears. "She fell asleep that day and…it wasn't her fault. I should have been there." She shrugged dully. "It doesn't matter anymore."

"Yes, it does." David had to make her see it. "It matters a lot. You cut your mother plenty of slack, but you can't do that for yourself?"

"I don't deserve it."

"Why don't you? You were a child." He swallowed hard, then spoke the words he knew in his heart were true. "She told you it was your fault, didn't she? Your mom blamed you?"

"Yes," Susannah whispered. "But she was right—"

"She was wrong," he said, his anger burning white-hot. "So wrong."

"No." Susannah shook her head. "She was in pain. She didn't know, didn't realize that I wasn't there—"

"But she should have, don't you see? She was the one who was responsible for taking care of the three of you and she dumped that duty on you, a young child." He could hardly speak, so infuriated was he at this woman who had so wounded her own grieving child.

"She must have thought I was home to watch them," she murmured.

"You told her you were leaving?"

"Yes, but I didn't make sure she heard. I wanted to escape." Susannah lifted her head and stared at him through her tears. "Why did God let my sisters die? Why didn't He let me die instead?"

"Oh, Susannah." He gathered her into his arms and held her tightly, trying to ease the burden of her loss. "God doesn't want you to die. He wants you to live and make something wonderful out of your life. And you're doing it."

"I am?" She lifted her head, her face inches from his, hope flickering.

It was all David could do not to kiss her. But he held back because he understood that now more than ever, Susannah needed to know about the kind of love that would always be there for her.

"Of course you are." He smoothed the tendrils off her face. "God has given you this opportunity and you're doing your best to make good."

"How?" she asked, forehead furrowed.

"You're making sure your baby has a good start, for one thing. You're eating right and exercising. You're seeing your doctor regularly, right?" He didn't like the way her gaze skewed away from his. "Aren't you?"

"I will go again, as soon as I can pay," she whispered.

"What? No, Susannah." David shook his head. He tilted her chin so she had to look at him. "You don't have to pay. Didn't the doctor's office tell you that?"

"No." She leaned back to look at him, her face troubled. "Why wouldn't I pay?"

"Because you have insurance. I bought it for you." He liked the way she fit in his arms—liked it a lot. "All of my employees have health insurance."

"Oh." A soft glow flickered through her eyes. "Does it cover sonograms?"

"It covers whatever you need," David said. He wanted to keep holding her, keep reassuring her. He wanted more. He wanted…everything.

The realization shocked him.

And terrified him.

He couldn't have love, or marriage and a family. The things other men took for granted—a wife, family— God had not chosen for him. He knew that.

So why this irrational need to protect Susannah, to make sure she was cared for, that her child was not given away to strangers?

"I had a sonogram a while ago," she was saying. "I was supposed to have another one, but I didn't have quite enough money saved." She explained that she'd paid for the first one.

David needed distance between them to calm his racing heart. He eased her out of his arms as he made a mental note to claim Susannah's money back.

"Make the appointment and have the test done immediately," he insisted. "If you need another doctor, special treatment, anything—I'll make sure it's covered. We want this baby healthy. Don't we?"

"Yes." She struggled to rise.

He rushed to help her, realizing anew how difficult her pregnancy was making things.

"Susannah, I want you to know something."

"What?" She peered at him warily.

"I've put away some money for you. In case you change your mind about the baby." He put one finger on her lips to stop her protest. "I don't want you to feel that adoption is your only option. If you want to keep your baby, you can do it." He slid the bankbook from his pocket and into her hand.

"You shouldn't have done this, David." She opened it and blanched at the amount, going even whiter than she was before. "This is wrong."

"I pay into a pension plan for my staff," he said quietly. "Think of that as your pension plan." When she still frowned, he folded her fingers around it. "I won't take it back. It's yours, to help however you want."

"It's unbelievable." Susannah was silent for several moments. Then she looked at him, her eyes glossy with unshed tears, and nodded. "I don't know how to thank you."

"You don't have to." He frowned at her pallor. "Are you certain you're all right to look after Darla? You're not overdoing it?"

"I'm fine. I shouldn't say this but it's a really easy job." She smiled. "Darla has changed a lot, hasn't she?"

"Thanks to you." He smiled at her, loving the way she glowed with pride whenever she spoke about his sister. "You've done a great job."

She lowered her gaze, shy as always when compliments came her way. His anger flared again at the mother who'd treated her so shabbily.

"I better go." She walked toward the door and paused. "Oh, one other thing." She fiddled with the strap on her handbag. "Darla wants to work as a junior assistant at the butterfly exhibit at the botanical garden. We've visited frequently and the director thinks she has a knack for speaking to the kids who visit."

"When? Her schedule already seems pretty full," David mused.

"It is," Susannah agreed. "But I think she can do this. I think she needs to do it, David. She needs the confidence this public responsibility will give her. Isn't that what we've been trying to achieve?"

He liked the "we" part of what Susannah said. But Darla on show in a public place? It was something he'd secretly avoided ever since her accident.

"She isn't the same girl, David. She's learned how to manage her feelings. This can only help her gain further control." Susannah's quiet plea reached into his heart and touched a chord there. "Darla needs to feel needed. This is her chance to prove to herself that she has a place in the world."

David hesitated. He didn't like it, would never have countenanced it if Susannah hadn't pushed. But so far she had been right about his sister.

"Are you going to be there?" How had he and Darla managed before Susannah's arrival?

"Of course. For the first time or two, anyway. Just in case she needs me." Susannah smiled at him. "She can do it?"

"Okay."

"Great!" She raced across the floor and threw her

arms around him in a burst of exuberance. "Thank you," she said, hugging him. Then she stepped back, cheeks hot pink as her arms dropped to her side. "Sorry."

"No problem." David grinned. She was truly the most beautiful woman—inside and out—that he'd ever known. "I enjoyed it."

That made her cheeks even pinker. David enjoyed seeing her so flustered.

"When is her first day?" he asked. "I'd like to visit."

"Probably Saturday." She checked her watch. "I have to go. Thank you, David, for everything." She started for the door.

"Susannah?"

"Yes?" She stopped and turned.

"Take these and read them." He picked up the sheaf of papers from the table and offered them to her. "Will you please think about what I said, about keeping your baby?"

She took the papers but shook her head.

"Why not?"

"It's better if my baby has a new mother." Then she hurried away.

It wasn't better at all, David fumed. It was wrong. Totally wrong that Susannah of the loving heart should give up her child. What kind of a mother had she lived with to skew her thinking so much?

He decided to find out. He sat down at his desk, picked up the phone and asked his research assistant to dig up everything on Susannah's mother.

"There has to be a way, Lord. You surely couldn't want Susannah to give up this gift You've given her."

Why do I care?

Because I love her.

The admittance knocked him sideways. It shouldn't have—he quickly realized that he'd been carrying strong feelings for Susannah for a long time.

She was gentle, loving and tender. She'd made a ton of mistakes and she knew it. Which meant she carried a boatload of guilt from her past.

None of which mattered one iota to him.

Susannah loved Darla. She'd gone beyond what any caregiver could be expected to do to help his sister figure out her world. David would have loved her for that alone. But he loved her for so much more.

He loved her because she didn't let him get away with anything, because she listened—really listened—to him, because she never once, in all these months, had asked for anything for herself. Yet he wanted to give her everything.

And because of that, David wanted—no, needed—to make it possible for Susannah to keep her baby.

He picked up the phone.

"Wade? Can you and Jared meet me tomorrow for lunch? I really need to talk to you guys. Thanks."

They were his best friends, they knew his history and most important of all, they shared his faith. David had no clear-cut answer from God on what to do with his feelings but they could help him figure out his next step.

Love was something that wasn't for him. He knew that.

Yet love was exactly what he felt for Susannah Wells. So what was he supposed to do?

Chapter Eleven

"So you've fallen in love with Susannah," Wade said and clapped him on the shoulder. "Congratulations."

"It's not that simple," David said.

"Why?" Jared demanded. "What's wrong with love?"

"It's not for me, that's what. It's not part of God's plan for me." David rose and paced around Wade's patio. But that silence got to him. He looked up and caught the puzzled look his buddies were sharing. "I've been engaged before," he reminded them.

"So?" Jared shrugged. "They weren't the right ones. Susannah is."

"But how can I be sure of that?"

"Dave, sit down and let's work this through. You care about Susannah, right?" Wade asked after he'd flopped onto one of the chairs beside the pool.

"Yes."

"Okay." Wade nodded. "And you want her and her baby in your life permanently?"

"Yes," he repeated with certainty.

"But you think that's somehow wrong?" Jared frowned. "Why?"

"Because I'm not good husband material. I have Darla to care for, I work long hours." He glared at them. "Two other women walked away from me."

"Yes, we know. And if they'd been God's choice, don't you think He would have sent one of them back?" Jared rested his elbows on his knees. "I'm no expert on love, but I've read the Bible and I can't find a place where it says you have no right to love. In fact, God is love. He patterns love for us. He doesn't place love in your heart and then demand that you ignore it. Where does it say that in the Bible, David?"

"I agree. If that's your thinking, you ought to be able to line it up against His word. Chapter and verse, buddy." Wade leaned back, waiting.

"Of course there's no verse," David said, irritated that they kept pushing. "It's just something I know."

"How do you know it?" Jared demanded. "Because you were thrown over twice? That's not proof that you can't have love in your life, that you can't love someone."

"There's one thing I've learned about love this past year, David." Wade's voice dropped but remained intense. "God gives us love to enrich our lives, so we can share with someone who will be there for us, help us through the good stuff and the bad stuff. It seems to me that's what you have going with Susannah. And I think it's wonderful. What I don't get is why you can't accept a gift like that from your heavenly Father."

"It's just—I don't believe He meant that kind of relationship for me." David didn't know how else to express it.

"Exactly. *You* don't believe. You." Jared glanced at Wade who nodded and began speaking again.

"Listen, buddy. Jared and I think that this so-called

truth of yours, that God doesn't want you to love, is something you've convinced yourself of. I know being dumped the second time, especially when she blamed Darla for your failing relationship, had to be hard on your ego." Wade winced. "When my first wife took off with some other guy, I felt gutted. I couldn't even imagine I'd be able to care for another woman, let alone love one again. I made up my mind that I would never get involved again. But God brought Connie into my life."

"And now look at him," Jared teased. "Seriously, though, just because Wade thought and felt like that didn't make it God's plan for him, Dave. It's the same with you. You wanted to avoid the hurt and embarrassment those fiancées brought you. That's understandable. But you don't care for either of them now, do you?"

"No." David was emphatic on that. The only woman in his heart now was Susannah.

"Because you love Susannah," Wade said.

"Yes." It felt so good to admit that aloud.

"There's nothing wrong with that," Jared insisted. "Love is God-given. You might also tell Susannah how you feel. Maybe she feels the same?"

How David wished that were true.

"But if you're still doubting," Jared said, "why don't you pray about it and ask God to work it out for you? If she's the one, don't you think God had a hand in bringing you two together? Don't you think He has a plan to make it all work out?"

"Is it God you don't trust, David?" Wade asked. "Or is it yourself?"

"Hello, baby."

Susannah blinked through her tears at the shadowy

image of her child on the sonogram picture the technician had given her. With her fingertip she traced the tiny head, the neck, two perfect arms and legs—her baby. The wonder of this life growing inside her blindsided her to everything else.

So tiny. So precious.

How could she let this child go?

How could I not?

Her baby would soon be born and she'd have to hand him or her over to strangers. Forever.

Susannah's heartache intensified as the desolating loss swamped her. Though she tried to suppress them, tears flowed in a steady stream down her cheeks.

If only David was right, if only she could keep her child. What a sweet and generous gesture to give her the money. Susannah's Baby, he'd written on the bankbook. Once again she marveled at his generosity and the way he saw beyond what everyone else did, probing to the heart of things. He figured out she didn't have anything and went the extra mile to ensure she could make her choice with no regret.

But it wasn't about the money, never had been. It was about her inability to handle such a massive responsibility without messing up. And so she decided that when she left Tucson she'd make sure he got his money back.

Susannah stared down at the picture again and new tears flowed. She was glad Darla was outside playing with Silver. She didn't want anyone to witness her weakness. Because it was weak to want what you couldn't have, what you knew you'd ruin.

"Susannah?" David stood before her. "What's wrong?"

He crouched down to study the paper in her hand. She watched him examine the image, a huge smile spreading across his face from one side to the other. Delight lit his eyes as he examined the picture in minute detail. Finally he lifted his gaze to meet hers.

"Your baby," he whispered. "It's perfect, Susannah. Is it a boy or a girl?"

"I didn't ask." She dashed the tears away. "I only asked if it was healthy," she said. The words dissolved into a blubber as her emotions seesawed again.

"And?" he asked, sitting beside her. Somehow she was in his arms again, and she didn't mind one bit.

"It is." She sighed as he gathered her close and let her rest against him. She was so tired. "The doctor says everything is great."

"Good. Then we should celebrate this gift of life God's given you. Not cry about it." His hand smoothed over her back in a soothing caress that made her feel loved, cherished, cared for.

"Celebrate?" She leaned back. "How?"

David chuckled as he brushed her cheek with his knuckles, drying her tears. He gently released her before smoothing the long strands of hair she'd left free. Susannah felt the faintest caress of his lips against her forehead before he rose.

"I'm not sure how," he said, staring at her. "But this healthy baby definitely deserves a pre-birthday celebration."

"Can we have a party, Davy?" Darla said from the doorway. "Silver is staying for dinner."

"I hope you have a lovely time," Susannah murmured, too tired to get up. Everything seemed to suck her energy these days. "I think I'll go home."

"Connie and Wade went out for dinner, didn't they?

So you haven't eaten. I could order in a pizza," David offered.

"No." Darla shook her head at him. "No pizza."

"I thought you liked pizza," he said, obviously bewildered.

"I do. But Susannah's baby doesn't like it." Darla moved to sit beside Susannah. She put her hand on her stomach and gently stroked. "It kicks her and upsets her stomach when she eats pizza. Then she can't sleep, and Susannah needs to sleep lots." She frowned at her big brother. "We have to have something else."

What a girl. Susannah smiled at her protector, glad she wouldn't be forced to eat the spicy Italian food she usually loved.

"Okay. What would you prefer, Susannah? I'm guessing sushi is out?"

She made a face.

"That's what I thought." He grinned. "Is that because you can't put peanut butter on sushi?"

"Ew, gross." Darla made a gagging motion.

"You don't have to order anything for me, but I'm sure the girls would love cheeseburgers," Susannah said, trying to get the focus off of herself.

"Too greasy. I think stir-fried vegetables would be good." Darla glanced at her friend. "We like Chinese food, don't we, Silver?"

"We like it lots," Silver agreed, grinning. "Especially me."

"Good. Chinese it is. How about if you two come with me to pick it up. Then Susannah can have a rest." David bent over Susannah, his nose a centimeter from hers. "And I do mean rest. Put your feet up and have a nap. No setting the table or anything else."

"It sounds lovely," she agreed, enjoying the way he slipped off her shoes and playfully placed them across the room. "Thank you."

"You're welcome." His toffee-toned eyes held hers for a moment.

It had been a very warm day, but Darla insisted on covering her with an afghan before they left. She tucked it around Susannah's feet, her face brimming with concern.

"You won't get up?" she asked anxiously.

"I promise." Susannah waved as they left. She'd intended to watch a documentary about childbirth, but somehow her brain began replaying that moment when David had kissed her forehead. She fell to dreaming about what it would be like to be cared for, loved, by a man like him, a man who wouldn't dump you the moment life took a wrong turn.

A man who would cherish you and protect you and make life fun again.

A man who would love a baby that wasn't even his.

"Davy, can you help me?"

"Sure, sis. With what?"

"Susannah." Darla frowned. "Me and Silver are worried about her."

"You are? Why?" He'd been a little worried himself when he'd found her weeping like that. "I think she was crying because she was so happy to see that picture of her baby," he said.

"I don't mean that." Darla shook her head. "Susannah gets really tired. Silver heard her tell Connie that the baby is moving around a lot and she can't sleep. One night Silver saw her swimming and it was really late."

"I think that's the way it is with babies," he said, wondering where she was going with this. "I think Susannah is okay though, Darla."

"But Connie said the doctor told Susannah to slow down, to stop trying to do so much, and she doesn't. Susannah thinks she has to do everything with me. It's my fault she gets so tired." She glanced at Silver who was playing at the juke box, then leaned closer. "Maybe if she didn't get so tired all the time, Susannah wouldn't want to give away her baby," she whispered.

"Sweetie, she doesn't want to give it away, exactly. She's just afraid she won't be able to look after it," he explained.

"She won't if she's too tired," Darla said. "We could adopt it. I would help."

"I know you would, sweetie," David said. He touched her hand. "But I don't think Susannah wants that."

"I guess not. We're not a family and Susannah wants a family." Darla sighed.

"Listen kid, you and I are a family. Always have been, always will be. Got it?" He bussed her cheek with his fist.

"Yeah, but we're not the kind of family that can take care of a baby, are we, Davy?"

He shook his head, unsure of how to deny that. So far he'd been focused on the two of them, not on including anyone else, though he'd wanted exactly that for years.

"Could you come with us to the botanical garden tomorrow?" Darla said. "Susannah says she has to be there, but it's hot in the butterfly exhibit and she might get too tired. She could go and rest if you were there."

"I have an appointment tomorrow afternoon. I was going to come after that," he told her.

"Could you put it off? Or send somebody else?" Darla asked anxiously. "We have to help Susannah now. 'Cause we love her."

Yes, we do, he thought.

"Okay, I'll do my best," he promised.

"And can we get a chair and an umbrella for soccer?" she asked. "There are only hard benches there and there's no shade."

"I'll figure something out, sweetie." He hugged her, touched by her compassion. "You just tell me when you see something we can do to help, and I'll do it."

"Well, we were talking about that," she said, waving at Silver to come over. "Tell him," she ordered.

"Susannah likes flowers." Having abandoned the juke box, Silver flopped down on a stool. "She told me nobody ever gave her flowers before. My dad gives Connie flowers lots of times."

"Hmm. How about if we pick up some flowers on the way home." David made a mental note to make sure Susannah got lots of flowers. Such a small thing. How sad that no one had been there to do that for her. He intended to change that.

Their food arrived and David carried it out to the car. On the way home he pulled into a flower shop and let the girls choose a bouquet for Susannah—a bright spring one. He also spotted a portable chair with a little umbrella attached.

"Perfect," Darla told him with a grin.

Satisfied, David drove home—and found Susannah sleeping on the sofa.

"She really is Sleeping Beauty," Darla whispered.

"No, I'm not. I'm a troll who needs her dinner. Grr,"

Susannah said, eyes closed. She grinned at them as she eased upright.

David extended a hand to help her to her feet, marveling at the difference a little sleep made. Her green eyes shone with life, her skin luminous.

"Feeling better?" he asked as they laid the table.

"Much." She blushed when he held out her chair for her and quickly sat. "Thanks."

"You're welcome." He couldn't resist touching the swath of golden curls that cascaded down her back.

"These are for you, from us." Darla held out the bouquet with pride.

"Oh. Thank you." Susannah glanced at him, startled. Then she accepted the flowers and buried her nose in the fragrant petals. "They're beautiful."

David could have sworn he saw tears in her eyes, but when she looked at the girls, she'd blinked them away and was smiling. He got a vase, filled it with water and set it in the middle of the table so she could enjoy her bouquet.

"Only two months till Easter," he said, holding up his water glass to toast her. "Not long to go now."

"That's easy for you to say. I have a quite different perspective." She peeked through her eyelashes, grinning.

And David lost his breath. She actually sounded happy about the future.

"I'm starving," Darla said.

"Me, two," Susannah agreed and winked at Silver.

"Me, three." Silver giggled.

They all looked at him with expectant eyes.

"Me, four?" Susannah burst into laughter.

"Say grace, Davy."

David offered a quick prayer of thanks then served everyone, enjoying the pleasure of making sure each had enough to eat. It had been a long time since a meal around this kitchen table had been so happy and he knew it had everything to do with Susannah's presence. He couldn't stop staring at her.

David felt compelled to study Susannah's radiant face as the girls teased her about her appetite. This afternoon Wade and Jared had helped David realize that he wanted this woman and her child in his life permanently. His friends had insisted there was no reason why David couldn't care for Susannah, that cutting love out of his life had never been something God had told him. Repeatedly they'd asked him to show a Biblical foundation for his belief that love was wrong for him. Wade had even said he thought David had made himself believe that after being thrown over twice.

But were they right?

And how risky was it to love her?

Susannah wasn't like David's former fiancées. He didn't have to wonder if she'd walk out because he worked too long, or because of something Darla did. Susannah knew what his life was like, knew he was committed to his sister. She was committed, too.

But could she love him?

"You're not eating," she said, frowning at him. "Is something wrong?"

"No." He felt the worries, the cares, the heavy thoughts go as he returned her smile. "Nothing is wrong at all."

Life seemed so simple, so enjoyable when Susannah was there.

"I'll help clean up," she offered when the food had disappeared.

"There isn't much to clean up." David chuckled at the one lonely chicken ball rolling in sauce. "I can load everything into the dishwasher. You go and rest."

"I did rest," she told him, a glimmer of spirit flickering in her gorgeous eyes. "And I'm fine. Perfectly able to clean up a few dishes. So don't argue," she added when he opened his mouth.

"Okay. You can help a little," he agreed, pretending he'd made the decision.

David enjoyed the camaraderie of working beside Susannah. He made a big fuss about giving her plenty of room for the sheer pleasure of watching her blush.

He drove back to Connie and Wade's enjoying the sound of laughter and happy voices. Darla raced out of the car and up the walk with Silver, leaving him and Susannah alone in the car.

"It was nice to have someone to share our table with," he said. "I'd forgotten how long it's been since Darla and I entertained."

"I hope you don't feel you have to entertain me," Susannah said, frowning at him. "I'm just the help."

"Susannah, you must know you mean a lot more than that to us," he said meaningfully. He held her gaze until she looked away.

"Thank you for these," she said, burying her nose in her flowers. "I've never had—well, thank you."

"You're welcome." David climbed out and went to open her car door. "What time will Darla be working at the butterfly exhibit tomorrow?"

"You're going to come?" She didn't look exactly thrilled at the prospect.

"I'll try to get there," he said. "I want to see how she does. Is that a problem?"

Susannah drew in a breath and stared past his shoulder. She wore a pained look that made him wonder if he'd said something wrong.

"Susannah? Are you all right?"

Finally she exhaled and nodded. "Yes."

"Did something just happen?" he asked as a wave of concern rushed over him. He grasped her elbow in case she felt faint or something. "You don't look pale."

She slid her arm out of his touch and smiled. "I can't get used to the soccer game going on inside me, that's all."

She let him escort her to the door before she hugged Darla and waved at him. "See you tomorrow." She inclined her head at Darla. "She'll be helping after school till five o'clock."

"Oh. Yes. Okay." David scanned her face once more. "You're sure you're all right?"

"I'm fine. Good night." She stood in the doorway, waiting for them to leave.

"Good night." He helped Darla into the car, and they drove away. Susannah remained in the doorway, her focus on the picture she clutched in her hands, the picture of her baby.

A wash of yearning swamped him. All down the block families were heading inside their homes, gathering their loved ones around them. David wanted to be able to do the same thing with Susannah. To protect her, to share her life, to have the right to help her with her child, and not just be an outsider.

He wanted to be able to kiss her good-night and wake up to her smiling face, to share his hopes and dreams with her, to discuss Darla and seek her opinion. He wanted Susannah to help him build a family.

God, please give me the sense to wait for the right time and find the words to tell her how much she means to me.

"I love Susannah, Davy," Darla said, yawning as she followed him inside their dark and silent home. "She makes everything happy."

"She sure does."

Darla stopped at the bottom of the stairs and frowned at him.

"What's wrong?" he asked.

"Susannah might come and stay with us forever if you kissed her like Prince Charming kissed Sleeping Beauty," she said. "Couldn't you kiss her, Davy?"

"We'll see," he said as he struggled to keep a straight face. "Have a good sleep, sweetie."

"Yeah." She hugged him, started up the stairs, then paused. "Davy?"

"Yes?" He waited, knowing something important was coming.

"Are you sure we couldn't adopt Susannah's baby?" Sadness drained the joy from her face. "I don't want that baby or Susannah to go away. I love them both."

"I know." David embraced her and tried to soothe her, but he couldn't tell her everything would be okay. Because he wasn't sure it would be—not for Susannah once she let her child go, and not for him if he let Susannah go.

"What can we do, Davy?"

"Pray," was the only answer he could think of.

Darla was doing an amazing job explaining the butterfly exhibit to the group of day-care children who were visiting the botanical garden. Susannah smiled encouragement when two older boys wandered in and began to ask Darla a hundred questions. Susannah listened but her mind was on finding somewhere to sit. She was so tired and the little butterfly gazebo was so hot.

Loud voices drew her attention.

Darla was supposed to inspect and brush off each person to ensure no butterflies hid in their clothes and escaped the enclosure. But the boys would not let her do it. In fact, they taunted her. Susannah stepped forward to intervene, but at that moment one of the boys jerked back and knocked her off balance. She reached out, desperate to grab on to a metal fountain to stop her fall.

Next thing she was lying on the ground, winded and dazed, and Darla stood over her, berating the boys.

"You hurt Susannah," she bellowed, her anger flaring. "Get out." She pointed to the door. As soon as they'd pushed their way through the hanging plastic panels in the exhibit, she knelt beside Susannah and searched her face. "You have a cut," she whispered fearfully, pointing to a mark on Susannah's arm.

"I'm okay, I think. Can you help me up?"

"Yes." Darla almost lifted her to her feet. Thankfully the enclosure was empty.

Susannah felt woozy and worried. Darla insisted she leave the exhibit and sit down on a bench outside. Once Susannah was seated she took her phone and dialed.

"Darla, no," Susannah protested, but it was too late.

"You said you'd come, Davy. Where are you?" Darla was angry, her brown eyes intense. "Some boys pushed Susannah and she fell down. She has a cut."

Susannah heard David's low voice assuring her he was on his way. She'd fallen so awkwardly—was the baby okay? It wasn't moving. She laid one hand over her stomach protectively and tried to form a prayer for help.

"We're really sorry." The boys had returned to apologize. "We didn't mean to bump into you."

Susannah opened her mouth but Darla spoke first.

"You should be more careful," Darla lectured. "A butterfly exhibit isn't a good place to fool around. And you shouldn't make fun of people, either," she added, her face very severe.

"Yeah, we know," the bigger one said with a sheepish grin. "You were just doing your job. Sorry, miss."

As they left, Susannah shifted, feeling bruised and uncomfortable.

"You shouldn't have phoned him, Darla. I'll be fine. It was just a little fall."

"At your stage, there are no little falls," David said, striding up to them. He knelt, touching the mark on her arm before his fingers slid down to thread with hers. He squeezed them and closed his eyes. "Woman, you scared the daylights out of me."

To her shock he gathered her in his arms and held her close.

"I'm sorry." Susannah marveled at how right it felt to be held like this. But then she noticed how pale he was, and that his hand trembled as it smoothed back her hair. "I'm fine, David."

"We're going to make sure of that," he said grimly. "You have a bruise on your chin." His jaw clenched.

"It's nothing." She wouldn't tell him how off balance she felt.

"Shall I carry you?" David held her as if he'd never let her go.

"Of course not. I can still walk." She touched his

face, smoothed away the lines on his forehead, completely overwhelmed by his concern. "I'm really all right, David," she whispered.

"I'd prefer to hear that from a doctor," he growled. "Darla, tell the lady you have to leave now."

"Okay." She hurried away but was back in a flash. "Ready."

"All right, you walk on one side of Susannah. I'll walk on the other," David directed. "We'll go slowly. Okay?"

At least he waited for her nod of approval, Susannah mused. But truthfully, she was very glad of his support. A hint of fear that she'd messed up again would not leave her.

Please don't take my baby, she silently prayed. *Please?*

Deep in her heart Susannah repeated the words Connie had been telling her ever since she'd arrived in Tucson. *God is the God of love.*

Chapter Twelve

God? Are you listening?

David waited outside the examining room, his heart in his throat.

She's so small, so delicate. That baby is all she has. Please, please don't let—

He couldn't bear to even let the thought develop as fear like he'd known only twice before burgeoned and clutched at his heart. The only time it had loosened its hold in the past half hour was when he'd had Susannah in his arms.

Where she belonged.

In that instant David made up his mind. He was going to tell Susannah that he loved her, just as Wade and Jared had advised. More than that, he was going to ask her to marry him.

"David?" Connie rushed up, laid a hand on his arm, her face worried. "Have you heard anything?"

"Not yet—" The words died on his lips as Susannah's doctor emerged from the room they'd taken her into. "Doctor?"

"You're David?" Dr. Grace Karrang smiled at him. "Susannah said you'd be hovering out here, waiting."

So she knew he wouldn't just leave her. Good.

"How is she?" Connie asked.

"Everything seems okay. I'll keep her overnight, just to make sure. But as far as I can tell now, Susannah and her baby are fine."

"Can I see her?" he asked.

"Yes. They'll move her to a room shortly, but you can all talk to her for a while. One at a time, though."

"You go first, Davy." Darla slid her hand into Connie's. "We'll wait."

"Thanks, sis. I'll hurry," he promised.

"It's okay, Davy." She touched his cheek, her eyes clear. "I prayed. Susannah and her baby are going to be all right."

"Yes." He kissed her forehead.

Susannah looked so petite on the bed, her skin ashen against the pristine sheet. Her hair had been pushed back off her face. Her eyes were closed.

David picked up her hand and threaded his fingers in hers.

"Susannah?"

She blinked a couple of times before those incredible lashes lifted and she smiled. His Sleeping Beauty.

"Hello, David. I guess I drifted off." Her soft, sweet voice sounded like music to him. "You're pale. Are you all right?"

"Me? I'm fine. It's you I'm worried about." He couldn't stop brushing his thumb against her skin, reassuring himself that she was alive and well. "How are you?"

"A little tired. The doctor said I have to stay here

overnight." She frowned. "That's going to be expensive."

"It's taken care of. Don't worry." When she licked her lips, David poured a little water from the carafe and held it to her mouth. "Sip slowly."

"Thank you." She leaned back, smoothed the cover over her stomach. "I'm sorry if I worried you."

"Of course I was worried."

"Because I let this happen." She squeezed her eyes closed. "You think I'll let something happen with Darla, too. You want me to quit." She stared at him. "Is that it?"

"No!" He frowned. "I care about what happens to you, Susannah. I care a lot."

"You do?" She stared at him in disbelief, emerald eyes wide in her pale face.

"Susannah, I'm in love with you. I have been for some time." David waited to see how she'd react.

"In love—with me?" She peeked at him through her lashes, then hid her eyes.

What if she still loved the baby's father? The idea hadn't occurred to him before. He couldn't think about that now—he just needed to show her.

"I've known how I felt for a while." He loved the way she let him finish his stumbling admission. "I just wasn't sure what to do about it. Until today." ·

"W-what have you decided?" she whispered, worry filling her face.

"Why do you always expect the worst?" he asked with tender mirth.

"I don't. Not always," she argued, her feistiness back.

"Susannah." He smiled, cupping her face in his palms. "I want to marry you, Susannah. I want you to stay with Darla and me forever. I want a future with you."

"And the baby?" she asked, fear in the shadows of her eyes. "What about my baby?"

"You'll have to learn to share because it will be our baby. Every bit as much mine and Darla's as yours," he said firmly, holding her gaze. "We'll raise him or her together. With love and laughter and faith in God."

"My faith in God isn't very strong right now," she whispered, tears welling in her eyes.

"It'll grow. We'll both work on trusting God."

Susannah studied him without speaking. David could see she was thinking deep and hard and he could only pray that she would at least think about his proposal.

"Susannah, you're not the only one who has made mistakes," he admitted, loving the feel of her skin as he caressed her face. "I let failed relationships from the past influence me into thinking God didn't want me to love again. I knew I was beginning to care for you, but I assumed I was supposed to remain single, for Darla."

"David, I—" she started, then faltered.

"You've shown me that Darla and I both need you in our lives." He slid his arms around her, drawing her close. Then he leaned forward and touched her lips with his. To his surprise, she returned his kiss with a sweetness he'd only dared dream about.

David felt relief wash over him. Maybe, just maybe, somewhere deep inside, she had at least some feelings for him. He felt joy welling up inside him.

"I love you, Susannah. And so does Darla. She would love to have a sister."

"She was like a mother bear today, protecting her cub." She smiled reflectively and reached up to smooth his hair. "Darla is amazing. You're pretty amazing, too," Susannah whispered shyly, brushing her fingers against his cheek. "Thank you for getting me here so quickly."

"I love you. How could I do anything else?" he asked, content to savor the pure bliss of holding her in his arms. "Anyway, I was scared stupid. You were so pale. Still are."

David waited but Susannah didn't respond with the words he wanted to hear. He told himself to be patient. She needed time, he reasoned. He'd sprung it on her. He kissed her quickly, then rose.

"Darla's champing at the bit to get in here. And Connie. I'll give them a turn."

"Okay." She let him go, her arms dropping to the bed.

"Susannah?"

"Yes?"

"Will you think about my proposal?" he asked, his heart jammed into his throat.

"I have to think it over. Marriage isn't something to be rushed into." Her green eyes held shadows. "I did that before and I made some huge mistakes. I'm not going to make them again."

She hadn't said yes.

But neither had she said no.

"Take all the time you need," he said as a giant geyser of hope flowed inside his heart. "I'll be waiting."

"Thank you." He turned to leave but she stopped him by catching his hand. "David?"

"Yes?"

"Will you do me a favor?" Her eyes grew huge in her small face.

He wanted to say yes, but he had a hunch he wasn't

going to like it. So he quirked an eyebrow upward and waited.

"Can we not tell the others?" Her eyes were turbulent like the sea during a tempestuous storm. "Not yet anyway."

The geyser of hope inside sputtered. "Because?"

"Because I need this to be between us for now," she whispered. "There's another life at stake. I have to make the right decision."

He wasted several moments studying her then nodded, squeezed her hand and left. "Your turn," he said to an eager Darla.

Wade stood in the hallway.

"Connie went to get some coffee," he explained. "So?"

"I asked her to marry me. She wants to think about it." David studied his friend. "She also wants to keep my proposal quiet. For now."

"So we'll pray. Hard."

"Thanks." David had laid his heart out there. What more could he do but trust that God would see him through?

While he walked on tenterhooks.

David loved her?

Susannah couldn't quite assimilate that knowledge and there wasn't time anyway. Darla burst through the doorway and came bounding over to the bed.

"Is the baby all right?" she whispered. "Are you?"

"We're both just fine. Thanks to you." Susannah hugged her. "I don't know what I would have done without you there, Darla."

"But I wasn't good," Darla countered, her face glum. "I got mad and yelled at those guys."

"You know, sometimes anger is a good thing," Susannah told her, patting the side of her bed so Darla would sit near. "Sometimes we have to get angry against injustice or when somebody does something wrong so that the wrong gets corrected. You did very well and I'm proud of you."

"Really?" Darla's huge smile lit up the room.

"Really. Thank you for protecting me. It's just the kind of thing one sister would do for another," she said quietly. "That's how I think of you, you know. As my little sister."

"I love you, Susannah." Darla hugged her enthusiastically. "And I love the baby, too." She patted her rounded stomach. "Hello, Baby."

Susannah listened to her talking to the child in her body and marveled at the love she felt for this wonderful girl. How was it possible to feel such a bond with Darla? What strange coincidence was it that Darla had slipped into her heart and nestled right next to her unborn child?

She said as much to Connie after Darla left. Her old friend simply smiled.

"It's not coincidence, Susannah," Connie assured her. "It's God."

Susannah wasn't sure about that. God didn't seem quite so personal to her, though she'd been trying to breach the gap between them by reading the Bible Connie had left in her room and taking time each night to pray.

"See, that's the thing about God," Connie said. "His love doesn't hiccup when we make mistakes or turn away from Him. His love isn't like human love, Susannah. And He never, ever turns us away."

Rick Green had said the same thing, Susannah remembered.

"God's love never changes, no matter what." Connie shook her head. "There's a verse in the Bible that says nothing can separate us from the love of God. The verse goes on to list a whole bunch of things and then repeats that none of them, nothing can come between us and the love God has for His precious children."

"I hear that" she admitted, "but then it sounds like there's a *but*."

"The *but* is us, Suze." Connie shook her head. "We forget how great the love of God is, or we think we're too bad, or that we've done something too terrible." A serious note lowered her voice. "But the Bible says nothing can stop God's love."

It sounded nice, Susannah thought. Comforting, if only she could believe it. But Connie had no idea about her past, about the things she'd done since she'd left the foster home. And Susannah had no intention of telling her.

"We need to move Ms. Wells to a room now. You can see her later."

Susannah was glad for the nurse's intrusion. She wished her friend goodbye.

As they moved her to her room, she couldn't shut out that inner voice that kept offering hope. Connie's words made her wish for the impossible. But in her heart of hearts Susannah couldn't quite believe that God's love extended to her.

David claimed to love her, too. His words pinged

into her brain. Was it real love he felt? How could he love someone like her?

You're pregnant with another man's child. You are so dependent on Connie and Wade you don't even have your own place. What is there to love?

But David *had* said he loved her.

And she loved him. Why deny it any longer? He'd snuck into her heart, a bit each day. She'd simply refused to let herself believe that such love could ever be returned.

For a moment, Susannah let herself bask in the knowledge of what David's love could mean. Happiness. Peace at last. Contentment. A home for her and her baby, a husband who cared about her, loved her and would help her make the right decisions for the future. A sister to share with—something Susannah had missed for so long. She wouldn't have to be alone.

But what if she failed him? What if she did something stupid, something that embarrassed him? What if he became ashamed of her? The thought made her physically sick. She admired David so much, but could she live up to what he'd expect? Did she dare risk loving again?

The pros and cons circled her brain as Susannah struggled to envision exactly how her life would change if she said yes to David. The images were dazzling, alluring and so far beyond anything Susannah knew that she could hardly believe in a life like that. He would come this evening, however. And by then she had to have her answer ready.

Connie had said God loved her. Susannah wasn't sure that was possible. But surely He could help her.

God? Don't let me make another mistake. Please?

* * *

Susannah curled up in the armchair behind the curtain and inhaled the heady fragrance from the lush bouquet of crimson roses David had sent. Her fingers trailed over the words on the enclosed note. *For Susannah. With love, David.*

To be loved just for yourself—how wonderful that would be. As she fingered the velvet petals, for a moment she let herself dream that she could actually live the happily-ever-after of Darla's beloved fairy tales.

Dare she dream?

"What does that hunky lawyer see in our white-trash girl?"

Susannah froze at the voices coming from the other bed in her room. She huddled tighter into the curtain and prayed they wouldn't see her.

"Watch it." A nurse's aide checked Susannah's bed. "She's not there. Be careful what you say, will you? She might overhear us."

"She's having a shower. Primping, no doubt," the other nurse's scathing voice condemned. "A man like him, from a wealthy family—he could have his pick of women. Why send *her* roses? She's nothing. Nobody. What's she got to offer him—an illegitimate kid?"

They left moments later but the damage was done. Even Susannah's gorgeous roses couldn't erase those harsh words from her brain. Over and over they replayed, driving the shaft of pain deeper into her heart.

Why did they have to ruin it?

Because they were right. Susannah Wells wasn't worthy of David Foster's love.

The harsh truth smacked her with reality. It was an illusion, a fantasy to think she could marry him. And she couldn't afford to deal in daydreams when her baby's future depended on her making rational, sensible choices.

Susannah shook off the fairy tale, rose from her dream world and prepared for her meeting with David. Her heart cried out to God, begging Him to help her say the hardest thing she'd ever had to say.

"You're a wonderful man, David." Susannah's voice was quiet yet he heard every word. "You're gentle, caring, kind. You'd make a wonderful husband."

"But not for you." He sat down, amazed by the decimation that rushed to swamp him. Was it possible for love to root so deeply in such a short time? *Yes*, his heart thumped. "Is it because you think I won't love your baby?"

"No."

He felt relief that she knew him that well, at least.

Susannah shook her golden head, her green eyes darkening. "That's the last thing I'd worry about. You would be the best father any child could have."

"You don't love me?" He noted the way her glance veered from his.

"I'm sorry, David. I can't accept your proposal."

"Why?" he demanded, ashamed of his desperate need to know.

"I can't use you like that," she whispered, her face sad.

"Use me?" He didn't get it.

"David, I'd ruin your life—embarrass you and Darla. Eventually you'd be ashamed when you realized I'm not someone worthy of being your wife." She put her hand over her mouth and looked down.

"Ashamed of you?" he scoffed. "That's ridiculous. I've always been very proud of you."

"Thank you for saying that." Susannah hesitated, then shook her head. "But I can't marry you, David. I'm sorry. I think the best thing is for me to give my baby a chance with someone who won't mess up as I have, someone who will make sure he or she grows up happy. That way I won't risk making another mistake."

"Won't you?" He studied her. "Or will you be making the biggest mistake of all?"

She met his gaze but said nothing.

So that was it? He'd gambled, taken a chance on telling her his true feelings, and lost. Now he was supposed to just give up?

"You haven't said anything about love, Susannah."

"I—uh—"

David tilted her chin so she had to look at him. "Do you love me?"

She didn't speak but her green eyes flashed a warning not to push.

"So you won't risk even saying the words, let alone allow yourself to feel love." He shook his head. "How sad that is—because I know you care for me. I think you love me almost as much as I love you."

"David—"

"Don't you see, Susannah? Your fear has taken over." He had to make her understand. "It controls you so much you won't let yourself believe that you can be more than the past. You won't stretch your mind and imagine yourself living with love, being the mother your child needs, being the wife I believe you can be."

"Don't waste your feelings on me—"

"Waste?" he scoffed. "It's not a waste for me to love

you, Susannah. It's a joy and a privilege. You enrich my life, you make it worth living. I finish work as fast as I can so I can come home and see you, talk to you and listen to your laugh."

She looked at him, eyes welling with tears. "I'm not worth loving."

"Then you don't know Susannah as I do because I find you eminently lovable," he insisted. "I can hardly wait to hear how you're feeling and learn what you did each day. I ache to be included in your life, to be part of it all, to help you plan for that child."

She was shaking her head but David couldn't stop. He was desperate to make her understand the place she'd carved out for herself in his heart.

"Do you want to know how much I care about you, Susannah?" He should have felt embarrassed to be so needy, but he didn't. He was fighting for his future and that demanded honesty. "I question Darla every night to make sure nothing's wrong, that you didn't get too tired, that you weren't bored. I make her repeat conversations just so I can be part of your world. I can't get enough of you."

"David—"

"I love you and your child, Susannah. So don't pretend it's to spare my feelings that you're turning me down."

"I am trying to spare you," she insisted. "My past isn't—"

"Your past is not you," he said fiercely. "Not who you are today, or who you could be tomorrow. You are not that little Susannah your mother blamed."

"Yes, I am."

"No. What you are is an amazing woman who doesn't

spare herself for others. You've made an endless number of good choices since you came here. But all you can do is look backward and focus on the past." Frustration surged inside him. "Why won't you risk being more than the old Susannah? Why aren't you willing to stretch yourself to be the mother your child needs?"

"People don't change, David," she whispered. "Not that much."

"You have."

"I fell for a man who lied to me, and I believed his lies." She sniffed, head bent, refusing to look at him.

His heart ached for her but he resolved to keep fighting.

"Okay, so you fell for the wrong man. Did you ever ask yourself why?" David grabbed her hands and hung on. "Because you didn't trust your inner warnings. That was a mistake people make every day."

"A bad one." Despair edged her voice.

"So?" He had to help her understand what she was throwing away. "You aren't that person anymore. You've grown, matured and taken responsibility for a baby. You've changed my life and certainly Darla's. You have a lot to give, Susannah. And by refusing to accept love, you're cheating all of us."

"I'm not cheating anyone." She yanked her hands from his. Bright spots of pink dotted her cheeks as she glared at him. "Don't you dare say that!"

Good, he wanted her to get worked up about her future and stop passively accepting what her mother had told her.

"You're cheating all of us, including yourself. But mostly you're cheating God." David hunkered down to see into her eyes. "He's given you a chance to change the course of your life, Susannah. He's given me a deep, strong love for you that can withstand your past. And I believe you share that love. Are you going to accept His gift, or throw it away?"

He held his breath, waiting, praying, hoping.

An announcement came on asking visitors to leave the hospital. David ignored it. A nurse ducked her head in and told him visiting hours were over. He ignored that, too. And waited.

Finally Susannah inhaled. Then she straightened, met his gaze directly and shook her head.

"I'm sorry, David. Thank you for your proposal, but I have to refuse." No quaver in her voice, no hesitancy— nothing that exposed what she was feeling inside. "You don't know how I wish that I could be the person you think I am. But I'm not."

"That's it? You're just going to walk away from everything—me, your child, Darla, your future? God?"

"No, I'm planning my future the best way I know how." Her voice was firm. "And I've made a decision."

David knew he wasn't going to like the next part.

"I'm resigning, David." Her big green eyes emptied of all emotion. "I promised Darla I'd take her to the pre-Easter presentation at the desert museum. That's in two weeks. It should be enough time for you to find someone else to work with Darla."

"And the baby?" he managed to choke out.

"I want to thank you for all your help, David, but I think it's better if I find someone to adopt my child on my own," she murmured. "But I will pay you what I owe you."

"Money? Will that make you feel better, Susannah?" he asked as bitterness welled.

"Yes." She lifted her chin. "Being able to pay what I owe is something I haven't always been able to do. That's just one of the things you don't know about me."

David couldn't think of a response that wouldn't dump all his anger and hurt and frustration on her, and Susannah, with her pale cheeks and hurting eyes, didn't need the extra grief.

So he did the only thing he could.

He leaned forward and kissed her, pouring all the love he felt into that kiss. To his joy, she responded. When he finally drew back, they were both breathless.

"I love you, Susannah. That isn't going to change, no matter what you do or where you go. And because I love you, I will support whatever decision you make." He smiled, touched her cheek. "You see, I have no worry about you. I know your heart. Maybe better than you do."

He walked out of the room without looking back.

But his soul wept for all he'd lost.

Chapter Thirteen

Tucson's warm desert wind stole moisture the way it stole energy. Susannah was drained.

She'd expected her last two weeks with Darla to be problematic, and they were. But not for the reasons she expected.

For one thing, Darla kept asking her about the baby and Susannah had no definitive answer.

Then there was David. He didn't press her to change her mind about marriage, didn't ask her why and didn't insist she rethink her decision. In fact, Susannah scarcely saw him, though each day there was some small reminder that he'd said he loved her.

A jar of the gourmet pickles she loved, a little book about the hilarious woes of pregnancy, a pretty bouquet in pinks or blues or both, a box of luscious chocolates, trinkets that were original and thoughtfully chosen, never duplicated.

Each one would appear with Susannah's name carefully printed on the tag in his precise writing with "Love, David" etched beneath. His manners were faultless when he arrived at home in the evening, and his demeanor as considerate as anyone could ask for. He was everything a good friend would be—kind, considerate and very gentle.

Except Susannah wanted more.

Which was totally unreasonable, and she knew it. She'd refused his proposal. She couldn't expect him to hold her when she felt ugly and horrible, or understand that she ached to hear a word of encouragement. She waited, but he never inquired about her most recent doctor's visit or commented on the fact that her feet had become all but invisible.

But she wanted that. She wanted all of it. Badly.

Each day when she left his house in the evening, he said the same thing.

"I love you, Susannah." Then he kissed her.

And each night she sat awake with her child doing acrobatics inside her, and wished the fairy tale she dreamed about could come true.

Susannah's days were full as she escorted Darla to her programs, watching the girl blossom with confidence in every activity. One evening she sat Darla down and told her she would be leaving shortly. Darla didn't argue, as she'd expected. Instead she accepted Susannah's words, hugged her tightly and told her she loved her. Then she'd disappeared to her room. Later Susannah heard her weeping.

Susannah found herself in tears often. It was so hard to think of never watching her child grow, take her first step, stumble and know she wouldn't be there to see that baby walk. Her heart squeezed tight whenever she realized she would never hear her child say "Mommy." She felt a special bond with her baby now, a secret flush of wonder each time a tiny leg stretched or a hand reached up. The wonder of this life had turned her prayers to God into pleas for help to do the hardest thing she'd ever contemplated.

But God didn't seem to be listening, because the ache intensified right along with her feelings of worthlessness. That, more than anything, reinforced her belief that she couldn't be a mom.

The warm spring air added a precious clarity to Susannah's days as the desert began to bloom and come alive in ways she'd never imagined. One afternoon Connie drove her out to the desert museum so she could get her bearings for her trip with Darla the following week, and to witness the first burst of cactus flowers.

"I never imagined there were so many cacti," Susannah said when they'd wandered the paths for a while.

"Those are hedgehog, those are fishhook and those are saguaro cacti," Connie pointed out. "Don't walk there," she warned, grabbing Susannah's arm and drawing her back. "That's a Jumping Cholla and its spines are nasty."

So many dangerous things in this world. Would her child's adoptive mother be sure to protect her baby from all of them?

"This will all be decorated for Easter. It's unbelievable. We came last year and Silver was tongue-tied for at least ten minutes." Connie chuckled and waved a hand. "There will be specially trained museum volunteers all over the place. They'll be wearing white shirts. They can answer questions about the plants and animals in the Sonoran Desert—pretty well any that Darla can think up, I'm sure."

"She wants to know everything." Susannah smiled

as pride swelled inside. "I think she wants to be a docent. Someday."

"It would be perfect for her." Connie took her arm to steer her away from the cactus garden. "You look tired, Suze. There's a café. Let's stop and relax. We can get some coffee. Or tea."

"And maybe some sorbet?"

"Sure." Connie giggled. "You and Darla seem to share a fondness for that treat."

"Yeah. Only she prefers pistachio and I love key lime." Susannah laughed and pretended everything was fine, but inside she wept. She and Darla had grown so close. Who would love and care for this sister of her heart?

David. At least she knew Darla would be safe with him.

It was a relief to sit in the shade of the cottonwood trees and sip their hot drinks in between spoonfuls of frosty sorbet. Nearby a rock-surrounded garden burgeoned with the buzz of bees from the pollination gardens and cut the stillness of the warm afternoon.

"How are you feeling?" Connie asked.

"Big. Ugly. Tired." Susannah forced a smile. "I don't seem to be able to sleep much at night anymore." She touched her stomach. "She's always dancing."

"Or maybe *he's* playing football," Connie teased. "Are you sure you'll be well enough to trail around here with Darla? You're getting awfully close to your due date, aren't you?"

"Not that close. The doctor says I probably have at least two more weeks, and I will most likely go overdue." Susannah made a face. "How much bigger can I get?"

"You're so small, it just shows a lot. You look beautiful," Connie reassured. She was silent for several minutes before asking, "How are things with David?"

Tired of being alone and struggling to sort out her confusing feelings, Susannah had confided in Connie after David's hospital visit. Connie hadn't been surprised to hear of David's proposal. Susannah had a hunch her friend had long since guessed at her feelings, too.

"He's fine, I guess. Very busy at work, I think, but he always takes time to compliment me about something each evening." She didn't tell her friend about the good-night I love you's that kept her awake. "He keeps leaving me little gifts." Susannah tipped back her head and let the breeze cool her neck. "I feel guilty but he won't stop no matter what I say."

"Don't you like his gifts?" Connie asked, frowning.

"Oh, yes. I like being surprised by them." Susannah called herself a fool to be so transparent. "Yesterday he left the catalogue from the college. He's gathered a lot of information on the courses I will need to take to get my degree. I didn't think he'd even heard me talk about it."

"Good thing you'll have the summer to get used to the baby's schedule." Connie smiled. "You can start your program in the fall and then add as you feel able."

"I probably should have told you this before," Susannah murmured, knowing it was way past time to tell her friend. "But I'm going to give the baby up for adoption."

"Oh, Suze." Connie's eyes brimmed with tears.

"I can't keep this baby," she said firmly. "I'm a horrible role model."

"That's not true." Connie reached out and squeezed her hands, her face serious. "Listen, Susannah, I know you've been working hard to rebuild a relationship with God. Well, part of that needs to include letting the past go. It says in the Bible that God remembers our sins no more. If He can forget, why can't you?"

"David said the same thing. I haven't thought much about it," she said.

"Well, think about it now," Connie insisted.

"Why?" Susannah asked. "What difference will it make?"

"It will help you understand why you shouldn't keep hanging on to guilt from the past," Connie said, her voice stern. "When God forgives, it's gone. He doesn't keep going back and harping on it over and over. What good does His forgiveness do if we keep bashing ourselves over the heads with our mistakes?"

"But you don't know—" Susannah gulped.

"No, I don't. But the thing is, God knows, Suze. And He's forgiven it all."

Susannah sipped her tea and wondered how it felt to be clean, forgiven, made all right.

"Suze, there's always been part of your story that you held back. All that time at the farm—I've always known you never told me everything that happened with that fire." Connie squeezed her fingers.

A shadow fell over them. They glanced up. David stood staring at Susannah. It was clear he'd overheard Connie's last remarks.

"David?" Connie blinked.

"Wade sent me. Silver fell off her bike. He wants you to meet them at the hospital." He shook his head when she rushed to her feet. "She's fine, just needs a stitch. Darla's with her but she's calling for you."

"I'll go with you." Susannah pushed away her glass.

"No, stay. David can bring you back." Connie glanced at him, waiting for his nod.

"Yes, I can. No problem. In fact, I could use a drink myself. It's hot this afternoon. Drive carefully," he said to Connie.

"I will. See you later, Suze?" It was a question.

Susannah knew Connie was asking if she'd be all right with David. "Go, Connie. And kiss Silver for me."

David hailed a passing vendor and purchased a drink. Then he sat down across from her, his stare intense.

"What?" she said, feeling as if she was under a microscope.

"I overheard Connie. And I agree with her. I think you have held back something that happened at that fire." He leaned forward, touched her cheek with a forefinger. "I think you need to say it, to get it out so you can forget it."

"I'll never forget," Susannah said bleakly.

"Why?"

"Because I was the cause of that fire." She couldn't look at David, couldn't bear to see the condemnation in his eyes. "I am the reason my sisters died."

"I don't believe it." He shook her head, as if that put an end to it.

"Believe it. I left a pan on the stove. It used to get so dry in our house in Illinois in the winter. I got nosebleeds sometimes. My mother told me that if I kept a pan of water on the stove, the moisture would help. So that's what I did." She gulped as the memories flooded back, then turned to look at David. "I didn't turn it off before I left. It must have burned dry, got too hot and caught on a dishtowel or something. I was mad, you see. I wanted to get away and I never checked…"

The tears would not be stopped, grief for years of trying to erase the images of her little sisters alone, crying for help.

"Oh, Susannah." David shifted his chair nearer and wrapped a loving arm around her shoulder. "Sweetheart, you were too young to be responsible for any of that—even if it did happen that way, and I'm not sure it did."

"It did." She scrubbed her cheeks, irritated by her emotions. Good thing she had said no to David. This was just something else he'd be ashamed of.

"It doesn't matter what happened. Don't you understand? God doesn't say that one mistake is worse than another, that He'll forgive some things but not all." David smoothed her hair, his voice brimming with love that soothed. "He says 'I forgive' and He means everything. Whatever it is. And He wants you to forgive yourself, too. He wants you to enjoy a full life, to experience love and joy. He planned that especially for you, Susannah."

"I've done a lot of things I'm ashamed of."

David only smiled.

"Doesn't matter," he said. "You asked for forgiveness and God gave it. He doesn't hold it against you. He knows you, Susannah. He knows you were young and mixed up and hanging with the wrong group. He knows who you are, everything that you've done, and He loves you anyway."

"I don't understand how that could be." Susannah listened as David explained more about forgiveness on the way home. And she promised him she'd try and forgive herself for her past.

But late that night, as she sat on the window seat

watching the moon slide in and out behind clouds, Susannah knew that while forgiveness might be possible,
forgetting was not. She would carry those scars of guilt
for the rest of her life.

And she couldn't bear it if her child found out. Adoption was the only way.

"So you're saying Susannah Wells's mother is still
in jail?" David scribbled the information on a pad to
study later.

"Not still—again. And not exactly jail," the social
worker said. "It's a facility to help Mrs. Wells deal with
her personal issues. But yes, she has been committed
to staying there until the doctors feel she can handle
life on the outside. Given her refusal to accept any responsibility for her recent actions, my understanding
is that she will not be leaving soon." The social worker
listed the most recent charges that had been added to
Mrs. Wells's latest sentence.

She wouldn't give him specific details, of course.
And David hadn't expected any.

"The lady has a problem with responsibility," she
finished.

"Me, too," David muttered after he'd hung up.

But his problem was of another kind. He'd been so
preoccupied with being overwhelmed with responsibility, he now realized he'd missed out on a lot of what
life offered. Now he desperately craved the opportunity
to be responsible for Susannah and the life she carried.
But she would have none of it.

And he didn't know what to do about that.

For years after his father's death, David had believed
he had to be in control of everything in his world. But

when Susannah came along, she'd inadvertently forced him to realize that he needed to surrender the controls of his life. Recently Wade and Jared, too, had helped him realize he needed to completely surrender his past, present and future to God.

"Jared Hornby is on line two." His secretary cut into his thoughts.

David picked up the phone.

"You called?"

"Yeah." David proposed lunch with his old friend. "I need to pick your brain again," he explained.

"Oh, so then you'd be buying," Jared said. "Great. I'm not far away. Fifteen minutes at Scarfies? We haven't been there in ages."

"Okay." David left the office immediately. He needed to get outside, breathe the fresh spring air and think as he walked the few blocks to their favorite lunch place. But when he arrived, his brain was more knotted than ever.

Jared sat waiting, his iced tea half gone.

"Hi." David hurriedly ordered the special. When Jared had placed his order and their server had left, he cleared his throat. "I feel like I'm drowning," he said.

"Susannah," Jared guessed.

"I believe she is God's choice for me, Jared. She's the only woman I want in my life."

"And her past?" His old friend hunched forward to study him.

David crossed his arms over his chest. "I couldn't care less about her past, except that whatever happened, it made her into the woman I love."

"You can't write it off that easily, pal." Jared shook

his head. "Susannah has had some bad things happen to her. It's got to impact her."

"Where are you going with this?" David frowned.

"Wade and I advised you to tell Susannah how you felt." Jared shrugged. "Okay, you did that. And she didn't respond the way you wanted. I think you have to accept her response, buddy. I think that you have to leave the future with God." Jared sipped his iced tea.

"Just give up. That's what you mean?" Even the idea left a bad taste in David's mouth.

"Give it up to God," Jared corrected. "If she's His choice for you, let God work it out."

David shook his head. "I don't think God expects me to sit back and do nothing here, Jared. I can't do that. What if she gives her child away?"

"David, she *is* going to give her baby away," Jared said.

"Her past and her mistakes are exactly why she has to keep that baby," he insisted. "If she doesn't, that will only be one more thing Susannah will regret."

Jared thought about it a moment. "You said her mother's blame is at the root of all her feelings of unworthiness?"

"I'm no psychologist," David said, "but I think her mother's accusation that Susannah caused her sisters' deaths left a pretty big wound, yeah."

"Maybe you should go see her mother, try and get her to show some compassion for the only daughter she has left?" Jared quirked one eyebrow.

"It's worth a try, I suppose." David hated the thought of it. Intruding into someone else's past, reopening old wounds—everything in him protested at the depth of involvement. Susannah would be furious. But if it would help her…

"I'll pray. So will Wade." Jared leaned back as their food was delivered. "We'll keep a steady line going to heaven while you talk to this woman. There's just one thing."

"Yeah?" Personally David thought there was a lot more than *one* thing, but he waited for his friend to finish.

"What if none of it makes any difference to Susannah?" he asked.

David stalled, taking a bite of his burger and chewing it thoroughly. Finally he met Jared's gaze.

"I don't know," he admitted. "I can't think that far ahead."

"I don't know you." The woman flopped herself into the easy chair, her silver-blond hair tumbling to her shoulders. A more mature Susannah. "Do I?"

"No. David Foster. I'm a friend of Susannah's."

A spark of interest lit the green eyes before she covered with a lackluster shrug. He held out a hand, which she declined to shake.

"Your daughter Susannah," he said as anger surged up.

"I haven't seen her in years." Sara Wells looked at him balefully.

"Since the fire." He nodded. "I know. Why is that?"

"Look," she bristled, "I don't know who you think you are or why you're poking your nose into something that isn't any of your business, but—"

"It is my business." David leaned back and chose another tack. "Do you know you're going to be a grand-mother?"

She leaned forward, intrigued in spite of herself.

"Congratulations." Her lips curled.

"It's not my child. But I would like it to be," he said. He felt a rush of love as the words resounded to his soul. "I love Susannah. I want to marry her. She's a wonder-ful woman—loving, caring, gentle and courageous."

"Everything I'm not, is that what you mean?" Her eyes darkened.

"This isn't about you," David assured her. "You cut your own daughter out of your life."

"I have my reasons."

"I know all about your reasons. To make yourself look innocent. To ease your own pain. You blamed Su-sannah for her sisters' deaths. That was a lie, wasn't it?"

Sara Wells remained silent.

"She was a child, a little girl with far too much re-sponsibility."

"Do you think I don't know that?" Sara's face tight-ened.

"Then why?" he asked quietly. "You weren't the only one who lost. She lost her sisters. And she's spent all these years believing the lie you told her."

Tears flowed down her cheeks unchecked, but she stayed silent.

"Everything Susannah does is colored by her guilt, her belief that she was responsible," he said, but he mod-erated his voice because her tears touched his heart. This woman had lost her children. There was enough pain to go around.

Sara still said nothing. David knew he had to jar her out of her silence.

"This is a picture of her." He slid his favorite photo of Susannah across the table. She was daydreaming about something, staring into the lens, a small smile lifting her lips. "She's beautiful inside and out. She'd be a wonderful mother."

One hand reached out to trace the features on Susannah's lovely face. The tears did not stop. A flicker of empathy rose inside David's heart for this woman— she'd never known the wonderful beauty of what her child had become in spite of her.

"She's going to give away her baby to someone else, to adopt, because she thinks she's unworthy and because she's afraid she won't be the kind of mother she wants to be," David explained.

"She thinks she'll be like me. A drunk?" Finally Sara looked at him. Her excruciating pain engulfed him like a tidal wave and sucked all his anger away.

"She needs your forgiveness," David told her. "She needs to hear you say that her sisters' deaths were not her fault. This pain, this hurt—hasn't it gone on long enough, Sara? Your daughter needs you. Susannah needs the mother who abandoned her all those years ago."

"I'm sorry but your time is up." A guard waited at his elbow.

David rose, but he left the picture on the table.

"Susannah's baby is due very soon," he said, keeping his voice soft. "If you're going to help her, it must be quickly, before the baby's born. Otherwise it will be too late to repair the past."

Sara simply sat there, staring at her daughter. He laid a hand on her shoulder.

"I'll pray for you, Sara. I'll ask God to heal your

heart and soul and show you that He has plans for your future, something beautiful that you can't even imagine."

As he drove home, he prayed harder than he had in his entire life.

For all of them.

Susannah was miserable.

"I'm tired all the time," she told her doctor. "I can't see my toes anymore, let alone polish them. I feel like a limp rag even first thing in the morning."

"It's spring and this is the desert. It's only going to get warmer. Rest," the doctor advised.

"That's what everyone says," Susannah complained. "I do almost nothing but rest, and I'm still tired."

"Then rest some more. You're carrying a baby, Susannah. That's hard work. Probably the hardest job you'll ever have. You have to save your strength. Did you go to those Lamaze classes?"

"Yes." She'd gone with Connie and Darla. Precious, poignant, bittersweet evenings, full of laughter and tears.

"So you're ready," the doctor said. "Now you're just going to have to wait patiently until this baby decides its arrival date. Relax."

Connie also kept telling her to slow down but Susannah was frantic to find a family for her baby, and without David's help she floundered. How could you know about anyone's real intent through an internet profile?

As she made her way to pick up Darla, Susannah realized anew how difficult she was finding it, keeping up with Darla's activities, though her charge was always solicitous about Susannah's health. Darla fussed about the baby constantly, monitoring what Susannah ate and when. She insisted Susannah take frequent rests and offered water so often Susannah worried she'd float away during soccer practice or while waiting for Darla at the botanical garden. She made her way into David's house with Darla dancing attendance.

"Sixty-seven percent of pregnant women do not drink enough water," Darla declared. She was quoting statistics less often now, but the odd one still popped out whenever she wanted to defend her actions.

"I'm fine, Darla. Oh." The Braxton-Hicks contraction grabbed and held on, forcing Susannah to sit down on David's sofa and wait it out. "We'll make cookies in a little while," she promised with a gasp.

"Okay." Darla flopped down at the coffee table. "I'm going to draw some of the butterflies from the botanical garden so I can show the people at the center what I do." She plugged in her headphones and began humming to the music as her fingers flew across the page.

Once the tension in her stomach relaxed, Susannah closed her eyes. Just for a minute. Then she'd get up and make the cookies Darla wanted to take to school tomorrow. As she lay there, the scent from roses David had cut from the garden filled her senses. How wonderful to have your own rose bushes.

It was just one of the things Susannah was going to miss about this job. Each day had proven harder than the one before as she realized exactly what she was giving up by refusing David's proposal. Once she took Darla to the desert museum, her lovely life here would be over and all she'd have left were memories.

"I'm only asking You for one thing, God," she whispered. "Just please make sure my baby is healthy."

* * *

The house was quiet when he arrived home. Too quiet.

David tucked the packet of key lime-flavored mints under Susannah's purse. She'd mentioned she liked them last week, so today, on the way home, he'd made a special trip to the candy store to get them for her.

Not that she'd said it specifically to him. She hadn't. Susannah barely said two words to him anymore, and if she did, she made sure to keep her gaze averted. Ever since he'd proposed she'd been shy around him—hesitant, quiet.

But that didn't stop David from noting her likes and dislikes—Susannah liked lime-flavored anything, and it gave him great pleasure to seek out little gifts and leave them for her enjoyment. He'd wait like a kid and watch for her to discover his surprise, and then treasure that moment when she closed her eyes and hugged the treat to her heart.

Those few seconds made the bereft moments in his life bearable. That and the way she leaned into his nightly embrace before she remembered and pulled away...

David was going to call out, but then he stepped into the family room and saw Darla flopped on the floor, her headphones in her ears, her eyes closed. Her chest moved up and down in a soft, rhythmic snore. He found Susannah lying on the sofa with her eyes closed and a faint smile on her lips as she dozed.

Darla's Sleeping Beauty.

One hand lay on top of her stomach, as if to protect the precious life within. Mother and child. Was there anything more beautiful?

He wondered again about Susannah's mother. Would

she do the right thing? Or would she stay in her self-imposed prison? Once more he prayed for the troubled Sara and asked God to release her heart so that she could reach out to the daughter who needed peace so badly.

David spent some time just watching Susannah, treasuring the moment because he didn't know when it might happen again. One more day, that's all she had left to work for him. Then—who knew?

"Oh, I didn't realize it was so late." She blinked at him, then struggled to sit up, grasping David's hand when he held it out, easing herself off the sofa. "Thank you. I feel like an elephant."

"You look beautiful," he murmured. He touched her cheek with his fingers and pressed a kiss against her forehead. "Very beautiful."

She gave him a look that said she thought he was fibbing.

"I mean it. Your skin has this amazing luminosity—it's very attractive," he said, finishing hurriedly, amazed at his newfound ability to be so poetic.

"Well." Susannah stepped around him. "I shouldn't be sleepng. Darla needs to take some cookies to school tomorrow and we haven't baked them yet."

"Let's have dinner, and then we'll make them together. I think Mrs. Peters left everything in the slow cooker."

"I don't need to stay for dinner," Susannah said. "I can come back later."

"Susannah, please. Just stay for dinner. It's not a big deal, okay?" He woke Darla, then followed them both into the kitchen.

Darla made short work of setting the table. She put the kettle on to boil for tea, lifted a salad from the fridge and a freshly made loaf of bread from the cupboard. "Everything's ready, Davy."

They sat, and as he held out his hand for Darla's to say grace, David also reached out for Susannah's.

Please let her stay permanently, he prayed silently. *She's a part of our family.*

Susannah bowed her head for the grace. The moment it was over she took her hand from his. She said little during the meal. She picked at her food, eating only a small fraction of what she was served.

"Are you all right?" he asked when Darla went to answer the phone.

"Fine. Just a little uncomfortable." She smiled ruefully. "I'll get in the pool tonight and stretch everything out. That should help."

"I'm sorry it's so hard on you," he said, touching her shoulder. "I'd do it for you, if I could."

She smiled faintly, her gaze finally meeting his. "Thank you," she whispered.

While David cleared the table, Susannah helped Darla assemble the ingredients for cookies. But when he thought it might be best to leave the two alone with their baking, Darla suddenly said she had to finish her homework. David waved her off, then noticed how Susannah flagged, leaning against the counter.

"Sit down," he ordered, easing her into a chair. "There's no need to bake cookies tonight. I can stop by a bakery tomorrow."

"Darla said everyone is bringing some from home. She wanted to do the same." She began pulling out ingredients.

"You are so stubborn." He rolled up his sleeves. "Okay, tell me what to do."

She would have argued but he guessed from the lines of weariness around her eyes that she was too tired. So he listened carefully and followed each step she gave until the batter was mixed.

"Darla and I will bake them later." David was inordinately pleased with his accomplishment.

"You don't know how to bake," she said with a frown.

"Three hundred fifty degrees for about eight minutes," he repeated, and then added before she could interrupt, "and watch they don't burn."

"But—"

"But now it's time for you to go home." He held up a hand so she wouldn't argue. "You need to take care of yourself, Susannah. And that baby."

"But this is my job," she protested, though it sounded weak.

"You have done an amazing job. Darla and I both know that. You've gone way beyond anything I ever expected." He drew her into the circle of his arms and pressed his lips against the top of her head. To his joy she rested against him and relaxed, letting him hold her. "I don't want you to overdo. Not now. So go home. Take the car. Please?" he asked, tilting her head back so he could look into her eyes.

"You're a very nice man, David," she whispered against his chest. "I wish…"

So did he. Unfortunately wishing didn't make your heart's desire come true. And he couldn't badger her about it now. So David kissed her tenderly, then set her away from him.

"Go home and rest," he ordered.

He waited while she gathered up her handbag. Her

hand paused on the mints. She lifted her head to stare at him, green eyes shiny with tears.

"Thank you," she whispered.

"It's my pleasure." And it was. Whatever he could do for her was so little and he only wanted to do more. "I love you."

She searched his eyes, touched his cheek with her small delicate fingers then reached for the door.

"Good night," she whispered.

He watched her get in the car, pull out and drive away as his sister emerged.

"Tomorrow is Susannah's last day, Davy. Then what will we do?" Darla's hand curved into his. Her troubled eyes searched his for reassurance.

"I don't know, Darla. Keep loving her, I guess."

"And pray."

Yeah. Pray.

Lord?

But the only answer David heard was "trust."

Chapter Fourteen

"I've got to get back to the office," David said Saturday morning.

"Today? Tomorrow is Easter Sunday." Susannah had been hoping he'd volunteer to take Darla to the museum, or at least accompany them.

Truth to tell, she hadn't felt well since she'd risen. Still wasn't. She had thought about backing out of this trip, but had been unable to deny Darla when she learned David would be working. Also, Susannah had greedily wanted a few more moments together before she was permanently out of their lives.

Like so many other things, that wasn't to be.

"I wish I could go with you, but I've got a big court case next week. It's my last chance to interview some people I intend to call as witnesses." He held out an envelope. "But I wanted to personally make sure you got this."

"What is it?" She stared at the plain white envelope curiously.

"A letter. Someone asked that I give it to you." He

tucked it into her purse. "Don't forget to read it, please. It might change your life."

Susannah puzzled over that and over the kiss David gave her. It was deep and rich and satisfying, but there was also a longing to it. She kissed him back in spite of herself. When he finally drew back, he kept hold of her and stared deep into her eyes.

"I love you, Susannah. I wish you could accept that, because it's not going to change." David laid a fingertip over her lips. "Don't say anything. Just know that if you ever need me, for anything, promise you'll call me. I'll come, no matter what. No matter what, Susannah."

She nodded, but she knew she would not be calling him. This was goodbye.

"The same thing is true of God," David murmured. "He's there waiting to hear from you. If you could only accept that God is about forgiveness, not condemnation. He loves you. He loves you so much He gave His only son for you. Because He thinks you are worth it." He cupped her cheek, brushed his hand over her hair and cupped the back of her neck in his palm. "All you have to do is believe it."

One last kiss, then he was gone.

"Did you see that?" Darla asked, hours later.

"Uh-huh." Susannah smiled but continued her search for a chair.

"I got that little girl to move back from the edge so she wouldn't get hurt and I didn't yell at all." Darla preened, her chest thrust out.

"I'm very proud of you." No longer appreciative of the vista in front of her, Susannah shifted from one foot to the other, trying to ease the ache in her lower back.

She wanted—no needed—to sit down after tramping around the desert museum for the better part of two hours.

"I got those kids to be quiet in the underground exhibits, too," Darla reminded. "They wouldn't listen at first, but then I explained how the animals like to sleep in the day and work at night, and the kids stopped making so much noise."

"You did a fantastic job." Susannah smoothed her hair and smiled at the triumph on Darla's pretty face. "Should we go have lunch?"

"Not yet. The docent—" Darla paused, serious. "That's what they're called, docents," she explained.

"Uh-huh." Susannah forced herself not to smile.

"Well, the docents said there is going to be a demonstration of the raptor free flights." She checked her watch. "That's in ten minutes."

Susannah wanted to groan. The raptor area was way at the back. She knew she could not walk that far right now.

"Listen sweetie, can you go with the docents and stay right beside them?" Guilt overwhelmed her at letting Darla go alone, but she'd waited so long to see the birds and the raptor flights were a seasonal thing. "I'll stay here."

"Are you sick, Susannah?" Darla tilted her head to one side and studied her with those wise-owl brown eyes. "I don't have to see the raptors," she decided.

"Yes, you do. And I'm fine. Just really tired and hot. I'm going to sit down right over there—" she pointed to the nearby coffee bar "—and wait for you. Okay?"

"Are you sure you're not sick?" Darla frowned.

"I'm not. I'm fine. I'm only tired," Susannah reassured her.

"Because of the baby," Darla said. "Pretty soon I'll see it, won't I?"

"I think so. Pretty soon." She rubbed her side as a funny little cramp uncoiled.

"I asked God to make your baby strong, Susannah. I pray for it and you every night." Darla trailed along beside her until they found a chair where Susannah could sit, still visible, but out of the hot sun.

"Thank you, sweetie. I appreciate your prayers." Susannah saw one of the many volunteers nearby. She handed Darla some money and asked her to buy two cold drinks from the vendor inside. Left alone, she waved over the docent and explained her situation.

"It's not a problem, ma'am. I'll be happy to take her to the raptors, and I'll bring her back when it's over," the girl said.

"Thank you very much." Susannah shifted, trying to find a more comfortable position.

"Are you okay? Can I get someone to help you?"

"That's very kind of you, but I just need to sit awhile. I'll be fine." When Darla returned, Susannah thanked her for the drink and introduced the girl. "You go with her and come back with her," she said firmly. "Don't wander away."

"I won't." Darla hugged her tightly. "You rest. I'll be back."

"Have fun." Susannah waited until they'd disappeared, then closed her eyes and sipped her drink. Five minutes later she felt much better.

Then she remembered the envelope in her bag.

Now Susannah lifted the envelope free and opened

the flap. A single sheet of paper was inside, plain white with writing scrawled across it.

Dear Susannah:
I write that because you are dear to me. So precious. You are the best thing to come out of my stupid, wasted life. I know that now. A daughter who took over when I wouldn't. How can I ever thank you? I can't. And I owe you so much. Most of all, I owe you an apology.

Susannah's breath jammed in her throat as she read on.

Susannah, I want you to hear me on this. And hear me well. You did not cause your sisters' deaths. I did. That night I was in a drunken stupor. Some ash from my cigarette fell on me and burned my leg and I realized the sofa was on fire, so was the carpet. I ran to the kitchen to get some water. I thought I could put it out. But it was in the drapes then and flaring. The smoke was so thick. I tried, but I couldn't reach Misty and Cara. They'd fallen asleep, waiting for me to tell them a story. A fireman told me later that they never woke up.

Every breath was agony as Susannah remembered their happy, smiling faces. How could God let two small lives be taken like that? The familiar tidal wave of loss filled her with pain that reached into her soul and squeezed.

Susannah wanted to stop reading. She wanted to fold up the letter and hide it away and never look at it again. But she couldn't. The past had dogged her for so long.

The desperate yearning to hear from her mother, long buried deep within, now would not be silenced.

The truth.

She needed to hear the whole truth about that terrible night.

Sniffing back her tears, she refocused on the scribbled words.

I wanted to die with them, Susannah. I wanted to go with Misty and Cara and be rid of my awful life. But you came and found me in the kitchen and pulled me out. I hated you for keeping me alive. I wanted to die and you wouldn't let me and the pain was excruciating. So I lashed out and said it was your fault they died—because I needed to get rid of my own guilt.

Oh, Susannah, until your boyfriend came to see me, I never realized that no one had ever told you the real truth of that awful night—that you were not to blame. All these years I've kept away from you, distanced myself because the guilt and the shame were so great when I looked at you that I knew I could never be the parent you needed, that I could never be worthy of being entrusted with another child. So I pushed you away and made sure you didn't come back. But I've missed you.

David? David had gone to see her mother? But then, it fit with what she knew of him. David Foster had shown time and again that he loved her. No wonder Darla liked fairy tales. Her brother was hero stuff through and through.

Susannah, you are not like me. You never were.
You are strong and courageous and the best mother
to your sisters that they could have had. They loved
you so much. And you loved them. It was not your
fault they died. You did your best, even tried to get
to them. No sister could have done more.

Susannah blinked through the tears as the devastating scene from that night replayed through her mind again. But this time it had a new part, a part she'd never recalled until now. A part where she remembered pushing open the back door, seeing her mother on the floor and dragging her outside. As if in a trance, Susannah felt the heat stinging her hands as she knocked away a burning chair and slapped at her mother's dress to put out the flames. And now she also remembered lying on the lawn, gasping for air, struggling to inhale enough oxygen to go inside and find her sisters.

She'd made it to the door before the firefighters had stopped her. They'd put a mask over her mouth and something cool on her hands. The next thing Susannah recalled was awakening in the hospital with bandages on her hands and face and a terrible sadness in her heart for the sisters she knew were gone.

For so long she'd forgotten those details. That's why her mother's screams of blame had stuck. That's why she'd never questioned that it was her fault that Cara and Misty had died. That's why she'd always felt so guilty.

Because she'd forgotten the truth. The truth.

Bemused by this new insight, she glanced down.

Your young man loves you, Susannah. Don't
throw it away because of my mistakes. Love

*doesn't come so often that we can waste it. Your
sisters would want you to be happy, to enjoy your
life. I don't know much about God, but your boyfriend has made me think that He might someday
forgive me.*

*You are more than I will ever be, Susannah. I
know that no child of yours would ever be without your love. And love, more than anything, is
what we need to survive. You were always fearless as a child, Susannah. Be fearless now and
embrace your life.*
Your mother.

She wasn't guilty. She hadn't caused their deaths. It
wasn't her fault.

The words kept racing around and around her brain,
rejuvenating her soul with relief and joy. After reading
the precious words once more, Susannah refolded the
letter and tucked it back into its envelope. A tiny slip of
paper lay there. She pulled it out and read it.

*It's in Christ that we find out who we are and what
we are living for. Long before we first heard of Christ
and got our hopes up, He had His eye on us, had de-
signs on us for glorious living, part of the overall purpose He is working out in everything and everyone.*
Ephesians 1:11-12 from The Message.

David. Dear darling David, who had gone to see her
mother, dug until he found the truth and made sure Susannah knew it. David who'd said he loved her so many
times and refused to give up on her. David—a man who
practiced love.

Carefully, Susannah placed her precious papers in
her purse. How could she ever thank him? As she sat

waiting for Darla, she tried to think of ways to tell him what his actions meant to her. And yet, she couldn't do that. It would be too painful and he might think that she'd changed her mind about marrying him. Which she hadn't. Not because she didn't love him, but because she did.

Her thoughts got sideswiped by a rip of pain through her midsection. It dulled to a steady ache that would not go away even after Darla returned and they went for lunch. Susannah ate a little to keep her strength up, but as the day went on, she felt progressively worse.

"Susannah, we should go home." Darla frowned when Susannah declined to enter the aviary but insisted Darla go without her. "You're too tired."

"I just need to walk a bit more. When I walk I feel better. Go ahead. I'll be out here." But eventually even walking didn't help and when the museum announced they would be closing in five minutes, Susannah was forced to agree that they should leave. But she asked Darla to buy her some bottled water first. "I'm really thirsty," she said.

"Because it's too hot for you," Darla said. She trotted off to get the water but quickly returned, her face showing her concern. "I wish I could drive."

"I'll be fine once I'm in the air-conditioning."

Only Susannah wasn't fine. She'd no sooner sat down in the driver's seat when her water broke. She turned on the radio.

"I need a minute to hear the news," she said, desperate to keep Darla from knowing how scared she was.

The baby was coming. Susannah had read enough to know that. It was simply a matter of how long she had before it arrived. She shifted into gear and began the drive home.

She'd gone only a few miles when a fierce contraction grabbed her. Susannah pulled into a vista point along the way and told Darla to go ahead and look. As soon as Darla left the car, Susannah began breathing the way she'd learned in Lamaze class. She puffed through the contractions before Darla returned.

It was well past six now. The road from the museum was almost deserted. Easter weekend. People were home with their families. Susannah bit her lip as another contraction hit. She tried to keep her concentration on the road but they were too strong and too fast and there was so little time to regroup in between. She veered sideways and felt the car lurch to a halt as the front wheel struck a huge stone at the side of the road. The grinding sound of metal made her cringe.

"Darla, are you okay?" she asked, fighting to breathe through the ferocity of this contraction.

"Yes. I'm fine." Darla touched her hand. "Susannah, what's wrong?" She had to wait while Susannah worked her way through the pain before she could explain what was happening.

"I'm so sorry, Darla. I should never have brought you out here today." She slid her seat all the way back and caressed her fingers over her stomach, breathing more normally as the skin grew less taut. "The baby's coming."

"Now?" Darla's brown eyes widened.

"Pretty soon, I think." Again she had to stop and work her way through another contraction. They were much closer together now. And getting stronger.

"We have to pray, Susannah," Darla insisted. "We'll

ask God to help us and help the baby. He loves us, Susannah. He knows about your baby and that we need help."

"Just another thing I've messed up," she muttered.

"God doesn't care about that. He always forgives, if we ask." Darla closed her eyes and began to speak to her heavenly father, asking His help. Then she opened her eyes and smiled. "God loves children," she said with supreme confidence. "In the Bible Jesus told His disciples they had to let the kids come to Him. He won't let anything happen to your baby."

Susannah wished she was as sure.

"I should never have waited so long," she said, tears slipping down her cheeks as the pain began with renewed force. "How could I make such a stupid mistake?"

"I'm going to call for help." Darla took Susannah's phone and dialed 911 and in a clear, precise voice told the operator what was happening. "I can't stay on the phone," she said. "I have to call my brother, Davy."

Susannah didn't hear the rest of her conversation—she was too busy managing her breathing. When finally she was through the contraction, she heard Darla say, "Susannah is having her baby, Davy. We need help. Hurry, okay? Susannah's really scared. But I'm not. I prayed. Davy?" She frowned, shook the phone then held it out. "Something's wrong with it."

"The battery is dead," she explained after glancing at it. Terror clawed at Susannah's throat. What if something went wrong with the baby?

"Darla, I'm so sorry. I should have left earlier." Susannah searched the girl's eyes, wondering if she would panic.

"It doesn't matter, Susannah. Davy will find us."
Darla used her scarf to dab some of the water from her
bottle on her forehead.

"I hope somebody does. It will be dark in less than
an hour. Ooh," Susannah groaned, losing a bit of her
focus as the pain grew.

Darla waited until the spasm was gone.

"I don't think you can have the baby sitting there,
Susannah. I think you should get into the backseat." She
scooted out and around the car and in between huffing
and puffing right along with Susannah, managed to get
her lying in the rear seat. "Put your feet in my lap," she
ordered after she'd closed and locked the doors.

Susannah got caught up in another contraction but
Darla was right there with her, encouraging her to fol-
low her breathing pattern as they'd done so often in
Lamaze.

"You're doing very well, Susannah," she encouraged, smoothing back her hair as she spoke. "Don't be
afraid. I remember all the steps they said you have to
go through before the baby comes. I'll help you."

"I know you will, sweetie. You're a great help."

She had Darla—and God. Trusting was so hard.

After several fierce contractions, Susannah was convinced her baby's birth was imminent. She had to count
on Darla's help and she had to prepare her before things
progressed any further.

"Listen to me, honey."

"I'm listening." Darla remained silent and attentive
as Susannah explained what she'd need.

"Do you think you can do all that?" Susannah asked.

"Yes." She nodded confidently and calmly. "I can
do it. And I won't get scared, Susannah. I'll keep pray-

ing." With that simple assurance, she began assessing their resources. "There's a blanket here. Mrs. Peters put it in last week. She thought it would be good for a picnic. And we have the water. Everything is going to be okay, Susannah."

There was no other choice, Susannah realized. She had to trust that God loved her. In that moment she realized the truth of that Scripture verse David had written. God was working out a glorious purpose in her life. He'd helped her during the fire; He'd sent her to a good home to grow up in; He'd led her to David and Darla.

"Susannah?" Darla touched her hand, her wise eyes soft. "Are you okay?"

"I'm scared, Darla. What if something goes wrong? What if the baby needs help?" She wanted to trust, but she hurt so much and now the fears and worries she'd kept tamped down for so long rose in a tumult of terror. "What if I did something to hurt my baby? What if God is going to punish it because of me?"

"No, Susannah." Darla shook her head firmly. "God isn't like that. He loves us. That's all. Love." She spread her hands.

And finally the truth penetrated to Susannah's heart. God was about forgiveness, not punishment. The guilt she felt, the condemnation she'd lived with for years— that didn't come from God. That was something she put on herself. She'd wanted her baby to be adopted because she was scared—scared to risk moving past the fear, scared to risk being hurt by loving David, scared to accept that she could be more than she'd allowed herself to dream of.

Susannah grabbed her purse and pulled out the note David had written.

It's in Christ that we find out who we are and what we are living for.

Doing things her way had resulted in nothing but trouble. Was she going to stay alone and afraid, and keep getting the same results? Or was she going to get some backbone, accept the love God offered and live her life in a newer, better way?

When she considered what was at stake, there was no contest.

"Please help me, God. Please help my baby. Please help Darla," she whispered.

A wonderful sensation of warmth suffused her, as if someone had drawn her into warm sheltering arms.

"Oh!" Susannah groaned. "Darla, I think the baby is coming. I have to push."

"That's okay," Darla said with a grin. "I'm ready. I remember everything the lady said. Seventy-two percent of births have no complications. And besides, we have God helping."

"Yes, we do," Susannah cried. And then she pushed.

Chapter Fifteen

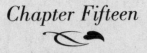

"Oh, Lord, be with them both."

David wove in and out of traffic until he was free of the city. Then he barreled through the desert like a madman, desperate to get to Darla and Susannah. He'd wasted minutes trying to remember where they were going today, only recalling the desert museum when a frantic call to Connie had reminded him.

He still felt the shock of Darla's message. Why hadn't he answered the stupid phone, instead of letting the call go to messages? Was work so much more important than the two women in his life? Why hadn't he gone with them today?

A big lump of fear stuck in his throat as he tried again to reach their cell phone. There was still no answer. He'd contacted Susannah's doctor and received some assurance that labor in a first birth usually took its time. He could only pray that was true because he was afraid to envision anything else.

Darla had gone to the Lamaze classes. She'd regaled him with all the knowledge she'd learned. But she couldn't handle a birth. Not alone. And Susannah—

this was her first child. She'd be alone, afraid and worrying she'd made another bad decision.

If only he'd—no. David wasn't going to doubt. Susannah, her baby and Darla were all in God's hands. He had Wade, Jared and Connie praying. He had to trust that God would show him how to help the woman who held his heart in her delicate hands.

Ahead David saw the flash of lights signaling an ambulance. He swerved to the side of the road before he leaped out and sprinted across. His heart almost stopped when he saw a small figure on the white stretcher.

"Susannah?"

"Davy!" Darla stood beside the ambulance. "We have a baby," she said showing him the tiny bundle tucked into Susannah's arms. "It's a girl."

"Grace," Susannah told him, her voice clear and her eyes sparkling. "Her name is Grace, David. Because of God's grace to me."

"Oh, Susannah." He bent and kissed her as his heart lifted with thanksgiving. "I love you." He gazed down at her and let the picture of mother and daughter frame in his mind. "She's beautiful, Susannah. As beautiful as you."

"We need to get them to the hospital now," one of the EMTs said.

"Yes. Go ahead." David touched her cheek with his knuckles, brushing one fingertip against the baby's velvet skin. "I'll see you at the hospital, Susannah." Then he bent and repeated, for her ears alone, "I love you."

She opened her mouth but the attendants whisked her away too quickly and he couldn't hear what she said.

"I helped get the baby, Davy! I helped." Darla danced at his side, yanking on his arm in her excitement. "Susannah said she couldn't ever have done it alone. I'm the first person Grace saw when she came in the world."

"You did really well, sis." He hugged her tightly. "I'm so proud of you."

"Me, too." She hugged him back but she couldn't stand still for more than a second. "Grace didn't cry at first. Susannah said she had to cry and she didn't so I prayed and said to God, 'God, can You make this baby cry?' And He did!"

"That's great, sweetie." He hugged her again. "You're quite a girl."

"I know."

While Darla related the events of the day, David glanced at the car Susannah had been in. He stopped Darla's story long enough to call a tow truck and his friends. Then Darla climbed into his car and they headed for the hospital.

Ecstatic over her role in the birth, Darla talked nonstop all the way. David heard little of it. He was too busy wondering how Susannah would react when the baby was adopted.

"Davy?"

"Yes?" He climbed out of his dark thoughts, noticing sadness creeping over Darla's face. "What's wrong?"

"Susannah's my sister, Davy. I don't want her or baby Grace to go away."

"Darla, honey, I explained to you about the adoption. Susannah wants another mommy to look after Grace." But Darla clamped her hands over her ears and refused to listen. She only dropped them when he stopped speaking.

"God made Susannah my sister," she said firmly. "Baby Grace is my family, too."

Nothing he could say could change her mind. But Darla didn't get angry and she didn't argue or yell.

When they got to the hospital she waited until he found Susannah's room.

"We must be very quiet when we see Susannah," he explained. "Don't ask her a lot of questions, okay?" He'd think of a way to explain it all later.

"I won't." Darla stopped a passing nurse. "Can you tell me where the babies are?" she asked.

"In the nursery." She pointed. "But only family can go down there. Are you family?"

"I'm the…aunt," Darla said proudly.

David winced. She was going to be so hurt when Grace went to another family. Maybe if he tried very hard, he could persuade Susannah to—

He pushed open her door and his heart stopped. Susannah lay still in the white bed. In her arms she cradled the baby. Both of them were sleeping.

"Kiss her, Davy."

There were times when Darla was absolutely right. This was one of them. So David leaned forward and pressed his lips against Susannah's.

"When will you wake up and love me?" he murmured.

She blinked. Then she lifted her incredible lashes and smiled.

"Right now. I love you, David." She lifted her head for his kiss.

"See? Sleeping Beauty. I told you, Davy." Darla smiled at Susannah. "Davy needs to listen to me more often."

"Yes, I do." He smoothed a hand over Susannah's

glistening hair, needing to touch her, to reassure himself that he wasn't dreaming.

"I'll hold Grace while you talk about the wedding," Darla said. She sat in a chair and held out her arms. "I'm ready."

David glanced at Susannah who nodded and smiled. He carefully lifted the tiny child away from her mother, feeling awkward and stupid and clumsy, but oh, so blessed.

"Hello, Grace," he whispered. "I'd really like to marry your mother. And I'd love to be your daddy. Do you think that would work for you?"

When he touched her cheek with his finger, the sleeping child lifted a hand and closed her tiny pink fingers around his. Tears welled in his eyes.

Oh, Lord. His heart overflowed with thanksgiving at the love that raced through him for this precious child. This Easter baby.

He handed Grace to Darla. Then he returned to Susannah's side.

"Please marry me, Susannah. Let me be a part of your life, and of Grace's. Be a part of mine and Darla's. Nobody could be a better mother to Grace than you," he added.

"I don't know if you're right about that, David," she whispered, wrapping her small hand in his. "But I'm going to give motherhood my very best effort.

"Darla was right you know," she said.

"She usually is." David loved the way her hand fit into his—he adored Susannah Wells. "But about what, specifically?"

"I was Sleeping Beauty. Well, maybe not the beauty part but I was sleeping, because until I met you, I didn't know what real love was. There are so many facets to love, but I know now that it all begins with God's love. That makes everyone worthy of love."

"Yes, it does. I believe God led you to Darla and me, that it was He who placed love in my heart for you. So—" David dragged out the word "—does that mean you are going to marry me, Susannah Wells?"

"Yes, please," she said with a smile.

"Finally." He wrapped his arms around her and kissed her the way he'd been longing to for weeks.

"But not right away." Susannah leaned back, her arms still circled around his neck.

"But—" He frowned when she placed a finger across his lips.

"I need time, David. Time to understand what it means to be a child of God. Time to understand what being your wife will mean. Time to understand how to be a mother to Grace and a sister to Darla."

"I'll be in a retirement home by then," he teased. But he loved her all the more for her wisdom. "Okay then. While you're figuring that out, I'm going to learn how to be a father. My first lesson will involve a trip to the toy store."

"I think you can start learning how to be a daddy right now, Davy." Darla held the baby toward him. "Grace needs her diaper changed."

Epilogue

Four months later, Susannah and David's wedding day dawned hot and glorious in the Arizona desert.

"I don't want all the frills and frou frou," she'd told David. "I've realized that it's what's in the heart that matters. Choose whatever you like for our wedding." Then she'd returned to walking colicky Grace across the pool deck.

David, being David, had gone beyond anything Susannah could have imagined and as she stood inside his house—their house—on her wedding day, waiting for the music to begin, she couldn't believe what he'd done for her.

For starters, David had asked Hornby to work magic on the backyard. Roses climbed and burst and bloomed everywhere, their fragrance filling the air. White chairs with bows dotted the lush green grass and nestled near a fountain that spilled water over desert rocks and stones. Fronting the fountain stood a white filigree bower decorated in more roses and Susannah's favorite—limelight hydrangeas.

"Aren't you glad I persuaded you to buy this suit?" Connie whispered. "You look gorgeous, a perfectly dressed bride at her garden wedding."

"I only got into it because of all that swimming,"

Susannah whispered back. "I don't know what I'd have done without Darla to egg me on." But the truth was, the ivory shantung skirt and matching jacket looked stunning on her and she knew it.

She'd decided against a veil and chosen instead to weave a few bits of baby's breath through her upswept hair. Diamond hoops in her ears—David's wedding gift—were Susannah's only jewelry, aside from the beautiful yellow diamond solitaire on her ring finger.

"Are you ready, Susannah?" Connie asked.

"Yes." She was ready to marry her Prince Charming and begin the life God had given her.

Connie gave the signal and the soft melodious sounds of a wedding song filled the air. Darla went first, wearing her favorite red in a stylish sundress that showed her beauty. In her arms she carried Grace, decked out in a white frilly dress with red trim that displayed her chubby legs, and tiny feet clad in white ballet slippers. David's idea. He was going to spoil his daughter rotten, Susannah had realized.

Connie walked out of the house, her dress also red. And then all eyes turned to Susannah.

She was nervous at first. But then her gaze met David's. *This is the man God chose for me*, she thought. *Because of God's grace I am worthy of love. I can give my heart to this wonderful man because I know that together we will share a future filled with joy and happiness. And love.*

She stepped confidently through the door and walked toward the man who'd taught her that love could grow to encompass everyone.

* * * * *

Dear Reader,

Hello there! I hope you enjoyed Susannah and David's story. I love the beauty and variations in Arizona and it was my privilege to set a story in this location. Susannah's story could be that of many women across North America—alone, in trouble and desperate to figure out the next move. She'd lost faith in everything and everyone except one old friend who had loved her when she needed it. David, too, fights a battle of loneliness. Loss and responsibility have bowed him with life's worries. It takes Susannah's special courage to open his eyes to possibilities. And Darla—well, what can you say about darling Darla? Darla faces bigger issues than many of us will ever know. But she keeps hanging on to her faith in our God who loves each of us dearly.

Thank you so much for your cards and letters. I love hearing from each of you and try hard to respond as quickly as I can. I treasure each kind word you've shared about my books. They touch me as I hope my books touch you. I hope you'll enjoy *A Family for Summer*, the next book in this series. Meantime, you can reach me at Box 639, Nipawin, SK Canada S0E 1E0, at www.loisricher.com.

Until we meet again, my prayer is that you will experience overflowing joy, hope that never dies and the kind of peace God meant us to celebrate at Easter.

Blessings,

Lois
Richer

A FAMILY FOR SUMMER

Every good action and every perfect gift is from God.
These good gifts come down from the Creator
of the sun, moon and stars, who does not change
like their shifting shadows.
—*James* 1:17

To Darcy, who's managed to make,
or should I say bake, a niche where once
there was a need. Way to go, girl!

Chapter One

The doorbell shattered his dream of Africa.

Jared Hornby shook off the blanket of sleep, raced for the front door and yanked it open. He stifled a groan.

She stood there—tall, capable and in control; Lady Justice come to dispense her judgment. Her pansy-blue eyes completed a quick survey of him before returning to his face. Jared found no emotion on her elegantly sculpted features.

Only the cascade of flaming orange-red hair that rippled past her shoulders in a waterfall of waves suggested that this woman might have a heart. That would make her substantially different from the other children's services people who'd contacted him.

He'd put them off as long as he could.

Today was D-day.

"Jared Hornby? I'm Ashley Ross." She thrust out a hand and shook his in a no-nonsense manner, apparently oblivious to the lightning jolt that shot from her slender hand up his arm. "I'm here because—"

"I know why you're here, Ms. Ross." Jared drew his tingling fingers away. Despite the "electrical" connection, he didn't bother to disguise his frustration with her visit.

"You do?" She blinked spiky golden lashes.

"Of course." He considered telling her to come back, but really, what good would that do? "Come in."

"Uh—thanks." She stepped into his sister Jessie's house, her long narrow feet clad in unbusinesslike red sandals.

Jared's attention strayed to the glittering turquoise polish that colored her toenails. It—she—was nothing like any of the previous social workers.

Ms. Ross shifted her stance, emphasizing her height and her incredibly long legs. She wore jeans, a T-shirt the color of her eyes and a fringed chambray vest. Even for Tucson that was casual dress for a social worker.

Jared had expected something else.

"Where should I start?" she asked. She set a metallic bag that looked like it could carry most of her worldly possessions on the dust-covered hall table.

"I don't know." Jared figured she was new at this. Not one of the other court people who'd shown up to discuss his parenting ability had ever asked his opinion—about anything. "Where do you want to start?"

"Wherever you prefer."

"The kitchen?" he said.

"Okay." Her gaze rested on his shoulder.

Jared tracked her stare to a stain on his T-shirt and immediately visualized a scoreboard with one mark deducted for lack of neatness.

"Breakfast is over?" Ms. Ross lifted an eyebrow. Her face was completely expressionless. So that tingle of awareness he'd felt hadn't affected her?

"Er, no. The twins are still sleeping," he explained.

"Well, I'll start in the kitchen." She moved forward.

"Wait!" Jared stepped in front of her, suddenly remembering he'd forgotten to clean up last night. Not a good place to assess his parenting abilities. Spaghetti for dinner had seemed such an easy choice. Of course, he'd never before made it with the help of two six-year-olds.

Actually he'd never made it at all.

"Uh, maybe the living room?" he offered.

"Fine." She turned and followed him there.

Jared blinked at the wall with the hole in the plaster he hadn't fixed. Then his gaze swerved to the pile of laundry he'd gathered but hadn't had time to wash. First impression—zero. He stopped so abruptly Ms. Ross ran into him.

"Sorry. I'm really sorry," he apologized.

She looked at him as if he'd lost most of his brain cells. He probably had. Instant fatherhood did that to a guy.

"It's just that— I wasn't expecting you this early— I mean, I'm a little behind—" He stopped because her wide blue eyes said she couldn't care less about his silly excuses. "Start wherever you want, Ms. Ross," he said, finally admitting defeat.

"It's Ashley and it really doesn't matter to me where we start, it's just that Connie said— Whoa!" She gaped.

Jared guessed that was a reaction to the plywood-covered opening where a door was supposed to go. Or maybe the mountain of dirty clothes littering the sofa shocked her.

But Jared's attention snagged on something else.

"You said Connie?" he repeated carefully.

"Yeah, Connie Ladden. Well, she was Ladden way back when we were in foster care. Now she's Connie

Abbot." Ms. Ross frowned. "But you know that—her. Don't you?"

"Yes, I know Connie." His brain couldn't make sense of this. Maybe because it got hung up on Ashley Ross's intensely blue eyes.

"Connie said you needed help." As she spoke, Ashley braided her masses of red-gold hair into two plaits and wound them around her head, like a crown. "She was coming herself."

"Yeah?" He remembered that offer.

"Well, she's not feeling well this morning. So I'm here to lend you a hand in her place." Ashley began to sort the laundry, assembling piles of clothes according to color. After a moment she glanced at him, one imperious eyebrow raised. "Don't you want to shower and change?"

"I guess." But Jared didn't move.

"Ew." Her pert nose wrinkled in disdain at mud-covered shorts. "These should have been soaked."

Jared thought the crown of hair made her look like a queen. Royalty vs. the mundane.

"You are *not* a social worker?" he asked carefully.

"Me? A social worker? Hardly. I'm a nurse. I told you, I'm Connie's foster sister, Ashley Ross." She checked her watch. "It's almost eight-thirty. If these people are coming at eleven-thirty—"

"Eight-thir—? But I thought—" Jared glanced at his watch, shook it, then realized it wasn't running. His mind did a video replay. The kiddies' pool. Eric and Emma giving their toys a bath and his watch?

"The washer's in here?" Ms. Ross stopped, surveyed the kitchen. "Oh, mercy."

"Yeah, it's in there." Jared winced at the look on her face.

"Somewhere in here," she muttered. "This is bad."

"Very bad," Jared agreed. He backed away. "Horrible. A mess."

"All of the above," she agreed, her eyes leveling with his, pink lips pursed.

"Yeah." He backed up. "So, um, I'll just go shower, then."

"You do that," she said, her forehead pleating in a frown.

Jared turned and escaped upstairs like the chicken he was. First he checked on the still-sleeping kids then took the precaution of calling Connie. "There's a woman here," he began.

"Yes, Ashley. I sent her to help you," Connie's husky voice assured him.

"That was nice. She, uh—"

"Jared, honey," Connie said, smothering a laugh. "Ashley's one of those people who can do anything in half the time it takes everyone else. If I were you, I'd just get out of her way and let her do her thing while you prepare for that meeting."

Connie's advice was usually good. He decided to take it.

"There is no way you can allow anyone to take the twins from you," she added.

"No," he agreed, "I can't. Thank you, Connie. I hope you feel better soon." Bemused by the morning's events he stared at the phone until the dial tone intruded. Then he hit the shower.

When was the last time he'd taken his time in the shower? Sobered, Jared stared at his freshly shaven face in the mirror and faced the answer. Two months ago. The day his twin sister, Jessie, and her husband, Jeff, had died in a car accident, the night of their annual Valentine's date.

The last sane day of Jared's life.

Ever since then he'd been running on adrenaline, trying to make the world okay for two little kids who didn't understand why their parents weren't around anymore.

Speaking of which, Eric and Emma should be up by now. Jared pulled on his only clean T-shirt and jeans— well, relatively clean. He yanked the quilt on his bed into place in case some nosy social worker checked his room later, and then headed down the hall. Both kids' beds were empty.

Fear gripped his heart and held on. He raced downstairs, yelling their names.

"Relax. They're in the kitchen having breakfast." Ashley beckoned to him.

Having jerked to a halt on the bottom step, Jared carefully stepped across the now-gleaming foyer tiles.

"It's dry. I washed it first thing." Ashley shrugged. "It needed it."

"Yes, it did." He followed the twins' voices.

The kitchen didn't exactly sparkle because unfinished oak floors couldn't, but it looked better than it had since—Jared forgot everything as a fragrant aroma assaulted his senses. Coffee.

"Have a seat," Ashley said.

Bewitched by the smell, Jared sat. She handed him a steaming mug across the clean table. His mouth watered as he lifted the cup to take a sip.

"Hey, Uncle Jared. We're having oatmeal. Can you

make oatmeal?" Eric lifted a spoonful of it to show him then slid it into his mouth. "I like oatmeal."

Since Eric hated almost everything, Jared could only stare.

"It's not my fave, but it's okay." Emma glanced around. "Did you know Ashley was coming, Uncle Jared?"

"No," he said, amazed by the results the redhead had achieved in such a short time. "But I'm sure glad she's here. Thank you," he said to Ashley.

"Not a problem. Your dad stopped by while you were in the shower. He offered to help so I asked him to spray wash the patio. He did but said he had to leave." She shrugged. "We used all the milk so I also phoned in an order for groceries. Okay?"

"I didn't know you could do that," he said, amused by the idea of saving a trip to the grocery store.

"You can if you pay a delivery fee," she said, starting another load in the washer.

It would have saved so much time if he'd only known that.

The doorbell rang. Jared looked at her.

"Probably the groceries." She opened the fridge to show off its sparkling depths. "Once I threw out the moldy stuff, you didn't have much left to eat besides the jars of condiments. You must really like pickles."

Not him. Jessie.

"I've been meaning to clean that," he said, gritting his teeth. Like he needed it emphasized that he didn't have the fridge loaded with healthy stuff. "Thanks."

"No problem." She smiled, her grin open and friendly.

Jared relaxed, just a little. So far nothing seemed to be a problem to Ashley Ross.

As fast as a procession of grocery bags were deposited on the counter, Ashley stored them, leaving Jared to pay. When the delivery boy was gone, she faced him.

"If the kids are finished eating, maybe they should get dressed?" Ashley checked her watch then shot him a pointed look.

Bossy. Pushy. A buttinsky. He knew what needed to be done.

"Their clothes are all laid out. They bathed last night." Jared wiped Eric's chin and dabbed at Emma's dainty nose where a spot of brown sugar had landed. "You guys go on up and get changed. Remember I told you a lady is coming today?"

"We know." A very adultlike Emma gripped his arms as he swung her off the chair then slapped her hands on her tiny hips. "Behave and remember our manners."

"And don't ask questions," Eric added.

"Right." Jared high-fived them. "Don't forget to make your beds, either."

It still amazed him that they could do that. The fluffy duvets were easier for the twins to manage than sheets and blankets. Jessie's idea. She'd been so smart about that kind of stuff, and Jared wasn't. But at least this morning the kids scampered away giggling and care-free—for the moment.

"I'm sorry for your loss," Ashley said quietly, blue eyes dark and serious. "Connie told me. It must be terribly hard for you."

"Yeah." Jessie's loss was profoundly tough, on so many levels. But Jared was not going into that. Not now. Not with her. "Anything I can help with?"

"The garage?" She quirked one royal eyebrow, once more projecting that imperious demeanor. "The door is locked—"

"As it should be," he said firmly. "It's off-limits to everybody."

"I'm not sure you should say that to children's services," Ashley warned, her tone mildly chiding. She tilted her golden-red crown to one side. "What's in there anyway?"

"Skeletons," he said.

"Uh-huh." Ashley's queenly jaw tilted upward. "Truthfully?"

"Actually they are skeletons—of cabinets I'm making for this kitchen. I thought if I could show my work, I could earn some extra money at night, while the kids sleep." His dropping bank account grew closer to red every day.

Judging by the way she narrowed her eyes, Queen Ashley wanted to ask more. But then the twins returned. And they were not happy.

"I can't find Mr. Mudrake, Uncle Jared," Emma told him, hands on her hips again. "He was on the sofa but everything's moved."

"I just tidied up a little, Emma." Ashley squatted so she was on the child's level. "Who is Mr. Mudrake?"

"A big ugly frog," Eric said.

"He's not ugly," Emma growled.

"I'll bet he's a handsome prince," Ashley teased with a wink at Jared. "I tucked him into the toy box. He was tired."

"Are you sure he's okay?" Miss Em questioned everything lately, Jared noticed.

"I'm positive. But you can check on him if you like," Ashley said.

"Okay." Emma raced away. She returned with a huge smile. "He said he's staying there. He wants a longer nap."

"Sleepyhead." Ashley touched her mussed brown hair. "May I comb your hair?"

"Well, are you going to put it in those knobs that Uncle Jared always makes me wear?" Emma demanded. "I hate those and the kids at school always laugh at me."

"What do you like?" Ashley asked.

"Ponytails?" Emma suggested after some thought.

"Good. I can pull them." Eric caught Jared's glare. "Kidding," he said.

"I hope so." Jared watched Ashley and Emma disappear upstairs. "She should have told me she didn't like how I did her hair." His ever-present parental insecurity multiplied. "Your mom always used to—" He stopped. Was it bad to keep talking about Jessie with them?

Another minefield Jared constantly tiptoed around.

"I think that's why Em doesn't like it," Eric said, his voice very quiet. "It reminds her of Mom." Then he smiled. "She was way better at it than you, though. You suck at doing hair, Uncle Jared."

"Thank you very much." Jared tugged his nephew's ear. "Could we please clean up our language? *Suck* is not on my approved list."

"Derek says it all the time at school. His dad doesn't care." Eric scuffed his sneaker toe against the floor.

"You're not Derek." In those words Jared heard echoes of his parents. "Let's clean up the backyard. Then we could shoot some hoops."

"You suck at that, too. And sometimes you don't keep score right." Eric waited for a reaction then shrugged. "I guess we could, for a while. But it's Saturday. We usually do fun stuff on Saturday, Uncle Jared."

"We have to wait until the lady comes, remember?

She made special arrangements to visit today so you guys would be home from school," Jared reminded.

"Why is she coming anyhow?" Eric followed him outside.

They couldn't play hoops because someone—Ashley or his dad?—had painted the cracked and broken patio with the gray paint Jared had bought last week. His dad hated painting.

Queen Ashley sure was thorough.

It took only a few minutes to pick up the things strewn across the grass. The sun shone strongly but Jared wasn't sure the patio paint was totally dry so he suggested they climb up on the big trampoline. They began bouncing while he struggled to explain in six-year-old terms something he wasn't sure he understood himself.

"They're coming because they need to decide if it's okay for you guys to live with me, if I can look after you all right." Jared wasn't going to tell the kid he was the only alternative to their elderly grandparents. "This lady has to make sure I'm up to the job."

"Are you?" Eric stood perfectly still, head tilted to one side.

"Yes." Jared faked confidence.

"Huh." The boy didn't sound convinced.

I don't blame you, kid. I'm not sure, either, but that doesn't mean I'm going to walk away from you and your sister.

They bounced and talked about school and baseball and summer's soon arrival until Ashley opened the patio door and waved at them.

"There's someone here to see you," she said. "In the living room."

Jared moved through the house, marveling at its organization. Jessie would be proud of her home today, even if it was an old fixer-upper. The worst of the unfinished repairs were now almost invisible thanks to strategic pictures, lamps and furniture that had been moved. Even a few bright flowers perched on the mantel, clipped from Jessie's wedding bush in the front yard.

The place looked like a home.

"Mr. Hornby?"

He nodded, stifling a groan. The children's services matron was everything he'd imagined she would be. Lean with a severe face that almost screamed judge, jury and executioner.

"I'm Loretta Duncan. I'm here to do an assessment."

"Hello." He shook her thin clawlike hand and waved at her to be seated. "Do we really need another assessment?" he asked just to let her know he wasn't backing down from his guardianship claim. He introduced the kids. From the corner of his eye he saw Ashley coax Eric and Emma from the room.

"Our assessments help us ensure you meet all the conditions required to care for these children," Ms. Duncan recited, studying her notes.

"Even though their parents made me their godfather?" Pain stabbed his heart and clogged it with burning loss. "And neither set of grandparents are able to do the job?"

"Even though," Ms. Duncan agreed, her voice firm. "Now, I see the house has been cleaned. That's good. Apparently it was a disaster last time."

"The last time someone from your office was here, the children were sick with colds. Hardly a good time to visit." Jared chafed at the need to explain.

"Hmm. Before we begin, may I look around?" she asked.

"Look wherever you like," he invited. He was going to say "except the garage" when he remembered Ashley's comment. "Would you like a cup of coffee?"

"I do not drink stimulants," she said in a stern tone.

"Oh." He wasn't exactly sure where to go from there, but Ms. Duncan didn't seem bothered. She rose and walked away. As she moved, she touched a surface here and there, making notes on her pad and murmuring something he couldn't hear.

The old house needed a ton of work. He'd slaved every free moment since he'd arrived and hardly made a dent. If you looked closely enough…

Jared felt the weight of his responsibility like a load of bricks on his heart, but no way would he give up. Not today, not next week—no matter how many "assessments" they did. The twins were his. Just let anyone try to take them away.

"I'll be outside when you need me," he said and received a grunt that he assumed meant Ms. Duncan agreed he could leave for now.

Squeals of laughter from the backyard drew his attention. Jared followed the sound. He stopped short when he saw Ashley parade across the grass, nose in the air, a long scarf draped around her neck and trailing behind her like a train as she moved regally across the lawn, one small fist pressed against her chest.

"A queen," Emma squealed. Her dark ponytails— perfectly combed ponytails—flopped up and down in her excitement. "You're being a queen. The Queen of Hearts—the one who ate tarts?"

"Yes. Now it's your turn." Ashley sank to the ground in graceful elegance, long legs bending under her like one of the kids' rubberized flexible toys. She winked at Jared and patted the grass next to her. "Join us?"

"Uh—" Jared was lousy at games. It was too hard to push away the anger that festered inside and pretend he wasn't furious with God for taking his loved ones.

"We're playing charades. You can be next," she promised. "Sit."

Jared sat.

The twins had been reticent to make new friends since their parents' deaths. In public, among strangers, they stuck close to him, as if afraid he'd disappear from their lives, too. Yet Ashley Ross had managed to feed them breakfast, comb Emma's hair and engage them in a game that they clearly liked.

Who was this wonder woman?

Emma now carried the same scarf Ashley had worn. But she chose to lay it on the grass, carefully stretching each corner to ensure the chiffon laid flat. Then she lay down on it, but only for a second. She got up; she lay down. Up, down.

"I don't get it," Eric complained. "Uncle Jared, what's she doing?"

"No clue." Jared noticed the flicker of a smile that tugged at Ashley's wide mouth. "Do you know?"

"Uh-huh." She chuckled when Emma folded her hands under one cheek as if asleep. *"The Princess and the Pea?"* she guessed.

"Yes!" Emma giggled like a carefree child should.

Which she would be, Jared reflected, once Emma got past her loss. Clearly Ashley helped her do that, royal manner notwithstanding.

"That's a silly one," Eric grumbled. "Who knows a story about dumb old peas?"

"I do. And I won." Emma did a little happy dance across the grass. Then she flopped down beside Ashley, face beaming.

"Well, it's my turn now and I'm gonna do something way better than dumb old peas." Eric grabbed the scarf and wrapped it around his head to make a kind of mask. Then he walked on tiptoes over to Emma, bared his teeth and growled.

"That's easy," Emma said. "The big bad wolf."

"Which one?" Eric demanded. "You have to say which fairy tale, don't you, Ashley?"

"Yes, I'm afraid you do. Which one do you choose, Emma?" She smiled at the little girl who looked deep in thought.

"I think it's the wolf from *The Three Little Pigs*," Emma decided finally.

"Wrong." Eric stood in front of Jared. "Who do you guess, Uncle Jared?"

"Me?" On the verge of backing out, he glanced at Ashley. No way she'd let him escape. "Uh, I don't know." He'd never dealt in fairy tales. Never wanted to after his dream of happily-ever-after had died in Africa. "I give up."

"You can't. You have to take one guess at least," Emma declared. "That's the rule."

"Oh." Jared tried to think of something but his mind blanked. "Do it once more," he said, buying time. He saw Ashley hide her smile. While Eric performed his act again, Jared leaned near her. "Hints?" he murmured.

"Against the rules," she whispered back.

"My house, my rules." He waited, pinning her with a dark look. "Help me."

After an imperial stare she nodded once.

"Red, with a hood." She didn't even move her mouth to say it.

"Who am I, Uncle Jared?" Eric was growing impatient.

"Uh, the wolf in *Little Red Hood*?" he said.

"*Red* Riding *Hood*," the woman beside him corrected. A strand of red-gold hair slipped forward. She slid it behind one ear. Her eyes mesmerized him.

"That's what I said," Jared muttered.

"Sure you did." Ashley tucked her chin to hide her grin.

"Uncle Jared wins." Delighted to have fooled his sister, Eric did his own little dance before holding out the scarf. "Your turn, Uncle Jared."

"My tur— No!" Jared shook his head as if that would help his case. "I mean, you guys go ahead. You're doing well. But I—"

"You what?" Ashley's big blue eyes held his, waiting. She glanced toward the twins who were whispering some secret. "Don't know any fairy tales?"

"Of course I know some fairy tales," he shot back, and then wished he hadn't. The truth was Jared's knowledge of fairy tales extended only as far as those DVDs Jessie had bought for the kids to watch, and that was because he'd played them over and over in the past two months whenever he ran out of ideas and needed something familiar for the kids. Well, he sort of "knew" them. "I can't think of any fairy tales right now."

Eric and Emma wore resigned faces. It occurred to Jared that he backed out of a lot of their activities because he was uncomfortable with acting as if everything was okay. That was probably the wrong thing to do, but then he was learning there were a lot of those when it came to parenting.

"I'll just watch," he said.

"I thought Connie said David and Wade had been helping you out." Ashley's head tilted sideways as she studied him.

"They have." Truthfully, Jared's two pals had been his lifeline to sanity since his sister's death. Two months and he still couldn't quite believe Jessie wouldn't come bursting through the door, demanding to know how he'd treated her "babies."

"And David's sister?" Ashley pressed.

"Darla? Yeah, she's been here a lot, playing with the twins." Jared frowned. "What's that got to do with it?"

"I met Darla. She's all about fairy tales." Ashley grinned. "How could you possibly forget a fairy tale given her, um, obsession over them?"

"Obsession?" Well, that made sense given that Darla had a brain injury that had left her with a mental age of around ten. Jared figured some of Darla's obsession must have rubbed off on the twins because they'd played some game about fairy tales for the past three evenings.

Fairy tales. Stories passed down through generations. Suddenly Jared was back in Africa, listening to the village elders recite past glories and tumultuous victories while the kids reenacted them. An idea clicked. He held out his hand.

"Give me that scarf."

"Attaboy," Ashley cheered.

Jared draped the scarf over his head so it fell to his shoulders. His discomfort at looking stupid melted when he caught sight of Eric and Emma's wide happy grins. Maybe he could get this part of fatherhood right.

A blanket they'd used yesterday lay draped across a picnic table. Jared grabbed it and gathered it like a cloak.

"King," Emma said immediately.

"But which one?" Ashley tapped her bottom lip with one slender finger.

"Not a king." Something he'd done had set them on the wrong track. Jared thought quickly before walking over to a blue paloverde tree. He selected a branch then stripped off one new shoot. He tested its weight and then began to parry and thrust.

"You're poking something," Eric yelled excitedly. "Stabbing?"

"Not quite." Jared felt like a fool but he'd started this and he was going to finish it. He stood straight, bowed in front of Ashley then pressed the hilt of the stick to his side. His audience remained silent, puzzled. "Second clue," he said. He drew a circle on the grass, marked twelve spots around it then sat down at one of them.

"I don't know any fairy tales about eating dinner, Uncle Jared." Emma's disapproval chided him. "Except the three bears and Goldilocks."

"Nope. And it's not dinner." Jared jumped to his feet and began moving the stick once more, frustrated that he couldn't get even a silly playact right.

"Excuse me." Ms. Duncan stood in the French door, staring at him as if he'd lost what little sanity he'd begun the day with.

Which he probably had.

"We were just playing a game." Jared slowly removed the scarf from his head and dropped his sword and cloak. His face burned with embarrassment. "Did you want to speak to me now?"

"If you have time." Ms. Duncan did not crack a smile.

Jared turned to go inside with her, but Emma raced over and tugged on his arm.

"That's not fair, Uncle Jared. You have to tell us what you were acting," she said with a frown at the social worker.

"Oh. I was Sir Galahad. One of King Arthur's knights. Of the round table." Both kids blinked in confusion. "You know—Camelot?"

Ashley's blue eyes widened. Then a tiny smile shaped her lips.

"I've heard of it," she admitted.

"Who?" Emma demanded.

Jared sighed.

"I'll read you the story later, guys. Maybe you can keep playing the game with Ashley for now?" He glanced the redhead's way. "Would you mind staying with them for a few minutes more?"

Ashley studied him for several moments. At first he thought she might refuse but then Emma twined her fingers into Ashley's and she finally nodded.

"I can stay a little while longer," she agreed. "But I do have an appointment to get to."

"Okay. I'll be done as quickly as I can. You guys play on," he said, sparing a moment to wonder what appointment the lovely Ashley had on a Saturday.

"I don't want to play anymore. I'm thirsty." Miss Em planted her sneakers on the grass in a way that told Jared she couldn't be cajoled.

"Me, too." As usual Eric followed his twin's lead.

"How about some juice? I saw orange, grape and apple when I unpacked the groceries." Ashley gave

Jared an outrageous wink. "Would you like a drink, ma'am?"

"Yes, actually I would," Ms. Duncan said, her face relaxing a fraction. "It's very warm for April. Orange juice, if you don't mind." She led the way inside.

Jared rolled his eyes at Ashley then followed Ms. Duncan to the living room, and sat down on a straight-backed chair Jessie had recovered last year.

"Shall we begin?" Ms. Duncan asked.

"Sure." Jared hoped he didn't look like he was sweating bullets. "I'm ready whenever you are. Ask me anything."

"All right." Ms. Duncan cleared her throat. "Tell me how you intend to care for these children, Mr. Hornby."

How would he care for them? Jared caught sight of Ashley tickling Emma under her chin and heard the little girl burst out in the giggles. Eric followed a minute later. For once the house sounded as it had when his sister was alive. He was so angry at God for taking Jessie.

Then an idea burst in Jared's brain as bright as any rocket during fireworks. In a short time, Ashley had straightened the house and engaged the twins, proving she wasn't just a very attractive woman—which Jared intended to ignore. He was never going to get involved again, no matter how beautiful the woman or how strong his reaction to her. What he was interested in was Ashley's skill with the twins.

He had a job lined up. What he needed was someone to watch the twins. From what he'd seen today, Ashley Ross would make a perfect nanny.

And with her in his corner, winning custody of the twins would be a cakewalk.

Chapter Two

"So far, so good, Connie," Ashley whispered into her phone. "The children's worker is here now so we'll see how it goes."

"That could last awhile and you have plans," Connie murmured. "I'll come over."

"No! Do not come over here," Ashley hissed. "You're probably contagious. I have a while before my interview. I can stay a little longer."

After coaxing Connie's agreement, she hung up, trying not to listen to the conversation in the next room as she got the children involved in coloring pictures to decorate the fridge. The grueling questioning Jared endured and his steady answers clearly showed how much the big man cared for the two munchkins now seated at the table.

She poured juice for Jared and Ms. Duncan and carried it into the other room. Jared rose and took the tray, setting it on the table. Typical Sir Galahad gesture.

A smile tugged at her mouth as he cast her a droll look that said he wanted to escape. Just as quickly she stifled her mirth. He was good-looking in a heartthrob kind of way, but she wasn't interested. Not at all.

"I brought a glass of juice for each of you." Ashley bent and placed the glasses in front of Jared and Ms. Duncan.

"I believe you've already met Ashley? She and I have a common friend," Jared explained to Ms. Duncan. "Connie Abbot. Maybe you've heard of her?"

"Oh, yes, we know Mrs. Abbot well at Children's Services." The woman actually smiled. "We often benefit from her charities." She squinted at Ashley. "Do you work for Mrs. Abbot?"

"I, um, help her sometimes," Ashley hedged. She quickly changed the subject. "I'm currently staying with her. I just moved back to Tucson."

"You have a job here?" Ms. Duncan asked.

Strictly speaking, Ashley knew she didn't have to answer. What she did was none of this woman's business. But Connie had told her how much Jared wanted to keep the twins and she'd seen for herself how hard he was trying to do the right thing, including playacting fairy tales, which he clearly abhorred. She couldn't do anything to jeopardize his chance at guardianship.

"Not yet," she said, lifting the tray and preparing to leave.

"Ashley's a nurse. I'm sure it won't be hard for her to find work," Jared reassured the nosy woman.

"Did the children *need* a nurse today?" Ms. Duncan's tone oozed innuendo.

"No. Of course they didn't." Jared tipped back his tousled head and looked at Ashley, his burnt chocolate eyes smoking black with temper.

Ashley frowned at the hint that Eric and Emma

weren't being properly cared for. According to Connie, this man would bend over backward for his charges.

"I came in Connie's place," Ashley butted in before Jared could say something he might regret. "Connie intended to visit with the twins this morning so the two of you could chat freely, but she fell ill. Jared has a lot of support from his friends, Ms. Duncan. Connie, her husband, Wade, and their friend David Foster have been helping the twins make the transition."

Okay, maybe name-dropping wasn't apropos, but it couldn't hurt to let this woman know that Jared had the influential support of both a well-known Tucson architect and a respected lawyer in his bid for custody. At least it silenced Ms. Duncan. For the moment.

"Excuse me." Ashley shared a look with Jared. "I'd better get back to the twins."

"Thanks a lot." He did look grateful. Sort of. Or mad.

Ashley left the room as a wealth of empathy surged inside. How appallingly agonizing to lose your sister and then have to step into her shoes. How honorable of him to even try. Parenting two six-year-old children was a lot to ask of anyone. Especially a single guy with no experience. At least Ashley didn't think Jared had experience.

But she didn't feel sorry for him. What was there to feel sorry for? Her entire life she'd begged heaven for two things—a home of her own and a family. As an adult she intended to make the home part come true, but inside she still yearned for that tangible connection with someone who would wrap an arm around her shoulders and say, "I'm here for you. I love you, no matter what."

Jared had that in his parents and the twins. They had Jared.

Ashley had no one.

An orphan for as long as she could remember, Ashley had found acceptance and love in her final foster home in North Dakota, the one she'd shared with Connie. But she'd always known the Martens weren't her *real* family. They were loving people who'd given her a wonderful home and plenty of love when she'd needed both. She had no doubt they'd be there to listen if she dropped by, but they had other needy kids. Besides, Little Orphan Ashley was all grown up.

Or she should be.

"You look sad, Ashley. Are you?" Eric's hand touched her arm, his brown eyes, so like his uncle's, brimming with compassion.

"Not really. Just thinking." She forced a smile to her lips. "Shall we play another game?"

"I'd rather make cookies." Emma climbed down from her stool at the breakfast bar, grape juice splattered across her shirt. "We used to do that with our mom sometimes. But she died."

"Daddy died, too," Eric added in a solemn tone.

"I heard about that. I'm so sorry." Ashley felt the anguish emanating from the two as they shared a sad glance. She crouched down and slid an arm around each waist. "But I know they loved you very much."

"Yeah." Emma sighed. "They're in heaven now."

"Yeah, in heaven," Eric echoed. He poked Ashley's arm. "Uncle Jared doesn't know how to make cookies. Do you?"

"Sure. Chocolate chip?" Both little faces lit up. For a nanosecond Ashley was relieved. Then she remembered the empty cupboards. Maybe there weren't any baking ingredients in the house.

"I like lots of chocolate," Emma ordered.

"I like peanut butter," Eric added.

"I think we'll have to check first to make sure we have what we need. Now let's see." Ashley rose and began opening cupboard doors. She heard snickers behind her and turned. Emma and Eric were almost doubled over with the giggles. "What's so funny?"

"The chocolate chips aren't in there," Eric hooted. "You have to look in the stash."

"The stash?" Ashley moved to check the corner cupboard where Emma was pointing. "Oh, my." An array of chocolate treats filled the lowest shelf.

"My sister had a sweet tooth." Shades of pain colored Jared's hushed voice.

Ashley caught herself wishing she could make it better for him. She studied him as he leaned against the door frame. His height topped her five feet ten inches by a good half a foot. It wasn't often she could wear heels and still be shorter than a man. She rather liked the dainty, protected feeling it gave her.

Her brain blasted a warning. *Do not trust him.*

"Ms. Duncan wants to talk to you two," he said to the twins. "Are you ready?"

"Are you going to be there, Uncle Jared?" Eric asked as his forehead furrowed.

"I don't think—"

"He's going to be there," Ashley butted in, pinning Jared with her gaze. "Your uncle is going to hear every question and if you have trouble answering, he'll help you. He won't let anything bad happen."

"Okay." Eric headed for the other room. "I'll talk to her."

"Me, too." Emma walked a little way then stopped and glanced behind her. "Come on, Uncle Jared."

"Coming." He waited till Emma was out of earshot. "I can speak for myself," he muttered as he passed Ashley. "Besides, she said she wanted to talk to them alone."

"You're their guardian, Jared." She gripped his arm. "You hear everything that's said unless a judge decides otherwise. That's your right. And your duty."

"And you know this because?" He didn't look convinced.

"Because I was a foster kid. Look, I'll explain later. For now, just be there. If you're uncomfortable with any questions, stop them." She gave him a tiny shove in the back.

"I suppose you'll insist on coming in with us?" Those dark eyes made it clear Jared Hornby never asked for help.

"Sure I will." She smiled. "You might need me."

"Doubtful. I can manage this on my own." He turned and walked out.

"Because you've been doing such a bang-up job so far," Ashley mumbled under her breath as she followed him. That probably wasn't fair, but having been through the foster system numerous times she was familiar with the kinds of questions that would be asked.

And the kind that shouldn't be answered.

"Good, you're back. Actually I have a couple of other questions for you first, Mr. Hornby." Ms. Duncan shifted her papers. "Where did you reside before the—er—"

"I was staying with my dad." Jared rushed to answer as he glanced at the kids. "I returned home before Christmas. Mom has been ill so I decided to move back—"

"From?" Ms. Duncan's pen scratched furiously.

"Australia." His voice altered, hardened. "I'd been living there for several years, working as a contractor. Before that I was a missionary in Africa. A high school teacher."

Ashley could tell by his pinched lips that he didn't like talking about that part of his life and wondered why. It sounded exciting.

"So you weren't intending to take up permanent residency in Tucson." Ms. Duncan scratched more.

Ashley took that scratching as a bad sign.

"Actually, yes. I was looking for accommodation before the accident," Jared said quietly.

"You've been looking since Christmas?" Ms. Duncan frowned. "It's April. Surely it doesn't take that long to find a place to stay in Tucson."

"For me it does. I like to do woodwork." He shot Ashley a glance.

She immediately thought of the locked garage door. His tools, she realized.

"And?" Ms. Duncan's pen tapped against her pad, displaying her impatience.

"I wanted a workshop. In fact, I am making cabinets for this house." His tone left no doubt that he'd prefer to be there now, working instead of answering a bunch of questions.

Careful, Ashley warned mentally. *Don't antagonize her.*

"Ah." Ms. Duncan studied him for several moments, made another note then lifted her lips in what might be called a smile. "Now, children, I'd like to ask you about living with your uncle."

"Why? Did we do something wrong?" Emma's fear was palpable.

"No, sweetheart, you didn't." Jared lifted her onto his knee. A moment later Eric joined his sister. They both clung to their uncle's big tanned hand.

Ashley's throat jammed closed at the heart-wrenching picture the three of them made supporting each other. Forget the appointment. She would spare whatever time it took for this hurting family.

But the interview dragged on until both kids were yawning and fretful. After the first half hour, Jared did little to hide his irritation at the woman's continued probing. He objected when her inquiries grew too intrusive so Ashley took it upon herself to interrupt and smooth the waters whenever tensions grew. Which was often.

"Are you Mr. Hornby's legal representative?" Ms. Duncan demanded, testy after several such disruptions.

"Goodness, no." Ashley laughed. "It's just that I grew up in foster care so I've heard all these questions before. I'm only trying to help."

"I see." Ms. Duncan was not impressed.

"I'm sorry, but when you called you said this would take under an hour. You've been here much longer." Jared's face tightened. "I'm not trying to be rude, Ms. Duncan, but Saturday is my day to run errands and do fun things with the kids. This isn't fun." He glanced down at the children. Bored, they'd dropped the plastic blocks they'd been playing with and now ignored the cars, dolls and other paraphernalia from their toy bin. "Could we continue another day perhaps?"

Ashley wanted to cheer. He'd phrased it perfectly.

"It's such a lovely spring day outside. Kids need fresh air and movement to stay healthy, don't they, Ms. Duncan?" His eyes gleamed with cunning.

"Well, yes." Ms. Duncan's face turned pink under his fulsome smile.

"I'm sure Ms. Duncan has her own things to do today," Ashley murmured, standing on one foot while the other woke up. "It must be inconvenient to work on your day off."

"We are compensated for overtime," the woman said stiffly. But she also rose. "I believe I have enough to fill out my assessment forms in the office. You will hear from me when I am prepared to do another assessment."

"Do you know when that might be?" Jared asked.

"We prefer to arrive unannounced. We get a better picture of the family then. Nothing is staged," she said, glancing around the room.

"Sure. No problem. Come whenever you like. I'll see you to the door now." Jared shot Ashley a look.

She translated it to mean "keep the kids here" and bristled a bit at the implication that she was here to serve. And then she remembered that she was.

Get rid of the chip on your shoulder, Ashley. Not everyone's out to con you.

"Okay, you two. Let's clean up these toys." Ashley began helping them restore the room.

A few moments later Jared returned. He looked frustrated.

"Go and wash your hands, guys," he said. "Then we'll go out for lunch."

"Yippee!" They rushed away.

"Is something wrong?" Ashley asked, concerned that the sparks in his espresso eyes had been snuffed out.

"Ms. Duncan wants three more inspections. Unannounced. At the end of August she'll decide whether or not I'm fit to take over permanent guardianship."

"Well, today went well." Ashley frowned when he shook his head.

"Because you were here. Yesterday I was offered a teaching job with the local school until the end of term. I start in three days. How am I supposed to keep this place pristine, teach, look after those two and finish the cabinets?"

Ashley watched a speculative gleam alter his incredible eyes.

"I don't suppose you'd consider hiring on as a nanny?"

"I can't. I need to work to keep my nursing license active," Ashley explained. "I don't know about teachers but nurses need a certain amount of work hours of nursing in order to stay registered. If I let it go, I'd have to retake my training. Because I was overseas—" She shrugged and clamped her lips together to stop revealing more personal information.

"The kids go to school. It wouldn't exactly be full-time." He raked a hand through his hair as if he was at his wit's end.

"But you can work during school hours and then you're free, aren't you? You don't need a nanny," she said, thinking he needed some training in housekeeping.

"Originally I thought that would work. But there's a lot of prep with this school. I've never taught young kids, always high school science, and this is a big class. I need time to prepare." He smiled as Emma hung one of her pictures on the fridge. "I need that income," he murmured.

"I see." She waited as he told the kids to put their crayons away.

"Everything happened so quickly." He sighed. "It's taken us a while to get adjusted," he said with a meaningful glance at the twins.

"Yes, of course." Ashley caught his wistful glance at the informal family photo that sat over the fireplace and felt a pang for his loss.

"I underestimated my savings account," he admitted with a wry look. "Okay, so you can't do it. But do you know anyone who could give us a hand? Your help here today has shown me that I'm going to need it." He brushed Eric's hair smooth with one hand while the other dusted off Emma's shirt.

"I haven't been back in Tucson long enough to know anybody like that," she said quietly, sensing that the children were now listening to their conversation. Ashley looked at Jared and inclined her head toward Emma.

He caught on immediately.

"Hey, guys, I need my wallet if we're having lunch out. Can you get it from my dresser?" Jared asked. He waited until they dashed off. "It's going to be a struggle. They don't like being away from me unless they're at school. I guess they're worried maybe I'll leave them, too."

Ashley's heart melted as his words. Poor little things. But because she'd been conned one too many times by someone's sad story she forced herself to remain steadfast.

"I'm sorry," she said, and meant it. "I'd really like to

help but I have an interview at the hospital this afternoon about a job. If I get it, I'll be tied up there."

"Don't apologize," Jared said. "It's just that the kids seemed to relate to you. They haven't relaxed like that with anyone since—but don't worry. I'll manage. I have been."

Not very well, she wanted to say. But that was unfair. The kids were healthy and as happy as they could be given the circumstances. He'd kept their family home and was doing everything he could to ensure they stayed in it. Sir Galahad—Jared—was keeping this family together to the best of his ability.

"Well, I'll see what happens. Maybe they'll have to come to my room and wait after school until I'm ready to leave." He shrugged.

But what if he had a meeting? Or one of the twins was ill and had to stay home?

The dryer buzzed so Ashley moved to change loads then began folding clothes. To her surprise, Jared pitched in right beside her, carefully folding the small clothes.

"How many loads so far?" he asked.

"Not so many that you can quit," she teased.

"I was afraid of that."

They shared a grin until the twins came tumbling downstairs, wallet in hand, and Ashley remembered that she was supposed to be leaving.

"It was under your bed, Uncle Jared. We had to look and look." Eric handed him the black leather.

"Well, I'm glad you did. I can't do anything without it." He stuffed the wallet into his pocket then led the way to the front door. "I owe you for a lot, Ashley, and I can't thank you enough. We finally made a good impression on someone from Children's Services thanks to you. I appreciate it."

"I'm glad I could help. And glad I could meet all of you." She smiled at the twins. "I guess we'll have to make cookies another time since you're going out for lunch."

"But you're coming, too. Isn't she, Uncle Jared?" Emma asked.

"No, I have to leave. But thank you for the invitation." Ashley looked at Jared, somehow loath to go. Oddly, he was smiling. "What's funny?" she asked.

He shrugged. "You're so organized, I guess I thought you'd be giving me advice or something."

"As a matter of fact—"

"Can we wait in the truck while you guys talk?" Eric interrupted.

"Sure." Jared nodded.

"Bye, Ashley. Don't forget about the cookies."

"I won't." She grinned. "You be good and help your uncle."

"We will." First Emma then Eric held up their arms for a hug.

Ashley reveled in the warmth of that embrace. It was so hard to let go and watch them rush away. Jared followed the twins as far as the front door and stood watching as they climbed into his vehicle. Then he faced Ashley. "Sorry. You were saying?"

"I was saying that, as a matter of fact, I did do some checking." Ashley withdrew a list from her pocket and held it out. "Those are some of the things the children mentioned they'd like to do. I phoned and the first two are possibilities as long as you arrive before two o'clock."

"I always was a good judge of character." He chuckled as he scanned the paper. His laughter died when he turned it over. "What's this list on the other side for?"

"Jobs that need to get done around here before the next inspection." It was aggressive, in-your-face and absolutely none of her business. Except that Ashley couldn't erase the image of two small sad children clinging to the only adult in their world.

"You think I need your list to tell me how to get this place squared away?" His long lean fingers crumpled the paper as he spoke, his voice a snarl of irritation.

"I think you have to get this house repaired however you can. The twins need you, Jared. They need you to get this guardianship thing settled and keep them safe, here in their home." Ashley spoke from her heart, willing him to listen. "You are what stands between them and foster care. You've got to make this work because you are their family now. You cannot let anything mess that up."

Family. It was always her passion and in that moment she got caught up in defending it. Until she glanced at Jared. His eyes had hardened to black flint. His jaw flexed. His shoulders went back and he drew himself to his full height.

"Look, lady," he said, his teeth almost snapping together. His eyes shot daggers at her. "Back off. I know exactly what I need to do. Make no mistake, no one will take these children from me. But what I don't need—"

"I know I'm nosy," Ashley interrupted, unfazed by his anger. "And pushy. But I care about those two kids." Maybe a little history would help. "I told you I grew up in foster care, Jared. I wasn't beaten or abused or anything like that. But I didn't have my own home or someone who would always be there for me, somebody who would love me even if no one else did. I was an orphan."

She paused, waiting for a reaction.

"So?" He wasn't giving an inch.

"So every orphan, every foster kid has the same dream. We hope for someone to show up in our lives and say, 'There you are. I've been looking for you. You're safe now. I love you and care about you. I always will.'" She pinned him with a look. "You can do that for the twins. Don't let them down." She didn't stick around to hear whatever he would say when he stopped spluttering. What he thought of her didn't matter. It was the kids that mattered.

Ashley grabbed her purse from the hall table and walked out. The twins waved from inside the truck. She waved back but kept walking to her car. Once inside it, she switched on the ignition and drove away. In the rearview mirror she could see Jared standing there, watching her.

Sir Galahad—the perfect knight. Perfect in courage, gentleness, courtesy and chivalry.

Nice to know he still existed.

Chapter Three

"How was the job interview, Ash?" Connie croaked from her seat in the living room.

Connie had been Ashley's foster sister in North Dakota and their bond remained strong even after being apart for seven years. It was Connie who had helped her adjust and refocus after Ashley's life had changed two years ago.

"You don't sound better." Ashley closed the front door. She walked into the living room and flopped on the sofa across from Connie. "The interview was okay. They'll let me know."

"You'll get the job. You're a great nurse." Connie poured a cup of tea from the white china teapot next to her. Connie's panacea had always been tea. "You should probably take some vitamin C since you're around me. This cold is awful."

"I don't catch colds. Don't you remember?" Ashley held out the box of tissues as Connie sneezed again. "Bless you."

"Thanks. And yes, I do remember. When we were

kids you were always immune to everything." She made a face. "Very annoying."

"Sorry." Ashley shrugged then slipped off her sandals.

"By the way, David Foster called. He has another stack of letters for you to go through," Connie murmured, holding out the steaming cup.

David was Ashley's lawyer, thanks to Connie's recommendation. He was also the husband of another of their foster sisters, Susannah.

"I wish people would stop writing and asking me for money." Ashley hated the rush of guilt she immediately felt. "Ever since Harry left me that money in his will, people have been after it." Ashley tore open one letter, scanned the words scrawled on the white sheet then crumpled it and tossed it in the garbage. "Same old, same old. 'I have a great idea for your money. I would do wonders if you let me have it. Blah, blah.'"

"You sound a little bitter, Ash," Connie said in a quiet voice.

"I am. I've been tricked by that line too many times since I inherited." Ashley shook her head. "But I won't be fooled again." She sighed, leaned her head back and perused the ceiling. "Sometimes I feel like people look at me and see a debit machine."

"I know Harry Bent left you money," Connie said then paused to clear her throat. "There was a lot about it in the papers, but you never told me much about him."

"Harry was a sweetheart." Ashley stretched, more tense than she'd realized. "I was a nurse in the palliative care unit where he spent the last months of his life. Liver cancer."

Connie winced. "That's a tough one."

"Very. He had a rough time." She stared at her friend, her anger surging. "Harry was a peach. He loved everybody and he loved to talk."

"No one visited?" Connie asked, her voice husky.

"He had very few visitors because he'd had to move away from home for treatment. Most of his buddies were too old or too ill to travel." Ashley bit her lip. "I don't think anyone suspected that he had a fortune. He was a fearless player on the stock market, you see. He loved the challenge of it and he did very well. But he used to say it was all a waste. He was afraid that whomever he left it to would blow it on stuff and Harry had this dream of helping people. He used to do that anonymously, before he got sick. But then he became too weak to go out and find people who needed his help. He didn't have any family. We used to joke that we were each other's family."

How she missed that wonderful laugh.

"I wish I'd known him," Connie murmured.

"You'd have loved him. Harry would ask questions and then listen. One day he asked me what I'd do if I had a lot of money. I've always had a thing about families," Ashley muttered. She peeked through her lashes at Connie. "You know that."

"I sure do." Connie smiled.

"I told him I'd like to make it easier for families in trouble to stick together. There were a lot of hurting families in my area of Detroit," Ashley said. "He gave me a task. Figure out how fifty thousand dollars could make a long-term impact on families in any community of my choosing. I did a study, found there were at-risk teens nearby who had nothing to do and no place to go. I raised some long-term funding, used his money as start-up capital and The Den opened about three months later. It's still running, thanks to the community who sees the benefit of helping teens help their neighborhood. After that I did a couple of other challenges. I did the legwork, he set things up."

"So that's why he left his money to you." Connie smiled. "He knew you'd use it well."

"I'm trying." Ashley frowned. "But Harry was very astute, plus no one knew he had money. It's just not that easy without him. When people learn how much I've inherited, they change. They always want money and they'll lie to get it. I've been hoodwinked so often."

"Ashley, give yourself a break. You've done wonderful things with Harry's money." Connie sipped her tea in thoughtful silence. "I could never have completed the center without your help and now so many are able to benefit from it."

"That was easy. I trust you. All I had to do was pitch in where you left off." She sighed. "My other ventures haven't done as well."

"You've run into some nasty people, true. But everyone's not out to get money from you, Ashley," Connie chided.

"Sure seems like it. Even my old coworkers in Detroit started asking me for loans. I tried to help and it was like open season on Ashley. When I refused it got even worse, personally and professionally. When I left that hospital, I felt like I'd been abused. I lost a lot of money in schemes where I got tricked." She cuddled the tea against her cheek, suddenly cold. "Sometimes I wish Harry hadn't left me that money."

"Oh, honey, don't say that. He's given you a great

opportunity to make a difference." Connie squeezed her shoulder. "And you will."

"I'm glad you think so because I have a new idea for my next project." Ashley's excitement bubbled. "Right here in Tucson."

"Already?" Connie grinned. "You've only been back in the country for a week, in Tucson for four days."

"And I've loved spending these four days with you, Connie. You and Wade have been great hosts. But it's your work at the center and my time touring Europe, thinking, that has helped me clarify what I want to do." Ashley inhaled. "I saw an old ramshackle house, Connie. It needs a ton of work. But I think it would make an excellent place for homeless families to stay while they get their lives reorganized."

"Ashley, that's a great idea," Connie enthused. "Tell me more."

"I haven't got anyone's opinions on renovations yet, remember," she warned. "But I think it could be made into several apartments, maybe with some common areas. It's got a huge yard for kids, plenty of possibilities. It looks gracious and welcoming, even in its current state." She smiled, imagining a yard full of kids.

"Best of all, it has a little house on the back of the lot. I'm going to make that house my home."

"And make your dreams come true," Connie murmured.

"Yes," Ashley agreed with heartfelt fervor. "I'm so excited I don't know where to begin."

"David might be able to help you," Connie suggested.

"Good idea. I can't thank you enough for putting me in contact with him. He's been wonderful about handling all the demands for money. I'm going to ask him

to find out about the house," she said. "You were sure
right when you said I could trust him."

"David is trustworthy. So is Wade. So is Jared. All
three are proof that there are good people in this world
who won't try to con you." Connie winked. "Speaking
of Jared, how did your time over there go?"

"The twins are so cute." Ashley stalled. "I adore
them. They play dress up a lot, I gather." She grinned
at the memory.

"Their mother was big on that. Jessie loved fairy
tales. I don't suppose Jared will continue her tradition
though." Connie leaned her head back and sighed.

"I think he might. Today he played Sir Galahad."
Ashley smiled at Connie's surprise. "He was pretty
cute."

"And the social worker? How was that?" Connie
asked.

Ashley filled her in on what had happened.

"You sent me to help and I did my best. The place
was a disaster but it looked pretty good when I left." She
paused, glanced at her friend. "Jared's got an awful lot
on his plate with that wreck of a house, parenting the
twins and a new teaching job he's taken."

"That's where we come in," Connie explained.
"We're his friends and we must help him. There's no
way I want to see those children go into the foster system. You and I both know the problems they could
find there."

"I don't think Jared is going to let that happen," Ashley mused. "But you're right, he will need help. Could
your church do anything? Maybe take over some meals?
Or babysit for him. He tried to hire me as a nanny." She
explained about his job.

"We can certainly take over food but our church is made up of mostly young professionals. I don't know about finding a sitter there." Connie scribbled a note to herself.

"I don't know how it would work anyway. He says the twins hang on to him pretty closely." Her heart pinched with sympathy for the motherless twins.

"Their world has been rocked off its axis, for sure." Connie studied Ashley with a knowing glint lighting her eyes. "Meanwhile, how are *you* going to help Jared and the kids, Ash?"

"Me?" Ashley shrugged. "The kids begged me to make cookies with them. I might go back and do that."

"That's it? Come on, Ash. You know you won't be able to leave it at that. You're the poster child for organizing other people." Connie chuckled.

"Yes, I am." Ashley squared her shoulders. "I'd like to get that man ultraorganized so he'll make sure those kids have the kind of home they need, but I don't think he wants my help."

"As if that will stop you," Connie said. "I think our Sir Galahad is in for a surprise. You're not just a teensy bit interested in him, are you, Ash?"

"Not the slightest bit," Ashley said vigorously. "When I discovered that Peter was only after my money, I realized that I need to focus my life on using Harry's money to help as many people as I can. Harry would have loved that and I believe that's God's plan for me, too." She blocked the familiar rush of pain that came from the mention of her ex-fiancé. Even after a year, the betrayal stung.

"Speaking of plans." Connie smiled.

"What?" Ashley studied her bright face. "Come on, spill it. What's up?"

"Wade and I are planning to take Silver on a summer visit to Brazil. You know that's where Silver was born?" Connie asked.

"I remember you told me. Your stepdaughter is one lucky girl." South America had been on top of Ashley's list of places to visit—until her yearning for family had drawn her back to the States. "When will you go?"

"The week after school is out. We were wondering if you'd mind staying here until we get back. Wade's stepmother will be visiting friends at the lake. I'd feel better if someone was here in case the staff needs something." Connie paused. "David will help if you need anything."

"I won't need a thing. And I'd be happy to stay here. This house is gorgeous." Ashley rose, hugged her friend and thanked her for the tea. "I'm going for a run before dinner."

"Okay." Connie touched her cheek. "Is everything all right, Ash?"

"Yeah. I just need some time to think about my project."

Funny though. The only thing Ashley thought about as she ran through the sun-dappled streets was a tall, grumpy, very handsome man dressed up in a cloak with a twig for a sword.

Sir Galahad.

Maybe for the twins.

Ashley wasn't looking for a knight in shining armor.

Chapter Four

"Look, Uncle Jared. I'm building a bridge." Eric piled another chip of wood on the already teetering stack.

"I'm building a house." Emma was not about to be outdone.

"Good job. You are both great builders." He watched them a few moments longer before beginning the tedious project of removing broken oak floorboards and replacing them. It was busywork. He was stalling and he knew it.

Jared had spent his entire Monday searching for after-school care for the twins. Neither solution he'd found appealed. Maybe he was being too picky but he didn't want to leave the twins in the care of a fourteen-year-old babysitter. But neither did he want them to stay with Mrs. Heffner next door. She was a dear old soul, had volunteered to help and Jared knew she would do her very best for the kids. But he feared the twins would run the frail old woman ragged.

Still, he started teaching tomorrow. He had to choose someone.

I could use some help here, God.

Heaven remained silent, as it had since Africa.

Jared sighed and reached toward the phone to call his neighbor. The phone chose that moment to ring.

"Hey, buddy. David and I feel like doing something tonight. If we can find a sitter for you are you up for it?" Wade sounded happy, carefree.

Jared envied him his happy carefree life with Connie, a woman who kept Wade's life sane. Must be nice.

Down, green-eyed monster.

"Jared? Are you there, buddy?"

"Yeah, I'm here. A night out sure sounds good." Jared let himself daydream for a moment. Once upon a time he'd had dates, gone out with women and partied with his friends.

That was then, his brain chided as a small brown head lifted to stare at him, eyes wide with fear.

"You're not going away, are you, Uncle Jared?" Emma asked. "You won't leave us, will you?" As she watched him the familiar hair twirling started, a visual sign of her insecurity.

"No, sweetie." Jared sighed. He covered the receiver. "I'm staying right here."

"Oh. Okay." After a tentative smile she went back to her building.

"So when should we pick you up?" Wade asked.

"It would be nice, Wade, but I don't think we're ready for that yet. Thanks for the invite though." He scrounged for a joke edged with the wit he'd been known for in college, but somehow nothing came to him.

"We could come over there," Wade offered.

"Maybe another time. I'm kind of in the middle of something." Mostly slivers. He nudged one out of his thumb. "You guys have fun."

"We'll miss you, man. Next time."

"Yeah. Next time, Wade." Jared hung up and took out his frustrations on the pry bar. The board came out so easily it knocked him on his rear. The twins roared with laughter as they raced out of the room to answer the doorbell. He sat there a minute, stunned.

"Having fun?" an amused voice inquired.

Jared lifted his head and turned. For the first time in twenty-eight years he forgot to breathe.

Ashley Ross stood in the doorway, a twin on either side. It wasn't the formfitting jeans she wore, or the thin white shirt she'd tucked into them. It certainly wasn't the small turquoise scarf around her neck. It wasn't even that regal braided crown on top of her head. It was more the whole fantastic package that made him gulp like a guppy.

"Sorry to interrupt." She smiled uncertainly when he kept staring. "It's just that I wanted to talk to you." She glanced distractedly at the twins who were begging her to see their creations.

"Okay." He glanced at the mess he'd made. "Can you give me a couple of minutes to fix this first? I don't want anyone tripping."

"Sure." As simple as that she walked to the kids' corner, sat down cross-legged and, red head bent, began to assemble her own structure.

It took Jared a minute to refocus. Then he cleaned out the remnants of the ruined boards and slid the new ones into place, gluing and nailing them securely.

"Once the stain is on, you'll hardly be able to tell you patched it." She rose and walked over to examine his work. "How did you learn to do that?"

"I've been working as a contractor in Australia for

the past few years." Jared grazed one hand over the wood. Satisfied it was smooth, he gathered his tools and rose. "If I'd have been here, I'd have advised Jessie and Jeff to run a mile from this place."

"Why?" She glanced around. "It's a charming house. It only needs a little work."

"Define 'little.'" He put the tools in the garage, locked it then washed his hands. When he returned to the kitchen, Ashley and the twins were discussing chocolate chip cookies.

"Can we make them tonight?" Emma begged. "Please?"

"I think it's a bit late for baking this evening, Emma," Ashley said, giving Jared a sidelong glance. "Maybe another time? I just stopped by to talk to your uncle."

"You two go and get ready for bed. You can come down and say goodbye to Ashley after you brush your teeth." He waited till they'd rushed away then waved Ashley to a chair at the table. "Coffee?" he asked, lifting the pot he'd brewed earlier.

"Uh, sure." She accepted a cup, took a sip and quickly set the mug down, struggling to mask her distaste.

"I guess it's a little strong," he said after he'd tasted his own. She looked so elegant, polished—and out of place in this house. "So, what do you need?"

"Need?" Ashley frowned, blinked. "Oh. No, actually I'm here to ask if you still need an after-school sitter."

"Yes." Jared tried not to let hope mushroom. "You know of someone?"

"I think I can help you." She sat erect in her chair, her eyes clear and focused.

"You?" He didn't get it. "Personally? But I thought you had to work."

"I do," Ashley agreed. "I've taken a job at the hospital. I'll be working seven to eleven three weekdays. Which means I'd be free to pick up the twins from school, bring them home and stay until you arrive." Her smile lit up her entire face.

"That sounds good." He told himself not to look a gift horse in the mouth, that there had to be a catch. "But after working so hard will you really want to come here and watch the twins? They can be a handful."

"They're delightful." She chewed her bottom lip for a moment. "I've given this a lot of thought and I'm sure it won't be a problem. Unless you've changed your mind?" Her blue eyes clouded over.

"I haven't. I think the twins will love spending time with you and it's a lot better than having our elderly neighbor watch them." He got lost in thoughts of having Ashley here, in his home, until a new problem dawned. "I can't pay you much."

"I don't want your money," Ashley told him, her gaze resting on the boards he'd just replaced. "Maybe we could come to some other arrangement."

"Such as?" Suspicion lent his voice a harsh tone he hadn't meant.

"I don't know. It's just an idea. For now, let's see how things work out. Okay?" She was glowing again, her skin picking up the rose hints from her hair. "I'll pick them up, feed them a snack and keep them busy until you get home. Is that what you need?"

"Sounds great," Jared said, and meant it. "And maybe help with homework, if they have any. Though I can do that in the evening also."

"We'll play it by ear the first week. Then you can tell me if you want me to change something or do things differently." As they hashed out the details, the twins came bounding into the room.

"Guess who's picking you up from school tomorrow?" Jared pointed to Ashley, chuckling as the twins whooped with excitement.

"You see what I mean about wearing you down," he said as Emma clung to one hand and Eric the other.

"I love it," Ashley proclaimed.

And, in fact, it did look to Jared as if the woman thrived on the kids' demands. She smiled, answered questions and generally reassured them, so that when she finally said goodbye, the twins were full of plans for the following day.

"Thank you hardly seems enough," he said as he walked her to the door. "I was dreading leaving them with a sitter."

"But isn't that what I am?" she asked, staring into his face with a perplexed look.

"You're different," Jared told her.

"Well, thank you." Ashley smiled, waved and finally drove away in her small compact car.

The twins went inside but Jared lingered in the doorway, thinking about how different Ashley was from some of the women he'd known in Australia. He couldn't imagine one of them volunteering to look after two kids for free. He still wasn't sure about not paying her. Maybe he'd insist. But something in the way she'd refused made him think that Ashley might ask for something in return for child care.

And that made Jared very curious about the tall, gorgeous redhead.

"Do you realize there are only two weeks of school left?" Connie shook her head. "I have hardly anything ready and we'll be leaving for Brazil the second of June."

"Can I help?" Ashley watched as the twins splashed and played with Silver, Connie's stepdaughter, in her friend's pool.

"You're already up to your neck, Ash," Connie teased. "Work, the twins and now this project you've taken on. I don't think you have time in your day for anything else."

"If this project doesn't get going, I'll have too much time on my hands." Ashley glared at the preliminary drawings she held. "I have so many plans. It's frustrating not to be able to get on with them."

"I take it you've had no luck finding a contractor?" Connie sipped her iced tea.

"Well, I found two who promised me the moon. But when it came time to talk contract, they backed out. A third one was interested but wanted to start immediately and I couldn't do that because the sale isn't through yet. I did get some estimates for cost though," Ashley told her.

"That's a start."

"Yes, and David says the property should be mine by the end of the week." She paused, then continued, "I've found lots of people who will do this job or that, but I need someone to oversee them. That person is hard to come by."

"You certainly want someone who is trustworthy and honest." Connie leaned over. "Tell me about these drawings, Ash. What's this in the corner?"

"That's my future home. I told you, remember?" Ashley tried to control the quickening thud of her heart. "When all is said and done, I'm going to live there. I can hardly wait."

"This looks lovely," Connie enthused.

"Well, it doesn't look like that now, I assure you.

Check this out." She handed Connie a sheaf of pictures. "Everything in the place is run-down, but I had an inspection done and apparently it's mostly cosmetic stuff so that shouldn't be a problem. I'm going to have it finished first. I want to get in there ASAP."

"Hello." Jared moved from behind them. He waved to the twins, who took a moment to acknowledge him before diving into the water again. "This is a good place for a Friday afternoon chat."

"Have some tea and relax with us." Connie handed him a long tall glass that clinked with ice cubes.

"Thanks." He sat down next to Ashley and pointed to the architect's preliminary drawings. "What's that? Or is it private?"

"It's a project I'm working on. A place for homeless families to come and regroup. It will be called Harry's Place. And this building—" she handed him the drawing and pointed to a sketch in one corner of the perspective "—this is my future home."

"Looks great. I like the way they've rendered things," he said as he studied it. "What's the current condition of the house inside?"

"Have a look." Ashley handed over her pictures.

"Wow!" He sorted through them quickly, pausing to whistle at one point. "A lot of work."

"It is. But it's going to be worthwhile when families get in there." Connie patted Ashley's hand. "This woman will make sure every detail is perfect."

"I'm sure you had inspections done?" Jared studied one picture for a very long time before he handed the sheaf back.

"Yes." Ashley accepted her pictures and tucked them into her bag. "Everything checked out."

"Good. Don't want any hidden surprises." He swallowed the last of his tea. "I'd better drag the twins out of that water and get going."

"Oh, won't you stay, Jared? Wade is barbecuing steaks tonight. We'd love to have you share dinner," Connie offered. "You don't visit Wade often enough."

"Steaks, huh?" Jared grinned. "You talked me into it."

"If that didn't do it, I had a backup plan," Connie admitted with a smile. "Ashley and the kids made a chocolate fudge cake this afternoon."

"Chocolate? I have no other plans for tonight," he said with a wink at Ashley.

"Good. I'm going to call and see what's holding up Wade. Excuse me." Connie walked into the house.

Ashley sat silent, wondering how to bridge the silent gap that now hung between them.

"I was—"

"Did you—"

They looked at each other and laughed. Jared waved a hand.

"Ladies first."

"Actually, I wondered why you studied that one photo for so long," Ashley said. "Did you see something wrong?"

"Not wrong," he said, his voice careful. "More like curious. The grounds around the house look uneven. That's all."

"I imagine a landscaper will have a field day." She picked up the big blue ball that had flown out of the pool and tossed it back in. "I can't think that far ahead. It's enough trying to figure out how to get the renovations done on time."

"On time? There's a deadline?" Jared frowned. "Whose?"

"The city's. Because it had been in arrears for years, the property was a really good deal. But they put a stipulation into the sale's agreement that the shelter for homeless families must be operationally ready by September 1," she explained. "Otherwise there's a big penalty."

"Very short time frame," he said, his forehead pleated in a frown.

"Yes, it is. I think some of the city councilors opposed the project and thought this short deadline might scare us off. And it might. No one seems to want to commit to it." Ashley sighed. "But this is a project I believe God wants done so I can't let a little thing like that hold me up."

"A little thing?" Jared shook his head and chuckled. "Pretty important. There are a lot of scam artists out there. Be careful."

"Oh, I'm well aware of that. I've been scammed by the best." She couldn't keep a hint of bitterness from leaching through.

"You have?" Jared looked confused.

"Oh yeah. But this time I intend to be very careful about who I choose," she assured him. "Besides, I'm counting on God to lead me to the right contractor."

"Good luck with that," he said very quietly. His eyes darkened with the same pain-filled shadows she'd glimpsed before.

"I don't need luck. God is on my side." Ashley could see skepticism roll across his face and quickly changed the subject. "How was school?"

"Good. It's a little nerve-racking to take on a class this young and keep them on task, especially at the end of the year." He rolled his head as if to stretch his neck muscles. "But I'm getting the hang of it. Thanks for the suggestion about kite-making. It forced them to use some math and to follow directions. We flew them this afternoon. It was fun."

Jared Hornby had changed a lot in the month she'd been watching the twins. Ashley had sensed a hesitancy in him before his first full day of teaching. She thought it was because he was anxious to prove himself so he'd get another teaching position in the fall. When he floundered with what to do with his fourth grade class at the end of the year, she'd suggested activities to fill up the last weeks before summer vacation. He seemed to appreciate her suggestions and often shared funny stories about his students with her and the twins.

Ashley had been surprised by just how much she enjoyed those times of sharing and laughter. It was almost like having her own family.

Wade arrived, bringing David, Susannah and family along and the conversation shifted. Connie called the kids out of the pool and dried them off while Wade hovered over the steaks, with Jared and David adding advice about the proper way to grill. Ashley was amazed by how easily they all blended old friendships with new.

"Seems funny for us three to be together again, doesn't it?" Susannah remarked as she set out the plates Connie handed her. "It's been a long time since we were foster kids at the Martens'."

"Some pretty good times there." Connie chuckled. "Did you ever learn to ride a horse, Ashley?"

"Yes, I did. And don't you dare bring up my past embarrassments," Ashley said, cheeks burning as the others turned to stare at her.

"I sense a secret." Jared winked at Connie. "Are you going to tell us?"

"Of course." Connie gleefully related Ashley's many attempts to ride the Martens' horses and the countless times she'd been thrown. "Let's just say it's a good thing she became a nurse. Her horse experiences have allowed her to empathize with hurting patients."

Susannah snickered. Ashley flushed even darker.

"How's your golf game these days, David?" she asked, desperate to change the subject.

"Golf? Who has time for golf?" David held up baby Grace. "This little sweetie takes up most of my free time, especially with Susannah so busy at college—" He stopped, blinking at his wife whose eyes immediately filled with panic. "Sorry, honey. I know you don't want to talk about school. Slip of the tongue, I promise."

"Did we tell you that our visas finally arrived?" Connie intervened. "We didn't think they'd ever get here."

Wade pronounced the steaks ready as they chatted about the trip. While Connie directed Jared to sit next to Ashley, across from the twins, Wade slid the succulent meat onto a platter and carried it to the table, which was already laden with delicious food.

"Let's join hands and give thanks," Connie said.

Ashley wanted to groan. She was already too conscious of Jared. Now, as his big strong hand slid over hers, her heart rate took a leap that made her catch her breath. She didn't hear what was said, didn't pay any attention to what the twins were doing. All she could focus on was the "Amen" that meant she could break contact with Jared.

Her reaction puzzled Ashley. Jared was the twins'

guardian, that's all. Why was she acting like a teen with a crush?

And yet, as his arm brushed hers, Ashley knew her daily interaction with Jared had attuned her to him. Now he laughed and teased as if he were carefree. But Ashley knew that when he thought no one was watching him, he'd lose that smile. Sometimes she'd seen him look straight through something, unmindful of anyone. Then his eyes would darken. Tiny lines of pain would crease the corners of his eyes and one hand would rifle through his sandy brown hair as if he couldn't quite reconcile his thoughts. In those moments something inside her yearned to reach out and soothe whatever hurt lay buried deep inside, away from prying eyes.

Ashley told herself to get a grip. She worked for Jared. That was all.

But his presence here tonight unnerved her. Those intensely brown eyes of his saw more than she wanted. Sometimes it was as if that pensive gaze could peer inside her and see how alone she felt, how deeply she longed for her own family. Being with the twins had only multiplied that yearning.

"Delicious meal," she said to Connie. "The ham in that salad reminds me of the farm in North Dakota. Remember when Dad wanted to roast a pig in the ground, Hawaiian-style?"

Connie, Susannah and Ashley looked at each other then burst into laughter. The men watched them with funny looks and demanded an explanation. Finally Connie sobered enough to relate what had happened, but the story was interrupted by bouts of the giggling women.

"Those were some pretty good days," Ashley said.

She rose to clear plates. "I must remember to send the Martens a thank-you."

"There must have been a lot of kids coming and going while you three were there. Do you ever have reunions?" Jared asked idly, his focus on the massive chocolate cake Connie set on the table.

A hushed silence fell.

"Genius," Ashley breathed.

"Thank you." He frowned. "Why exactly am I a genius?"

"Dude, you *never* ask that question," David scolded. "Anytime a woman pays you a compliment, take it and run."

"Have we taught you nothing?" Wade mourned.

"Oh, be quiet you two. You're just jealous of Jared's brilliance," Connie said. "I think we should do it. Ash? Suze?"

"Yes," Susannah voted.

"Ditto. When?" Ashley asked.

"Next summer?" Susannah bit her bottom lip. "I don't think I'll be taking classes in spring again, but if I am, I'll need a break. A reunion would be perfect."

"We'll have to make a list of names and try to get addresses for everyone," Ashley suggested. She went in search of a pen and paper. When she returned the three women huddled together, shooting out ideas in rapid-fire succession as the kids bounced a ball to each other.

Ashley was lost in thought when she saw Jared glance at the cake. She had to stifle her laughter as longing washed over his face. Wade and David looked just as bad.

"Maybe we should talk later, girls," she said. "It looks like that cake has drawn a lot of attention."

"Is it for eating?" Wade asked Connie. "Or are we just going to admire it?"

"Personally, I could admire it more if it was in my mouth and my stomach," David murmured. "But that's just me."

"Food," Susannah grumbled to Ashley. "That's all these three think about."

"Not all, honey," David corrected. "But the thing is sitting there, tempting us to enjoy it and—"

"And we want to enjoy it. What's wrong with that, huh?" Wade demanded.

"Nothing wrong that I can see. Food is supposed to be eaten." Jared's staunch support of his friends made Ashley laugh.

"You'd think the poor things hadn't eaten in months." With an exasperated look Connie cut three large wedges and passed them to each of the men. She handed her husband a carafe full of coffee. "Will that keep you three busy for a few minutes while we talk?"

"Yes, thank you, dear," he said, beaming a smile at her. "But you'd better cut some cake for the kids, too, because I'm not sharing."

"Let's finish dinner, Connie," Susannah suggested. "We'll talk about a reunion later."

So they sat around the table, enjoying the cake until the stars finally came out. Once cleanup was finished, the kids began to yawn and Jared declared it time to leave.

Ashley bent to embrace Emma and Eric, loving the sweet hugs they lavished on her.

"Are we going to go for our bike ride tomorrow, Ashley?" Emma demanded.

"I'm not sure." Ashley glanced at Jared. She'd meant

to confirm it with him earlier and forgotten. "You said you had some work to do on the house tomorrow. I was wondering if the twins could come for a bike ride with me. There's a really nice trail at Mount Lemon we could go on. I thought maybe a picnic?"

She saw his eyes widen. A moment later his reaction was hidden.

"Can I think it over and call you in the morning?" he asked.

"Sure. No problem." Why did he need to think it over? He must have a list a mile long of stuff to do on that house. But Ashley kept silent.

"Great. Thanks again for all your hard work. We appreciate it." A few moments later Jared left. The twins waved out the back window of his truck.

David and Susannah quickly followed. Then Connie led a yawning Silver up to bed.

"It's a nice thing you're doing for Jared," Wade said as he helped her straighten the patio. "He's had a tough time of it lately."

"I imagine it was very hard to lose his sister like that," Ashley said. "And taking over the twins has to be taxing."

"Yes, all of that," Wade agreed. "And even more. It's become a real struggle for Jared to believe that God is working in his life. I'm hoping your presence will show him that."

He excused himself to say good-night to his daughter, but Ashley stayed on the patio until darkness fell and the night cooled as she puzzled over Wade's words.

Everyone had faith issues at one time or another. Jared had been a missionary. He must have had a close relationship with God. But somehow she sensed from his dark moments of introspection, when he thought no one saw, that his faith wasn't helping him. She had a hunch something had rocked his world beyond anything she'd ever experienced.

Ashley couldn't help wondering what that something was, and how it had changed him from the laughing, carefree friend Wade and David had described.

Chapter Five

"Come on, guys. A little farther and we'll meet your uncle with our picnic."

Ashley waited while the twins stored their water bottles in their backpacks. Then they all climbed back on their bikes. The bike route was a workout, especially for her because she rode so seldom. But the twins seemed to enjoy the exertion and pedaled happily, their cheery voices chiming in with whatever song Ashley began.

"Hey, look!" Having caught sight of his uncle at a picnic table ahead, Eric began to pedal furiously. Emma, not to be outdone, also sped up.

Ashley moved more slowly, content to take her time. The lovely mountain area with its Ponderosa pines had her spellbound. She'd chosen Rose Canyon because of its purported beauty and because of the lake where the kids could swim and cool off. She'd worn her own swimsuit under her clothes for just that reason.

"Hi." Jared held the bike while she dismounted. "Jessie's old bike work okay?"

"It worked perfectly. It's been a wonderful afternoon. I see you got the best picnic site. It's beautiful here." She handed him her helmet and brushed her hand through her loose hair, letting it spill over her shoulders so her scalp could cool. Self-consciously aware of his scrutiny, she paused, let her hand drop and looked around.

"Wade, David and I used to come here to fish sometimes," he told her as they walked toward the table. "We're lucky today. It's often very crowded."

"I can understand why," Ashley said. "It's gorgeous." She sat down and rubbed her calves. "I think I'm going to ache tonight. How high are we anyway?"

"We're at about seven thousand feet now, but because the trees are so thick in this canyon, we don't have sweeping vistas like some of the other picnic sites." He poured her a glass of something and held it out. "Lemonade. It should help ease your thirst."

It did. In fact, the whole picnic was delicious. The twins, having exhausted their energy on the afternoon's ride, quietly cooked their hot dogs over the small fire Jared had built.

"I thought it would be too dry for a fire here," Ashley said, relieved when he offered to cook her hot dog with his. The ride, the heat of the day and the odd way he kept glancing at her sapped her energy.

"It's only because of the unusual amount of rain we had this winter that they're allowing fires in these grills. I had to get a permit." He pulled out a piece of paper and waved it. "If we don't put it out properly, I'll get a fine."

"Then we'll put it out properly." She glanced at the lake. "I just want to dive in."

"Sorry." Jared shook his head as he handed her a hot dog with all the fixings. "There's no swimming in this lake." He chuckled at her moan of dismay. "There's a swimming place we can go after we eat, if you like."

"That'd be good." She munched happily on the food he'd brought. "Did you get much work done while we were gone?"

"I got a door replaced. And some stain on the floor. It should be dry before we get back. It's a start." He shrugged. "I think I've quit obsessing about the house since I started at the school. I finally figured out I can only do so much every day. I have to make time for the twins and Mom and Dad."

"How is your mother?" she asked, smiling as the twins tried to coax a chipmunk to take a bit of their hot dog buns.

"About the same. She seems happy enough, especially when Dad goes to visit her." He smiled but a flicker of tension wove through his words. "They've been married forty-five years and they still hold hands."

"I think that's so sweet. Love should last like that, don't you think?" He didn't answer but Ashley grabbed at the opportunity to know more about Jared. "Did you and your sister have a happy childhood?"

"The best." He forced a smile. "They were the kind of parents who gave you boundaries and then stood back and let you figure out life. I never felt there was anything I couldn't do." His face got that distant look again. "I'd like to do that for the twins. I think it's what Jessie would want."

"I envy you the opportunity to impact their lives," she murmured.

"Envy me?" Jared's gaze slid to her, intent and serious.

"Yes." Ashley shifted under that steady scrutiny. She twisted a little to watch the twins scamper among the trees before facing him again. "I know it probably sounds silly but I've always longed for a family, children to love and nurture. I don't think there is anything more worthwhile in life. You're lucky because you get to do it at school and at home."

"And you won't?" he asked, one eyebrow lifted.

"Doubtful," she said, keeping her gaze down so he couldn't see how much that hurt.

"Why not?"

"I don't know much about the kind of love your parents share, Jared. I've been in love twice," Ashley admitted. "Both times left me feeling like I'd been in a battle."

He leaned forward, his attention fully focused on her. "Tell me."

"Well, the first time I was naive and fell for a doctor while I was in training." Ashley grimaced. "Dr. Don wasn't looking for a wife or anything to do with permanent."

"Creep. And the second time?" Jared turned at a shriek from the twins, who were pointing at a fawn. He nodded then turned back to Ashley. "What happened then?"

I believed in a lie called happily-ever-after.

"I'm sorry if that was too personal," he said when she didn't immediately answer. "You don't have to tell me anything, Ashley."

"It's okay. I'm over it." She inhaled. "I was engaged to a man I adored."

"Sounds good so far."

"It was so far from good." Ashley wished she'd never started this. She didn't want to go back, dwell on the past or even let that old negativity tarnish the project she was about to start. Most of all she didn't want to talk about the man who'd stolen her confidence so completely that she now looked at everyone through the jaundiced eye of distrust.

"He was that bad?" Jared joked.

"He was much worse," she told him as a wave of the old anger surged up. "It's a long story I don't want to go into. Let's just say one of us wasn't getting married for love."

Jared frowned but said nothing.

"Anyway, I've come to the conclusion that I have to start looking to myself for happiness. I'm okay," she told him, forcing a cheerful tone into her voice. "I'm getting on with my life. I'm going to have a home and I'll make a family for myself. It might not be a traditional family, but it will be mine. Are those marshmallows for roasting?"

Jared blinked at the sudden change of topic but nodded. "S'mores."

"Chocolate. Just what I need." She straightened her backbone and met his stare head-on. Nobody was going to pity Ashley Ross. "Shouldn't you call the twins to share them?"

"Yeah, right." But Jared studied her for several moments before he called Eric and Emma.

The two came running and had their marshmallows roasting in minutes.

They spent the rest of the afternoon prowling through the woods. Ashley was amazed by Jared's knowledge as he explained habitats and species to the children.

"What did you teach in Africa?" she asked while he checked that the bikes were secure in the back of his truck.

"High school science," he said. "Dad's love of plant

life got me interested early. I had my own garden when I was four."

"Ah. Hence the little garden plot in the backyard." She smiled. "You're passing it on to the twins."

"I'm trying." He grinned, shrugged. "Dad was a great teacher, patient and so knowledgeable. I guess I inherited my love of botany from him and over the years it has mushroomed."

"He does an amazing job at Connie's. I don't think I've ever seen roses to match the ones he grows." Ashley debated the wisdom of continuing and decided to go for broke. "Didn't you like teaching science in Africa? Is that why you left?"

"No." Jared said nothing more, merely continued tying down the bikes.

"Sorry. I shouldn't have asked." He didn't counter her so Ashley turned away to coax the twins to help pack up their collection of pinecones, leaves and nuts.

Soon everything was stowed. It seemed the afternoon was over. Ashley realized how much she'd enjoyed it, doubly so since Jared's arrival. Too bad she had to put her foot in her mouth by asking the wrong question.

"I'll give you a ride back to your car," Jared offered without looking at her. He seemed distant, withdrawn.

"Thanks." She climbed into his truck.

The twins in the back of the cab, buckled into their booster seats, were continuing an animated discussion about who had the biggest pinecone. A sidelong glance at Jared's face told Ashley he wasn't in a chatty mood, so she limited her remarks to the twins. It seemed to take forever to get to the parking lot. She was relieved to arrive.

"Thanks a lot for the ride. I'll see you all at church

tomorrow." Ashley blew kisses to the twins then quickly climbed out of the truck and fished her keys out of her pocket. "Thanks for lending me the bike," she said to Jared. "It was fun."

"I thought you wanted to swim." He frowned at her.

"Maybe another time," she said. "See you."

He nodded, but remained in place, watching as she drove away.

On the drive home, images of Jared and the twins arriving home, preparing dinner, sitting around the table, filled Ashley's mind. To distract herself she drove past the house she had just purchased. It still looked derelict and sad, but that would soon change.

Remembering Jared's overlong contemplation of her pictures, Ashley climbed out of her car and walked around the lot, studying the house from different angles. The land was chewed up and neglected, but she couldn't see anything wrong. The big house in front and the small one at the rear still drew her even if both needed a lot of love and attention.

"And that's what you'll get," she promised. "We'll fill this place with laughter and happiness," she pledged to herself. "And I'll finally have my home."

But the question remained: Would that be enough to satisfy the insatiable longing she'd carried for so long?

"This is getting to be a habit," Jared told his friends a week later as he kicked back on a lounger on the pool deck and savored his coffee. Somehow the stuff he brewed never managed to taste like this. "Wade might come home from South America and find me camped here."

"You couldn't sit still that long." Wade rubbed the

side of his knee. "Anyway, I might need you here if you tag me again the way you did today."

"You were trying to steal second base. Jared had a perfect right to stop you." Connie kissed his cheek then handed him an ice pack. "Keep that on it for a while," she ordered before she went back inside where the kids and ladies were watching the end of a movie.

Jared leaned back in his lounger, listening to David and Wade talk baseball and thought how lovely it would be to sit here and watch the sky darken and the stars come out. Since he'd taken on the twins, he'd had precious few moments alone to just sit and think. Even fewer since Ashley had arrived. She seemed to always be there, helping with this, suggesting a new way for that. Except this afternoon.

Well, her absence this afternoon didn't bother him. Friday afternoon's argument still rankled. The one thing Jared couldn't abide was someone touching his precious tools. Not only had she breached the inner sanctum of his garage on Friday, she'd dusted and vacuumed! And in the process she'd wrecked his best saw.

Ashley was a beautiful woman. She was also very nice. She'd helped him a lot with the twins and he appreciated it. But Ashley was bossy and she never backed down, like insisting that the garage should be clean and tidy in case Ms. Duncan wanted to look out there. As if! Ashley's obstinacy bugged Jared. Just about as much as that sketchbook she'd forgotten at his place bugged him.

And you called her intrusive, his brain jeered.

Except he hadn't meant to go through her personal stuff. When he'd first seen the book, he'd wondered if it belonged to the twins. Of course, at the first page, he knew it didn't, but he'd kept turning the pages, examining each one, stunned by the lists, the decisions, the pictures she'd placed in it. Her plans for the project she'd titled Harry's Place were detailed in the extreme. Seeing the exacting minutiae she'd included, Jared realized just how near and dear the project was to her heart. Especially the smaller house, across which she'd written "my home."

He'd looked at that and recalled her words the afternoon she'd taken the twins biking. She was going to have her own home, she'd said, her own family. So this house was to be her home? He'd puzzled over it all weekend and called himself a fool for doing it. Whatever was going on in Ashley's private life was none of his concern, no matter how much his brain kept asking questions. And it asked a lot of them.

Shame rushed over him as he recalled the scads of rough drawings and sketches tossed in the garbage. He'd waited till after the kids were in bed before he pored over each one. The scope of her project intrigued him. Apparently construction was still in his blood.

As if he'd conjured her, Ashley appeared in the center of Wade's patio doors, her hair loose and mussed. She wore jeans, of course, and a colorful cotton shirt that had bits of plant matter clinging to it. A smudge of dirt darkened one porcelain cheekbone. Was she working on the house herself?

Butt out and mind your own business, his subconscious ordered. Good advice. Jared wanted to take it.

But then Ashley sauntered toward him.

"The twins say they need cupcakes for school. They want to bake them tomorrow night. Is that all right with you?" she said.

No, it did not work for him. Jared had already lost

too much time daydreaming about this woman in his kitchen, a smear of flour on one cheek, her blue eyes dancing with laughter as she told him he'd have to eat the dinner she and the twins had prepared outside because the house was full of smoke thanks to a pan he'd forgotten in the oven.

"Uh—"

"Or did you want to bake them yourself?" she asked.

Like that was going to happen and she knew it. But Jared found no guile in her gaze.

"Sure, tomorrow night is fine," he said. "If you can afford the time." *Tell me something about that project,* his brain begged.

"I can spare the time." Her voice could have chilled ice cubes.

"Okay." Jared nodded. "See you then."

"Fine." She strode away, her long legs eating up the distance to the house.

"Brrr. You wanna tell us anything, buddy?" David asked, his voice soft so it wouldn't carry.

"Nope." Jared closed his eyes, leaned his head back.

"Like maybe discuss one very hot lady who's giving you the freeze but still wants to bake cookies for you?" Wade added, his voice brimming with innuendo.

"Cupcakes. And she's not baking them for me. She's making them for the twins to take to school." Jared opened his eyes and gave his two pals a dark look. "Which is great because while they're busy at that, I can lock myself in the garage and get some work done on the new cabinets."

"Lock yourself in the garage?" Wade sniped.

"Missed opportunity if you ask me, dude." David shook his head.

"I didn't." Jared knew what they were insinuating. His friends were blissfully happy in their marriages and they wanted the same for him. Only it wasn't going to happen. "Ask you, I mean."

"And they called him a genius." Wade sighed.

"Mistake." David sighed. "Dumber than dirt, our Jared."

Maybe he was. Maybe Wade and David had changed so much they liked being bossed around and told what to do by busybody females. Maybe they enjoyed having someone organize them to the nth degree.

Jared preferred to make his own thought-out decisions.

That way he avoided regret.

"Something happen between you and Ashley?" It would be David the peacemaker who couldn't leave it alone.

"A slight disagreement on Friday. Nothing serious." He closed his eyes and pretended to ignore them.

"How slight are we talking?" Wade asked.

"She's so bossy." Jared winced as the words left his lips. Ashley had just stepped onto the patio with Connie. It was clear by the upward jerk of her head that she'd heard him. She stomped clear around to the other side of the pool and sat on the diving board, ignoring him as she watched the kids jump into the pool.

"She's trying to help you," Wade soothed. "She likes to organize."

"I'm already organized," he said through clenched lips. "My tools are exactly where I can find them."

"Uh-oh," David groaned. "She touched his tools. Didn't you warn her, Wade?"

"What was I supposed to say? 'Our buddy Jared is

over-the-wall paranoid when it comes to anyone putting a finger on his precious tools'?" Wade shook his head. "Ashley's gone out of her way to help you with the twins, Jared. The least you could do is say thank you."

"I did say thank you for that. Many times. I did not say she could go in my garage and totally rearrange my work space." He jumped up. "I'm going to get some more coffee."

"There's a carafe right here." David held up the thermal jug.

Jared ignored him. He didn't want more coffee. He wanted some time to cool off. He stormed into the kitchen, rinsed out his cup and set it on the counter. Two pieces of pie sat there. He took one, grabbed a fork and sat at the breakfast counter to eat.

"I said I was sorry." Ashley stood in the doorway. "Several times. I didn't mean to damage anything."

Do not speak. Do not open your mouth. Concentrate on eating this pie.

"I was only trying to help."

The softly voiced apology was his undoing. Jared raked a hand through his hair and slowly nodded.

"It was just so messy in there," she continued and sent his blood pressure soaring again.

"It's messy because I'm working," he said, hoping that the amount of teeth gritting he'd done this weekend hadn't ruined his molars. "It's a *workshop*. Or it was. Now it's lovely and clean but I can't find anything and my best saw blade…"

"You know," Ashley sputtered, hands folded across her chest, blue eyes blazing, "if I had someone offer to help me, I'd take it and stop being such a grouch."

"Really?" Temper got the best of him. That and the

fact that a new blade was going to dent his shrinking wallet big-time. "You're saying that if I told you that the sketch someone made for the portico that you left behind at my place is completely wrong—you wouldn't take offense at that?"

Ashley blinked. Her face went white.

"Is it wrong?" she whispered.

"Yes." She looked so devastated he temporized. "I'd have to see how they built it to be sure, but, yes, I believe it is wrong."

"Come on." She took the fork out of his hand, grabbed his arm and tugged.

"What? Where?" He rose, frowning at her. "What are you doing?"

"Taking you to the scene of the crime. So to speak." On their way out they met Connie. "Can you watch the twins?" Ashley asked. "We won't be long."

"Sure." Connie gave them both a funny look but after a moment she turned and went back toward the pool.

"I knew a man from Texas once," Ashley said as she switched on her car motor and shifted gear. "He told me about this saying. Big hat, no cattle. It means—"

"I know what it means," Jared assured her. "And I do know what I'm talking about when it comes to construction."

"I hope you don't. I hope you're very, very wrong." Ashley glanced his way. "No offense."

"None taken." Jared could not get comfortable. The seat belt cut across his windpipe and his legs felt like they were folded in two in her compact car. They hit a dip in the street and his head slammed against the roof. "Aren't there any shocks in this thing?"

"If they put shocks in cars, then there are some in

here. Bessie is very dependable." She whipped around a corner and pulled to a halt next to a construction fence.

She named her car?

"It's going to be dusk soon. We won't be able to see much," he warned. "Besides, the gate is probably locked. At least it should be."

"Fortunately, I have a key and a very good flashlight." Ashley flashed him a grin before she bounded out of the car.

"I don't get it." Jared winced as he unfolded himself. "You're not that much shorter than me. How can you ride around in this thing and not have a back injury?"

"Clean living," she shot back from her position by the fence. "Yoga and learning to keep my temper. Come on, Grandpa."

Stung by her remarks he walked toward her quickly, grabbing the gate as she unlocked it. Then he swung it closed behind him and snapped the padlock shut.

"Why are you locking it? I'll only have to undo it when we leave."

"Construction sites are a haven for troublemakers," he told her as they tromped across the unkempt yard. "Trespassers can do a lot of damage that will up your costs so fast it will leave your head spinning."

"Oh." She studied him for a minute then pointed. "There it is."

Jared tore his gaze away from her glowing blue face and the dust spot on her nose and studied the portico. He took the flashlight from her fingers and swung it over the structure, pausing periodically to examine load-bearing points.

"Well?" Ashley was almost dancing from one foot to the other.

"It has to come down." He read the panic in her eyes and regretted he'd stated it so baldly. "It's not structurally sound. Look." He banged one hand against a support. Ashley's gasp told him she got his point.

"Then this is all a waste?" she whispered, bitterness edging her voice. "But he said it would last forever. He told me over and over that he knew what he was doing. You're saying he lied? Deliberately cheated?"

"Maybe not. Maybe the guy who put this together was in over his head. Your general contractor would probably order it down tomorrow."

"He was here with me today. He said it was great work." Ashley's blue eyes blazed.

Jared scrounged for something to say that would wipe that devastated look off her face. Instead he saw another problem. And another. He wouldn't say anything about them, not now when she was already reeling.

"Why would he do that?"

"I don't know," Jared said, though he could think of several reasons. "It's getting dark. We should go."

Ashley stayed silent as they walked back. She unlocked the gate and relocked it when they were on the other side without saying a word. Then she strode back to the car and got in. Jared stifled a groan and folded himself inside again.

To his surprise Ashley didn't immediately start the car. Instead she switched on the interior light and studied him.

"Are you absolutely sure you're right about that?" she asked, tilting her head to one side, toward the house.

"Yes."

"You don't think that if you saw it in daylight, you might—"

"No. It's wrong, Ashley." Jared knew his words hurt her by the way her head bowed, but he wasn't going to give her any false hope. "Have you got a piece of paper? I could show you."

She dug in her bag, handed him a sketch. "Use the other side."

"This is what should happen." Jared quickly drew the big house, outlined the supports and showed her how the whole thing should tie together. "When it's finished it should look less bulky, but it will be a whole lot stronger."

"I see." She sat silent for a few minutes, then inhaled. "Okay. Thank you. I appreciate your honesty."

"I'm sorry. I know this project means a great deal to you."

"Yes, it does. I want the house to be perfect. It's not starting out that way." She switched on the motor and headed for Connie's. "By the way, I replaced your saw."

"What? Ashley, no. There's no need for that. I'll get another blade—" He felt irritable and stupid for making such a big deal of it now. Especially when she'd only been trying to help.

"From what I learned at the store, I ruined more than the blade. So I replaced it. End of story. Okay?" She flashed him that wonderful grin of hers as she pulled into Connie's driveway. "Am I forgiven?"

"Of course. Nothing to forgive." How could he not be honest? "I'm afraid I was already in a vile temper on Friday. I didn't get the summer school position that I was hoping for and then a cabinet commission I was counting on fell through. I am paranoid about my tools but I took my disappointment out on you. I should be the one asking forgiveness."

"Okay, we're both forgiven," she said, climbing out of the car. "Plus, there's only a few days of school left. It's not like we'll be in each other's faces for much longer anyway."

"No." Jared followed her through the house.

"Thanks for the advice," she said, pausing in the doorway to the patio. "I'll get someone to check things out tomorrow. If it's as bad as you claim, I don't want this guy doing any more work." She turned to walk across to where Connie and Susannah were seated but Jared grabbed her arm.

"As I claim? Ashley, I'm not lying," he said, surprised she'd think so. "Why don't you believe me?"

"I do." She flushed a deep dark pink. "It's just that I like to make sure. Really, I appreciate your help, Jared." She patted his arm then walked across the deck.

"So did you two kiss and make up?" Wade asked, tongue in cheek.

"Oh, shut up," Jared told him.

But as he drove home later the words came back to haunt him. The idea of kissing Ashley Ross skittered through his mind long after he'd tucked in the twins. So he went out to the back deck and cuddled a cup of tea. At least it didn't taste like his acid coffee. He didn't bother with a light, content to watch the night sky as the constellations emerged.

His mind's eye tantalized him with a picture of Ashley, lit by moonbeams, singing one of those happy songs she always had at the ready. She was so—nice. It would be easy to coax the awareness he always felt around her into something stronger.

But then Jared's brain kicked in and reminded him that getting involved meant loss. The wounds from his past were too fresh and too deep to let him risk it again.

Keep your distance. Just for a few more days.

Simple to say. Harder to do when Ashley made it so easy to laugh. But he would have to because there was no way Jared would get involved again and risk losing someone else. No way at all. That was his choice and he'd stick to it.

As Jared sat in the dark, loneliness settled on him like a quilt. His life was brimming with responsibilities but his job would be over soon. Then what? How was he supposed to keep the twins if he couldn't get a job?

Worry battled with anger and as always, the same question bubbled up.

"Why did you abandon me, God?"

And like always, God didn't answer. That's what bothered him the most.

How could God—the same God of love he'd preached about to the Africans—leave him hanging with so many questions?

Fed up, Jared carried his now-cold tea inside and tossed it down the drain.

Ashley might have problems, but at least she had big dreams for her future.

All Jared had was worry that he'd lose the twins, the house—everything he loved.

Chapter Six

"It's exactly as Jared said, David." Ashley pressed her phone against her ear as she quickened her pace across the street. She was running late. "The building inspector told me nothing they'd put up could be saved. I fired them. I've got to find another contractor to manage the site. And soon."

"That's tough." David was silent for a moment. "You could ask Jared for a recommendation. He did a lot of construction in Australia. Maybe he's made some contacts since he came back."

"Thanks. I'll think about that. In the meantime, I have to go. Last day of school and I've made a little party for the twins." She hung up and racewalked the last block to the school.

"Ashley!" Emma came running, her smile stretched from ear to ear. "I passed. Next year I'm going to a new class."

"Good for you!" She hugged the little girl then did the same with Eric. "Ready to go home now? I've got a surprise."

"Can I share?" Jared asked. He stood behind her, a smile on his face. "I got to leave early."

"That's nice." Ever since he'd told her the building was incorrect, Ashley had struggled to ignore her extrastrong awareness of this very handsome stand-in daddy. "Shall we go?"

They walked two abreast, Ashley and Emma in front, Jared and Eric behind. The twins were full of talk about the summer ahead and all the things they wanted to do. As they approached the house, Eric spied the streamers and balloons. He and Emma scampered away to inspect.

"You made a party for them." Jared looked at her; his brown eyes creased as he smiled. "That was nice."

"When I lived in North Dakota, our foster mother always had a party for us on the last day of school," she told him. "After we'd presented our report cards, she'd get us to help carry stuff out to a table she'd set up under the trees. We'd play games, run through the sprinkler, stuff ourselves on her delicious baking and then she'd give each of us some small gift and tell us to enjoy our summer. It was such fun."

"Sounds like you had a very rich childhood," Jared said.

"I wasn't there the whole of my childhood, but I don't remember any other place. I went to live with the Martens when I was three and stayed till I graduated. I loved it there." She sighed. "I loved them. They were wonderful to me."

"Do you ever go back?" he asked, walking with her around the house to the back patio where the twins were trying to touch the swinging piñata she'd hung.

"I went for a visit after I finished nurse's training. But not since." She shrugged. "They were there for me when I needed them, but now it's time for another kid who needs their love."

"That doesn't mean they don't still care about you," Jared said.

"I know. But I'm older now. I need to take care of myself." She smiled as Emma ran over and grabbed her legs, grateful for the change of subject. "Ready to get this party on the road?"

The games were a hit. For once Jared joined in without complaint. The twins loved that and did their best to beat him. Ashley couldn't dampen her sense of pride as they sat around a small campfire later. This was what she wanted, this sense of togetherness that family gave. She could hardly wait to get into her new home and start working to create that.

"How's the building going?" Jared asked as she handed him a freshly brewed cup of coffee.

"It's not. I fired the contractor." She stuffed down the rush of panic she felt every time she thought of the September 1 deadline. "A building inspector for the city pointed out several other things he'd done wrong. I couldn't trust him."

"I see." Jared studied the flickering flames. "So now what?"

"I was going to talk to you about that. David said you might know someone, since you used to work in that field." She leaned back in her chair. "It's a problem I need to fix soon, so any help you can offer would be gratefully appreciated."

"I know a few guys and I will ask around, but I'm pretty sure you're in for a wait," Jared told her. "Most I've talked to have already committed their summers to projects they've had on the books."

"I cannot lose that property," she said. "I've got to get things finished by that deadline."

"Well, I will ask around," he promised. "But in the meantime, maybe you could hire some jobbers to do the preliminary work."

"Preliminary work like what?" Ashley leaned forward eagerly. She was desperate to try anything that would move things forward.

"Have you got those pictures?" Jared asked.

"Yes." She dug in her purse, handing him the sheaf.

Jared rifled through, noting things on each one. He waited as she scribbled herself notes on each point and patiently answered her questions.

"Thank you very much," she said.

"You're welcome. If you can get those things done, it will ease things a bit for your contractor. Of course, you'll have to be there every morning to let people into the site. And in the evening," he added. "Don't leave anything unlocked at night."

"You already warned me of that," she said. "And I'm there most days anyway. I want to get this project on the road. Since I won't be coming here anymore, I—"

"You're not coming anymore?" Emma's face crumpled. "But I like having you here, Ashley."

"Oh, sweetie." Ashley gathered the child in her arms. "I've loved being here. But your uncle will be home with you now that school is out. You don't need me."

And wasn't that the truth of her entire life. No one needed her. Not yet.

But Ashley aimed to change that as soon as her project was open.

"I'd better go. You munchkins need to get to bed." She rose, hugged both children. "Sleep tight."

"I can't thank you enough for your help, Ashley," Jared said, his voice sincere. "If there's ever anything I can do to repay you, let me know."

"Be careful," she teased. "I might hold you to that."

"Good because I mean it. Anything. Just ask." With the twins in tow, Jared walked her to her car. "Thanks hardly seems to cover it," he said.

"Tell the truth," she teased. "You're glad to have me out of here, cleaning and organizing. Tomorrow you'll have that garage turned upside down."

"I hope so." Jared's eyes sparkled with humor. "I want those cabinets finished."

"Just don't track the mess into the house," Ashley ordered. "Ms. Duncan could show up anytime."

"Good night, Ashley." In spite of his straight face a tiny smile tugged his lips upward.

"Good night." She climbed in her car and drove back to Connie's with a flicker of sadness. She was going to miss seeing those kids every day. She was going to miss Jared. A lot.

"Focus on the future," she told herself. "Focus on Harry's Place."

But at the back of her mind, a tiny voice wondered if even that would ease the longing in her heart for loved ones of her own.

In three days of being a stay-at-home dad, Jared learned a whole new appreciation for parents who did this every day of their lives. It was only four-thirty and he was exhausted!

"Uncle Jared, Ashley's here."

A scamper of feet and the creak of the front door told him the twins had let her in. Jared steeled himself for the reprimand he knew would come his way for the stack of dishes he hadn't washed today.

"Hi," he said cheerfully. He noted her weary smile. "You okay?"

"Lonely in Connie and Wade's big old house. And frustrated." She glanced at the coffeepot. "Mind sharing?"

He didn't. But he had a hunch his coffee would make Ashley feel even worse. That hunch was confirmed when she took a sip, blanched and quickly swallowed.

"What do you call this?"

"Coffee." He turned away, embarrassed by his inability to make a simple tasty cup of coffee. Somehow he'd never been able to get it right.

"In my world this doesn't qualify as coffee." She dumped the contents into the sink then filled her mug with water. "I see you put back the dishwasher," she said, noting the gaping hole had been filled. "Having trouble loading it?"

"I can't get it to work," he admitted.

"It looks new." She peered inside, shrugged and sat back down.

"I think it is. Someone gave it to Jessie. Apparently they changed plans in the midst of remodeling and decided to go with a new drawer kind of dishwasher. Jeff was going to connect it but…" He let it go. He and the kids had fun this afternoon. What did a few dirty dishes matter?

"Did you come to make cookies with us, Ashley? You said you were going to do that, remember?" Eric managed a woebegone look that usually got him what he wanted.

"I did say that, didn't I?" Ashley glanced at Jared. "You don't mind?"

Jared couldn't say no. More than that, he didn't want to. He loved the twins but he craved some adult conversation and something other than kids' games and cabinetwork. He also craved more of that tasty food Ashley had always had waiting when he came home from school. Hot dogs were fine but he didn't want them every day. And his cooking repertoire was limited to spaghetti, hot dogs and chicken nuggets.

"Why would I mind?" he asked. "I like cookies as much as the next guy."

"Okay, but I think you should eat your dinner before you sample the cookies." She glanced at Jared. "What if we get dinner started and then we'll bake? You can eat dinner and have the cookies for dessert."

"Sounds like a plan."

"What were you going to have?" Ashley asked.

"Uh, I'm not sure." He opened the fridge and peered inside as if it would yield answers.

"You have the makings of a taco salad if we cook the hamburger," she said, peering over his shoulder. "And I have a bag of taco chips in my car. Does that sound good?"

"Yeah," Eric cheered. Eric, who'd never met a vegetable he actually liked.

"I like taco salad," Emma agreed.

"And you?" Ashley studied Jared with a half smile. "Is that okay with you?"

"Perfect. We could eat outside." Then he wouldn't have to remove his cabinet drawings from the dining table.

"Okay. Let's get to work. So—aprons." Ashley set her handbag on one of the kitchen chairs.

Jared pulled open a drawer and selected the kids' aprons and a pretty blue one for Ashley. Jessie's creations. He stuffed down the pang of loss. He didn't bother with an apron for himself because he had no intention of cooking—only eating. But when he went to close the drawer, Ashley reached in and grabbed a fourth apron, which she handed to him. Jared almost balked at wearing it until he caught Eric studying him. The boy would copy his actions so he daren't refuse. Besides, aprons could help save on the monstrous laundry pile. He was all for that. Jared tied the apron around his waist.

"Now, Eric, you can be in charge of tearing up the lettuce. Make it like this." Ashley demonstrated. "Emma, you can shred the cheese. Jared, you cut up the tomatoes and I'll season and cook this hamburger. Everybody good?"

They were. The twins laughed and joked as they completed their tasks. Jared probed Ashley for details on her project.

"It's not happening at the moment," she told him. "I did what you said about the little jobs but I haven't been able to find anyone to take over as supervisor."

"That's too bad." He didn't know what else to say so he concentrated on his tomatoes.

With the salad quickly assembled and resting in the fridge, Ashley moved on.

"Now let's get out our cookie ingredients," she said to the twins.

Jared figured Ashley assumed he would sit and watch them, or find something else to do. But he had an idea. This was an opportunity to learn how to make the kids a treat with their help. Ashley could hardly tell him to get lost, though she looked confused when he began plying her with questions about each step.

"Can I mix the eggs and sugar stuff?" Eric asked.

"Yes. You'll have to really use those muscles though," Ashley teased. "Baking is hard work."

"It sure is." Emma huffed her bangs off her forehead as she plopped the last egg into the bowl, along with half of its shell.

Ashley reached in and fished it out. A second later she caught Jared's grin.

"Isn't there calcium in eggshells?" he asked, tongue in cheek.

"Maybe a little too much for our purposes." Ashley tried to control her smile but the corners of her mouth twitched and he could tell she struggled to remain serious. She let Eric have a turn stirring then pushed the bowl to Jared. "Okay, now we're going to add the flour. You can have that job."

"Me?" He clutched the bowl so he wouldn't drop it. "I don't know how."

"Put it here," she said, easing the stainless steel bowl back onto the counter. She added flour, a little at a time, as he mixed then frowned. "It's not really different from making meals."

"Uncle Jared makes cereal. And grilled cheese sandwiches," Eric said happily.

"And hot dogs and spaghetti," Emma chimed in.

"Well, that's good." Ashley glanced at him then got the kids busy measuring chocolate chips. "You don't cook much?" she whispered when the twins weren't listening.

"Never really learned how. Cafeteria in college. Restaurants. Whatever." He shrugged. "Is this stirred enough?"

Ashley glanced down, obviously distracted by what she'd learned.

"Yes. What about in Africa?" she asked, wrinkling her nose so the smattering of freckles across it joined together.

"A woman named Keshia cooked and kept house and I did some house repairs for her in exchange. When I came back home, I ate at my parents. My mom's been sick lately, but she comes over from the care home and my dad is a great cook. So was Jessie." He glanced around. "Somehow the gene never got passed on to me."

"Well, lucky for you, it's never too late to learn." Ashley smiled at him.

Jared's knees wobbled. He pretended the strong scent of chocolate caused it and not the way her golden eyelashes fluttered.

"I'll put in the chocolate chips," Eric volunteered.

"No, I want to!" Emma argued.

The tussle ended up sending the jumbo-size bag of chips into the mixture, which Jared immediately began to blend.

"No, stop! That's too much. Oh, dear." Ashley laid her hand on his, halting his stirring and his heartbeat, though she didn't seem to notice. She frowned. "Now it's impossible to pick out the chips and use them later," she said sadly. "They all have bits of dough on them."

"So?" He thought that was the general idea.

"So if the twins eat that much chocolate, they'll probably go into diabetic shock," she said with a grimace.

"Hmm." Jared tilted his head to one side. "Now that

you mention it, it doesn't look quite the same as Jessie's used to," he agreed.

"No wonder." Ashley thought for a moment. "Set that over there," she ordered. "We're going back to the beginning."

Jared wasn't exactly sure what that meant but he followed her directions without complaint. He and the kids mixed and mixed and eventually Ashley said they had three recipes of cookie batter.

"Now we'll put this together with the chocolate chip mixture," she instructed.

He was huffing by the time he'd mixed it all.

"That's going to make a lot of cookies." Eric's brown eyes grew round as saucers.

"It is, Eric. But you know what?" Ashley tweaked his and Emma's pert little noses. Her blue eyes sparkled when the children giggled. "We're going to freeze some of this dough. Then when you eat all the cookies we make today, and you want some more, all you'll have to do is defrost the dough, bake it and voilà! Fresh cookies."

The twins cheered their approval of this plan. They followed Ashley's example and scooped spoonfuls onto cookie sheets then parked themselves in front of the oven window to wait. But after the first sheet was removed and pronounced too hot to eat, they lost interest and wandered away.

While the rest of the cookies baked, Jared found some containers, which Ashley then filled with the excess dough. She labeled each one, adding the oven temperature and how long to bake, then lined them up in the freezer.

"That's three more batches," she told him. "Now, let's clean this mess up."

"Sure." Jared began filling the sink with hot water.

"You know, this kitchen is very well laid out," Ashley said. "Your sister knew how to make the cabinets work for her."

"She'll never get to see the new ones I'm making though." There were so many things Jessie would miss. In that moment Jared felt swamped by the pain.

"It must be very difficult for you to live here and face those memories every day." Ashley touched his arm for the briefest moment, her voice very soft. "Sometimes it's so hard to understand why God allows people we love to go."

Sometimes? Jared didn't understand anything God had done since Africa.

"I haven't figured out how to connect the dishwasher yet, but I will. I'm too stubborn to pay for a plumber." He averted his face as if he thought Ashley would comment on that.

"Not really a priority, I'm sure," she said quietly. "It can't be easy keeping everything together. I'm sure you're doing a great job."

"I'm trying." Jared exhaled the spicy fragrance of her scent and concentrated on cleaning. He might not be able to cook but he scrubbed the baking utensils with surgeonlike precision.

"That didn't take long." Ashley dried the bowl then removed the last sheet of baked cookies from the oven. "And there we are."

"Aren't any cool enough to eat yet?" Emma stood on tiptoe to peer with longing at the first tray of browned cookies.

"I think they might be soon." Ashley winked at Jared.

"But first dinner," he said. He glanced at Ashley. "You are staying?"

"Oh." She blinked. "I wasn't angling—"

"I know. But you will stay?" He wanted that. He wanted her to stay very much. And if he was truthful with himself, adult conversation was only part of the reason.

"Then thank you. I'd love to." She smiled at him and suddenly his troubles seemed insignificant.

"Great. Who wants to help?" Jared gave each twin something to carry while Ashley assembled the salad and carried it outside. A second trip brought everything else and soon they were seated, munching on her delicious meal.

"I like this salad, Ashley." Emma's empty plate proved her words. "Can we have cookies now, Uncle Jared?"

"I think we'll need more milk to have with them."

"I'll get it." Eric raced inside. He returned with the milk jug but tripped on a crack in the patio. The jug went flying and the little boy landed hard on his face.

Immediately the yard was filled with wails of pain.

While Jared rescued the child, Ashley sent Emma for a clean tea towel to stop the boy's nosebleed. Then she washed the milk off the patio.

Jared cuddled Eric while guilt and responsibility tore at him. He was supposed to keep them safe. Why hadn't he? He tamped down the anger. It wouldn't help. This was always the hardest part of parenting Jessie's kids. Was he doing the right thing? Was he parenting the way Jessie would have done? Was he failing them?

"I've got a cut, Uncle Jared. Will I have to go to the hospital?" Eric wailed, thrusting out his legs to show the spot of blood.

Jared didn't get to answer.

"I'm a nurse, Eric. Could I take a look, do you think?" Ashley waited for permission to look at the boy's knees. He glowered but finally nodded.

"Emma, can you go get the first aid kit?" Jared asked. "It's in the bottom cupboard in the bathroom. In a red box with a white cross on it."

Emma scurried away on her mission.

Jared held Eric, murmuring reassurance while Ashley, armed with a bowl of warm water, a cloth and antiseptic from Emma's kit, gently cleansed the wound. He liked the way Ashley asked Emma to be her assistant so she wouldn't feel left out or afraid. As Ashley worked, she spoke quietly and calmly.

"I used to work on the emergency ward," she said. "That's the place in the hospital where you come if you've had an accident. The doctors always asked the nurses to clean up scrapes like this. Sometimes they look really bad, but when you get them clean, you can tell it's not too bad. See? There are just a few marks here. We'll put some special salve on it and a bandage and it will heal very nicely."

"My arm's hurt, too," Eric sniffed.

"Really? Well, Nurse Emma, let's have a look at it." Ashley smiled at the little girl then bent over the cut. "Yes, I see. I'll pour on a little of this stuff. It chases away any germs that are trying to get in there. Oh, that's much better. Now it seems there are two kinds of bandages in here. I wonder which bandage we should use."

"Emma's are the pink ones. My mom got me the

green ones. They're frogs 'cause I like to hop." Eric hiccupped a sob. "She used to stick them on and then she'd kiss it better. I want my mom." He tucked his head against Jared's chest and began to cry.

From the way Ashley was staring at him, Jared figured he wore the same look of sorrow as Eric. He felt like bawling right along with the kid. All he could do was hug him because a lump wedged firmly in his throat, choking off any words he might have uttered to soothe the hurting child.

Ashley seemed to realize his inability to articulate and took over.

"I'm sure your mom is watching you now, honey. Your mom loved you two so much. You're her babies. I know if she could, she'd tell you how much she loves you, Eric." Ashley smoothed her fingers over the wounds, gently applying salve as she spoke.

Jared saw Emma's sad face and beckoned her over into his other arm. Ashley kept talking.

"There's nothing more important to a mommy than her children. That's how God made mommies. They love their kids no matter what."

"What about when I get big?" Eric sniffed.

"A mother's love never changes. It doesn't matter how big you get. That's the way mommies are," Ashley said as she covered the injuries with two bandages.

Jared stared at the golden-red mane of hair in front of him and wondered if Ashley ever questioned why her own mother hadn't loved her enough to keep her.

"If Mommy loves us, why doesn't she come back?" Emma said.

"Oh, sweetie." Ashley scooped the little girl into her

arms. "Your mom would be here, holding you as tight as this if she could."

"Why can't she?" Emma stared at her, big brown eyes puzzled.

"Because when people go to heaven they can't come back, even though they really love their kids. They have to stay with God." Ashley smoothed the brown hair.

How did she know all the right things to say? Jared struggled to soothe their pain and yet Ashley seemed to have no trouble finding the right words to ease the twins' sad little hearts. She was as deft at that as she had been treating Eric's wounds. He could feel the twins' fears lessening as she matter-of-factly dealt with their questions.

Quite a woman was Ms. Ashley Ross.

"I know it's hard to understand, Emma," she was saying now. "But don't worry about it. Just remember that your mommy and your daddy loved you more than anything."

"But sometimes I can't remember what they look like," Eric whispered. He angled his head to frown at Jared. "Is that bad?"

"No," Jared assured him and wondered how long Eric had been harboring these worries. "It's not bad at all. When we don't see someone for a while, we forget what they look like. You didn't see me for a long time so you forgot what I looked like, didn't you?" He waited for Eric's nod. "That's why we have pictures. You can look at your mom and dad's pictures and remember how they looked. Okay?"

"I guess." Eric tilted his head sideways, studying him. "Do you get sad sometimes, too, Uncle Jared?"

A wave of agony clenched his gut in a fierce wrenching pain. But Jared kept his voice soft and answered as gently, as reassuringly, as he could manage.

"Yes, Eric, I get very sad. Jessie was my twin sister, just like Emma is yours. We were each other's best friends and we did everything together. I miss her very much."

"I'm sorry, Uncle Jared." Eric reached up and wrapped his arms around his neck, squeezing tightly.

"Me, too." Jared closed his eyes and bent his head to rest on the boy's.

When Ashley turned her head away, Jared realized she was probably uncomfortable. This was a family moment, one of those times when a family drew into a circle and strengthened itself. She probably wished she was somewhere else rather than watching this.

But when he glanced up a moment later he noticed Ashley had her eyes closed and had Emma wrapped in a fierce hug, until the little girl finally wiggled free and demanded, "Are we ever going to eat those cookies?"

Ashley looked at Jared and burst out laughing.

"I think we could have some now. I'll pour what's left of the milk." She moved quickly to fill glasses. "There we go."

"We forgot to say grace. Don't we hafta say grace?" Eric asked.

"Sure." Jared knew it had been Jessie's habit and that she'd passed it on to her kids, but he didn't feel like talking to God; not when he missed his sister so badly. "Why don't you and Emma say your grace?"

They recited the little poem together, their voices clear in the silence of the yard. Then they each reached for the same cookie and burst into the giggles. Back to normal.

"These are very good," Jared said, finishing his third. "They'd go better with coffee," he murmured with a disparaging look at his milk. "But still—excellent."

"I'm glad you like them." Ashley had poured a minuscule amount of milk in her own glass and she sipped it as if it were scorching hot.

"Can we play now?" Emma and Eric, their faces wreathed in chocolate, stood grinning at them.

Jared was going to send them in to wash, but what was the point? They'd only get dirty again.

"Half an hour," he agreed. "Stay in the yard."

"Thank you for making us cookies, Ashley." Emma held up her arms.

In that instant, Jared saw Ashley's face transform. Her solemn expression melted; her eyes deepened to a rich royal blue. She knelt and enveloped the little girl in an exuberant hug. A surprised but delighted smile curved her mouth when Emma kissed her cheek. Not to be outdone, Eric eased in, too. She brushed a featherlight touch against each forehead.

"You are so welcome," she whispered. Her arms fell away as she watched them scoot across the yard. When Ashley finally turned to face him, the joy still lingered in her expressive eyes, but a touch of wistfulness lay under it.

"How lucky you are," she murmured.

Lucky? Him? He had a clunker of a house, two needy kids and a bank account that shrank so fast it left his head spinning.

"I'd give anything to have what you have," she whispered.

Jared didn't know what to say so he stayed silent, watching as she regained control. A glossy sheen washed over the blue irises. Ashley dabbed at one eye with a fingertip and laughed a self-deprecating, mocking little laugh.

"Sorry, Sir Galahad," she said with a wink. "It's just that they're such sweet kids."

Sir Galahad. Why couldn't she let that silliness die? He turned to watch the twins, smiling as they climbed up the little wall he'd erected as part of their play set.

"That's new." Ashley squinted for a better look.

"I finished it this afternoon." He followed her as she walked over to examine the structure. "It's not complicated, but they should have fun without hurting themselves."

"It's very clever." She remained oddly silent as she walked around the structure.

"Not compared to some things I've built. Like the cabinets. They take way more time." Why was she looking at him like that?

"Those drawings on your table—what are those?" Ashley wore the strangest look.

"Oh, just some changes I want to make to the house. Someday, when I can afford it." He shifted, discomfited by her odd behavior. "Do you want to see them? I'll get them and bring them out if you'd like."

"I would like to, yes."

"Uh, okay." Jared rose, walked inside and gathered up his drawings. He didn't understand what was going on, but talking about his love of building was not a hardship. "Here we are." He explained what he wanted to do.

"But this is major—moving walls, restructuring the upstairs. Have you built a lot?" she asked, blue eyes now blazing.

"I started when I was in high school." He shrugged. "I knew Mom and Dad couldn't afford to send me to college so I worked construction. It was great. Came in handy when I went to Australia. A buddy helped me get my license."

"I see." Ashley rose and began gathering the used dishes and stacking them. "You don't have any pictures of those Australian projects you worked on, do you?"

"Yeah. Sure." He frowned. Something was going on in that red head. Something he didn't understand. "Why?"

"Could I see them? Please?" She looked at him without flinching but Jared couldn't discern what was going on that made her blue eyes darken to a deep electric shade. "I'll watch the kids while you get them," she offered.

"Yeah, okay. I guess." Jared went to the garage and rummaged through some boxes before he found a couple of pictures he'd had enlarged and the little albums of snapshots he'd taken as work progressed. He carried them back to the deck. "Here are three projects I was in charge of."

Ashley bent over the pictures and examined them in great detail. Then she picked up one of the albums and began eagerly leafing through it. She spent so long in her study that Jared finally joined the twins for a game of tag. Eventually the half hour was up.

Jared shooed the children upstairs to brush their teeth. When they'd left he approached Ashley, who was staring into space. He touched her arm.

"Sorry. What did you say?" She blinked at him as if emerging from a haze.

"Is everything okay?" he asked.

"Fine. Fine. Let's get these dishes cleaned up." She scooped the dishes into her arms and carried them into the kitchen. She ran hot water and added detergent, but again she seemed to drift into a daze as the suds multiplied exponentially.

"Whoa!" He grabbed the soap from her hands and turned off the tap. "Overkill. Ashley, what's going on? Tell me. Come on, don't wimp out on me now."

She straightened, her manner that of the regal Ashley he'd glimpsed that very first day.

"I do not wimp out," she said. "On anything."

As if Jared didn't know that. It was obvious by the way Ashley tackled the twins, this house and her project. This was no fainthearted lady.

"I don't know why it didn't occur to me before." Ashley began washing the dishes with lightning speed. "I guess I just didn't realize—" Her voice trailed away. She finished washing then unplugged the drain. She barely waited till he'd removed the last dish before she began spraying the other sink down. Then she turned and faced him.

Jared inhaled. Now what?

"What are your plans for the summer, Jared?" she asked.

"My plans?" He frowned, hoping she wasn't going to talk about the mess in the living room. "You mean since I didn't get that summer school job I applied for?"

Ashley nodded.

"Well, I'd like to get those cabinets done. Maybe I can find some tutoring. Of course, I'll look after the kids." He stopped when a smile spread across her face. "Why?"

"Because." Her blue eyes turned almost navy. She was gorgeous. And smart. And incredibly appealing.

Ashley brought out weird feelings, made Jared think about the past. And the future. She disrupted his world and kept him off-kilter. Which was why he'd felt a sense of relief when school had finally ended and she didn't invade his world every day.

Except every morning he fought a sense of loss that he wouldn't see her that day.

"Because?" he repeated.

"Because I have a proposition for you, Jared."

"Really?" The sound of the twins jumping down the stairs brought clarity to his muddled state. "Which is?"

Ashley straightened. Her gaze riveted on him. She radiated beauty and independence. What could a woman like her possibly want from him?

"How would feel about coming aboard as the general contractor of my project, Jared?"

Chapter Seven

There. She'd said it.

Ashley waited anxiously for Jared's response to her offer.

Except the twins were there and ready to say goodnight.

"I've got to tuck them in," Jared told her, obviously surprised. "Can you stay for a while, so we can talk?"

She nodded, bent to wish each child good-night, then stood in place and watched Jared follow the kids upstairs. When he paused once and turned back to look at her, Ashley's heart gave a bump of recognition. Something about this man spoke to that secret part inside of her, the part she kept hidden from everyone else, the part she'd thought her ex-fiancé, Peter, had killed.

After going through that awful time, having everything she believed about love torn apart by Peter's greed—how could she allow herself to be vulnerable to that kind of betrayal again?

And yet Ashley knew this awareness of Jared she kept tamping down was not like what she'd felt for Peter. Jared was not like him at all. Jared was strong, determined. Money was not his god. Jared had put his life on the back burner to take over the twins. Those unselfish actions were miles beyond Peter's avarice.

So as not to disturb the twins, she walked back to the patio, sat down and studied the sky.

I think he's the right man for the project, God. I think this is the right move. Isn't it?

"Do you want some coffee?" Jared stood in the doorway, his eyes unreadable in the shadows.

"Yes—" Recalling previous cups, Ashley rethought that decision. "No, thanks."

"Chicken." He walked over, sat down opposite her. "But probably smart. I know my coffee is awful."

"At least you're truthful about it." She chuckled at his pretend chagrin. "I always prefer the truth."

"So do I."

Silence stretched between them.

Ashley cleared her throat.

"About the job."

"You want me to take it over," he said, his face thoughtful. "Why?"

"Because I believe you have the knowledge to do so. Your past projects show that. Because I think you understand what it means to me and because I believe you would do the work well. Your cabinets prove you're a stickler for details." She told him exactly what she could pay.

"Are those the only reasons?" he asked softly.

"I have a lot of reasons for asking you, Jared." Like she almost trusted him. At least she trusted him more than any man since Peter—besides David. "Aren't you interested? Do you no longer need a job?"

"Yes, I do." He studied her now, his dark eyes intense as they burrowed into hers. "The deadline bothers me."

"First of September." She nodded. "There's no wiggle room on that. The city is adamant. I think they've had too many projects started and not finished. And they did give me a whale of a deal on the property."

"And the budget?" She told him and he nodded. "That's for both the main house and the one you want to live in?"

"Yes. That's also nonnegotiable." Ashley didn't flinch when he frowned. "The project cannot go over budget, Jared. There is no way. That's a deal breaker."

"Ashley, renovation is always about going over budget." He smiled. "It's all part of not knowing what you'll uncover."

"This one cannot go over," she repeated. "And there's no reason it should. I've had engineers, inspectors and architects examine those buildings. No one has found anything problematic."

"Doesn't mean it won't be there," Jared said, flashing a grin.

"Doesn't mean it will." She was not going to let him think he could con more money out of her. Harry had taught her to budget and then stick to it in every project.

"Don't let anyone think there's a bottomless pit they can draw from," Harry had often said. "Otherwise you'll end up spending way more than you planned, which means that some other worthwhile project will have to be denied or shorted. If people know you'll budge, they'll find ways of increasing the amount they want from you."

Ashley had her own negative experiences of people who realized she had a lot of money and found ways to get it from her. A car she'd considered purchasing had shot up in price when she'd returned to buy it. Later she learned the owner had looked her up on Google, found out about her inheritance and thought he could benefit. She had walked away. But he was not the only one and Ashley was sick of it. By coming in on budget, she would ensure that Jared couldn't con her or work some deal with the suppliers to overcharge her.

Not that she thought he would, but prevention was better than disappointment.

"Okay, so tight budget and short timeline. That's tough enough, but I still have to think about the twins," Jared reminded her. "School was familiar. They knew their teachers and their peers so it wasn't an issue. But there's no way they're ready to go into day care. They fuss if I even talk about leaving them with a sitter for an evening."

"Let's focus on the job first. We can deal with other issues after that." At least, Ashley hoped they could. "Can you do it?"

The darkness hid his expression. For several moments Jared didn't answer her. He rose, paced the patio. Ashley remained silent. Finally he looked at her.

"Do you have blueprints?"

"In the car. Want to see them?" She waited for his nod, then walked to her car and retrieved the thick cardboard roll with blueprints inside. She flicked on the outside lights, unfurled the papers and set them on the patio table. "Have a look."

"Harry's Foundation." Jared finger hovered over the name at the top of the sheets. "That's who is funding this? Harry Somebody? You know him?"

"I did. He was a good friend. He's gone now." A fresh

wave of sadness threatened to swamp her but Ashley controlled it the way she always controlled her emotions. That way no one could see the longings she kept tucked inside.

"I'm sorry." Jared studied her for several moments then turned his attention to the details laid out on each page. He shot questions at her in rapid-fire sequence. How did she see this bay window being used? What were her plans for the two dining areas? The bedrooms?

The grilling lasted for almost an hour. It was clear Jared wasn't satisfied with some of her answers, but that's why she had architects and engineers involved.

"I can't tell you more than that," she said finally. "But I can arrange a meeting for you with the people who will be able to answer your questions. Tomorrow?"

"I don't know." Jared scratched his chin. "I still have the twins to think about."

"Maybe I can help there."

"Ashley, you're working. You can't possibly fit all-day child care into that." Jared sighed. "It's tempting, a project like this. These buildings are gorgeous old structures. To see them come to life again would be—" He paused, shook his head. "But not at the expense of the twins."

"Of course not." An idea glimmered at the back of her brain, but she'd have to do some research first. "Let me get the meeting arranged so you can see if this is something you want to tackle. Then we'll think about the twins."

He thought about it a long time before finally nodding.

"It would be good to have a steady income for a while

at least," he muttered. "If only I could be certain about work in the fall."

"One step at a time." Ashley smiled. "And we can pray about it."

"I guess." But he didn't look like he thought praying would help. Which puzzled Ashley. Jared was a former missionary. Where was his faith?'

She glanced at her watch and blinked, surprised by the time.

"Tired?" he asked. "It's not much wonder. You've had a pretty full day with work, baking, making dinner. Thank you for that, by the way."

"It was a joint effort." She slipped the blueprints into the cardboard roll, then had second thoughts. "Should I leave them?" she asked.

"Sure. I wouldn't mind taking a second look." He took the roll from her and tucked it under one arm. "You seem to come to our rescue on a regular basis, Ashley."

"Actually, if you can take over as foreman on Harry's Place, I'll be the one who is rescued. I couldn't bear it if this project had to be abandoned because there was no one to manage it." She should have shut up, but the words came tumbling out in spite of herself. "I have a lot of dreams for that house. I intend to make it my home, but that's only the beginning. I'm going to make it into the place I've always longed for."

"I see." Jared smiled but she glimpsed uncertainty in those dark eyes.

Time to go home, Ashley.

"Thanks for rescuing me from boredom today. With Connie, Wade and Silver gone, the house is so quiet. But according to Connie's emails, they seem to be having a wonderful time in Brazil. And it's probably a lot cooler there than here."

"Yes. And Tucson will only get warmer as summer arrives." He kept studying her with those enigmatic dark eyes that gave away none of his feelings.

"I'll see what I can arrange for tomorrow and let you know. Good night." She turned to leave but his hand on her arm stopped her. She glanced at it, then him.

"Thank you, Ashley." Jared's voice fell softly in the night air. "Thanks for thinking of me for this opportunity. I appreciate it. If I could do it, it would completely change our situation."

"Mine, too. I hope it works out. For both our sakes." There was nothing more to say so Ashley smiled, waggled her fingers and left. But as she drove away, the memory of Jared's face when she'd spoken of praying stuck with her.

What could have happened that had desolated him so much he thought prayer couldn't help? The answer to that question bothered her all night long.

Inside the house Jared stored the tube of blueprints then walked to the window. He watched Ashley drive away, unable to sort through the puzzle that was Ashley Ross. A job. She couldn't know how desperately he wanted to accept, how close he was to broke. She offered him work and even offered to help with the twins. She just kept giving. How rare was that?

"Uncle Jared?" Emma crept down the stairs. Her hand curled into his.

"Yes?" He lifted her up and peered into her eyes. "What's wrong, kiddo? Bad dreams?"

"Kinda. I was thinking about Ashley. Why is she so sad?" she asked, wrapping one arm around his neck.

"What makes you think she's sad?" He snapped the lock on the front door then climbed the stairs with her in his arms.

"The way Ashley hugged me. Mom used to do that sometimes when she was sad." Emma pulled back to stare into his eyes. "Is Ashley going to go away, too?" Fear threaded through the words.

"No, sweetie. She's not going away." He could see Emma wasn't sure what to believe. "In fact, Ashley was telling me about a job. She said she might be able to come and see you guys more often if I took it. Would that be okay?"

"Yes." The little round face beamed with happiness. "When would she come, Uncle Jared?"

"Yeah, when?" Eric chimed in, also awake.

"You wouldn't mind staying with her some more?" Jared asked in surprise.

"With Ashley?" Eric frowned at him. "She's our friend."

"So when will she come, Uncle Jared?" Emma plunked herself on the bed and waited.

Clearly there would be no sleeping until this was resolved but Jared had no firm answers yet.

"I'm not sure. It's just something we're talking about. If I read you a short story do you think you can go to sleep?"

Both dark heads nodded. Jared opened the book about Camelot that they'd borrowed from the library and almost groaned at Emma's next words.

"You can talk to her when we go to church. Ashley said she'll be there. Okay, Uncle Jared?"

They wouldn't settle down until he promised. And it took forever for them to fall asleep.

But as he trod downstairs and inhaled the sweet aroma of freshly baked chocolate, Jared couldn't dislodge the image of Ashley laughing as she organized the ingredients. And later, that odd yearning that filled her face as she'd talked about the house she wanted to make into a home.

When she'd said it, he'd wanted to hug her and tell her everything would be all right.

That reaction alone was a very good reason to avoid the woman. She drew him like a magnet, even though he didn't want to be drawn. Fatherhood of the twins wasn't a part-time job and even if he wanted to get involved with someone, which he did not, Jared knew he couldn't take his focus off the kids.

He'd lost part of his heart, part of his very soul in Africa. It had taken him years in Australia to ease the pain enough to allow him to sleep through the night without seeing the faces of civil war casualties. Of Fran. As always, anger at her death festered beneath the anguish he kept locked inside.

No way would he allow himself to suffer such loss again. It was better to keep his distance, be friends with Ashley but allow nothing else.

No matter what his reactions to her.

"So is it a deal?" Ashley toyed with her soda on Monday afternoon, afraid to look up into Jared's face lest he say no. "Will you take over the project?"

"You're sure you can handle those long nursing shifts on the weekend and still watch the twins during the week while I'm at the site?" he asked, plopping a fry into ketchup and twirling it around. He lifted his head to check on the twins, who were in the kids' play section of the restaurant, burying themselves in multicolored balls.

"It's not every weekend," Ashley protested. "And besides, twelve-hour shifts mean I only have to work one long day to make up for three of the shorter ones I used to work. Plus they're day shifts so it's not like my sleep pattern is disrupted or anything. I'll be fine."

"Can I give you my answer tonight?" he said.

"Sure." Ashley frowned. "Is something wrong, Jared? You seem kind of—upset."

"I had a visitor this morning. Ms. Duncan stopped by." He frowned. "It wasn't the best of timing."

"Uh-oh." She studied his face. "What happened?"

"Nothing major. Just a lot of little things that she wants changed." He lifted his head to peer at her. "I am trying, but I can't do everything at once."

"I'm sure she knows that," Ashley reassured him, hating that he looked so down.

"She said she's trying to make sure I have every base covered so that when the time comes for the judge to decide, there won't be any sticking points." He raked a hand through his sandy-toned hair. "It's good of her, I know. And I sound like a whiner. It's just that sometimes that house swamps me. The moment you fix one thing, another pops up needing attention."

"You're not whining. What are friends for if not to talk to? And I hope that we're friends?" She smiled while wondering what Jared would think if he knew how often she thought about him and the twins.

"You've been a great friend to us, Ashley. And I appreciate it. Venting with you always seems to give me the courage to push on through the next hurdle." He pushed away his plate, leaned back and fixed her with an intense stare. "Who do you vent to?"

"Connie, mostly."

"But she's away." His brown eyes narrowed.

"I know. So I talk to Susannah. Or you. You're both good listeners." She glanced at her cold fries then abandoned them. "So is David. He's given me a lot of good advice."

"Yes, he's been very helpful in handling my petition with the court, too. David's one of the good guys."

"You and Wade are, too." She paused, bit her lip. "Jared, if you decide to take this job you should know something else." Ashley had been struggling with how to say the words. Now she decided to just say it and see what happened.

"Which is?" He frowned as if he expected the worst.

"I am in charge of this project. If you want to make changes to the plan, you consult me first. If there's a problem, you inform me. I am the go-to girl." She saw his irises flare but that didn't stop her. "Nothing happens that I don't approve. That's very important."

"You really think you can handle all that, and watch the twins, and do your nursing job?" Doubt creased his forehead into a series of furrows.

"That's the way it has to be," she said firmly. "Maybe that will change your mind about taking it on, and I would be very sorry about that. But it's best if you know the truth up front."

"Okay. Now I know." But that speculative glint didn't leave his dark brown eyes. "I'll think about everything and I'll let you know tonight."

"Great." Ashley rose, gathered her bag and smiled.

"I need to get going. I'm filling in for someone on a shift this afternoon."

"Have a good afternoon then."

"Thanks. Bye." She tried to wave at the twins but they were too busy jumping into the balls to pay her any attention so Ashley left.

She'd left enough time before work to stop by the site. She wandered around the grounds, changing and altering the structures in her mind until all she saw was the finished product, her dream come true.

If Jared took the job.

"This project is for You, Lord. Please help me get it done."

But her brain chirped a reminder as she focused on the small house at the rear. Not all for God. That house was going to be her home.

That would be the first task she'd give to Jared.

One day at Harry's Place and Jared was already butting heads with Ashley. He hoped that wasn't a portent of things to come.

"The bigger house must be done first," he insisted.

"If you recall, you agreed that this project is mine and you would follow my will," she snapped. "Why are you arguing this?"

"Because, as your foreman, it doesn't make sense." Jared yanked off his hard hat and tossed it into the back of his truck where the twins immediately argued over who could wear it. "It's a matter of timing and budget."

"What about the budget?" she demanded as if he'd just told her it was all gone.

"Ashley, the way we handle these renovations makes a difference. If we do the biggest building first then any material odds and ends we have left over can be used on the smaller building. It allows us to plan a little more tightly. That's just good sense."

"Oh." She glanced at the tired old house sitting on the back of the lot, her gaze wistful. "You're sure?"

"Yes. Besides, the bigger one will take longer, provided those inspections you had done are accurate." Since he'd found several unreported issues in the bigger building, Jared intended to go over the little house himself, after he got his crew working smoothly. Bringing a lot of new people together didn't always work right away. "So can we start demolishing what we need to on the big house so we won't waste more time?"

Ashley sighed but she did nod.

"Thank you." He glanced at the twins and grinned at their dirty faces. "You might want to get them out of here. It's not a safe playground."

"Yes," she murmured. "We were on the way to the zoo."

"We're going to see the giant anteater, Uncle Jared." Eric hopped off the truck. "Did you ever see a giant anteater?"

"Grandpa took me once." He ruffled the boy's hair and crouched down to look him in the eye. "Have a good time but listen to what Ashley says and obey, right?"

"We will. Come on, Ashley." Emma grabbed her hand and pulled.

Ashley went but it looked to Jared like she had to force herself to leave the grounds. She kept glancing back over one shoulder at the little house.

He recalled their conversation in which she'd told him her two confidants were Connie and Susannah. From what Jared had seen Ashley was popular at church. People came up and talked to her, she talked back. He'd never thought of her as a wallflower. So why didn't she have more than two close friends from the distant past to talk to?

"Hey, boss," one of his workers chided. "She's very pretty but we still have to get this work done." The other guys snickered.

"I'm down with that." Jared forced his attention off the tall redhead and onto his men.

"So where do we start on this old house?" they wanted to know.

"Up there. First floor. Let's get the bathrooms gutted. Then we'll take a better look at what we've got." But for the rest of the day Jared couldn't get the picture of Ashley out of his mind. Or the way she'd looked at that house.

As if it held all her hopes and dreams.

The knowledge that he could make or break those dreams made Jared very nervous.

Chapter Eight

It was hot and it was late. Ashley checked on the twins again. They were happily involved on the play set Jared had built in the backyard.

Speaking of Jared—where was he? It was well past his usual arrival time, well past dinner time even. What was he doing?

In the two weeks since he'd begun work on Harry's Place, Ashley had checked the site every day. Sometimes more often. She had to continually fight her misgivings and irritations at delays he insisted were normal. But every time she struggled to quash the feelings of distrust buried inside, relics of her past she longed to be rid of, they came surging back up.

She'd prayed over and over to be freed from this hovering sense of suspicion, of always expecting the worst. But each time Jared told her of some new issue with the project, she felt herself holding her breath, wondering when he'd tell her the budget wasn't enough, when he'd ask for more money. Those niggling uncertainties made Ashley expect the worst of him, and he'd done nothing to deserve that. He'd been honest about each step along the way. Jared was a man of integrity who didn't deserve her suspicions.

So why couldn't she trust him completely?

A truck revved then stopped.

Ashley glanced out of the window. Jared sat behind the wheel, his head tilted back as if he were too weary to move.

She started the coffee brewing, and then checked to see that his dinner had not dried out in the pan where it was warming. A moment later the door opened and he walked in. He was filthy.

"Hi." His slow grin slashed a white banner across his dusty face. "Sorry I'm so late. I had a little issue I had to fix before I could leave."

She itched to ask what issue, but he was so clearly worn out she held her tongue.

"No problem. Do you want to have a shower before you eat?" she asked instead.

"The twins?"

"In the backyard. They're fine." She waited, wondering why his tall, rangy stance leaning against the door frame always sped up her heart rate. "Go and shower. Take your time."

"Thanks." He smiled that weary smile again, pushed himself away from the door and clumped upstairs.

Ashley went out to talk to the kids.

"Uncle Jared is really tired tonight. He's been working so hard. Do you think I could give you your baths while he eats his dinner?"

Both children nodded.

"Only I'm having a shower, like Uncle Jared does. Because I'm a man." Eric thrust his chest out proudly.

"Yes, you are," Ashley agreed.

"Well, I'm a girl. And girls have bubble baths," Emma declared. "Don't they, Ashley?"

"Sometimes. And sometimes a shower is fine." Ashley smiled at them both. "You can each have whatever you like. How about ten more minutes of playing, then it's upstairs and into the shower. Or bath."

"Okay." They raced off, squealing with delight when a neighbor's cat hopped off the fence and into the yard. A chase ensued that left Ashley chuckling as she returned inside.

"They sound happy." Jared poured himself a cup of coffee and inhaled. "I don't know why I can never make coffee smell or taste like yours. I do exactly what you do."

"It's a gift," she teased. "Sit down before you fall down. Your dinner is ready."

"The kids already ate?" He sank onto a chair with a heavy sigh as he glanced at the clock. "Stupid question. They probably ate a couple of hours ago."

"Yes." Ashley set the meal before him, poured herself a glass of water and sat down. "You look beat."

"After today, I'll be ready for the weekend, that's for sure." He savored his food and repeatedly told her how tasty it was.

She told him about the zoo, how the hot afternoon had driven them inside, how they'd begun to remove the tattered wallpaper in the hallway. Ashley described the twins wallpapering their arms and legs, hoping some comic relief would help Jared relax. A moment later the twins burst through the door, chattering about the cat. Ashley waited a few minutes before shooing them upstairs.

"I'll bathe them while you eat," she said. "There's a

pie in the oven if you want some. Be warned, it's a long time since I baked a pie. I'm out of practice." Then she scurried away, half-embarrassed that she'd wanted to make something nice for his dinner.

She'd finished drying Emma's hair and had read a story by the time Jared came upstairs. He lounged on Eric's bed, legs stretched out with Eric curled under one arm and Emma under the other as he discussed their day. Ashley went downstairs to give them some time alone. She'd tidied up the kitchen, swept the floor and put together a fruit salad for morning when Jared reappeared.

"I made some tea, if you want some. I'm not sure you want to drink any more coffee now," she said.

"I don't think even a whole pot of coffee could keep me awake tonight." He sprawled on the family room sofa. "You don't have to rush away yet, do you? Sit down and relax for a bit. Tell me about your day."

So she sat and related more funny stories about the wallpaper adventures. But finally she had to ask the questions foremost in her mind.

"What happened today?"

"I knew you could hardly wait to ask me that." He smiled. "Nothing serious, just a whole lot of demolition that needed to be done if we're to keep on schedule. Including a bunch of rusted plumbing that had to be taken out so we can reframe."

"Are you on schedule?" She almost wished she hadn't asked when his eyes opened wide. "I'm just wondering."

"You're always wondering," he said, his voice very quiet. "You ask me every night. Ashley, we're doing the best we can. I know you want everything done and I'm doing my best to make it happen, but there are going to be times when we get behind." He made a face. "There might even be times when we get ahead. We do what we can do."

"It's just—hard for me to stay back and let you put it all together," she murmured.

"Why?" Jared leaned forward, elbows on his knees. "Are you expecting something bad to happen?"

"Yes," she wanted to yell. Instead she kept silent.

"I've worked on a lot of projects. This isn't the worst, you know." His reassuring smile sent her heart tripping over itself.

"Have some faith, is what you mean." She made her own face. "I am trying. It's not that I don't believe God intends to use this project. I know He will. It's—" She wasn't sure how to explain.

"Because you've made a lot of plans for that house." He had a speculative glint in his eyes.

"And for the big house," she said.

"But it's the little house that you're itching to move into," he guessed. "That's understandable, especially since you say you've never felt as if you've had a real home."

"Yes, it's partly that." Embarrassment kept her from continuing.

"And part what else?" Jared held her gaze with his darker one. "Talk to me, Ashley. You're entitled to your dreams just like everyone else."

She longed to share what had been building up inside ever since Connie had gone. Of course, Susannah was fun to talk to, but she was so busy with her baby, her husband, his sister and her studies. Susannah didn't have a lot of time to listen and even if she had, Ashley felt like she was whining when, truthfully, she had a lot to be thankful for.

"I'm not going to judge you, Ashley," Jared said quietly.

"I guess it's not just a house I'm craving," she admitted. "It's the feeling of being home, of knowing you are where you belong. I did have a home with the Martens when I was in foster care, but somehow I missed feeling a connection—like it was my home that I could leave and return to anytime and still feel the same. That's what I'm trying to create."

"You'll do it," he said, certainty in his voice.

Gratified but curious she asked, "What makes you think so?"

"Take a look around. Look at the changes you've made here. Everything has a place in this house. You've organized and structured this house so no one has to go chasing stuff down like we did before you were here." He smiled. "This has always been home for the twins, but it hasn't for me. I always felt like I was babysitting. Keeping the place going until Jessie and Jeff got back."

Ashley wasn't sure what to say. His sense of loss and grief had lessened, she knew that. But this was far more than she'd ever expected to hear.

"Of course I always knew they weren't coming back," Jared admitted. "But I think I sort of delayed making the changes I needed to make because I subconsciously felt I needed to get her approval, to make sure it was what she wanted."

"But Jared." Ashley frowned. "I'm quite sure Jessie wouldn't have cared about anything as long as her kids were loved and cared for."

"See, that's what I mean. You intrinsically know

that, but I had to get that through my thick head." He grinned, shrugged. "And what I was trying to say is that you waltzed in here and made this place home by changing things the first day you arrived. You didn't ask."

"Sorry." She blushed.

"No, don't be. You saw what needed to be done and you plunged in and did it. I needed that wake-up call." He glanced around, grimaced. "The only thing is that now I see the light, but I don't have time to fix it. Pun intended."

"You'll get to it." Ashley chuckled. "If I may quote you to yourself—we do what we can do."

"Yeah." He grinned. "Thanks for the pep talk."

"Back 'atcha." She rose and hunted for her purse. "I thought I'd take the kids over to the center tomorrow. Before she left, Connie told me about some changes and I'd like to see them."

"How are the twins doing in public now?" he asked, rising, too.

"They're getting better. They don't hang on to me as if I'll run away. But Emma especially keeps a close watch. They never wander too far. I figured that if we spent the odd day out, it might help them realize they don't need to fear being abandoned." Ashley stood in the doorway. "I want them to lose those feelings."

"You're a very nice woman, Ashley Ross." His hand touched her cheek. His fingers grazed her jawbone. "You don't give up and you don't give in. I like that. Thank you for taking such excellent care of my family."

"You're welcome." Her skin burned where he touched. She wanted to lean in closer, yet at the same time, she longed to jerk away and run until she'd regained control. "Oh, speaking of family, your dad wants you to call him about the Fourth of July."

"Ah, the old Hornby family Fourth of July celebration." He grinned and let his hand drop away. "I'll give him a call. Thanks."

"You're welcome." She turned to leave and then turned back. "Oh, and Jared?"

"Yes?"

He was so close she could have brushed his chin with her lips. Ashley struggled to remember what she'd been going to say.

"I, uh, haven't had any receipts from you for the project this week. I like to keep a running tally. Can you give me what you have tomorrow morning? I'll work on them over the weekend."

"While you're nursing? Ashley. Ashley." He shook his head. "You do so much worrying. Don't you trust anyone?"

"I have to keep tabs on things. So, can you?" She knew she was being stubborn but she had no intention of letting Harry's Place run out of control.

"It will have to be tomorrow night. I left them in a folder at the site." He smiled but there was a dimming to his brown eyes. "Everything is in order. Don't worry."

"I'm not worried."

But she was. She was always worried, always maintaining a barrier. Always afraid someone was going to breach it and see that instead of cool, controlled Ashley, there was a woman hiding inside who desperately wanted to feel safe.

Frustration lent an edge to his voice that Jared didn't bother to disguise. Ashley's repeated second-guessing of his decisions was severely testing his patience.

"Why did you reverse my orders to my men?" He glared at her. Irritation vied with admiration at the way the evening sun blazed on her long wavy hair. He swallowed and ordered his senses to get a grip. "I was hoping to move on to the second floor today, but now we'll have to backtrack because what you told them to do will have to be undone."

"Undone?" She frowned at him, her brows pulling together in a line of annoyance. "Why?"

"Because it's wrong. We need the electrician and the plumber to check everything before that wall goes up. Now I have to waste time undoing what shouldn't have been done in the first place." His irritation shriveled when her blue eyes lost their sheen.

"I was only trying to keep them busy," she murmured. "You weren't around and they were wasting time."

"How were they wasting time?" he demanded. He shook his head as she described his men's actions. "I asked them to do that. For a reason."

"But—"

"Ashley, did you or did you not hire me to do this job?" he demanded.

"Of course. But I'm in charge of this project and it's my business to keep everything progressing." She straightened, lifting her chin to glare at him. Queen Ashley.

"I want the same thing," he said quietly. "But your micromanaging is slowing things down and that gets worse when you countermand what I say."

"I never meant to do that," she said, blue eyes solemn.

"I know you didn't but the effects are the same."

He decided to be blunt. Maybe then she'd understand. "When you interfere, you challenge my authority with the men and cost us extra money. It has to stop, Ashley. We can't afford either the time or the money we're wasting if we're to finish on schedule."

"I'm sorry." She ducked her head.

"I know and I understand, but please, it has to stop." He pushed his forefinger under her chin and pressed up to get her to look at him. "You're wearing me out with these constant questions about what I'm doing. Don't you trust me to do this job? Are you having second thoughts about offering me the position of foreman?"

"Doubts? About you?" She frowned, but it took a moment before she shook her head. "No."

"Then let me do the job, okay?" Jared noted that Ashley hadn't said she trusted him but he didn't have time to puzzle that out now. "I promise I will tell you if a problem arises, or if we need to change something. But unless I do, what we really need is to focus on the job and get it done without interference."

"And the little house?" Her eyes never left his face, but she nibbled on her bottom lip as she watched him.

"We'll get there, Ashley," he promised. "We will get your dream home finished."

"Just not yet." She sighed. "Okay. I promise that I'll come to you with all my questions from now on. And I'll rein in my impatience."

"I know it's not easy. I know you want to get in there, but I don't want you to get in and then have to get out." Jared softened his voice because he knew how much having that home meant to her. "When you walk through that door, I want you to be able to say, 'I'm home' and stay there knowing that there isn't any more work that needs doing. I want you to come home. Okay?"

"Okay." Ashley's swirling blue gaze met his.

Jared could feel the magnetism in that look and fought to remain detached, but it was a losing battle. Ashley drew him with a power he hadn't expected. It was growing harder and harder to remember why he couldn't reach out and touch her cheek, hug her when disappointment overwhelmed her, wipe away the tears of frustration he knew she wept when no one watched.

"Did the kids eat yet?" he asked, deliberately switching subjects so he could get his mind off how good she looked in the pretty flowered sundress.

"No, they wanted to wait for you. It's so warm I didn't want to heat up the house for dinner. I thought we could grill." *We* could grill.

"I'll shower and be right down." Jared hurried upstairs like a chased rabbit thinking how easily she'd become part of their family. He liked the work at the site, liked the challenge of pushing ahead, of making something old and crumbling new and useful.

But mostly he liked walking in the door and seeing Ashley standing there, waiting for him with her pretty smile, good food and restful conversation. He liked it a lot. Too much. When the end of summer rolled around, he would miss her smiles, her teasing and her generosity.

Life was so much easier with someone to share it. His friends were great, of course. But they had their own lives. Ashley did, too, to a point. But a lot of her life revolved around this house and the twins, and like it or not, him.

Jared had to keep reminding himself not to get used

to her because it could never be permanent. Losing Fran had been gut-wrenching. His life had been ripped apart. People in that African village that he'd known and loved had disappeared just like his wife—as if they'd never been there. As if they didn't matter. That was the thing that ate at him. Why?

That question gnawed at his soul like cancer. Why hadn't God stopped it—the rebels? Why had He let it happen? Why hadn't Jared been able to find her in time?

"Jared? Are you about ready?" Ashley's voice rippled up the stairs, jerking him out of his memories. "The kids are starving."

"Coming." He tucked in his shirt and took the stairs two at a time. "Hey, guys. How was your day?"

They followed him out on the deck, chattering like magpies as he grilled the chicken Ashley had prepared.

"Did you know most hummingbirds go to Mexico for the winter, Uncle Jared?" Emma was full of facts and figures and she listed them all, interspersing them with "did you know."

Jared listened and nodded, but he also noticed that they'd left the yard a mess.

"How about if you put away your toys before dinner?" he said. "I have to cut that grass tonight."

"I'm too tired." Emma stayed where she was. Of course, Eric followed. "Ashley can do it."

"Sure I will." Ashley moved from the doorway.

"No. Ashley's tired, too. So am I," Jared told the child. "But I still have to cut the grass. They're your and Eric's toys, so you go and put them away."

"I don't want to." Emma's brown eyes waited for a reaction.

"Me, too," Eric said.

It was the first time one of them hadn't rushed to do his bidding. Jared had a hunch this was a test to his attempt at fatherhood. They were challenging his authority. He didn't feel like battling, not tonight. But he couldn't let this go.

At least Ashley was smiling encouragingly at him.

"You may not want to, but you are going to pick up your toys, children. We're not going to eat dinner until you do."

"But I'm starving." Eric glanced at Emma who gave him a glower. "Couldn't we pick them up after dinner, Uncle Jared?"

"No. I told you, I want to cut the grass tonight. Go on now."

Emma didn't move and when Eric tried to rise she grabbed his arm.

"You're not my daddy," she said to Jared, her cheeks red with anger.

"No, I'm not." Jared switched off the grill, lifted the meat and placed it on a plate. He handed that to Ashley, then hunkered down in front of the little girl, tempted to weaken when he saw the distress on her face. "But I'm the one your dad and mom told to take care of you two."

"So?" She glared at him, obviously in a bad mood.

"So your parents wanted us to be a family. We live together. We also have to work together and help each other." Jared glanced at Ashley, who'd returned from the kitchen. She gave him a cheering nod. "In families we all pull together because we love each other."

"I love you, Uncle Jared." Eric threw his arms around his neck and hugged tightly. "I'll pick up my stuff." He scooted off the bench and across the yard.

Emma did not follow.

"What's wrong, Em?" Jared asked quietly.

"Ashley's really nice and I like her lots," the little girl said, her eyes tearing. "But I want my mommy and daddy to come home. I'm tired of this."

"Oh, honey." He gathered her weeping body into his arms, brushing a kiss on the top of her head. "I miss them, too, but they can't come back. I told you, remember? They're with God."

"God doesn't need my mom and dad," she said, eyes flashing. "He has lots of other people. I need Mommy and Daddy to live with me."

Emma's words were so close to Jared's own thoughts about Fran and God's part in her death that they resounded to his very heart. He wasn't sure exactly how to handle this; he only knew he had to comfort her. So Jared closed his eyes and held her close.

"Did you ever want something really, *really* bad, Uncle Jared? Did you ever pray and pray for God to make it better, and He didn't?" Emma whispered in his ear.

"Yes, I've done that." How many times he'd done that.

"I did, too. I've been praying and praying, just like Mommy said I should. But God doesn't make it better." She drew back, her mouth turned down in a frown. "I don't like God, Uncle Jared."

He sat stunned by her words, which so exactly echoed his own thoughts that he couldn't think of anything that would soothe her hurting heart.

"God's supposed to be nice. And good. So why does He take mommies and daddies away, huh?" Emma sat waiting for his response.

But Jared didn't have any. If he had, he could have silenced his own questions ages ago.

"Can I say something, Emma?" Ashley knelt down beside them after the little girl nodded. "God is good. In fact, the Bible says He is love. Everything He does is for our good. But sometimes we don't understand why God does things. Sometimes we can't understand because we don't know the other things that are going on in the world."

"But God does, right, Ashley?" Eric had come to join them, his hand sliding into Ashley's with unspoken confidence.

"Yes. God always does what's right," Ashley said, her voice tender. "Think about you two and Uncle Jared," she said with a smile at him. "Sometimes you don't know why he says you have to go to bed early, or pick up the toys, or not watch something on television. But Uncle Jared knows why he says it and he does it for your good. So you won't get hurt or your nice toys won't get ruined or you won't have nightmares from watching bad things. Your uncle is a very smart man."

"Yep." Eric grinned.

"Well, God is very smart, too. We can't always understand why He does some things, but because we know God loves us, we have to believe that what He does is the very best for us." Ashley brushed the bangs off Emma's forehead. "Honey, even though God knew how much you and Eric would want your mom and dad, God had to do something else. And when you hurt, He hurts. But if you pray, He can make it better."

Relief filled Jared as Ashley continued soothing the twins and answering their questions. Thank goodness Emma had asked her question when Ashley was here to bail him out. Jared knew he couldn't have answered in a way that soothed her, as Ashley was now doing. That knowledge brought him a wave of shame.

How could he let this distance between himself and God continue? He knew the truth, had told it to others a hundred times. But he never embraced it himself. The time had come. Either Jared had to accept that God was in control and that what He did was the ultimate best for him, for Fran and for the village, or he had to turn his back on everything he believed. It was high time he chose which side of the fence he was going to stand on. Trust wasn't going to get any easier, no matter how much anger he clung to.

"Do you think you can pick up your toys now, Emma?" Ashley asked.

The little girl frowned. Then she turned her head to study Jared. He saw that the questions were still there, that her little heart still yearned for her mommy. Her trust would take time to build—as would his.

"Come on, Em," Eric said. "I'll help you."

"No." She stood and moved out of Jared's embrace. "I can do it myself. I'm a big girl and this is my family." As she stored them she asked, "Can we eat now?"

"Yes." Jared rose. "As soon as you're finished."

"Good job," Ashley murmured as she walked with him into the house. "That was a hard one. You were great with her."

"How can you say that? I didn't have any answers for her. I'm only glad you were there to say the right thing," he said.

"Jared." She rested a hand on his arm. "It's not a contest. There is no 'right' way to answer and anyway I don't have any more answers than you. Besides, I don't think parenting is a matter of having the right answers. I think it's more like helping the child discover the answers she needs and you did. You're doing that."

"Thanks," he said, humbled by her words. "I'm trying. Sometimes I get overwhelmed."

Ashley grinned.

"Welcome to the human race."

How did one woman get so smart? And why did he want to lay his head on her shoulder and find the same comfort Emma had?

Didn't matter why because it wasn't going to happen.

Jared would work out his faith relationship. Somehow.

But he would not let his heart get involved again.

No way.

Chapter Nine

"I've never had a Fourth of July like this," Ashley muttered. Her fingers trembled as she clutched the fishing rod Jared had planted in her hands. "What am I supposed to do if something bites?"

"Reel it in." He laughed at her look of horror. "It's simple."

"Like that strawberry eating contest at the restaurant where we had breakfast was simple?" She sighed. "I've never eaten so many strawberries at one time."

"A bird could have eaten more," he said in disgust. "I entered you because you said you loved them. I was hoping you'd win first place and get that pie. Strawberry pie is my favorite."

"I don't care if I don't see another strawberry for years." She yawned. Though they'd come back to the same picnic site on Mount Lemon, the morning had started far too early for Ashley.

"Sore loser," he grumbled.

"Tired loser. Is there a reason we had to be up here at the crack of dawn?" She yawned and eased back against a rock.

"The crack of dawn?" He hooted with laughter.

"Uncle Jared," Eric chided, "you're scaring the fish."

"Sorry." Chastened, Jared motioned to the water. "We had to get here, Ashley, because the fish are more active when the water's cooler. As soon as it heats up, they go to the bottom. Of course, you need to actually have your line in the water to snag a fish." His hand closed over Ashley's, correcting her grip.

The only thing that snagged was Ashley's breath as Jared leaned over her, his spicy aftershave tickling her nose.

"Okay?" he asked, his grin more relaxed than she'd seen in days.

"Yes. Thank you." To her relief, he moved away to help the twins with their rods. So far Eric had caught two fish and Emma one. Ashley was good with that—as long as they stayed away from her line. To make sure, she wound the reel hard, then relaxed. No fish could swim that fast.

No sooner had the thought left her than her rod jerked in her hands. She almost let go of the thing, but managed to hang on as she yelled for help.

"Jared! There's, uh, something wrong."

"No, there isn't. You caught a fish. Now bring him in." He stood beside her, a huge smile on his face.

"How do I do that?" she asked through gritted teeth.

"Don't let go!" he cautioned. "Just wind slowly. Lead him in. I'll get the net."

"How do you know it's a he?" Ashley asked, trying to do as Jared had said. But the fish had other ideas and every time she thought he was close, the line squealed and fed out. "Why don't you just go away, you old fish?" she muttered to herself.

"Don't you want to catch a fish, Ashley?" Eric looked stunned by the thought that anyone would want to avoid her predicament.

"She loves fishing, don't you, Ashley?" Jared teased, watching in amusement as she drew in a little line and then lost twice that much as the fish fled again. "I think you've got a big one there."

"Couldn't you catch it?" she asked, her body rigid with the stress of fishing.

"You can do it." He hunched down beside her. "Fishing takes patience. Just like house building. Think of the fish as me. You have to keep wearing him down a little at a time."

"You are just so funny," she said sweetly. "I'm tempted to lay down this rod and leave."

"No!" The twins and Jared were unanimous in their protest. All three looked horrified.

"The things I do." Ashley heaved a heavy sigh and began winding again.

"Slowly, slowly. Steer him this way. Okay—ah!" Jared reached out with the net, but the fish took off again.

After three more tries, Ashley felt nothing but relief when the animal finally escaped for good.

"He was a big one, too." Jared set the net down, his mournful expression echoing the disappointment of the twins.

"Well, I didn't catch him, but there's no reason you can't." She held out her rod. "I'm finished, anyway."

"I would, but I promised Dad we'd meet him and Mom at the house for lunch. The Hornby Fourth of July picnic will take place as usual." He directed the twins to store their rods in the truck and began packing his own tackle box.

"Okay. Well, you can drop me at Connie's on your way back." She rose, rubbed her tired back and sipped the last of her water. "I've got some—"

"Oh, no. You're going to attend our picnic. It's imperative. All our games take six people. Besides, I want you to meet my mom." Jared grinned as the twins added their support. Before long, they were all in Jared's truck heading down the mountain.

"What exactly goes on at this picnic?" she asked, but the others only laughed.

"You'll see."

And she did. Ashley saw how much Jared adored his mother, how he hovered over her as she pushed her walker slowly and carefully to the patio. She saw how he and his father kept checking to be sure Susan Hornby was comfortable. She also saw the shared glances of love between father and son, and the smile that spread across the grandmother's face as the twins tried to outdo each other on the play set.

"You're very fortunate," Ashley murmured when Jared and his father left to get lunch from a nearby deli. "You have a wonderful family."

"Yes, I do." Mrs. Hornby's smile reached her dark brown eyes.

So that's where Jared got his eye color from.

"My family is a precious gift from God that continually sustains me. I try to thank Him every day that He's blessed me so richly. Especially since Jared's come back. He had such a terrible time in Africa. He lost so much. For a time I thought he'd never come home."

What happened? Ashley wanted to ask.

"It's good to see him laugh again. To enjoy life as he used to." Susan's hand patted hers. "I think much of that is due to you, my dear. Thank you for helping him with the children and for giving him that job. I think he's no longer so overwhelmed by life."

"He's very good at building. And I love the twins. They're very precious."

"They talk about you all the time. I think you'll make a great mother for your own children one day," Susan said quietly.

Ashley let that go because it was too nice a day to ruin with discussions of why she would never have her own children. Besides, Jared and his father returned with enough food to feed an army. But as she watched the family interact, the same old longings rose up inside, the same old cry raised silently to heaven.

Why couldn't I have had a family like this, God?

After lunch Susan Hornby needed to return to her care home to rest. She embraced the children and held each for a few moments, whispering something in their ears that made them giggle. Then she hugged Jared and teased him about the amount of chicken he'd eaten. She also embraced Ashley.

"It's been so nice to finally meet the woman my family can't stop talking about," she said.

"The same for me. I hope we can talk again soon." Ashley saw the quick glance Susan gave her son before she nodded.

"We will. I'm sure of it," Susan said.

After the couple left, Jared loaded the dishes into the dishwasher. He grinned at Ashley's surprise.

"I finally got it working," he said, his voice full of satisfaction.

"Good for you." Surprised by the pride she felt for him, Ashley busied herself cleaning up the twins while she reminded her subconscious that she had no business feeling proud of Jared Hornby.

"Okay, everything is shipshape here, sort of," he said when they reappeared on the patio. "Now grab your stuff and let's go see what the town is doing today."

"The town? Do they have special events planned?" Ashley asked, wondering if she was properly dressed to go anywhere. She'd dressed for fishing.

"Tons of them. We'll head out to watch the water fight between fire departments first," he said, helping her into his truck.

"We went there last year, Uncle Jared. Daddy got sprayed." Eric giggled. "I hope we get sprayed this year. It's hot today."

"They often spray some of the crowd." Jared leaned over from his seat, his words meant for Ashley's ears only. "I hope that won't ruin it for you."

"What's to ruin? These shorts can take it." She shifted when his gaze lingered on her legs. "What else?"

"Then we'll visit one of the hotels. They always sponsor stuff for kids like face painting, crafts and watermelon eating contests." He chuckled at the twins' yahoos.

"No more strawberries," Ashley told him firmly.

"No," he agreed with a grin. "But there is a cupcake walk and a splat attack. And a rubber ducky derby. That should keep us busy until dinnertime."

"I wonder if I'm looking forward to a splat attack," she mused.

"You're not one of those women who is always worried about her appearance, are you?" Jared asked as he pulled into a parking lot that was teeming with people. "Because you shouldn't be. You always look fantastic."

"Well, thank you." The thought of that strawberry contest with juice spraying all over made her grimace. How fantastic had she looked then?

"C'mon. Everybody out," he ordered, holding her door open.

Ashley was too conscious of his big hand grasping hers as she stepped down. His touch unnerved her and she stumbled, bumping into him.

"I didn't know you were so eager to see the water fights," he teased, bracing her until her balance returned.

"It's the lure of water," she shot back. "Though I like swimming better, especially when it's this hot."

"Did you follow my directions and bring your suit?" He smiled when she patted her backpack. "Good because they have a waterslide, a lazy river—a whole ton of stuff."

"Great." She couldn't look away from him, couldn't help the tiny shiver of anticipation that bubbled through her blood at the prospect of spending the whole afternoon with him.

"Can we go now?" Emma demanded.

Ashley blinked back to awareness and flushed when she caught Jared watching her. She got hold of herself. She was going to enjoy herself and forget about all these weird conflicting emotions racing through her.

And she did. She enjoyed the three-legged race she and Jared lost. She enjoyed the face-painting contest in which she painted his face in stars and stripes. She especially enjoyed the poolside oasis where they could cool off.

"I can't believe we're eating again," she said as they waited in line for the barbecue buffet. "I'll have to do laps at Connie's for the next month to work all this off."

"We have a table for your family now, sir," the waiter said and led them to a place overlooking the pools.

Your family.

Ashley sat down, her breath suspended as she glanced at Jared. He'd noticed the mistake, too.

And apparently decided to ignore it as he told them to leave their backpacks and follow him to the buffet.

Ashley helped Emma while Jared focused on Eric. As they worked their way down the food line, she peeked at him and found his gaze on hers.

"What?" She lifted one hand to touch her hair, which she'd braided into plaits before swimming. "Am I a mess?"

"You look great," he said quietly.

It wasn't so much the words, it was the way he said them with such intensity that shook Ashley. She smiled, said thank you and got back to helping Emma, but as they ate their meal and drove back to his house, she couldn't erase the memory of that brooding look.

Or what it meant.

As she was tucking in the sleepy twins while Jared threw in a load of laundry, Ashley noticed that the kites the twins had purchased with their allowances were still in their packages. She remembered their excitement and Jared's promise to take them to the park to fly the kites.

"I thought you were going to try those out last evening," she said.

"Uncle Jared had to work. Again. Grandpa came over but he doesn't know how to fly kites." Eric's face turned down in a frown. "Uncle Jared always has to work."

"Oh." She didn't ask more because Jared arrived. But she did stand in the doorway, watching as he read the twins a story and puzzling over why he'd had to work late. And when they returned downstairs she decided to ask him about it.

"You don't have to go yet, do you?" he said, motioning to the back patio. "We have a pretty good view of the fireworks from here. Besides, you deserve to sit and relax after today."

"It was fun. Thank you for including me."

"Thank you for coming." There it was again, that speculative look that made her nervous.

Ashley sat in the chair he offered and stared into the darkening sky while he brewed some tea and brought out two mugs.

"Here you go."

She accepted the cup, sniffed and smiled. "Mmm, mint, my favorite."

"Mine, too." He sat next to her, his shoulder brushing hers as he shifted to get comfortable. "It's a beautiful evening."

"It was a great day, too. I think the twins wore themselves out having fun." She searched for a way to ask about the late night.

"Yeah, too bad they couldn't stay awake long enough for the fireworks." He leaned his head back and closed his eyes.

"Tired?"

"Yeah." He straightened, smiled at her. "Guess I'm out of shape for this parenting business."

"Or maybe you're working too many hours," she said softly.

"What do you mean?" Jared frowned.

"The twins said you went back to work last night, that your father stayed with them." She waited for his nod. "Was anything wrong?"

She waited a long time before he answered.

"A couple of issues from the afternoon needed correcting. I wanted to get things back up to speed before we start again on Monday."

"Issues?" She knew she wasn't going to like his answer, but she had to hear it. "What issues had to be 'corrected'?"

"Why are you asking, Ashley?" he said, his eyes narrowed.

"It was me, wasn't it? I mean it was my fault. Because I changed the order. Again." Her face burned with shame as she saw the truth in his eyes. "I'm really sorry, Jared."

"It's fine. I dealt with it." He shrugged as if it didn't matter.

But it did. He'd had to give up time with the twins, time he needed to strengthen their family bond, because she thought she knew better, because she obsessed, because she didn't trust him.

"You shouldn't have to have dealt with it," she said, furious with herself as she clearly saw the havoc her interference created for him. "I apologize. And I'm telling you it won't happen again. If I have a question, I will talk to you first."

Jared smiled, but he didn't believe her and she knew it.

"I'm telling you the truth," she said, desperate to make him see her commitment.

"You're actually going to trust me in the day-to-day running of the place?" He smiled, shook his head.

"Don't promise what you can't deliver, Ashley. I know what the project means to you. I understand why you need to make sure every detail is covered—even though I've already covered it," he added with a grin.

"I can deliver," she insisted. "And to prove it, I will no longer be checking out the site on a daily basis. If you need me to deal with something, tell me. Otherwise I'll only go there once a week."

"If you want. Either way, I'll make it work."

And that shamed Ashley even more. Jared would make it work. Jared with the crumbling house that needed repair, the two kids who needed him to gain permanent custody, a sick mother and a father—none of whom saw him much now, thanks to her.

"I'm serious. I won't be there unless you ask. I'll be too busy anyway." She made up her mind the instant she said it.

"You'll be too busy?" He frowned. "What have you taken on now?"

"When I started at the hospital, I was asked to work in pediatric oncology," she told him, embarrassed but determined not to hide anymore. "It's a tough ward. Hurting kids really tug at your heartstrings."

"I can imagine." He studied her face. "You turned it down?"

"Yes."

"Why?" he asked.

"I didn't want to let myself care," she admitted honestly. "I didn't trust myself to keep my emotions out of my work, though after nursing so long I should certainly know better."

"I don't think it's in your nature not to care, Ashley." Jared wrapped one arm around her shoulder and squeezed. "You care too much about people to forget about the job when you walk out the door. That's what everyone loves about you."

"Maybe." She longed to snuggle into that arm, to shift closer and let herself relax against him. Instead, Ashley settled for relaxing the stiff front she usually kept in place and letting her heart speak. "But caring comes with a price, Jared. And sometimes the price is very high."

"Are you talking about your former fiancé?" he asked, squeezing her upper arm before he drew away.

"Not really." Ashley missed that connection but she continued speaking anyway. "Or rather, not just about him. You already know I have trouble trusting people. I've been disappointed too many times to blindly trust anymore. I guess that's why I'm so obsessive about the project. Or I was. I'm stopping that now."

"Uh-huh." He grinned. "But why did you mention the oncology ward?"

"Because I'm going to ask for a transfer. They're terribly short staffed. I could ask for my same hours and probably get them, which will still allow me to care for the twins."

"And you're going to do that because—?"

"Because I need to stop being afraid. I need to stretch myself and start trusting people more. If life bangs me up a little, fine." She inhaled and twisted to look straight at him. "I need to be where God can best use me, Jared. If that's in oncology, so be it. I have to trust God more fully and put my actions where my mouth is, believe He will see me through whatever comes along. I have to stop being afraid."

He was quiet for a long time. Ashley didn't know

what else to say so she simply sat there, watching the night sky appear. A slight breeze rustled through the yard, cooling her so that she shivered. Without a word, Jared got up and went inside the house. He returned with a crocheted afghan, which he spread over both of them after he'd pulled his chair nearer hers.

"Better?"

"Yes, thanks." She smiled at him, wondering why he looked so serious as he returned to his chair. "What are you thinking about?"

"I haven't been able to trust God for a very long time." His voice came out hard. He kept his gaze averted as he spoke. "I'm not sure I'll ever be able to."

"Why not?" She had a hunch he didn't want to tell her, but that he needed to, needed to talk to someone. So Ashley sat silent and waited, praying silently for this hurting man.

"I was a missionary. I constantly told people over and over that they should trust God with everything. I preached it almost every day." He voice cracked a little and he paused. "I said it so many times it became a habit. 'Trust God and He will see you through,' I'd tell people. 'Trust God and you won't be sorry.' Well, I was sorry."

The intense pain in his words reached out and grabbed Ashley's heart in a vise. She ached to comfort him, but something told her to let him spill out the festering anger and hurt. So she waited.

"I trusted God with the most precious thing in my life and He did nothing. He let her die even though she'd given up everything to serve Him." Jared turned to look at her, his brown eyes glassy with anger. "She was my wife. We were going to have a baby. She was so excited about it."

"What happened?" Ashley whispered, steeling herself.

"I was away from the village. Off at another place, telling people to trust God with everything." His lip curled. "Bolstering their faith in God and His love for them."

She reached out and clasped his hand in hers, trying to infuse courage into him. Jared drew in a ragged breath.

"While I was away, insurgents intent on inciting civil war went through the village. They shot everyone. Men, women, children." His voice dropped to an undertone. "All of them mowed down as if they were no more than dust. Fran was shot in the back, turned away from them, holding two babies, trying to keep them safe. She died saving their lives. They were the only two that lived."

It was too much. Ashley wrapped her arms around him, trying to ease his burden of pain.

"I'm sorry," she whispered. "I'm so sorry."

He didn't say anything, but his arms wove around her waist and his forehead leaned against hers. Ashley could feel the heat of his breath brush her neck.

"He could have saved her," Jared said, his voice hoarse. "God could have stopped it and He didn't. How could He do that? How can I trust Him again?"

"Who else can you trust?" Ashley asked. She drew back, not just to see his face when she spoke, but to create some distance between them. "The thing is, Jared, God is love. Always. Forever. What He does is for our best. I don't know why Fran died. I don't know God's plan and I'm not sure you'll ever learn that."

"You're going to say God's ways aren't our ways," he said, anger feathering his voice.

"I wasn't," she said with a smile. "But it's true. They aren't. We can't understand everything that happens in the world because we're not God. All we can do is hang on to His promises, trust in His love for us and move on believing that there is a purpose, because God loves us."

Jared was silent for a long time. Then the first crack of fireworks lit the sky and he drew away, turning his head to watch them. Ashley couldn't see his face clearly, but she could feel his tension. In the bursts of light from the explosions she took in the rigid line of his shoulders and the clench of his jaw and knew he was fighting a spiritual battle.

So Ashley prayed for him to feel God's love more strongly than he ever had.

Finally the world was silent again, the last golden burst flickering into nothingness. She could feel Jared staring at her and knew he wanted to be alone, to work through his pain and anger.

"I better go." She rose, folded the afghan and handed it to him. "It was a great day. Thank you."

"I should be thanking you," Jared said as he stood. "I'm sorry I dumped my angst all over you—"

"Jared." Ashley placed a finger across his lips. "Don't ever apologize for being honest. It's the one thing I value more than any other." Her fingers burned at the contact with him so she let her hand drop. "I think God does, too. Talk to Him. Ask Him for help. Let His love heal you."

"I don't think I can forget that easily." Bitterness edged his hard voice.

"I don't imagine you'll ever forget Fran," she whispered. "Why should you? But you can't go on with this anger and hurt built up inside. You can't go on hating God."

"No." He leaned down, touched his lips to hers in a kiss so swift she had little time to react. "Thank you, Ashley. For everything."

"Good night." She hurried out of the yard and into her car. On the way home, her fingers touched her lips, trying to recapture the wonder of being kissed by Jared.

And then, in an instant, she traveled back in time to the moment Peter had confessed he only pretended to love her. The devastation of that realization had knocked her world off-kilter and she'd taken a long time to get her bearings again.

Ashley couldn't, wouldn't allow that to happen again.

Not that she had to worry.

Jared Hornby was still in love with his wife.

Chapter Ten

"You've done an amazing job," Ms. Duncan said from her position in the doorway. "I know there's a ways to go, but you have made progress. I'm looking forward to my next visit."

"Thank you very much." Jared stood in the doorway and watched her leave, the weight on his shoulders suddenly lighter by half.

"So that was good." David said.

"Very good." Jared closed the door, grabbed the pitcher of iced tea from the fridge and ordered David to bring the glasses. "Let's sit on the deck and talk."

Finally, finally he was going to unload on his friend. He hoped David had some good advice.

"Where are the twins?" David asked.

"Ashley's trying to get them to relax around other people so she's got them in Vacation Bible School this week. It seems to be helping. They're not so clingy anymore." He poured the tea, handed one to David and then sat down. "I called you because I wanted to talk to you about something."

"Shoot."

Jared told him about Africa, about Fran, about the murders. Finally he admitted his anger against God.

"You never told Wade or me this before," David scolded him. "Why not?"

"I couldn't talk about it, Dave. Not to anybody. Until Ashley the other night." He raked one hand through his hair. "She was right, though. I need to get past this, work it out somehow. My faith has always been part of who I am. I can't simply abandon that."

"A crisis of faith is often when we really discover what we think about God," David said as he leaned back in his chair. "If we let it, it can push us into a deeper relationship where we learn more about the nature of God."

"You went through this with Darla's accident?"

"Yes." David nodded. "The injury from that accident damaged her brain so badly, she was left permanently childlike. I couldn't understand why He'd let a beautiful young woman be broken into a child who will never realize her full potential. And yet, it was because of Darla that I met Susannah."

"So you think that was God's reason for Darla's accident?" Jared frowned.

"No. God could have found any number of ways for us to get together. And I never said God caused the accident. That's not what I meant." He smiled. "What I'm trying to say is that I didn't understand then and still don't today. Not any more than Wade understands why his first wife, Bella, left him and Silver behind for another man. But the Bible says God will make things work together for good if we follow Him. Somehow He will bring good from bad because God is love. That's all I know. That's what I trust in."

They sat together in silence, each busy with his thoughts. Eventually David leaned forward.

"Jared, what are your feelings for Ashley? You can tell me it's none of my business if you want."

"It isn't, but—" Jared tilted his head back to let the evening breeze brush his face. "I like her, Dave. I like her a lot. She's funny and pushy and forthright and, at the same time, a bit secretive. She finds it hard to trust me, but we're working things out."

"You're talking business and I meant personally." David scratched his chin. "You don't mind working for a multimillionaire?"

"Who's that?" Jared didn't get it. "Oh, you mean the project funder."

"Ashley. Yeah." David gave him an odd look. "You don't mind working for her?"

"Wait a minute. Are you telling me Ashley Ross has money?" He couldn't get that through his brain.

"You didn't know?" David bit his lip. "I shouldn't have said anything. She's a client and I don't discuss my clients. Ever."

"Too late. So Ashley is rich?" Jared couldn't comprehend it.

"Very. She was willed it by a guy she looked after. He had cancer." David picked up one of the twin's toys and fiddled with it.

"So that's why she finds it hard to work oncology." Jared fought to make sense of it.

"I guess I can tell you what is common knowledge. If you did a search on her on the internet, you'd find out this guy got her started in philanthropic work. He had her develop ideas for several benevolent projects while he was alive. When he died his money went to Ashley." David shrugged. "That's it in a nutshell."

"So she's funding the project—Harry's Place—herself?" Jared asked.

"Yes. Harry Bent. That was the name of her benefactor. She intends Harry's Place to be a tribute to him." David frowned. "You really didn't know?"

"No clue." Shame suffused him as he thought of Ashley cleaning his house, making him meals, watching the twins. "She could have hired anyone to come here but she stayed and did it herself. Why?"

"Because she loves the twins. Susannah told me Ashley always talked about having a family. Always." David sighed. "When she got engaged Ashley told Susannah she figured she'd finally have the family she's always hankered for. Until she found out the guy was after her money."

"Ah." Jared nodded. Several things became clear. Ashley never talked about her money—because she thought he'd try to get some of it, con her? He tried to remember what she'd said about her fiancé but drew a blank.

"Ashley was badly hurt by this guy. She had so many dreams and they all came crashing down. And that was after she'd had to deal with friends and coworkers turning on her because she wouldn't hand her money over to them." His friend shook his head. "Ashley's heart is so tender. She wants to help everyone. At first she believed their hard-luck stories and they took advantage of her, used her to scam thousands. It left her reeling. That's where I came in."

"What do you mean 'you came in'?" Jared felt like he didn't know Ashley at all.

"I deal with all the money requests now. They all go through me. I shield her from the money-grubbers. Ashley lives on her salary and uses her inheritance to fund projects she believes Harry would have approved of." David shook his head, his smile wide. "She says the money isn't hers, that it's a legacy to make other people's lives better. She's quite a lady."

Jared had a thousand questions he wanted answered about this amazing woman, but he had to swallow them because the twins were back, with Ashley.

"Hi, Uncle David. Did you come to help us eat our ice cream?" Eric asked, holding a large white tub. "We got lots."

"Yep, that's why I'm here. I sure will have some."

"He'll have more than some, trust me." Jared looked at Ashley, heart thumping as he took in her flushed cheeks. "Everything go okay at Bible school?"

"Perfect." She smiled at him.

Jared's brain fogged over. He somehow couldn't see her as an heiress. All he saw was a woman in jeans with a great big heart who kept giving.

"Just in case bubble gum isn't your favorite ice cream flavor, I bought some chocolate, too." Ashley beckoned the twins. "Come on, you two. Let's go dish it up."

She and the twins disappeared into the house. Jared noted David was watching him with a tiny frown pleating his forehead.

"What?"

"Be careful," David murmured. "She's vulnerable and she's got a lot emotionally invested in this project."

"Believe me, I know. She talks nonstop about all the things she's going to do with her house." Jared sighed.

"I just hope reality lives up to her dreams. And that I can get everything done in time."

"You have some doubts?" David stared at him. "But I thought everything was going well."

"It is," he agreed. "But there are always delays in construction."

"I heard that." Ashley appeared. She handed a huge dish of ice cream to David and then held one out for Jared, her smile dimpling her cheeks. "He means I kept butting in and slowing him down. Most of the delays were my fault, I admit. But not recently," she said, one eyebrow arched as she winked at him.

"No, not recently." Jared gulped, took his ice cream and concentrated on spooning some of it into his mouth. Maybe that would cool off his runaway reaction to her. "But we're still not where I'd like. Aren't you having any ice cream?"

"No. Iced tea is all I want." She helped the twins sit at the picnic table. "How's Susannah doing with school, David?"

"Driving us all batty with her worry," he said cheerfully. "But so far she's aced every exam. One more and she's finished. Next year I'm putting the kibosh on summer school. We need a break."

"Actually, Susannah sounds a lot like you in college," Jared teased.

"I was never that obsessive."

"Ha!" Jared laughed at his friend's pretend outrage. "You were worse."

"Go ahead, insult me, but I'm going home." David adopted a wounded face. "Thanks for the ice cream, Ashley. It was great."

"You don't have to rush away," she told him. "I'll

make Jared behave. I'll threaten to visit the site every day."

"No, not that. Stay, stay," Jared begged, his hand clutched against his heart. Something about Ashley made him want to laugh, to relax and enjoy life. "Please?"

"Can't. It's my turn to bathe baby Grace." David's face shone with love. "I'm not giving that up for you, buddy, no matter how much you beg." He waggled a hand and disappeared.

"You two need to get to bed, too," Jared said to the twins, who had finished their ice cream and were visibly drooping. He overrode their protests, waited for them to say good-night to Ashley then ushered them upstairs. He hurried them through the shower and into bed with no shame because he wanted, needed to get downstairs to talk to Ashley. "Did you have fun tonight?"

"It's awesome there," Emma told him, brown eyes huge in her small face. "They have puppets and everything. Aisha and me love puppets."

"Who's Aisha?" Jared asked as he smoothed the duvet over her.

"She's Aiden's sister. They're twins just like us." Eric held his arms up for a hug. "They're our friends."

So they'd made friends. Love surged up for these two precious ones who were gradually finding their way back from their sorrow.

"I love you guys," he said as he kissed them good-night.

"Me, too," Eric chirped.

"Me, three," Emma added.

"Have a good sleep." He switched on the night-light.

"We hafta," Emma said. "'Cause you know what happens tomorrow?"

"No. What?" He stood in the doorway, partly listening to them, partly wondering if Ashley had left.

"Tomorrow some people are coming to fly little airplanes. It's gonna be great." Eric snuggled down. "Good night, Uncle Jared."

"Good night." He drew the door almost closed. The twins were getting over their loss. Now if only he could.

Downstairs, Ashley had loaded the dishes in the dishwasher and wiped down the counters. She had a load in the washer, too.

"Multitasking," he said and shook his head. "I can't seem to make it work when it comes to housework."

"Well, I couldn't do it with building so I guess we're even." She glanced around the room then smiled at him. "I should go."

"There's no rush, is there? Let's sit on the patio for a while." He led the way, holding the door so she could duck under his arm.

"You like the patio a lot, don't you?" she said, swinging her feet up onto the chaise she'd chosen. "Why?"

"It reminds me of Africa, sort of. At the end of the day, everyone in the village sat outside, chatting, sometimes singing, while the sun dipped down over the horizon." Jared closed his eyes and jetted his brain back to a time when life had seemed so simple. "Those evenings lent a great sense of camaraderie to the village. I miss that."

She didn't say anything, simply stared at the sky, her pert nose tilted up.

"Ashley, I learned tonight that you are rich."

In an instant her relaxed stance disappeared, her

shoulders went rigid and her chin tucked into her neck. Jared noted that she did not look at him.

"And?"

"And nothing. I just never knew. I assumed you had a job with the foundation that's funding Harry's Place." He waited but she said nothing, simply sat there, waiting.

David's words came back to him. She'd been hurt, decimated by other's greed. Did she think he was the same as her former fiancé? As those others who'd conned her for the money?

"Your inheritance doesn't make any difference to me," he told her. "You're still Ashley. I just wanted you to know that I knew."

"Okay."

"Don't think I'm going to ask you for more money or anything, okay? You've set a budget. You were very clear we cannot exceed that." He kept his voice firm and even, trying to reassure her. "I intend to stick to that."

Ashley said nothing.

"I expect you'll still drive me nuts with all these plans you have for Harry's Place though," he joked.

"And my house." She did look at him then. She smiled, but her lovely blue eyes were clouded.

"And your house," he agreed. He needed to lighten things up. "Of course the house. Do you think you might possibly be a little obsessed about that place?"

"Not in the least." She got up, retrieved her woven bag and drew out a tablet. "I had an idea for those windows in the kitchen. Do you think this is doable?" She held out the book.

"A window seat?" Jared studied the detailed drawing of the kitchen she'd rendered. "Sure, I don't see why not."

"I want the kitchen to flow into the family room so that when I have people over, I won't feel cut off working in the kitchen." Her eyes began to shine. "Don't you think this island would make a perfect place for buffet dinners? I'm not really into formal meals so I may turn the dining room into a kind of office. You could build some cabinets for a desk and filing, couldn't you?"

"Ashley, let me finish one job first, will you?" He chuckled at her crestfallen look.

"Of course." She looked at him, flushed a deep rich red, then looked away. "It's just that those cabinets you're building here are so unique. I always hated lazy Susans. But your idea makes a lot of sense and you don't lose precious space."

"Thank you. Now you can't pretend you haven't been snooping in the garage again," he said in a mock serious tone, loving the way she peeked at him through her lashes.

"Just a little," she admitted with a giggle. She spread out her hands. "I'm curious. So sue me."

"I don't mind if you look, but don't—"

"—touch the tools," she finished for him in a droll tone. "Been there, done that. Don't need to repeat." She raised one imperious eyebrow. "Speaking of people who are obsessed..."

"Not in the least. I just like my tools." Jared didn't want to get started on his faults. But he was worried about something she'd said. "Ashley, these people you're going to invite over to your house—you're not thinking of people from the shelter, are you?"

"Sure. Why not?" She frowned at him. "They're

going to become my family while they stay. Why shouldn't I make them welcome?"

"You don't think they might see your place and feel—jealous?" He hated saying it, hated bursting her bubble. But she had this rosy view of the future and now that he knew about her money, well, Jared just couldn't see her impossible dreams matching reality.

"I don't know." She frowned at him, her blue eyes full of storm clouds. "All I know is that I want to make a place where people can be happy, enjoy life and, for a little while, be free of their worries. I think Harry's Place will be able to do that, don't you?"

"Yes, I do." He had no doubts of that. Ashley would make the place as welcoming as any place could be. But he was worried now, more than he had been, that some unscrupulous person would come to the shelter to take advantage of her generosity.

Somehow he was going to have to make sure that didn't happen.

"It's been a great week for them, don't you think?" Ashley stood with Jared in the church's fellowship hall on Friday night, her eyes on the twins, who were chattering with their new friends as they nibbled chocolate squares after their final Bible school program. "I'm glad you could come. They've been working hard to memorize their verses."

"They did well." Jared sampled the treats on his own plate. "Jessie was always better at memorization than me. I was kind of surprised Eric won that prize. He seems to have a knack for it."

"Emma was a little disgruntled by his win, but don't tell her I told you."

"I won't," he promised, "but I'm glad they're learning they are individuals. Twins have a tendency to stick together a little too much sometimes."

Families had gathered at the church for the final night and now stood around them chatting, mothers, father, grandparents.

"I'm glad your dad could bring your mom to see them even if she couldn't stay for the entire program. She was pretty proud." So was Ashley. She watched Emma and Eric interact with those around them and noted aloud that they didn't once check to see where she or Jared were.

"That's due to you," he said, studying her.

"No, it's due to them. And I have another idea that might help them learn to feel more secure." She'd debated asking him, especially since it would cost money. But the twins had come so far.

"You've got that look on your face again," Jared said, his handsomeness stirring a chord inside her.

"What look?" She tilted her head to one side and wondered why it was so easy to talk to him, to be with him. She didn't want her emotions involved, and yet, every time she was near Jared she found herself feeling things she hadn't allowed in a long time.

"The look that says you're about to spring something on me. Out with it." His brown eyes sparkled, his mouth tipped up in that crooked grin he used whenever he was trying not to laugh at her.

"There's a day camp in two weeks," she said softly. "A special one that's only four days long. They leave Monday morning and return Friday at noon. It's geared to kids who are five and six years old. I think if we could get the twins to go, they'd lose that last bit of reticence."

"Where is it?" Jared bent his head nearer to hear as she gave him the details she'd learned.

"It's a church camp and the twins they met here will be going. Emma was listening to Aisha and her brother talk about how they went last year. I think the twins would like to go, too, but are afraid to ask. The details are there." She pointed to a stack of flyers on a nearby table. "What do you think?"

"I knew you'd tire out eventually," he said, that same old teasing grin daring her to argue. He tucked a pamphlet into his shirt pocket. "Why don't you just say you need a week off?"

"I do not!" She thunked him on the arm. "I love those two."

"I know." He grabbed her hand and closed his fingers around it. His eyes darkened, his voice dropped. "I know that you've gone way out of your way to help them. And I appreciate it, Ashley. A lot."

"Well, it's been a lot of fun for me, too." She wasn't exactly sure how to continue. On one hand, she was thrilled that he kept hold of her hand—as thrilled as any teenybopper would be, she mocked herself. His smile dazzled her, the low growl of his voice made her skin prickle. She was quite content to stand next to him for however long he'd let her.

But that was stupid. She wasn't a teenybopper, or a silly schoolgirl who didn't know what happened when you trusted your heart to another. In the back of her mind she heard Peter's words over and over.

Of course our marriage is about the money, Ashley. How could it not be? Who could ignore the kind of dough you've got? Any man who says he could is a liar. But that's no reason we shouldn't get married. He'd laughed then, perfectly sure that she'd carry through with the farce of their engagement.

And when she wouldn't, when she'd said it was over, Peter had told her how he'd manipulated, cheated and lied to her—all because he wanted that money.

You're a nice girl, Ashley. We could have made a good couple, but truthfully? You're a little too holier-than-thou for my taste. What's wrong with making life fun?

Jared made life fun. He teased her and the twins, planned special surprises, showed two orphaned kids how much he loved them every day.

But can you trust him? There was the same old niggle of distrust that kept resurfacing, kept her from fully enjoying this relationship. If she wanted her bond with Jared to grow and change into something more personal, she had to change. Easier said than done.

"Ashley?"

"Yes?" She blinked, refocusing on the tall handsome man whose sunburned face peered into hers. "Sorry. Daydreaming."

"About the project?" He made a face when she nodded. "I figured. C'mon. Let's collect the kids and get out of here. I have something to show you."

Bemused by the glint of excitement sparkling in his espresso eyes, she let him draw her toward the kids, helped gather up their craft projects and Eric's little trophy. She walked with them out to Jared's truck, well aware of the stares they generated and caring not a whit. When Jared held the door, she climbed inside, her anticipation rising.

"Where are we going?" she asked when it became clear he was not heading home.

"I have a surprise for you." He twisted to grin at her, then turned forward and refused to divulge anything else. A few moments later they pulled up to the project site. He held out a hand to help her out of the truck before freeing the twins. "Follow me."

Ashley did, taking in the changes on the site as she went. She'd deliberately avoided coming here for the past two weeks to prove to Jared that she trusted him, but also to test herself. When he unlocked the house, she was prepared to rush inside, but his hand on her arm stopped her.

"Close your eyes and let me lead you," he ordered.

"But—"

"Trust me, Ashley."

Could she? Ashley closed her eyes and held out her hand.

"Okay, first we're going up the stairs. Emma, you go on one side, Eric on the other. Go slowly so she won't trip," Jared ordered.

"Uncle Jared, what are those big—"

"Shh!"

"Is this necessary?" Ashley stumbled, felt him hold her steady. "I have been in here before, you know."

"Just concentrate on walking," she was told.

Ashley heard much whispering as she was guided up the stairs, but most of it was indecipherable. She walked slowly, feeling each step with her toes. Finally they reached the second floor. More whispers as she was led forward. Then a click.

"Okay. Now you can look."

She blinked at the bright lights then gasped, eagerly glancing in every direction to get a good look.

"Do you like it?" Jared asked. "It's not quite finished. We have a few touches here and there. Some tiling isn't complete, but overall—"

"It's fantastic." The hall was open and spacious and roomy. She walked through it to the first suite. "This looks amazing," she murmured, grazing her fingers over the wall. "And the color is exactly what I wanted."

"Did you think I'd change it?" he asked.

"No, but—oh, the alcoves are perfect. A family could stay in here, don't you think? There's enough privacy?" When Jared didn't answer, she looked up and saw him grinning. "I'm gushing."

"Yes, but go ahead," he invited. "My ego can take it."

"It's just so incredible. I mean I imagined it would look like this, but it's something different seeing it all done. You've certainly made progress."

"Not as fast as I'd like. In fact, things are considerably behind where I'd expected to be at this point. It's going to be hard to meet that deadline."

"You'll do it. After all, you did this." She waved a hand to encompass his work.

"It's not that simple, Ashley. There's a lot of damage—"

"Which you'll fix. I know it."

"But can we do it all in time?" He paused, then sighed when she nodded. "I'm glad you trust me that much. And we are working to catch up. Want to see the bathrooms?"

She nodded and he led her through them, pointing out each special feature she'd insisted upon. Then they moved on to the next room and the room after that. She could hardly contain her excitement.

"At last the dream is coming alive," she said. "At this rate you'll soon be able to start on my little house."

"Well that won't be until we're into August," Jared warned. "The kitchen here needs a ton of work, as does the basement, if we're to put in what you requested."

"I know. But still."

While he bent to answer one of the twin's questions, Ashley began a second, closer inspection. The place looked even better than she'd imagined it would now that all signs of neglect and decay had been erased. She twirled around, thrilled by what she saw.

"Happy?" Jared asked.

"Yes." The excitement of finally seeing her dream live was heady. In a burst of enthusiasm she threw her arms around Jared and hugged him. "Thank you so much."

"Oh." He seemed to freeze, then his arms came around her and he held her close, his chin resting on her head. "You're welcome." She felt his chest shake as he laughed. "If I'd known I'd receive this bonus I'd have worked harder."

"Ha ha." She pulled away, embarrassed by her own exuberance. "I really do thank you, Jared. You've managed to do exactly what I wanted here. I was right when I asked you to manage this job. The finished project is going to be great."

"I think you'll make it great." Jared jerked a thumb over one shoulder, indicating the twins, who were now seated on the floor, leaning against a wall, sound asleep. "I think we should get these little ones home."

"Yes." She lifted Emma; he lifted Eric. They walked

slowly down the stairs, turning off lights as they went. Before they stepped out the front door, Ashley turned for a second look. "I feel like there should be a banner across it that says, 'For the glory of God,'" she told him.

"You can hang one the day I give you the keys," he promised. Then he eased her out the door and locked it. "But that's going to be a while yet."

"You keep saying that. Do you doubt the deadline?"

"I'm concerned," was all he would say.

Ashley plied him with questions about what was left to be done on the ride home. Funny how she'd come to think of his tumbledown house as her second home. Was that because it was there she felt comfortable enough to be herself?

"How's oncology?" he asked after they carried the kids upstairs and tucked them into bed.

For once the twins had no questions, no requests and no ability to stay awake for a bedtime story. They were asleep before their heads hit the pillow.

"It's fine. I got the office to let me rearrange things a bit so the kids can have a little more interaction with each other. It helps if you can find a friend to chat with." She tidied away the pots and pans she'd used for supper and started the dishwasher while she talked about the parents of her patients. "Most of them are in shock and find it hard to ask the questions that bother them so I try to take some extra time and listen."

"I'm sure they appreciate your extra efforts."

"It doesn't take long to listen to someone," she said, brushing off his compliment. "The easier flow on the ward got me some praise from other staff so I got to-morrow off."

"Lucky you."

"Yeah. Oh, I stopped by to see your mom yesterday, while the kids were at Bible school. I took her some of Connie's roses. It's a shame they're away and can't see how wonderful your dad has those gardens looking."

"Mom loves roses. Thank you." He poured two glasses of iced tea and, as usual, headed for the back patio. "What did you two talk about?"

"Another nurse told me about a mobility program that might suit your mother. I wanted to pass on the information to your mom. She seemed interested." Ashley peered upward. "You know, I've heard all about the monsoons they get in Tucson, but so far I haven't seen much sign of them. If it does start to rain a lot, will that affect your work at the project?"

"No, because we turned that sieve into a real roof." He shrugged. "This summer has been unusually dry. I'm just glad we got so much rain last winter. Otherwise, the valley would be a tinderbox. Still, the rains will come. One morning it will start out clear and warm and then the winds will shift to the southeast, the clouds will build and suddenly it will pour. Be very careful if you're out during one of those storms," he warned. "We get flash floods that can sweep away your car in minutes."

"Really?" She could hardly imagine the dry desert surface awash with water.

"Trust me. It can get bad fast. If it starts pouring heavily, get to very high ground and stay there," he ordered seriously. "And if there's lightning, stay inside."

"It will be interesting to see that. At least the camp I was telling you about is in the hills so the twins wouldn't get washed away. If they go." She peered at him through the gloom. "Are you going to let them?"

"Why not—if they want to?" He smiled at her. "I'm sure you could use the break, too."

"Me?" She frowned. "Why?"

"Well, you've been going nonstop with work and the twins and the project. I'm sure you could use a break and do something for yourself," Jared said.

"You mean, like shopping or something?" she asked, confused by his remark.

"Or a manicure. Whatever women do to relax." He leaned forward. "You're always so busy giving, Ashley. The twins, your patients, their parents. My parents. You're running constantly." His voice dropped. "Is it enough?"

"I'm not sure what you're asking?" Ashley murmured.

"I'm asking you what you do to refill your well and replenish your soul so you can keep on giving." Jared studied her intently. "If there was one thing I learned early on in the mission field it was that I couldn't keep being there for everyone else if I hadn't taken time to, for lack of a better phrase, restore my soul. To grow as a person."

"You're afraid I'll get stale," she teased. But Jared didn't smile.

"I mean there's a whole world of things out there waiting for you to discover, Ashley." His eyes held hers. "How can you do that if you're always taking care of everyone else? I'm not putting down what you do. Frankly, I don't know how you do it. But I'm worried that you seem to be cutting yourself off from people and things that could enrich you, and that you use the excuse of busyness with the twins to do it."

"I'm happy with the status quo," she said, defending herself. "I have what I want."

"For the rest of your life?" he asked. "How do you know that? How do you know you'll be content at Harry's Place, that you won't want your own family, your own kids?"

"I thought you knew." Ashley wished she'd seen this coming. Then she could have avoided it. But Jared might as well know the truth. "I will never get married, Jared. Children, a family—that's not for me."

"What? Why? Because one messed-up guy ruined your fairy tale?" He frowned, shook his head. "There are other men out there who aren't jerks, you know."

"I haven't met any I could trust," she told him, the words bursting out of her in frustration.

"You don't trust any men?" he asked in disbelief.

"No." Okay, that sounded juvenile. "Maybe it's that I don't trust myself to distinguish between the creeps and the good guys," she admitted, jumping to her feet. "I haven't been very good at it so far."

"Thanks a lot." Jared grimaced.

"I didn't mean you. Or David, or Wade. You three are different." She bit her lip and then came clean. "I don't want to go through what Peter put me through, not ever again."

"So you're hiding?"

"No!" Exasperated, she glared at him. "I'm living. My way. On my own terms."

"Without anybody else?"

I have you and the twins. Only she didn't. She was a stop gap, a temporary measure in their lives, as they were in hers. She'd leave once her project was ready. She'd be alone. That thought shocked her.

"Ashley, you're a giver. You go out of your way to help people," Jared said, his voice warm and sweet. His fingers pressed under her chin, forcing her to look at him. "You're fixated on your project because you see it as a solution to your longing for a family. But I think you're selling yourself short."

"Because I want to help others?" She didn't like the way he stared into her eyes, as if he could see straight through to her soul.

"Because you don't see yourself," he said softly. "You are an amazing woman, Ashley Ross. But you can't keep giving without giving to yourself. You need to care for people and love them. Don't settle for less than your heart's desire."

Then he leaned forward and kissed her. And Ashley kissed him back because she could no more deny herself the luxury of his touch than she could deny herself breath. She reveled in that kiss, and she sensed that Jared, too, was not holding back.

And then a niggling voice in the back of her mind whispered, *Is he kissing you or is he kissing your money?*

Startled and chagrined that she'd let down her defenses so easily, Ashley drew away.

"I have to go home now," she said without looking at him. "I'll see you Monday."

"Uh-uh." He followed her to her car, his voice clear and firm. "You said you're off tomorrow. I'll pick you up in the morning. Five-thirty. Wear something casual."

"Why? Where are we going?" She thought about the laundry. "The twins—"

"Aren't coming. It's just you and me. We're going to do something you've wanted to do for a long time, but haven't even attempted." He took her keys from her nerveless fingers and unlocked her door. "Better get to bed early. You'll need your rest."

"Jared—"

He pressed his finger over her lips, then replaced it with his mouth. A second later he stepped away.

"Good night, Ashley."

"Yeah. Okay. Good night." She climbed in the car, utterly bemused by the look of pure satisfaction on his face. "Are you sure—"

"Yes. Bye." He waved once then sauntered back to the house.

Ashley put her car in gear and drove away with her lips tingling and her mind brimming with questions.

Why had he kissed her?

Where was he taking her?

Why had he kissed her?

One finger traced the path his lips had taken. A smile dawned.

Why he'd done it was anyone's guess. But she'd liked it.

A lot.

Chapter Eleven

"I appreciate this more than you know, Susannah."
Jared hugged her then headed out the door as light crept
over the horizon.

Okay. Phase one in his effort to show Ashley that
caring for needy families, though laudable, wasn't all
she needed to make her life complete was now in gear.
Ashley's ache was soul deep and Jared didn't believe
it could be filled by strangers who would come to her
shelter for a short while. She needed—*deserved*—more.

If he closed his eyes, he could visualize the wide-
eyed wonder that would swell in her blue eyes when he
showed her Saguaro National Park. She'd tilt her head
back, purse her lips and—those lips.

Jared hadn't meant to kiss her last night. Heaven
knew he'd thought about it a thousand times, but he'd
told himself he wouldn't go there. He didn't want her to
expect more than he was willing to give. He certainly
didn't want to hurt her. A romantic relationship was not
in his future. No way.

Yet he had kissed her. More than once. And enjoyed

it. It felt right to hold Ashley in his arms, to share her dreams. But nothing could come of that. He knew that.

"So what am I supposed to do?" he asked aloud.

Maybe not spend the day alone with her?

But he had to. If he could get her to let go of the fairy tale for a while, maybe other dreams would emerge.

He pulled into Wade's driveway and rang the bell. Ashley answered, but she didn't look like she'd been awake long.

"I wouldn't mind sleeping in on my day off," she said, her voice crabby.

"You can sleep anytime. Bring a cup of coffee and let's go." Jared chipped and chided at her until she was finally in the truck, wearing a pair of sneakers.

"I don't do sneakers," she said holding out her leg. The blue eyes glinted with temper. "Ever."

"You're doing them today. You can thank me later." He'd insisted she borrow a pair from Connie.

"I didn't realize you were so bossy. Is that how you get so much done on the project?" She sipped her coffee, her eyes closed.

"Must be."

That project. He'd hemmed and hawed, trying repeatedly to make her understand his worry that it was behind schedule and he was no longer sure they'd make the deadline. Problem was Ashley heard what she wanted to hear. He'd have to tell her again today. She had to be prepared.

"Hey, wake up," he said when her head tilted to one side. "You need to be awake to see this."

"Sure I do." She blinked, yawned then gasped. "Wow!"

"Welcome to Saguaro National Park, named for these

giant cacti which are only found in Arizona." He helped her climb out and led the way over a small path that ended in a spectacular viewpoint. "Aren't you glad you got up early?"

"Early?" She treated him to a scathing glance. "Try before dawn." Then she smiled. "But, yes, it was worth it. This is beautiful. Untamed, as if no one's been here."

Jared watched her experience the desert sunrise with every sense. Her eyes shone with life, flashing here and there as she took in the sights. She moved carefully, examining the cactus flowers that had started blooming thanks to the last few evenings' rains. Her nose twitched as she breathed in the aromas—sage, mesquite, moss and the leftover moisture. She'd brought along a cup of coffee for him and Jared sipped it as he waited, wondering again how God could have created such a variation in landscape in Arizona. For that matter, how had He created as complex a woman as Ashley?

"Thank you, Jared." She stood before him, eyes wide in her lovely face, her body bathed in the peach-pink light of dawn. Together they watched the sun climb over the craggy mountains. "I'm glad I got to see this in the morning. It's spectacular."

"Well, it's only the beginning. Let's go for breakfast." He took her to a historic resort hotel spread over fourteen acres of gardens, fountains, flowers and lawn.

"It's hard to believe this big resort is located in the middle of Tucson, right downtown." She forced him to stop as she savored the arrays of spectacular blooms filling beds and dressing walkways. "Marvelous."

"The inn was founded in the 1930s and has been maintained in the old casita style. I haven't been here in years, but the food was always magnificent." He watched her as the waiter offered his suggestions.

Judging by her selections, Ashley wasn't afraid to trust when it came to food. It seemed to be people in her general life that she had a problem with. Jared wasn't sure how today would help that, he only knew he wanted to show her his town and repay her for her generous care of his house and the twins. And for the job she'd given him, though she wouldn't be pleased if she knew how his doubts about finishing her house on time magnified with every working day.

"This place seems very busy. I'm surprised you got us in," she said as she sipped the last of her coffee.

"Reservation." He checked his watch. "Are you finished?"

"No time to relax, huh?" She grinned as she laid her napkin on the table. "What's next?"

"Kartchner Caverns State Park." He paid the bill and caught up with her outside where she was exploring the grounds. "If you want to see more, we'll have to come back because we have reservations for two tours and it's a bit of a drive to get there."

"Okay." Ashley used the time to quiz him about the project and how long he expected to spend on the main building.

"I can't be that specific," he told her for the third time, glad they were finally turning into the grounds. "I just don't know."

"But you will finish."

"I'm trying, Ashley. We might just squeak under the wire if there are no issues with that house you're so crazy about," he said. "But barring anything catastrophic Harry's Place should be done in time." *I hope.*

"You'll do it." She smiled. "I'm trusting you, Jared."

He was going to do his utmost to make sure she didn't regret that trust. He almost groaned when Ashley began describing the idyllic life she'd have when the project was finished.

"Hey, today is supposed to be about having fun and forgetting work."

"I'm sorry," she apologized sweetly. "You're there all day, every day and here I am bringing up work again. You must need a break."

"This is supposed to be your day," he reminded her. Rain began to fall. "Remember those monsoons you wanted to see?"

"Yes."

"We're about to get caught in one. It's a bit of a walk to the entrance. Are you up for it?"

Thankfully she was. He spread his jacket over their heads and jogged in step with Ashley, who giggled at the water that splashed all over her jeans. That was just another thing to add to the list of Ashley's admirable qualities. She could even enjoy a downpour.

"Why did we bring jackets? Besides the rain, I mean?" she asked when they had picked up their tickets.

"It's quite cool in the cave. You'll see."

Since they had some time before their tour began, Jared followed her around the exhibits, enjoying her expressions as she examined the displays. Then their numbers were called. He followed her outside and opened the door so they could duck inside a tram that would take them to the top of the hill and the first cavern. As they rumbled up the rocky road, his shoulder bumped hers and more than once he steadied her on the slippery seat.

Ashley grinned and thanked him, but when their gazes met and held, she was the first to look away. And her cheeks turned pink.

Jared was just as aware of her in front of him as they climbed the inclines and paused to hear explanations about the formations of the caves. On one particularly steep rise he offered his hand and she took it. It felt right to hang on to it while they stood inside the massive inner chamber and studied the immense formations as the lights flickered from one to the next.

"It's amazing in here," she murmured. "Can you imagine slogging through that muck to find this?"

"Those first explorers wouldn't have had these lights to show them what they'd found, either. They only carried small lanterns." He was enjoying this more than the first time he'd visited.

On the ride back down the hill Ashley turned her little camera on him and snapped several pictures. Jared made faces at the lens and laughed at himself for doing it. He hadn't felt so carefree in ages.

"We have time for a drink and a snack before the next tour," he told her.

"I can't believe I'm hungry again." Her red-gold hair gleamed in the overhead lights. She'd left it free today, a blue ribbon tied on the top of her head. "I'd love one of those exotic-sounding teas."

"Sure. Will you share some nachos with me?"

"I'll force myself," she agreed with a grin.

While he got their order, Ashley snagged two seats in the tiny crowded cafe. They sat watching the rain outside pour down in sheets and discussed the beauty of what they'd seen.

"I don't know how people say there is no God." She

waved a hand. "When I see things like this place, I am more certain than ever that He designed this world. And us. But better than that, He didn't abandon us to figure out life on our own."

Jared leaned back, content to listen to her melodic voice. Besides, he was interested in her faith view.

"Harry, the man who left me the money," she said, "used to say that humans always want to attribute wrong things to God. We think He's standing there with a big club, waiting to bop us into submission or punish us because we did something wrong."

"You don't think God punishes?" Jared watched her eyes flash.

"Yes. I think He sometimes does. But not as often as we believe. I think He's a lot bigger than that. I think it's mostly our guilty conscience that makes us expect God is going to nail us when we mess up." Ashley lifted her narrow shoulders in a shrug. "God knows us, knows exactly who we are. He's like a parent. Like you."

"Me?" He blinked. "What do you mean?"

"Well, you're a father to the twins now. Do you stand there, waiting for them to make a mistake so you can get them?" She shook her head. "Of course you don't."

At least she had that much confidence in him.

"The problem is that we think God's love changes, and it doesn't. His love is constant." She leaned nearer, her spicy floral scent enveloping him. "God's love isn't based on feelings or on perfection. It's based on His promise to us, His covenant to be our God. Always."

Their number was again called so there was no time to question her further. But Jared didn't want to. As they walked a different path and saw new calcite formations, he puzzled over her words.

God was there—even when Fran died He was there? Loving her? Loving the babies she had cradled and tried to protect?

It was an idea he hadn't before explored, but now he found truth and a measure of comfort in the thought. God didn't love and then stop loving to abandon His children. That was the antithesis of everything Jared had studied and experienced in his faith.

Part of him heard the guide's explanations about the various stalactites and stalagmites, but part of him couldn't stop thinking about what Ashley had said, about how God was relevant in his own circumstance. The deep loss he'd felt after Fran's death and the fears that had mushroomed after Jessie had died happened because of his wrong thinking.

"Jared?"

He blinked, felt Ashley's tug on his arm and realized he was holding up the line.

"Sorry," he apologized to those around him and quickly followed her lead out of the cave.

"I'm not sure you got as much out of that as I did," she said in a teasing tone. She looked straight at him and her voice altered, softened. "Are you all right? You've gone quite white."

"I'm fine." He glanced around. "It's still pouring but not as hard. Do you want to stop here for coffee or should we tough it out?"

"I'm always game to tough it out." And in fact she looked excited by the prospect. "But can we check the bookstore first? I'd like to get a couple of things for the twins."

If anyone personified God's love it was Ashley Ross.

"Sure, let's go take a look."

In the end it wasn't just the twins she bought gifts for. There were gifts for Wade's daughter, Silver, David's sister, Darla, and the baby. And she found something unique for her oncology patients—each one of them.

"You're going to blow all your wages," he said, groaning as she added to the pile in his arms.

"I don't have any living expenses since I stay at Connie's for free," she reminded him, her arched brows pulling together. "I can afford a few trinkets. Aren't these T-shirts cute? I'm going to take one for each of the twins. They're growing so fast this summer. They can use a couple of new shirts."

Jared had noticed and wondered how much he could stretch to spend money on kids' clothes. The dishwasher was acting up again, in concert with the washing machine. And he was fairly certain the water heater was on its last legs.

"I meant to ask you." Ashley paused in the middle of her shopping and turned to face him. "Have you had any news about a teaching job for the fall?"

"Nothing yet." He was getting desperate with only a little over a month till school began.

"Well, don't even think about dragging the project over schedule," she teased, a big grin slicing across her face.

"As if." He freed one hand and tweaked the end of her elegant nose. "Who would deliberately add nagging time to a job?"

"I'm not that bad!" She glared at him, then frowned in uncertainty. "Am I?"

"Oh, Ashley." He chuckled. "You make it so easy."

"Oh." She pinched her lips together and returned to

selecting her shirts. As if to punish him she put a great big kit for a balsa wood airplane in his arms.

"Who's that for?" He tilted his head, trying to read the box.

"Someone who's nice to me," she retorted in a pert voice.

"I am very interested in balsa wood airplanes," he said, trying to keep a straight face.

"Then you'd better start being nice to me. Very nice." She adopted what he termed her snooty pose but spoiled it by laughing. "Let's go pay for these, grumpy."

"Grumpy? And here I've gone all out to give you this lovely afternoon." He waggled his eyebrows. "Which we have not yet finished, I might remind you."

"We haven't?" She paid for her purchases then batted her golden eyelashes. "Well, where to next?"

Her Mae West impression was too cute and Jared could have watched her bat her lashes all day, but he did have plans for the rest of the afternoon. So he grabbed the large box and two of the bags, leaving the third one for her.

"It's still raining," he grumbled as they left the building and stood under the portico. "Stay here and I'll go get the truck."

"What am I, tissue paper?" Before he could say anything she was off across the lot, the bag held over her head for protection.

Ashley didn't dodge the puddles, but went right through them just as the twins would have done. No wonder they loved her.

"Smart-aleck show-off," Jared grumbled. The rain hadn't cooled things off much. He flicked the unlock button then followed as best he could, her bags bumping his legs with every jog.

Once the packages were inside and Ashley had shed her sopping jacket, she looked at him, her curiosity evident.

"I'm not telling," he said as he started the truck. "So don't bother asking."

He switched on the radio as they rode back toward Tucson. But when he took a detour around the city Ashley could contain her curiosity no longer.

"Where are we going?"

"It's an old mission, the oldest one in the U.S., actually. It's called San Xavier and it sits on the Tohono O'otham Indian reservation." He pulled into the long drive, pleased by her wide-eyed appreciation of the gleaming white buildings rising up from the reddish-brown desert floor. "If I've timed this right, we should still be able to enjoy their fry bread tacos."

They did. By then the rain had stopped and it was time for Jared to face the past and tour the site. Being back in San Xavier brought him both joy and pain. He wandered through the courtyard, the historic church and the restoration areas with a full heart.

"You seem sad. Is anything wrong?" Ashley asked when they emerged from the church into the massive courtyard.

"This was Jessie's favorite place. She used to come here to pray or think things through. She brought the twins here, too." He smiled. "I was just remembering how she'd twirl around with her arms stretched up to heaven. She'd say her happy basket was overflowing."

"The twins have a memory of that." Ashley nodded at his surprise. "I didn't know what they were talk-

ing about when they said 'the white church,' but they
were very clear that their mother loved it. Apparently
she once told them she felt very close to God when she
climbed that hill to pray." She pointed to the rugged little path that led to a white cross on the top of a craggy
hill to the side of the mission. Then she looked at him.
"It's a great memory for them to treasure, Jared."

"Yeah." It took a minute to get past the emotion but
finally he turned to Ashley. "Want to climb it?"

"Yes."

They climbed the dry dusty trail single file. Occasionally they stopped to take in the view or inspect the
little stations the faithful had made on their trek up
the mountain. When they finally reached the summit,
Ashley's hand crept into his. Jared was grateful for her
touch because he'd just seen the small marker where
his little sister had carved her initials.

J.H. Loved by God.

I miss you, Jess.

"Doesn't this remind you of the Old Testament pas-
sages about Moses going up on Mount Sinai?" Ashley
gazed down at the landscape below. "It's like we're in
a cloud here, isolated from people but close to God."

A reverence seemed to descend on them. Jared remained silent as awe crept into his heart. Was God here?
Was that why the hard knot of anger tucked inside him
seemed to soften?

God is always nearer than we think. Jessie's words
from when they were kids, the very first time their
parents had brought them here. Jessie—whose faith
in God had always been unshakable. Jessie who'd said
only one thing when she hugged him goodbye, before
he'd left for Africa.

Trust God, Jared. Always.

A splat of rain broke his concentration. Jared glanced up.

"Ashley, I think we should get back to the truck." He tugged on her hand, urging her down. The first few drops fell on the last steps of their descent. They raced across the parking lot hand in hand and climbed into the truck as the first flash of lightning speared the sky.

"Wow! That's magnificent." Ashley twisted to see the display. "I'm glad we're not in the city. It's so flat here you can see everything."

Jared remained silent, his thoughts still on the mountain as he struggled to align his feelings with his sister's words.

"Jared?" Ashley's hand touched his shoulder. "What are you thinking about?" she whispered.

"My sister. My beautiful, wonderful, very clever sister." In that second, tears came that had been suppressed too long. He sat there, staring through the windshield at the rain and let them fall, a catharsis that cleansed and purged the wrenching anger at his loss.

"Oh, Jared." Ashley's arms went around him and she cradled his head on her shoulder. "Don't cry for her. She's happy now."

"I know." His arms wrapped around her, drawing her close. He shifted so she could snuggle close, grateful that she was there. "I'm not mourning her," he said. "I'm mourning my own stupidity in not listening to her."

As the storm around them raged, the battle inside him quieted. Jared wasn't sure he could trust God in the same way he had before. But he was ready to try.

"Jared?" Ashley's hesitant voice broke the silence.

"Yes?"

"Can you move a little? My arm's asleep."

He burst out laughing and shifted so she could ease away. Her eyes met his, their navy depths searching his face.

"Are you okay?" Hesitancy clouded her voice.

"I'm fine. In fact, I'm very fine." He leaned over and kissed the tip of her nose. "And hungry."

"Again?" she teased. "Where to this time?'

"Do you feel like Mexican food? I know where they make the best chile rellenos and the Topopo salad is amazing." He waited for her nod, reminded her to do up her seat belt and started the truck. "You'll love the atmosphere, too. There's a real mariachi band."

Because it was Saturday, the place was hopping and they had to wait. It didn't seem to matter to Ashley as she soaked in the vivid Mexican decor. The band serenaded them and she swayed to the music, her smile broad.

At last they were seated. Jared helped her negotiate the menu since Ashley claimed she had little experience with authentic Mexican food. Once their order was in, they crunched their way through chips and freshly made salsa with amazing speed.

"You'd think I hadn't eaten for weeks. But I'm starved. This has been the most amazing day." Ashley clasped his hand in both of hers. "I don't know how to thank you."

"You just did." Jared couldn't tear his gaze away from her. She'd taken a moment to freshen up and now her hair shone a vivid red in the shadowy light of the stubby candles. He didn't pull away from her touch until their meal arrived.

They spoke sporadically as they enjoyed the food

and the festive atmosphere around them. Ashley kept saying she had to remember the comfortable aura here when it came time to decorate the shelter. Once dessert was finished, they lingered over coffee, listening to the music. Jared was loath to end the day just yet.

"Tell me about your dreams for the future, Ashley."

"My dreams?" She tipped her head to one side and gave him a quirky smile. "I haven't rambled on enough about my plans for the project?"

"Besides that."

"Well, I'd like to learn to snow ski," she mused, leaning back in her chair. "Is that what you mean?"

"Not quite." He searched for a way to make her really think about what her future would look like. "How do you see yourself in ten years? Will you still be running Harry's Place?"

"I don't know." A little furrow of concentration appeared between her arched brows. "Yes, I suppose so."

"Won't there be other projects? Wasn't that what your bequest was about?" As soon as the word *bequest* left his lips she stiffened. "I mean, are there going to be other Harry's Places?"

"You're looking for more work?" she teased, but her grin didn't reach her eyes.

"If I don't soon get a teaching job, I might have to," he joked. "But, no, I was actually thinking about you, trying to imagine what you'd be doing ten years from now."

"I guess I'll think about the future when I get Harry's Place up and running." She pushed away her coffee cup. "I'm finished if you're ready to leave."

So much for his plan to get her to consider her future. Jared escorted her to the truck. Once inside, he explained the last thing he'd planned.

"We're going to Gates Pass. It's the best place to watch sunsets." He accelerated around a curve then cut his speed. The Pass was known for its dangerous route. Besides, he wanted Ashley to appreciate the view. "I hope you're not too tired to walk because we have to park in the lot and then go on a bit of hike on a dirt path to get to the best spot. I think we should be early enough."

"It's at least an hour till sunset," Ashley said with a frown, stretching to peer down the sheer drop on her side. "How early do we need to be—" She stopped, gasping as they rounded the final corner. "Look at all the cars."

"Saturday is one of the busiest days at Gates Pass. Tourists and residents come here." Finding a spot wasn't easy, but soon they were climbing the dusty trail, past folks who had already found their perfect perch. "How about here?" Jared asked. When she nodded he spread the blanket he'd brought and helped her sit.

They chatted a little but mostly they watched the sky. Slowly, vivid streaks of red, oranges and yellows spread across the now clear blue sky then gradually melted into a molten red-orange mixture as the sun dipped inch by inch below the horizon and left the craggy mountain peaks outlined in black.

Other sunset watchers left, but Jared waited until Ashley finally turned to face him. Her face gave away her thoughts. A single tear dribbled down her cheek.

"Think of it," she whispered. "A Creator who could envision the sheer beauty of that and then bring it to fruition. That's our God." She sighed. "I am humbled that He allows me to be one of His children."

The drive back was silent, introspective. Jared moved slowly down the Pass, reflecting on the spiritual experience the sunset had offered. He hadn't intended that, but Ashley's appreciation had opened his eyes to something he often took for granted. When he finally arrived at Wade's, Jared didn't want the evening to end.

But he had duties, responsibilities.

He helped her carry in her packages and wondered how best to end the day. With a friendly handshake? Who was he kidding?

"Thank you for the most wonderful day I can remember," Ashley said. Her eyes were on level with his as she stood on the doorstep. "I loved all of it, even these sneakers." She stuck out one foot and giggled. "I could never have done those climbs in my sandals, so thank you again."

"I'm glad." He stood there stupidly, staring at her, wanting, wanting...

Ashley leaned forward to brush her lips against his cheek. Jared deliberately turned his head so his mouth met hers. He felt her quick gasp and then she was returning his kiss. His arms slid around her waist, his head angled as he deepened the embrace. Ashley met him with her own enthusiasm. Several moments passed and then the image of the devastation in Africa that had wrecked his life forced him to draw back. He could not go through that again.

He met her dazed look.

"Good night, Ashley. Sweet dreams." Then he left.

Jared drove home while his brain did battle with his emotions. He listened half-heartedly to Susannah and

David's explanations about their day with the twins. He agreed baby Grace was growing. But he was irrationally glad when they'd left, he'd ensured the twins were fast asleep upstairs and he could find his favorite spot on the deck.

He sat there, peering at the stars, reliving his day with Ashley.

"She's fantastic and I care about her a lot," he whispered and wondered if God thought it was funny when people said what He already knew. "I'm trying to trust You. I'll try harder. But I can't risk loving her."

What he really meant was, *I can't risk losing her.*

Chapter Twelve

"I'm so glad my exams are finished." Susannah leaned back in a lounger on Connie's pool deck and sighed. "I am enjoying the break from studying. And a break from the rain. Today is glorious."

"And I'm glad we're back," Connie added. "Although it was a great trip, it's nice to be home. And I'm glad Silver could go to camp with the twins. How are you doing now that they're gone, Ash?"

"Truthfully? I'm bored. I've loved spending time with them." Ashley had no intention of telling how bored she was—bored enough that she spent hours planning dinner for Jared each night. Okay, that wasn't boredom. It was fun. But still.

"Well, I suppose this camp time is good preparation for you," Connie said.

"Preparation? What do you mean?"

Susannah frowned at her friend. "She means it won't be long until the twins go back to school and you won't be there anymore." Susannah rubbed lotion on her skin. "You'll be busy at Harry's Place."

"Yes, I will." The thought didn't bring as much joy

as it should have. Was that because she couldn't quite picture the future without seeing Jared and the twins every day? "If it ever gets finished," she grumbled. "He hasn't even started on my house yet."

"Is there a problem?" Susannah asked as she closed her eyes.

"I don't think so. Jared hasn't said anything specific though I know a couple of jobbers have held up some of the work." She bit her bottom lip, remembering. "He told me several times that he wasn't on the schedule he wanted to be, but I think he's being cautious about making false promises. And I'm trying. At least I've stopped asking for constant reassurance that he'll be done on time. I'm trying to relax and just trust him and God."

"And how's that going? The trust thing, I mean?" Connie asked.

"I do trust him. How can I not? He's done nothing to destroy the faith I've put in him." Yet, a voice inside her head kept advising caution. Ashley shoved it away. "Jared takes real pride in doing this job. I can't believe how fussy he is about the details."

"Worse than you?" Connie smiled at her nod. "That is fussy." She frowned then looked directly at Ashley. "What are your real feelings for Jared, Ash?"

"I'm curious about that, too," Susannah added, sitting up.

"I like him. I think he's a great father to the twins and a good teacher. He's amazing as a foreman. No one could have a more dedicated crew than he's made of those men." She was stalling, and judging by her friends' rolling eyes, they knew it. "Okay, I care about him."

"You do?" A big grin spread over Connie's face. "How wonderful!"

"Is it?" Ashley shook her head. "What future is there in it?"

"Who knows? But aren't you curious to find out?" Connie frowned.

"I'm afraid," Ashley confessed. "He's stuck in the past, Connie. He's mourning the loss of his wife and he's fighting a battle with God." She remembered his misery when he'd talked of his wife's death in Africa.

"But that's not the only thing holding you back, is it, Ash?" Susannah leaned forward and took her hand. "You said you trust him."

"I do." She sighed. "I know I'm a dummy but I can't get rid of the memory of Peter telling me all he cared about was the money."

"Peter's in the past. And good riddance to him," Susannah said, wiping her hands as if to rid them of something nasty. "Jared doesn't care about your money, does he?"

"I don't think so."

"So?" Connie raised an eyebrow. "Problem?"

"I'm afraid I'll let myself care too much for Jared, I'll be vulnerable again. Then if something does happen—well, it's taken me a long time to trust again," she whispered, baring her heart to the only people she trusted without reservation.

"Aw, honey. You can't live being afraid that someone somewhere will disappoint you. Someone will, be assured." Connie moved to sit on the end of Ashley's chaise. She brushed a wisp of hair off her face. "Human relationships require trust. Besides, you have God to protect you. That's mighty big protection, if you ask me."

"Yes." They were right and Ashley knew it.

"But? I hear a but." Susannah joined them on the lounger.

"I can't get rid of this voice inside my head that keeps warning me that Jared is no different than Peter," Ashley admitted. "Every time he kisses me, that voice squeals its reminder."

"Kissing, huh?" Connie winked at Susannah.

"Kissing is good." Susannah chuckled at Ashley's red face. "Can I tell you what I learned from David? Love is a process. It grows and changes. I believe that if this love for Jared is God's will, He will help you overcome your barriers until you feel secure."

"Our sister is right. There's no rush, honey." Connie patted her shoulder. "Take your time and just enjoy being with him. Eventually that little voice will shut up."

"Thanks, ladies." She flung an arm around each of their necks and hugged. "You're geniuses."

"Yes, we are." Connie rose. "I've had enough of this heat. What do you say we go shopping together?"

"I say yes." Susannah swung her legs over the chaise. "David's on vacation this week and is taking care of Grace. Darla's gone to a birthday sleepover so I'm free."

"What are we shopping for?" Ashley asked, trailing them into the house.

Susannah and Connie stopped dead, stared at her and then shook their heads in pity.

"You need a reason to go shopping?" Connie asked.

"I guess I could pick up a couple of things for the twins," Ashley mused.

"She's got it bad," Susannah whispered to Connie. "Can't stop thinking about them for a minute."

"I know. And if we need a reason for shopping,

well, I'm going to need some maternity clothes in a little while." Connie blushed at their whoops of joy and gladly joined in the three-way hug.

"We're going to be aunties." Susannah cheered.

"Well, not for another six months or so. Hey! It's almost five. Nobody will be working at the site after five, will they?" Connie asked Ashley. "Can we stop by? You could show us around."

"Great idea," Susannah seconded.

"Okay. Sure." Ashley hadn't stopped by in a while because she wanted to prove how much trust she had in Jared without checking on him. It would be interesting to see the changes he'd made. Maybe the progress on the site would silence that itch of envy that both her foster sisters were busy with their families and Ashley didn't have one.

Yet.

"So everything is good in your world," Wade said as he helped carry tile for the kitchen into Harry's Place.

"Pretty good. I'm still behind, but this place is shaping up." Jared wished he felt as confident as he sounded.

"The kitchen and the basement to finish. That's it for this place?" David asked. He set down his boxes then checked to see if baby Grace was still asleep.

"There is some exterior work to be done," Jared told him. "And I haven't started on Ashley's house yet."

"Why not?" Wade asked.

"Because the city's stipulation was that Harry's Place be finished by September 1, and being a very clever lad, our boy Jared is making sure they will have no grounds to deny a permit on that condition. For which I applaud him." David high-fived Jared. "However, the city put no time constraints on the house at the back."

"But you've only got a little more than two weeks left till the deadline. I know Ashley thinks it's all going to be done by then." Wade frowned. "Is that going to happen?"

"What's left here is mainly fiddle work," Jared explained. "That is time-consuming but I'm hoping to dig into that house next week. We should have enough time to get it so she can move in—if the reports and inspections she got are accurate."

"How's it going with Ashley, by the way?" Wade poked the pacifier back into Grace's mouth.

"Fine." Jared knew that wasn't going to satisfy them. "We have a great time together. She's fun and interesting and I like her a lot."

"But?" David frowned. "You're not still battling that bugaboo of fear, are you?"

Jared shrugged.

"He is," Wade confirmed. "What is your worst fear about Ashley, Jared?"

"That something will happen to ruin things." He beckoned for them to help him bring in another load of supplies, but when they were back in the house, David stopped.

"You mean that she'll die? You can't live like that, Jared," he said firmly. "Nobody can live a full life with fear hanging over their heads. Let's take a break and you tell us what's really bothering you."

"Fine." They wouldn't give up so Jared did his best to put his worries into words. "Thanks to Ashley, I know in my brain that God isn't out to get me."

"But your heart doesn't accept that." Wade nodded.

"I can understand that, I think. I went through something the same with Bella. When she left me and died with that other man, I spent a long time feeling guilty."

"Guilty? Why? She left you," Jared reminded.

"But I lived." Wade stared at him.

"I don't get it." Jared was totally confused.

"I think it's called survivor's guilt. I lived but Bella didn't. You lived. Fran didn't." Wade touched his shoulder. "The mind does funny things with grief, Jared. Sometimes it twists reality because it's easier for us to deal with it that way."

"He's right. The way you talk about Fran—" David paused. "Well, it's almost like you think you should have died in her place."

"I would have if I could," Jared said quietly.

"That wasn't your decision to make. Is that what you're really bugged by? That no one consulted you?" Wade shook his head. "God decided otherwise. Fran is gone, buddy. You can't change it, you can't make it go away and you can't bring her back. All you can do is get on with your life. And Ashley helps you do that, doesn't she?"

"Yes," Jared agreed, because it was true. Ashley was hope, hope that his life wasn't a waste, hope that he could make a difference, hope that the twins would grow up strong and beautiful, like their parents.

"So?" Both of them stared at him.

"She has a lot of money. I don't have any," Jared reminded them.

"Money? You're using money as a barrier to a relationship with Ashley Ross?" Wade guffawed. "Ashley could not care less about money."

"Anyway, she doesn't even think of it as hers. It's a

resource she uses to help others," David added. "Love is a gift, Jared. A gift God gives because He loves us. Don't fear it, embrace it."

"The question is," Wade said quietly, "are you going to trust God enough to leave the past in His hands and move to the future?"

"The other question is—do you love Ashley?" David demanded.

"Man, you two are pushy."

"Answer the questions." David looked like he was in court arguing a case.

"I'm learning to trust God," Jared said quietly.

"And? Do you love Ashley?" Wade's face was implacable.

"I think so." He saw their exasperation. "Okay. Yes."

"Then do something about it!"

Jared was going to tell them to mind their own business, but there was a noise in the foyer. The three of them investigated and found the girls admiring the new light fixture.

"This is where you bring our baby?" Susannah asked David. "Why?"

"Wade and I wanted to give Jared a hand here," he explained. "Isn't this place amazing?"

Jared watched them pair off as they went to explore. He grinned at Ashley. She grinned right back then frowned.

"Working late? Again?" She shook her head. "Jared, even you need to take a break occasionally."

"I'll take my break on September 2," he told her. He knew she was pleased by what she saw. Her eyes gave that away. But she was also troubled. "What's wrong?"

"The other house," she murmured. "I know you've

had your hands full with this one, but when will you get to the other house?"

She wasn't referring to the city's deadline, she was referring to the one she'd imposed, which he'd agreed to.

"I'm hoping to begin tearing things down there this week," he told her.

"I'm not pushing, it's just that there's not much time left." She slid her hand over the polished banister. "Now that Connie and Wade are back and expecting, I want to get out of their way and into my own place. I want to get on with my future."

"Expecting? Wow." Jared smiled, truly happy for his friend. He stuffed down memories of another child, a child he'd never know. His buddies were right. The past was over. It was time to embrace the future. "Let's go look at your house while the others are checking out Harry's Place."

"Okay." She waited till he'd told the others then walked with her across the yard. "The rain has made the grounds so mucky I've started keeping a pair of rubber boots in my car."

"I noticed." He made a face at the bright orange boots. "They're not subtle, and your legs look better in those sandals you usually wear, but I suppose the boots are functional. You better leave them on when we go inside."

Jared pulled open the door and held it so she could enter. Ashley had torn down the blinds the day the property became hers. Light flooded the rooms, but they were also stifling.

"First thing to check is the AC," Jared grumbled.

Ashley didn't seem to notice the heat. She almost skipped from room to room, describing what she saw in her mind. Though she'd talked about the place a million times before, it had always been about how she'd use the place, who would visit, how she'd reach out to those who needed her.

Now Ashley talked specifics and her descriptions surprised Jared. He'd assumed she'd lavish the place with the best of materials, but that was not the case. Instead she described ordinary flooring, counters and finishes. When he asked she frowned and shook her head.

"This is just a place for me to stay," she said. "I don't need fancy, I need comfortable. I think if these old hardwood floors were sanded and varnished they'd do just fine. Don't you?" she asked. "Then it wouldn't matter if a guest spilled something."

That was Ashley—always focused on others and her goal of helping them. But Jared wondered how she'd feel when she returned to her house alone at the end of the day, with no one to talk to, share her work with or dream together about future goals.

And yet, he knew she'd make it work. And he loved her for her determination. Besides, what did he have to offer—a crumbling house, two kids who demanded attention, a bank account that was in the black—barely?

Love, his brain reminded. *You could offer her love.*

"Jared?" She'd been speaking and he hadn't heard.

"Yes?"

"The floors?"

"I can't say yet." He glanced down. "I'll have to pull all the carpet and get a better look, but in this room it appears in good shape. Your reports don't indicate anything major."

They talked about moving a wall and opening up the kitchen. As usual, Ashley had very specific ideas about what she wanted. He was trying to explain that major changes here would add precious time to the project but the others arrived and he gave up.

"Harry's Place is marvelous, Ash. Did you choose everything yourself?" Connie asked, wide-eyed at the mess they were now standing in.

"It started out that way. But Jared convinced me I needed some professional help with the fixtures and fittings. After all, it's not an ordinary house but one that will have to serve many people over the years, I hope." She grinned at him. "I hired a designer, gave her my input and she and Jared have worked out how it's all come together."

Jared loved the pride in her voice.

"It's amazing. But you've got your work cut out for you here." Susannah's nose wrinkled. "What's that smell?"

"Old house smell. Unused for years." Ashley laughed. "Don't worry. Once Jared gets finished with this place, you won't recognize it."

He hoped he could live up to her faith.

A cell phone rang. Everyone reached for their pockets simultaneously.

"It's mine," Jared said with a laugh. "Hello." He listened, said yes a couple of times then hung up.

"You look happy," Ashley said, staring at him. "Want to share?"

"I have a full-time job for the fall teaching sixth graders at the twins' school. I start September 5." His soul sent a thank-you heavenward.

"Jared, that's great." In a second Connie the hugger had him enveloped in an embrace.

His buddies clapped him on the back, Susannah kissed his cheek. Ashley just stood there, smiling at him.

"Didn't I tell you God would work it out?" she said.

"Yes, you did. And you were right. Does that feel good?" he teased.

"Extremely." She winked at the others. "He seldom says I'm right."

The others glanced from her to him. Jared shifted under their knowing looks.

"This calls for a celebration, don't you think?" Ashley took in the affirming nods. "At Jared's place."

"Pizza. Good idea." He tried to remember how clean the place was and came up blank.

"Not pizza. I put a roast in the Crock-Pot. And potatoes and carrots. It should be done about—" she checked her watch "—right about now, actually."

"It sounds like fun, Ash. But maybe another time." Susannah pointed to the fidgeting baby. "She's teething and, believe me, you do not want to be around when she starts the usual evening fuss routine."

"Yes, it does sound good, sweetie. But Wade and I made plans to eat with his stepmother tonight." Connie smilingly accepted Jared's congratulations on her pregnancy.

"You two go ahead and enjoy that roast," Wade said with a meaningful glance at him.

"Yeah, go ahead. We'll all get together another time." David inclined his head toward the mess. "I'll be here tomorrow morning bright and early to give you a hand. Wade, too."

"Really, I appreciate it," Jared stammered. "But you guys have your own jobs."

"I'm off for the week and Wade is taking time off,"

David said, brushing off his refusal. "We want to be a part of Harry's Place, too. Whatever we can do to help, you just let us know."

"It's very kind of you both," Ashley said quietly. "Thank you."

"This heat is a killer. We better go before the munchkin lets loose." David took Grace's carrier from Susannah and held open the door. "See you tomorrow."

Wade and Connie followed, leaving Jared alone with Ashley.

"Ever feel like you need a bath?" he said, referring to his friends' hasty exits.

"Or maybe we have bad breath." She giggled.

"Either way, I'm roasting. Let's get out of here." He led the way then locked up behind her. "Should I meet you at my place?" he asked, smothering a grin as she clomped her way through the mess of the worksite.

"I'm going home to change first. I'll see you in—" she checked her watch "—half an hour?"

"Good." He smiled when she hesitated. "What?"

"Are you sure you wouldn't rather eat alone?" she asked, her voice uncharacteristically timid.

"I'm sure. Besides." He forced his face to remain expressionless.

"What?"

"I don't know how to make gravy," he said.

"Ooh. Is that all I'm good for?"

"No," he said. And meant it.

"See you." She waggled her fingers and walked away, carefully sliding off her boots and donning her favorite sandals before she drove off.

In that moment Jared knew what he was going to do. He was going to tell Ashley he loved her, but he was going to do it when nothing else would interfere. He would wait until after the grand opening of Harry's Place, when they could have some time together. Though he wasn't sure how, he was going to make that moment special, something Ashley would treasure for years to come.

In the meantime, he was going to let his work show how much he wanted to give her each and every one of her dreams.

For the first time, after months and years of living with the past, Jared knew he was ready to embrace the future.

With Ashley.

Chapter Thirteen

"Ashley, my jeans don't fit! And they're my favorite." Emma's panicked voice echoed through the house as she hopped down the stairs from her bedroom. "Look. What will I wear to school next week?"

"We'll have to get you some new ones. In fact, we already did." Ashley pulled a bag out of the closet. "Your uncle and I went shopping while you guys were at camp. Try these on. There's pair for you, too, Eric."

In fact, she and Jared had done a lot of things while the twins had been away, and all of them had been fun. Ashley wasn't sure whether to attribute Jared's change in demeanor to his new job come September, or to the work at Harry's Place, which thanks to Wade and David, was going more smoothly. Of course, there was still the house but—she pushed the anxiety away. She was leaving that in God's and Jared's hands. She could trust them both.

"Will you still come here after we start school, Ashley? Like you did before?" Eric showed her his new jeans fit perfectly. He'd already told her he was saving the T-shirt she'd bought from the caverns to go with it on his first day of school.

"I'm not sure what will happen," she told him as she cut off the tags and helped him fold the new clothes. "We'll have to talk to your uncle. How about if you and Emma take your new clothes upstairs and put them away now. Then they'll be nice and clean for school." She made a mental note to pick up a couple more pairs for each twin, now that she knew they fit. "Then you can help me start dinner."

They raced upstairs, each trying to outdo the other. Ashley was on the way to the kitchen when the doorbell rang.

"Hello, Ms. Duncan. Come in. I didn't expect you today. Jared's still at work." She waved the children's services woman inside and offered her iced tea. "Not cooling off, is it?"

"Not at all. I'm glad you got the air conditioner fixed since the last time I was here. It was horribly hot in here." She accepted a seat and the tea with a smile.

"Yes." Ashley didn't want to talk about that. Jared had been furious when he learned she'd finally called in a handyman to fix both the AC and the dishwasher, until she'd reminded him that both were for the twins' sake. "They sleep better at night because the air is working and they're learning how to clean up after themselves by putting the dishes in the dishwasher. What's wrong with that?" she'd asked him.

Thankfully, he'd finally given up. Even apologized to her. And kissed her.

She'd enjoyed those kisses.

"Sorry," she said to Ms. Duncan, blinking as the returning twins disturbed her introspection. "I was day-dreaming."

"I said, it's nice to see the twins so happy. Did you both have fun at camp?" She listened and nodded as the two told her of their adventures. "Wonderful."

"Could you two set the table, please?" Ashley asked when they'd finished talking. "And then you can play outside until I need your help with dinner."

"Okay." They raced away, vying for jobs.

"They seem very well-adjusted and ready to embrace a new year at school. I'm glad of that. It's impressive to see the way they've changed," Ms. Duncan said.

Ashley heard a "but."

"I am, however, still concerned about this house." She glanced around. "It hasn't improved as quickly as Mr. Hornby said."

"Jared has been putting in a lot of overtime at a project," Ashley defended him and then wished she hadn't said it quite like that as Ms. Duncan perked up.

"You mean he doesn't spend as much time with the twins?"

"Oh, he spends a lot of time with them. He schedules his work around them." She smiled. "In fact, last evening he took them for a bike ride and ice cream. When they came back they had a little campfire. The twins loved it."

"And you, Ms. Ross? Did you love it also?" Ms. Duncan's gaze narrowed.

"Me? I—I don't know what you mean?" Ashley stammered.

"In the beginning I understood that you were here simply as a caregiver for the twins."

"Yes." Ashley felt like more than a caregiver, but where was this going?

"Lately you seem to have taken on the role of their mother." Ms. Duncan frowned. "Is there something between you and Mr. Hornby? I only ask," she hurried to say, "because I'm concerned that the twins may feel abandoned if or when your relationship with him ends."

"Ms. Duncan, Jared and I are friends. But I am committed to the twins. I would not do or allow anything to hurt them. Emma and Eric are like my own children. I love them." She forced the words out, accepting the truth as she did. "They'll start school soon and I won't be here as much, if at all."

"That's what I'm worried about," Ms. Duncan said, frowning. "Separation anxiety."

"A few minutes ago they were asking if I'd still be caring for them after school," Ashley admitted. "I'm not sure yet what will happen. I do know that I have been working all summer with Jared to help the twins deal with people coming and going from their lives and I think they're ready for a sitter or an after-school program. I can only tell you that it doesn't matter whether I come every day or not, these children will always matter to me and if they need me, I will be here. I love them." *I love Jared, too.*

"That's admirable." But Ms. Duncan didn't sound convinced. Nor was she particularly impressed by the section of new cabinetry Jared had found time to install in the kitchen. "Like the rest of this house, it needs to be finished."

"It will be," Ashley assured her. "But it may take a little longer now because Jared begins his teaching job right after Labor Day. They really liked the way he handled his class in the spring and offered him a job. He is determined to make a stable home for the twins. I think he's doing a fantastic job of it."

"Uh-huh." The woman's inscrutable face and dead-pan voice made Ashley nervous. "I'll just look around, shall I?"

"Please, go ahead. I'll be in the kitchen." Ashley left her to it. She called the twins in from outside and gave each a job—Eric peeling carrots, Emma peeling potatoes. "We're going to have a barbecue tonight."

"Hot dogs?" Eric's eyes lit up.

"No, chicken. But you'll like it," Ashley assured him. "The sauce has ketchup in it." She kept them busy all the while wondering what Ms. Duncan was writing down in that ever-present notebook of hers.

By the time the social worker finally left, Ashley was second-guessing every word she'd said. She was very glad when Jared drove in, desperate for his take on the visit. But she waited until he'd showered, they'd eaten and the twins were loading the dishwasher before she beckoned him outside.

"What's wrong?" he asked, smiling at her with that grin that made her knees weak.

"Ms. Duncan was here." Ashley studied him, loving the way he held a chair for her before he sank into his own. He was such a good man. "I think I might have goofed."

"You? Ashley the Perfect?" He chuckled, brushing her cheek with his knuckles when she glared at him. "Never. Tell me what happened."

"She was asking whether or not I'd be here when the twins started school." Ashley related the rest of the conversation as best she could. "Maybe I made things worse for you. She didn't sound very impressed when she left."

"Ashley." Jared's big hand closed around hers. His thumb brushed the top of her palm. "We have done the best we could. There's no point in second-guessing. The rest is up to God."

She blinked.

"I know. Doesn't sound like me, does it?" He smiled, shrugged. "I think I've begun to see the light when it comes to God. I don't always see why, but I'm trying to trust His ways. He loves the twins, more than I do. He will protect them."

"You're right." Ashley sighed, loving the curl of his fingers against his. This sharing of burdens—that was what she'd most missed when she'd begun to keep people at bay. "I'll keep praying and Ms. Duncan will just have to come around in time for your court date."

"Two weeks away. Don't remind me." He leaned over, brushed his lips against her hair. "Dad called my cell, said you'd taken the kids to see Mom today. Thank you for caring about my family."

Because I care about you, her heart whispered.

"Man, it's hot. Want to go to the movies after dinner? There's a new kids' flick the twins have been nagging me to see." He held out a hand and drew her up from the chair. "Come on. It'll be fun."

Yes, it would be. Movies, dishes—Ashley didn't care what she did as long as she could be with him.

So they went to the movie, but in the middle of it Ashley received a text message. She pretended everything was all right until the twins were in bed, but kissing them good-night only made it worse and she escaped to Jared's beloved deck to allow a few tears as she struggled to regain control.

"They're asleep." Jared grasped her shoulders and turned her to face him. One thumb lifted the tear from her cheek. "What's wrong?" he whispered.

"A patient died tonight. Eli." She put her head on his shoulder and sobbed for the sweet little boy who'd never complained no matter how many needles she'd had to give him. "I loved that kid so much."

"He's the little guy you took the twins to see?" Jared murmured, his hand smoothing over her hair. "The one with no one but an elderly grandma?"

"Yes." She sighed, burrowing against his chest as his arms closed around her. "I should have been there," she whispered sadly. "Maybe I could have done something—"

"Aw, honey, you can't be there for all of the hurting children, though I know you'd like to be." Jared nuzzled her head against his neck, his breath warm against her forehead. "Anyhow, Eli's with God now. You have that."

"Yes," she whispered. A smile escaped as she remembered the little boy's determination to talk to God about his arrival in heaven. "So I will see him again one day. That's some consolation."

"Oh, Ashley. That heart of yours." He rested his chin on top of her head and held her, just held her as she said a private goodbye to the little boy. Then when she finally shifted, he brushed his lips against hers for a quick kiss. "Do you want to hear about my day?"

"Sure." She eased away from him, peered into his face and tried to discern why his voice sounded so— blithe.

"I started on your house today." He laughed when

she threw her arms around his neck and hugged him. "I'll assume you're happy about that."

"I'm delirious. Thank you." Kiss. "Thank you." Kiss. "Thank you."

Jared captured the third kiss and deepened it until Ashley was left gasping for breath when he released her and the world spun around her.

"You're welcome." He smiled when she lifted a hand to touch her mouth. "One week is all that's left. I hope it's enough. I want to make sure your dreams come true, Ashley."

"Really?" She stared at him, entranced by the way he was looking at her, as if he couldn't get enough of seeing her.

"Really. I'm going to prove to you that when I give my word, I keep it." He grasped her chin and planted another kiss, a hard one, on her lips. "I'm going to prove that to you if it's the last thing I ever do."

"I'm not trying to kill you, Jared." She laughed but the sound came out oddly. Because she was nervous. Because he kept looking at her like that. Because she wanted more from him than she'd realized. Because she didn't want to say good-night. "Anyway, I trust you."

"Do you?" He hugged her again then let her go. "Thank you."

"Don't thank me," she told him seriously. "You've more than earned it. I've never seen anybody try so hard to make things work. The project, the twins, this house—you give your best. Always. You're nothing like the cheaters I knew, Jared. You couldn't be. It just isn't in you."

Silence stretched between them until finally Ashley knew she had to leave. She couldn't stand here a moment longer and not tell him how much she loved him. But she wouldn't do that because she was pretty sure Jared wasn't ready to hear it.

Yet.

"I have to go. I'll see you tomorrow morning." She stood on tiptoe to kiss his cheek.

"You couldn't make it a little earlier—say, two hours?" he asked. "I know I'm pushing it. You've been great and it seems like I keep asking for more, but that way I could get in a couple of hours outside, before the heat kills us."

"Of course I'll be here. Name your time." He did and Ashley blinked and made a mental note to arrive half an hour early so she could make him breakfast. He was going to need it. "I'll be here." She smiled, her heart almost bursting with love. "See you."

"Wait!" He walked up to her, bent and kissed her so sweetly she wanted to cry again. "Good night, Ashley."

"Good night." Ashley drove away with his face lingering in her mind.

It was late and she was tired, but she drove past the site anyway. Harry's Place looked majestic in the moonlight, its walls now sturdy and strong against whatever nature threw its way. And behind it, her little house huddled, waiting for Jared's magic touch.

But tonight Ashley felt no yearning to be alone in it. Tonight she could only imagine life with Jared and the twins there, filling it with their laughter.

"There's nothing wrong with that, is there, Lord?"

Her cell phone rang. Jared. She flipped it open.

"You're there, aren't you?" he said. "At the project?"

"Yes."

"I knew it. And?" he demanded impatiently. "Notice any difference?"

I notice that I love you. I notice that because of you I can't imagine loving anyone else.

"Ashley?"

"The landscaping will look wonderful, Jared. Thank you." She paused. The words were bursting inside, waiting to be let out. She whispered, "I love you."

Ashley didn't wait for an answer. She closed the phone and turned it off.

"I trust him, God. And I love him. Please let him love me." She caught her breath then hurriedly whispered the last part of her plea.

"Please let this be the family I've prayed so long for."

"Good morning, gorgeous." Jared wrapped an arm around Ashley's narrow waist and pulled her to him for a sweet kiss. His head rang with her words of love from last night.

Soon, sweetheart. Soon I'll tell you how much you mean to me. Then I'll ask you to marry me. Soon. Until then he'd play it cool.

After returning his kiss to his complete satisfaction, Ashley finally pulled away, her cheeks almost as red as her hair.

"You'd better sit down and eat if you're going to get an early start," she said. She held out his chair and, when he sat, served him bacon and eggs and a mug of steaming coffee. "Yes, I made extra for you to take along with you," she said, grinning when he inhaled the fragrant brew.

"Smart. So smart." He tweaked her nose then began eating. "What's on your schedule for today?"

"I thought I'd take the kids to pick up school supplies. Then maybe we'll stop by to see your mom for a bit, take her some of your enormous daisies from the backyard. After that, it's a dip in the pool at Connie's where you're invited for a barbecue."

"Sounds like a plan."

"Did you take a cold shower again this morning?" she asked, flicking drops of water that fell from his hair to his shoulders.

"Yes. That stupid hot water tank is on the fritz again. One of these days I'm going to have to take it apart, but at the moment, I'm not complaining. With this heat, a cool shower feels great." He grinned. "See. Blessings from heaven no matter which way you look."

"Hold on to that thought," Ashley said as she handed him an insulated mug full of her special brew. "Have a good day."

"It's off to a really good start." He kissed her again, thoroughly, mussed her mane of shining waves then headed for the door. "Be good."

"Jared, I'm always good," she said smartly.

"I know," he said and wiggled his eyebrows. "Bye." He left to the sound of Ashley's musical laughter.

Little traffic impeded his progress so he arrived at the project well before any of his workers showed up. He got to work organizing the bricks for flower beds that his father was going to plant. His two newest employees arrived a little later. He'd hired them out of his own pocket, but Jared was glad to pay the price. He was going to come in on time and under this budget one way or another. Ashley trusted him and Jared was steadfast in his determination to earn that trust.

"Hey, boss. What's on for today?" Wade and David

appeared as Jared climbed down from the loader he'd been using to transport pallets of brick.

"The little house. Today I want to finish demo and get to building." He set them to work cleaning the debris, then left to organize his crew. By the time he returned his friends had the main floor clear and were pulling up old musty carpet in the bedrooms. Jared chose the living room.

The first section came up easily. But after that it was a matter of removing staples, nails and three layers of underlay somebody had thought would level the floor. He called in the others to help.

"Why'd they do it like this?" David asked, out of breath.

"I'm guessing the floor is really uneven. Ashley wants to save the hardwood but I'm—" He stopped as a bug scurried across his boot.

"What's wrong?" Wade asked.

"Help me clear this section off, will you?" Fear clutched his heart and squeezed the very breath out of him. "Tear up the floorboards, too. I'll worry about replacing them later."

The three of them worked hard, sweating profusely as they tugged and pulled. The deeper they went, the bigger Jared's fear grew until his heart hammered in his ears, almost drowning out the prayer he sent heavenward.

No, God. Not this.

"Jared, what's wrong?" David glanced from him to Wade. "You know?"

Wade nodded. "Termites."

"But you can get rid of termites," he said, looking from one to the other. "Can't you?"

"Did you check outside?" Wade asked, not bothering to answer David's question. "It may not be that bad."

The three of them walked out into the heat. Wade showed David the easiest way to get off the stucco at the base of the house.

"It's two layers deep," Wade said.

"Or more." Jared kept plying his crowbar, his teeth clenched as he tried to stem the despair waiting to swamp him. Finally they pulled a six-foot section from one side. What it revealed left him speechless.

"The wood's gone. It's all rotted." David shoved his hammer into the powder that had once been a foundation. "What's holding this wall up?"

"Good question." Wade looked at Jared. "Inside?"

"Might as well. I'm going to call someone, too." He made the call while the others went inside the house. Wade must have explained the situation to David because the lawyer now looked as grave as Jared felt. And he didn't ask any more questions, just ruthlessly pulled up floorboards.

They took a coffee break while the exterminator examined what they'd uncovered.

"Well?" Jared felt like smashing something when he heard the results.

"It's extensive," the man said with a shake of his head.

"Repairable?" he asked, clinging to hope.

"I wouldn't go inside that thing unless it was to rescue someone. I did a couple of probes. There's nothing left. It's rotten. Knock it down and start over," he suggested.

Jared thanked him for his time and wrote a check.

"I'm sorry, man." Wade grasped his shoulder. "I'm so sorry."

"Yeah. Thanks." What good did sorry do?

"Ashley's going to be devastated," David said.

"I know." It was near the end of the day. Jared told them to go home.

"When are you going to tell her?" David asked.

"As soon as I'm finished here."

"We could tell her," Wade offered.

"No. It's my job. I'll do it." But his heart ached for what it would do to her. The project was one thing, but this house—this was going to be her dream home. She'd planned, color-schemed, even chosen furniture for this house. "Maybe—could I leave the twins at your place while I bring her here to show her, Wade? I have to make sure she realizes that there's nothing that can save this building."

"Do you even need to ask?" Wade shook his head. "We'll pray, buddy."

"What good will that do?" Jared tried to smile. "Is God going to miraculously restore the wood? I don't think so."

"You don't know what He'll do," David reminded him. "You don't know what His plans are for you, except as the Bible says, to prosper you."

"Prosper me?" He snorted. "Sure doesn't seem like it."

They left urging him not to give up yet.

It was hard not to. Jared realized that all the things he'd said to Ashley last night were now moot. He couldn't keep his promise, the deadline or the budget. The money he'd earmarked for the house wouldn't begin to cover costs to erect another structure, even if he had the time—which he didn't.

Jared walked back to the main building to check on his crew. The odds and ends were almost finished. One day, maybe two and Harry's Place would be ready. He wished desperately that he didn't have to be the one to shatter Ashley's dream. But she'd never been anything but open and honest with him. He had to do the same.

"Why?" he asked as he closed down the site that evening. "Why have You left me to handle this?" His anger grew as he arrived home and stood beneath the icy shower. It no longer seemed like fun and he wondered if it ever would again, without Ashley to affirm his blessings.

Because no matter how positively Jared tried to look at this, he knew two things.

Ashley had trusted him to keep his word.

He'd failed her. Whatever had been growing between them was now over.

Chapter Fourteen

Ashley didn't understand why the atmosphere was so heavy. The children's high spirits had drained away during a meal in which laughter felt forced. Jared wouldn't discuss any of her questions about the house and after his terse answers, she didn't press him.

After they'd finished dessert, which no one really ate, Jared asked her to go with him. He drove to the site. So there was a problem, Ashley figured. Well, she'd deal with it—with his help.

"You'll probably want to come back in the morning when you can get a better look," he said as he unlocked the house door. "But I need to tell you tonight."

She blinked when he flicked on a huge string of construction lights that lit up the interior.

"You pulled up the floor," she grumbled.

"We had to. We noticed something when we removed the rug. Actually several layers of rug. And underlay." Jared tilted the lights down.

Ashley's throat tightened. "What are those bugs?"

"Termites. The place is crawling with them. It would be best for you not to come in here after tonight, but I had to show you." He stood there, looking at her, his sweet chocolate eyes dispassionate.

"Okay. So how do we get rid of them?"

"You don't understand." He flicked off the lights and drew her outside. The wind was blowing, hard. Jared didn't seem to notice. He switched on another set of lights to pinpoint the problem. "It won't help. It's wrecked. The house cannot be repaired."

She didn't understand the words or the way he growled them at her. "What are you saying?"

"I can't finish the house on schedule, Ashley. Not on time and not on budget." He didn't flinch when she glared at him and he didn't back down. "I'm sorry."

The words inflamed her.

"You're sorry? You want more money, is that it?" she demanded, hating the thoughts of betrayal that rushed to fill her head. He wasn't like Peter. She couldn't have made that mistake a second time. Could she? "You're saying it's going to cost more to give me a place to live in?"

Jared nodded.

So it was the money. Her dream crumpled, dragged her down toward despair. Suspicion reared its ugly head and grew into a full-scale monster as she assessed Jared's unemotional response. Ashley fought them back.

"How much more?"

"A couple of hundred thousand, maybe more if you want this nice of a house. Probably at least six months to complete it." He said it with a careless sort of nonchalance that irritated her.

"You're kidding."

Jared didn't smile.

"You're serious? But—hundreds of thousands?" She

couldn't make it sink in. "Surely it's more economical to fix this house."

"No."

It was her worst nightmare come true. Anger, hurt, disappointment and an unbelievable sense of betrayal vied for supremacy. Ashley found it hard to speak past her bitterness.

"But you promised, Jared. You knew my terms, you knew the budget and you promised, over and over."

"I'm sorry I've disappointed you, Ashley." He did sound regretful, but was it real? "I wanted you to have this dream as much as you wanted it, I assure you. But I can't make it work because this house—"

"Is perfectly able to be repaired," she stormed. "I have the inspection reports, four of them. All from reputable firms." She glared at him. "Each one says there's nothing wrong with this house that can't be fixed."

"I—"

"Don't bother hunting for excuses," she stormed. "The truth is, the money got to you, didn't it? I should have expected it, actually. Everybody who looks at me sees that money." Bitterness rose in a wave of fury. "I've got news for you, Jared. You undertook a contract. You cannot get out of it just because I won't up the ante."

He got that puzzled look that always made her want to brush the hair off his forehead.

"I wasn't—"

"Don't bother pretending, Jared. I'm not buying. You're not going to get one more dime out of me," she promised, swallowing her tears until she could be alone. "Leave the house as it is. I don't want you working on it, anyway. You'd probably find a way to sabotage it.

But you are going to keep your word and finish Harry's Place. It will be done before September 1 as promised."

"I always intended—"

"To finish?" she demanded in disbelief. "Ha! Then why make excuses all along, finding reasons why you couldn't get to work on that house? Did you need time to get close to me, to make me think you cared about me?"

"I do—"

"Stuff it, Jared. I don't want to hear it. Finish your job then get out of my life." She gulped, regrouped. "I'll give you the two days until your contract ends. I'll look after the twins till then but after that I'm gone."

"I thought you cared about them," he muttered.

"I love those kids," she shot back. "I'm just sorry they've landed with someone who would renege on a contract as you've done. Make sure you don't hurt them," she said, her teeth clenched. "Because I will never ever allow that to happen."

Jared stood there staring at her, his face a mask of inscrutability.

"Stop looking at me like I've stolen your favorite toy." *How could this happen, God? How could You let it happen again?* "You're the one who's manipulated me, but it ends now."

"You won't give me even one minute to explain? Isn't it funny?" he said so softly she had to lean forward to hear. "Last night you told me you loved me. Your love didn't last very long, did it?" Then he walked to the door and waited for her to leave.

Ashley cast one longing look around, flicked off the light and locked the door. Then she climbed into his truck. The ride home was silent. Ashley seethed at the reminder of that stupid utterance. Why hadn't she shut up? Why did she always lead with her heart? Why did she always trust too easily?

She didn't wait for him to help her out of the truck, didn't bother to speak to the others. Instead she went directly to her room and locked herself inside, pretending to be asleep when Connie later stopped by.

But in fact, Ashley was awake long into the night as she examined the dreams she'd built—dreams of Jared, sharing the twins and the future. Slowly, one by one, she tore them out of her heart.

"He will not spoil my plans," she said when morning finally dawned. "The inspections said there was nothing wrong. He's playing me. I will keep to my budget and my plan," she told the mirror as she dressed. "I will not let my plans die because of his greed."

She drove to Jared's, determined to keep a bright cheery smile on her face while she was with the twins. It was only two more days, after all.

How hard could it be?

How hard it was to see the disappointment in Ashley's eyes when she arrived the next morning. Not that she spent much time looking at Jared. Nor did she bother making him breakfast. Instead she went out to the small garden and began pulling weeds as if they were the posters of wanted criminals he'd seen in the post office.

Jared made his own coffee, tasted it and tossed it down the sink. He ate some toast but his appetite was gone. If only he could explain. But Ashley wouldn't listen to him. The wound was too fresh, the disappointment too great.

Maybe later on, after other contractors backed his

claim, Ashley would listen. But would she let go of her conspiracy theory—the reason she thought he delayed work on her house? Determined to do his best for her, he focused on work and poured every ounce of effort into perfecting what was left to be done at Harry's Place.

The next day was a repeat of the one before. Ashley ignored him. Jared grimly completed his final inspection, signed off the crew's pay stubs and thanked them all for their hard work. He was ready to lock up when he saw his dad still working on the flower beds in the back.

"I thought you'd finished," he said, squatting beside his father.

"I had some extra grafts from my roses. Since you can see this area from inside, I thought I'd pretty it up, make a memorial garden for Harry Bent. After all, it's his house. You can help me if you have time."

"I have lots of time. My part in this project is finished." Sadness engulfed him at those words.

They worked together, side by side for at least an hour before his father leaned back on his heels.

"Next spring this will be amazing. Kind of reminds me of God when I do this."

"God?" Jared lifted an eyebrow. "How?"

"Every time I plant something, I have expectations in my head of how it will turn out." His dad fiddled with the mulch around each plant then gave him a sideways look. "But I can't force them. I can't make them grow into my dreams for them. Somebody might forget to water them. Someone else might walk on them. Somebody might even pull them up or a frost might kill them. I can't help that."

"I guess not." Jared didn't get where this was going.

"All I can do is take whatever plant lives through the

winter and do the best I can to encourage its growth. That's my part. But the result is up to Him."

Jared met his father's pensive gaze. "Meaning?"

"People die, son. They lose homes and family. They get sick with incurable diseases. Some suffer terribly. But all of that is beyond our control. All we get to do is lean on God for the courage to deal with it." He rose, dusted off his pant leg then smiled. "When you renovate, it's not all smooth, is it? Problems happen, people make mistakes, issues arise. We call it life."

"What are you saying, Dad?"

"Just because we serve God doesn't make us immune to bad things, son." His father's dark eyes held his. "But He will see us through whatever life brings if we keep trusting in Him, if we keep following the path He's set before us."

Jared helped him carry his tools to his truck. His father climbed in, slammed the door then rolled down the window.

"You've done a good job of playing the hand you've been dealt, son. Your mother and I are proud of the way you've taken over the twins, Jessie's house and managed this job. In spite of what you think, God has blessed you. You might want to think about those blessings and others He's given you." He patted Jared's shoulder. "See you, son."

Jared watched him drive away, his brain swirling with his father's words. When he couldn't discern the meaning, he pushed them away and took one more tour through the project, making special note of the places where his plans had taken a detour, where things hadn't worked out as he'd expected. But they had worked out, he realized. Things had come together. The place was finished, ready to be used to glorify God.

Because God had worked it out? Could he finally and totally accept that God knew what would happen with Ashley's house, knew he'd fail with her dream house and had let him try anyway?

Jared wanted to accept that, but somehow he couldn't. Ashley's scathing words would not be silenced. If God had known, why had He let him proceed? Why had He let her dream?

With a sigh, Jared finished his inspection, locked the door and exited the property. Then he drove home, steeling himself against what he knew would be Ashley's loathing and disgust. Explaining to her didn't matter anymore. Her dream was dead and she was hurting inside. She blamed him.

He wanted to hold her and ease her pain, but he couldn't do that.

This one was up to God.

The sultry afternoon heat dragged at Ashley. The twins had been more mischievous than usual, taxing her patience. She'd let some of their poor behavior go because this was her last day with them and she wanted the pair to remember her with fondness.

At the slam of Jared's truck door, her backbone stiffened. She'd hoped he'd apologize; she loved him enough to consider trying to forgive and forget if only he'd admit his guilt. But he hadn't. And in the past twenty-four hours Ashley realized she couldn't find forgiveness. The betrayal went too deep; the death of her dreams was too sharp. It wasn't just the house. It was that he didn't understand that she'd put all her hope in him, counted on him to make her dream live.

How silly to have imagined she could become part of this family. She was alone. Period.

"Hi." He greeted the twins then sent them outside again. He stood watching her.

"Supper is in the fridge," she said, ignoring the wave of yearning to be in his arms that threatened to undo her. "All you have to do is put the meat on the grill. I need to go."

"Not yet."

The twins burst through the door, carrying a bouquet and a small package.

"Here are some flowers for you, Ashley. Roses, because those are your favorite." Emma held out the sheaf, her grin wide. "We picked them out with Uncle Jared last night."

"And these are cookies we made ourselves," Eric said, thrusting out the box. "Well, with Uncle Jared's help. Because we love you."

"Oh." She knelt to accept the gifts and then set them aside to embrace the twins. "Thank you so much."

Jared had done this, after everything she'd said? Her heart began to thaw but she froze it with the thought that he was still trying to get to her.

"Thank you for looking after us, Ashley." Emma clung to her, big tears welling. "I wish you could come back."

"Oh, hush now." Ashley forced down her own emotions as she wiped away the tears. "I'll be around. I'll see you lots. And you just have to call my phone and we can talk anytime." She drew Eric close, pressed a kiss on his cheek. "You're such a strong, good boy, Eric.

Just like your daddy knew you would be. Your parents would be so proud of you."

For some reason that seemed to help dry tears. Both children finally drew away, brave smiles on their faces as they clung to her hand.

"Harry's Place is finished," Jared said when she finally rose. "I want to thank you for giving me the opportunity to work on it. I can't express my thanks for the time you've spent with the twins, but I do appreciate it. Very much." He held out the keys and let them drop into her outstretched palm. "I hope the project will be everything you hoped."

"It will be." But that wasn't true. Could anything ever fill that fantasy? She took one last look at him, the man she'd let into her life and her heart. She ached to let it all go, to pretend nothing had happened to ruin what they'd shared. But that was a fool's paradise. No one could live with a lie. "Thank you for everything you've done. I'm sure David will write a check for whatever the foundation owes you."

She couldn't stay there anymore. It hurt too much.

Ashley quickly knelt and hugged the twins.

"Be happy," she whispered.

Then with a last glance at Jared she hurried out the door and away from the place where she'd found such joy.

"Help me," she prayed as she drove to Connie's.

But the heavenly solace she craved did not arrive and Ashley was left wishing, wishing, wishing…

Chapter Fifteen

"But you can fix this, right?" Ashley was determined that neither Jared nor anyone else was going to kill her dream for her home. "That is what you do, isn't it?"

"Look, I'd like to help you, lady," the contractor said as they stood outside looking at what should be her dream home. "The termites have finished this place. It's ready to fall down. There's no way I'll risk a man's life to go in there."

"But I have plans, dreams." She struggled to make him understand.

"Are they worth killing somebody? Because the timber holding up the second floor has been compromised. The whole thing could come down on you if you move a single board. You were lucky your guy stopped when he did. The structure of this place is toast. Who was your contractor on the other house anyway?"

"Jared Hornby," she said quietly. Even uttering his name hurt.

"Jared? You're kidding! I had him work for me when he was in high school. He's smart and knows what he's doing. I can't believe he didn't tell you the place wasn't worth repairing."

"Well, he did, but I had inspections done. Several. They said it was okay," she explained.

"Sometimes that happens. Doesn't change the truth. You can see where previous contractors covered up the damage. This isn't something that happened overnight. It's been going on awhile," he said, showing her. "Some guys don't care about integrity, they're just after the money and they'll do anything to get it, even cover up rotten foundations. Jared isn't like that. I'd stake my life on his judgment." He frowned at her. "But he worked for you. You must know Jared's a straight shooter. Surely he told you the place was a write-off?"

"I just wanted a second opinion," she said. So the dream was really dead. Ashley was less hurt by that than the knowledge that she'd wrongly accused Jared. He hadn't lied to her. "How much would it take to knock this down and rebuild something similar?"

"I'm not giving you a quote because I'd need blue-prints to do that, but I'd estimate—" He named a price.

Ashley couldn't believe her ears.

"You should go after whoever gave you the inspec-tions," he said. "They gave false reports or they didn't look deep enough. Either way it's negligence. That's the way some folks are, don't want to dig down far enough to uncover the truth. Don't want to face it, I guess."

Like she didn't want to face the truth.

He agreed to demolish the house the following day, before the grand opening of Harry's Place, then left. Ashley stood alone on the site, her thoughts racing.

She'd condemned Jared, brushed him with the same tarnish as Peter, and yet he'd done nothing wrong. Nor had he defended himself. Yet, how could he? She hadn't given him an opportunity. She'd assumed all the wrong things. Why?

Your love didn't last very long, did it?

A tsunami of shame engulfed her. She'd claimed to trust him, told Jared he should trust God. But where was her trust in either of them? Was that trust—rushing to condemn without giving someone you cared about even a chance to explain? She talked about trust, but she'd never really trusted God or Jared.

"I'm so sorry, Father." Her heart wept for the pain she'd inflicted. "I let my silly dreams get in the way. I was so sure I knew Your plan that I didn't stop to listen to the caution when he tried to tell me. I wanted my own way."

She had to apologize to Jared. It wouldn't erase the horrible things she'd said; it wouldn't restore the precious relationship they'd begun to build. But she still had to do it. She owed him at least that much.

Ashley drove to the little house where she'd found love. She walked to the door and knocked, but her heart sank when she noticed Jared's truck wasn't in the yard. The shades were down, too. No one was home. She'd have to come back.

She returned to her car and sat there, remembering all the happy times she'd spent here. Like a video she saw the twins move from grief to joy, saw Jared resist his depression from the past and gradually accept his new role. She remembered the feel of his arms holding her close, the touch of his lips on hers, the way his mouth tipped into a grin whenever he teased her.

She loved him. It was too late for them, but that didn't diminish the love that glowed inside.

"Please, please, let me make it right," she whispered. Then she drove to Connie's. It was time to lean on her friend and stop being a loner.

Connie sat under an umbrella by the pool, her face a distinct shade of green.

"Hi." Ashley frowned. "Morning sickness?" She checked her watch. "It's after two."

"Tell that to the baby." Connie patted the chaise beside her. "Are you finally ready to talk, Ash?"

"I've been such a fool." Ashley poured out the whole story, shame filling her as she recalled the awful things she said. "Why did I do it, Connie? What's wrong with me?"

"You want a family, Ash. There's nothing wrong with that." Connie hugged her then leaned back, her face sad. "But wanting a family and trying to fill that hole in your heart without listening to God is a mistake."

"You mean God doesn't want me to have a home?"

"I'm not saying that. I'm saying that sometimes you have to put your plans aside and listen to what God wants." Connie squeezed her hand to soften her next words. "God knew the house wouldn't work, Ashley. He knew when you started that project that it was rotten."

"So why—"

"Maybe because He has other plans. But you weren't prepared to listen to those plans," Connie said. "You wanted the house, done your way, in your time frame. It's like you think that having that money entitles you to command the world to do your bidding. When they don't, you judge them and discard them. As you did with Jared. He didn't meet the standard you set out so you immediately decided he was after your money. I'm sorry if that's harsh."

"It's honest," Ashley admitted. "I know I'm paranoid about that money. I keep hearing Harry's voice telling me to be cautious, to make it stretch, to make a difference."

"It's a heavy responsibility to live up to all that," Connie agreed. "But you can do what he wanted, make a difference and not be suspicious of everyone. Don't expect people to fill the hole in your heart, Ashley. They can't. Because that's God's job. God will be your comfort if someone betrays you. He is the closest family you'll ever have."

"I see that now." How could she have been so stupid, expecting humans to heal her orphan past, to give her the security she'd always longed for?

"Don't run away from life because you fear being hurt. Don't miss out on love because you're afraid of losing a few dollars. Losing out on love and friendships will cost you much more than that."

Connie went to answer the phone. Ashley thought about what she'd said. Realization that she expected people to let her down, expected the worst, humbled her. She'd tried to cover that by constantly checking on Jared. She was afraid to trust with her whole heart and leave the consequences up to God. But if she really loved him, she owed him the truth. All of it. Whatever happened, she would have to deal with it, with God's help.

"I went over to Jared's to apologize," Ashley admitted when Connie returned. "There was no one home."

"He took the twins on a camping trip up to Mount Lemon," Connie said. "The last one of the summer. I think they're coming home the day before school starts."

The day of the grand opening of Harry's Place.

Ashley would have to wait. Wait and pray for God to mend what she'd so stupidly crushed. Or pray that somehow she would learn to live without Jared and the twins in her life.

Jared sat on the sand, watching the twins spend the last few hours of their holiday scampering along the lakeshore, trying to call the fish. If Ashley were here she'd—

He cut off the thought. Ashley wasn't going to be there anymore.

He wasn't sure how he was going to handle the loss. So many images, memories and sounds filled his mind, though he'd come here to get away from them. Love for her burned deep inside. It would take a long time to extinguish.

"Why didn't You stop it?" he asked bitterly. "Why can't I have anyone in my life to love and share with? Why are You punishing me?"

Punishing him? Jared's brain was bogged down on that thought.

Had God said he couldn't love Ashley? Had He taken her away? Or had Jared simply let her go because he accepted that it was over as he'd accepted her anger at him, accepted her blame for the failure of her dream, accepted that God didn't want him to be happy?

Whoa! God hadn't said that. God was all about love and joy and peace. He fulfilled dreams. Okay, He'd taken Fran. Jared didn't get that, but it didn't mean his life was cursed, that he wasn't allowed to find happiness with someone else.

He'd thought he hadn't defended himself against Ashley's charges because he didn't want to cause her more pain, and that was true. But what about later? Why hadn't he taken her back and shown her exactly how bad it was, how damaged the structure was?

Because he was afraid.

"I'm afraid to love?" he asked himself. "I can't be. I already love her. I know that."

You're afraid to lose at love, his brain shot back. *You're afraid that God will take away this love, that He'll leave you alone again.*

The truth hurt. Jared knew he'd kept that kernel of doubt buried deep inside. That's why he'd put off telling Ashley how much he cared for her. He wasn't afraid she wouldn't love him; he already knew she did.

He was afraid God would betray him again.

But had God ever really betrayed him?

Jared struggled with the question until the twins came racing up to him. Then he knew what he had to do.

"Okay, you two. Time to head home." He packed them into the truck and drove down the mountain, half afraid of what he was about to do, and half glad he was finally facing his fears.

"Your will be done," he whispered as he pulled into the driveway. "I'll accept whatever You bring."

In half an hour people would begin to arrive for the grand opening of Harry's Place.

Even though Ashley knew everything was ready, she toured the house a final time. As she moved through the rooms, she couldn't help but admire the details Jared had labored over.

"It's good, isn't it?" The man standing on the stairwell had been Jared's second in command. "He was determined this attic space would be exactly how you envisioned. He kept making us redo that window seat until it was just the way you described. He even put off his prep work for that school he'll be teaching at to search all over town for doorknobs to match the rest of the house."

"I didn't know that," she murmured.

"He was pretty insistent that this place match the standard you'd set. I think we achieved it." He glanced around, pride on his face.

"I think you surpassed it. Thank you."

He nodded. "I'm glad I had a part, but the end result is really due to Jared. He doesn't take shortcuts and he doesn't believe in shortchanging. I'm going to remember that on my next job site."

So already Harry's Place was having an impact on the community—because of Jared.

Ashley sat on the beautiful hand-rubbed oak seat and studied the Tucson skyline. How could she ever have thought Jared was like Peter? Jared cared about things that mattered. He'd sacrificed his time with his teaching job to give her what she'd dreamed of. He'd tried to warn her so many times that her dream might not match reality. But she hadn't listened.

And now it was too late.

A noise somewhere below her disturbed Ashley's contemplation. A tapping sound. When it came again, she decided to investigate and walked downstairs.

Jared stood in the foyer, a hammer in his hand as he lightly tapped a nail above the hall table. She watched as he carefully hung a framed photo of her, standing amid the chaos of the site before the transformation had begun. He straightened the edge of the frame then stood back to look at it. That's when he saw her.

"I'm sorry I disturbed you," he said quietly. "I wanted to make sure this was in place before the ribbon cutting." He studied her, his dark brown gaze moving from the top of her head to the tips of her toes poking out from her red sandals. "Is Harry's Place everything you dreamed of?"

She shook her head.

"I'm sorry," he said quietly. "I tried hard to achieve your dreams. Sometimes—" He shrugged. "I'm sorry."

Ashley moved down until she was on level with him and could look directly into his eyes.

"Harry's Place is more than I ever dreamed it would be," she said. "You've done a wonderful job and your work is beyond what I expected."

"Oh." His eyes brightened for a moment.

"But it's not everything I dreamed, Jared."

"I know. The little house—" He stopped when she laid a finger across his lips.

"The little house could never have lived up to my dream," she told him softly. "I dreamed of a family, a man who loves me no matter what, children to love and protect and kiss good night. A place where love for God and each other holds everything together and makes each moment special. That little house could never have done that."

He didn't move, didn't say a word. But his dark chocolate eyes began to melt.

"But you can." She moved her hand to cup his cheek. "You see, somewhere along the way to making Harry's Place a reality, God gave me a new dream. It took a while for me to let go of the old and realize that my dreams can only come true if you're there helping me achieve them. Without you and the twins in my life, my dreams are colorless, empty. You are what makes them live. I love you, Jared. I trust you with my life."

"I love you, too," he said. His hands slid around her waist and drew her to him. "I need you, Ashley. I need you to remind me that I'm a child of God, subject to His decisions. I need you to help me raise the twins to love God, to trust Him. And I need you to help me learn to live one day at a time, and be grateful for what God gives me."

Ashley caught her breath as he leaned in and kissed her so sweetly the tears piled up at the corners of her eyes.

"I don't have a lot to offer you," he said, fiddling with a tendril of hair that had escaped her updo. "You already know how bad the house is, that I'm trying to adopt the twins, that I haven't got two nickels to rub together. And that's not a hint at your money. I don't want it, Ashley. I know you want to use it for God's glory. I'm good with that. We can make our own way, though you might have to endure cold showers for a while." He smiled.

Ashley smoothed her fingers over his face, loving the way his eyebrows sloped, his eyes crinkled at the corners, loving his nose, his cheeks and, most of all, his smile. There was no lingering doubt. She trusted this man completely.

"They are going to be our projects," she insisted. "I'm the dreamer. You're the dream builder. I think that's what God intended by bringing us together." She smiled. "And if that was a proposal, I'm accepting."

"It wasn't," he told her, bussing her nose. "When I propose, you'll know it." Then he kissed her again.

When he finally drew away, they were both breathing hard. "What changed your mind about me?" he asked.

"God finally made me realize that a house doesn't make a home. People do. You do. You and the twins." She touched his cheek in wonder. "He is the giver of dreams. I have to look to Him and stop expecting others to make them come true."

"Well, I hope there are one or two dreams I make come true," Jared teased. Then he sobered. "I got a little wake-up call myself. I've been living in fear, Ashley. Fear that somehow God would betray me again, that if I told you my feelings, He would do something to take you away." He shook his head. "I'm going to need your help to shake that fear permanently and learn to accept whatever He gives."

"I'll be there," she promised. "For as long as God gives us."

"And I'll be here to share your dreams, no matter what they are."

They sealed their pledge with a kiss that could have gone on forever if noises behind them hadn't intruded.

"Let's get this place opened," Jared whispered. "I have plans for later this evening."

"Your wish is my command, Sir Galahad." Ashley grinned, her heart bursting with joy that her own private fairy tale was coming true. "I love you."

"My heart is yours, my queen." He kissed her hand and bowed, as any gallant knight would do.

Epilogue

"So is it okay with you two if we get married?" Jared asked the next afternoon. He'd arranged to come home after school with the twins so he and Ashley could tell the kids their plans.

"You mean Ashley's going to live here? All the time?" Emma and Eric hooted with excitement when he said yes.

"We'll talk more about it later, after you two get cleaned up," Ashley said as she ushered the muddy kids upstairs. "What is the attraction with you guys and mud puddles?"

"They're fun!"

She turned on the shower. There was a burst of water, a long, low squeal and then it stopped. She was about to call Jared when she heard him yell. She and the twins hurried downstairs and found him standing in a puddle in the kitchen.

"The water heater burst a pipe. We've had a small flood." Jared was splattered with water. It dripped from his lashes and hair.

"Small?" She glanced at the heap of towels he'd piled

on the floor and the puddles around them. "Noah didn't float on that much water."

"Ha ha." He made a face as he tugged his sopping clothes away from his body. "It gets worse."

"How could it possibly get worse than this?" she asked, taking in the extent of the mess.

"Easy. I just saw Ms. Duncan drive up."

"Do not tell me that." Ashley groaned. "Besides the water, this place looks like a bomb went off."

"Ashley." Jared's eyes shone dark with love.

"I know." She nodded. "All things work together— Hello, Ms. Duncan. Come in." She smiled. "We've just found the problem with the hot water tank."

The severe lines of the woman's face deepened as she took in the devastation. Her mouth tightened when she saw the twins, covered in mud from head to toe.

"Sorry, we're not at our best right now," Jared said. "We just finished telling the twins we're getting married."

"I see." Loretta Duncan didn't even blink. "As you know, this is my final inspection before your court date next week when I submit my suggestions for custody of the twins."

Jared wanted to groan. Of all the lousy timing. He glanced at Ashley. She winked—their signal to each other to remember who was in control of their lives.

"Ms. Duncan," Ashley began.

"I'm pleased to say that I will be recommending permanent custody of the twins to you, Jared, and after you're married, to your wife." Ms. Duncan's grin stretched her firm thin lips into the biggest smile Jared had ever seen on her face.

"But what about—?" He gestured at the surrounding chaos.

"A broken pipe? Stuff happens in everyone's life, Jared. It's the way you deal with it that matters. I have watched you handle adversity that would have decimated others. You have proven to me that you are a parent worthy of the care of these two." She giggled as she flicked a finger at the mud dotting Emma's cheeks. "I have no doubt that together you and Ashley will survive whatever the future brings. Congratulations to all of you. I know this 'summer family' will strengthen and grow through the years ahead."

Jared couldn't help it, he hugged her, swinging her off her feet and soaking her with his wet clothes. He quickly set her down, aghast at his temerity. But Ms. Duncan seemed amused as she glanced at her damp clothes.

"Were you going out to celebrate your engagement?" she asked. "Or do you have time for tea? I'd like to discuss Harry's Place. I intend to volunteer there, if you'll have me. My family was homeless when I was a child. I've never forgotten the kindness of others."

"Tea is out," Jared told her with a grimace. "I had to shut off the water."

"But we have soda," Ashley said. "And cookies. Would you care to join us? I'd love to talk to you about Harry's Place."

"Soda will be perfect."

It was all perfect, Jared mused, watching the twins munch on their cookies. Perfect because it really was the people and not the house that made a place home.

His glance slid to Ashley, who was bent over a notepad, earnestly describing her next project to help families. His heart swelled with love.

The future would be perfect, too, not because there wouldn't be bad times, but because God would work all things together for good. Jared would face it with Ashley by his side, confident that with her love he would have everything he needed to care for his family.

* * * * *

Dear Reader,

Thank you for joining me in another season of love. I hope you enjoyed the twins, Ashley and Jared as they each found a new life together. It's hard when our dreams die and we realize all our striving has been for nothing. Or has it? The mind of God is infinitely complex, far beyond our limited ability to understand. But if we wait on His timing, we can be assured He will work everything out for our eternal good.

I love to hear from you. Feel free to contact me at loisricher@gmail.com or via my website, www.loisricher.com. If you prefer snail mail, I'm at Box 639, Nipawin, SK. S0E 1E0.

As always, I wish you unending joy, ever deepening faith, abundant hope and love that spills out from your heart onto those around you.

Blessings,

Lois Richer